Jam

"QUITE POSSIBLY THE BEST HORROR NOVEL SINCE *SALEM'S LOT*. Will grab you and horrify you while maintaining a death grip on your interest throughout. This is the ultimate page-turner . . . Fully fleshed, well-developed characters. Immerse them in a great plot and superb action where the menace and mystery increase with each paragraph and you have a truly important novel. James A. Moore's *Serenity Falls* shows some of the strength of a young Stephen King, some of the flavor of the current Bentley Little, and a dash of the wit and perverseness of Dean Koontz. In the end, *Serenity Falls* is a major accomplishment in the horror field. Read it and you will echo my praise."
—Jim Brock, *Baryon*

"INTENSIFYING TERROR."
—*The Best Reviews*

"A TREMENDOUS HORROR STORY WORTHY OF THE MASTERS. James A. Moore is perhaps the most talented writer of this genre to date." —*Midwest Book Review*

Now available
Writ in Blood: Serenity Falls, Book I
The Pack: Serenity Falls, Book II

continued . . .

DARK CARNIVAL

Serenity Falls, Book III

JAMES A. MOORE

JOVE BOOKS, NEW YORK

THE BERKLEY PUBLISHING GROUP
Published by the Penguin Group
Penguin Group (USA) Inc.
375 Hudson Street, New York, New York 10014, USA
Penguin Group (Canada), 10 Alcorn Avenue, Toronto, Ontario M4V 3B2, Canada
(a division of Pearson Penguin Canada Inc.)
Penguin Books Ltd., 80 Strand, London WC2R 0RL, England
Penguin Group Ireland, 25 St. Stephen's Green, Dublin 2, Ireland (a division of Penguin Books Ltd.)
Penguin Group (Australia), 250 Camberwell Road, Camberwell, Victoria 3124, Australia
(a division of Pearson Australia Group Pty. Ltd.)
Penguin Books India Pvt. Ltd., 11 Community Centre, Panchsheel Park, New Delhi—110 017, India
Penguin Group (NZ), Cnr. Airborne and Rosedale Roads, Albany, Auckland 1310, New Zealand
(a division of Pearson New Zealand Ltd.)
Penguin Books (South Africa) (Pty.) Ltd., 24 Sturdee Avenue, Rosebank, Johannesburg 2196, South
Africa

Penguin Books Ltd., Registered Offices: 80 Strand, London WC2R 0RL, England

This is a work of fiction. Names, characters, places, and incidents either are the product of the author's
imagination or are used fictitiously, and any resemblance to actual persons, living or dead, business
establishments, events, or locales is entirely coincidental.

DARK CARNIVAL

A Jove Book / published by arrangement with the author.

PRINTING HISTORY
Jove mass-market edition / August 2005

Copyright © 2003 by James A. Moore.
Book design by Stacy Irwin.

ISBN: 0-515-13985-8

JOVE®
Jove Books are published by The Berkley Publishing Group,
a division of Penguin Group (USA) Inc.,
375 Hudson Street, New York, New York 10014.
JOVE is a registered trademark of Penguin Group (USA) Inc.
The "J" design is a trademark belonging to Penguin Group (USA) Inc.

PRINTED IN THE UNITED STATES OF AMERICA

10 9 8 7 6 5 4 3 2 1

WHAT'S GONE
BEFORE

In the very distant past, Serenity Falls was just a place of wilderness. Not long after Europeans started colonizing the land, that changed as it did in many places. In the interim, a lot had occurred, but really, not nearly all of it has to do with our story. Let's just hit the high notes. Over the centuries since the town was founded it has gone through name changes and seen the population grow to a height of close to ten thousand and down to a relative low that was just over five thousand.

The number of inhabitants has been on an upswing lately. The quarry that was closed fifteen years earlier has reopened, and the locals have started experiencing a concept that had, until only a few weeks ago, seemed completely foreign to a lot of the people in Serenity: prosperity. But it hasn't all been easy. Several deaths have haunted the town of late, and vandalism has definitely been on an increase. Twice in the last month or so the cemetery has been vandalized, the second occurrence leading to large numbers of the inhabitants of the Powers Memorial Cemetery being shipped away after their remains were disinterred. Funny thing about corpses: they aren't as easy to identify after decomposition has set in.

There have been other problems in town, almost as a counterpoint to the good news. Not too long ago a young girl was sexually violated, mutilated, and abandoned in the woods. It happened after her boyfriend dropped her off for not letting him do more than touch her panties. Currently that girl, Terri Halloway, is back at home and recovering, which is a pretty good trick when you consider that she was dead when her assailant was finished with her. Mind you, it's not the first time that sort of thing has happened in Serenity Falls. Nor the last, for that matter. Just a few days ago there was a problem with a pack of dogs that just plain refused to stay dead. Oh, to be sure, a few of them seemed to get the idea after they'd been shot into so much bloody confetti by the local constables, but most of them just kept getting back up, even after major organs had been removed.

They finally decided to call it quits when a stranger in town tore the hearts from their bodies, even as they were tearing the flesh from his. Jonathan Crowley got better. The hounds just got dead. Crowley wouldn't have been in town at all, but something from his past has been taunting him, driving him to come into Serenity Falls, doubtless with plans of retribution. Just what those plans are remains a mystery, but at the present time he believes he's found one of the sources of his troubles in the form of a twelve-year-old boy named Joey Whitman.

Jonathan Crowley is not a nice man. He intends to find out what is searching for him using any methods that he finds necessary. Of course, there are complications above and beyond the enemy he knows is out to get him. Because

Serenity falls has been under a curse for a long, long time, and the curse is finally coming to fruition.

And anyone caught in the way is almost certain to get burned when the promise made by the man who placed the curse is that every soul will scream . . .

CHAPTER 1

I

Nick Muller was not having fun. Having fun simply wasn't a possibility when he was busy identifying the remains of somewhere in the neighborhood of two hundred people, piece by piece. There were a lot of things he could think of that he'd rather be doing, but this was his job.

Forensics wasn't quite as exciting as he'd hoped it would be when he was growing up and watching *Quincy* on the tube. Jack Klugman solved a crime a week and almost never made mistakes. All Nick was doing was taking care of cataloguing body parts and hoping he didn't screw up too much in the process.

He wanted to wipe the sweat from his eyes, but that wasn't really possible. Biohazard suits made it difficult to reach the offending drops of perspiration, but they were necessary at this point. Every corpse in the warehouse where he and five other local coroners were sorting and resorting the grisly puzzles was riddled with decay and like as not crawling with every disease known to man. He wasn't really willing to take any chances. Still, the sweat was doing its best to make him want to damn the consequences and start wiping.

It was late, and everyone else was either gone for the day or was taking a break. If he'd been a little less eager to just finish up the task—and to his credit he never once considered doing slipshod work; that would be a violation of his personal ethics, and he wasn't really willing to throw his morals aside, even if he really, really wanted to call this job finished—he would have been with them.

Normally the idea of being around corpses didn't bother Nick. He'd been a coroner in Utica for fifteen years and had seen a lot of dead people in his time. The one truth he'd learned along the way was that they were just meat. Whatever made them living, breathing beings left them when they died. He made sure he told himself that every day. It made the job easier.

And really, it was important to make the job easier, especially on the occasions when corpses played dirty and made sounds or moved. Decomposition produced gas in the torso of the average corpse. That gas caused the dead to move, moan, and break wind, at least until the chest cavity was opened to let the gases out. The first time it'd happened around him he'd wet himself. A woman who would have been alive if she hadn't been on the wrong end of a speeding bus lifted herself halfway off the table where she was lying and let out a long, slow moan that sounded uncomfortably like she was having an orgasm. A lot of people might have laughed at him, but no one in the coroner's office was quite that callous. They'd all been through it before, and while it was humorous in its way, not a one of the forensic specialists working in the morgue had forgotten their own experiences with moving bodies. It was okay to laugh later, after the fact, but not right when it happened.

He got over it. Mostly. It hardly ever bothered him anymore.

Except when he was alone with a corpse or two, and the sky outside was dark. It wasn't nighttime, the sun hadn't set, but heavy clouds that were as black as ink blocked the light.

And he was alone with over two hundred dead bodies.

Major league chill factor, when he let himself think about it. And he was thinking about it now. Why? Because, damn it all, a few of the fresher ones still had gas problems, and they were moving around just enough to make him want to run screaming for the door. Nick Muller was a proud man. He stayed right where he was, unwilling to move a single inch away from his post, because that would be admitting that the fear was real.

He reached over to the radio and flicked the On switch. Classic rock from the early part of the seventies spilled into the air, easing a little of his tension. Jethro Tull's "Locomotive Breath." A good, solid beat and enough noise to let him ignore the sounds the dead made when they settled in for the afterlife.

Muller looked down at the partial remains of the man in front of him. He had no eyes left, and his lips had pulled away from his teeth, despite the staples meant to keep his mouth shut. From his dental records, Nick had determined that his name was Samuel Michaels. He'd been dead for a few years but was mostly intact. He made a few notes on his clipboard and then wrote down the proper name on the blank toe tag he'd set on the left foot.

And as he was finishing, the foot twitched. Muller stifled what his son would have called a "girly scream" and backed away, his eyes wide and bulging. Corpses do move from time to time, true enough, but the thing is, the corpses that do that are normally fresh. They usually lose the whole moan-and-shake stage around the same time they're opened up enough for the gases to escape from the chest cavity.

Nick wiped one hand across his faceplate, forgetting about the plexi between him and the world outside for a second. He blinked irritably at the interference. "Okay, that's enough of this shit for one day." He spoke aloud, startling himself. Nick closed his eyes and counted to ten, hoping to calm his nerves enough for him to act rationally. He was being positively juvenile, and he hated it.

After the ten count he opened his eyes and turned, ready to leave the room until he was feeling a bit more like an adult. Everyone wigged now and then. It proved he was still human, he supposed.

And as he walked his eyes scanned over the bodies in their various spots around the refrigerated area. He managed a total of four paces before he froze in place, his face paling under the plastic hood.

They were all in different positions. Some of them had shifted only a little, others had moved a great deal. What they all had in common was that the ones with heads now had their faces turned toward him. He didn't think or even attempt to rationalize what he saw. Nick Muller ran like hell for the door of the refrigerated room and damn the consequences.

OhGodohGodohGodPleaseletthefuckingdooropen!

His thoughts were as frantic and desperate as his heartbeat. No way in hell was he going to take the time to look behind him. He'd seen enough movies to know that was a certain way to get toasted.

His hand grabbed the handle on the insulated door, and he yanked it hard toward himself, getting it halfway open before it was stopped by his foot being in the way. He hopped back, fully aware that he was whining in the back of his throat and not caring in the very least. The door swung the wider, and he pushed through, desperate to get as much room as he could between himself and the heads that had turned to follow him.

Nick turned only for an instant, long enough to slam the door. His eyes scanned the room, taking in details that he really didn't want to process. Things like the bodies that were struggling up from their prone positions, some of them actually losing chunks of flesh as they jerked and stuttered into activity. The sounds of flesh splitting and bodily fluids spilling across the ground. He wondered desperately how much of the noises he was making up, as he could barely hear through the gear on his head under the best of circumstances, and the noises seemed far too clear.

Nick dragged the door back to him, wishing it swung the other way so he could press his own body against it as an extra defense against whatever might want to come out and see him. His gloved hands scrambled for the heavy padlock they used to close up and secure the bodies every night, and he felt it drop from between his fingers, slipping on the rot and embalming fluid that covered his gloves.

"OhshitohmanohpleaseGOD!" His voice didn't sound right, but then not much did at the time. His heartbeat was getting in the way, and so was his ragged breathing. He grabbed the lock again, all but juggling it as he tried to force it into the proper place. Finally it hooked through the eye of the lock, and he slammed the stainless steel hoop back into the locking mechanism.

Nick Muller stepped back from the door, his whole body shaking with unspent adrenaline. He backed away, too scared to look at anything else. He felt his way along the wall, leaving a trail of filth to mark his passage.

When he felt the hand on his back, he shrieked and felt his bladder give way. He looked back, his legs already starting to run for all he was worth, and realized that it was only the janitor—he couldn't think of the man's name to save his life—and stopped himself.

"You've got to get out of here! They're *in* there, and they're *moving!*"

The old man looked at him with a vacant expression, rather like someone waiting for the punch line to a joke that had gone on too long. "I'm sorry?"

"The corpses! The goddamn corpses are alive!" He started running again, this time toward the custodian, ready to call it quits.

The man let him pass, and Nick put on the speed. It was time to be somewhere else, like maybe Alaska. Sadly, his goals and his abilities didn't mix well. Had he been in a better frame of mind, he might have noticed that the man he'd pushed past was mopping the floors. He might have seen the bucket for mop water and avoided the spill that came. Nick did his best to keep his balance, but the wet floor, the barking pain in his shin, and his own speed worked against him. He bounced off the wall, his head slamming into the painted cinder blocks with enough force to crack the shield over his face.

When he hit the ground he was doing his best to remain conscious and would have been happy if he could have remembered his name. Warm, dirty water slopped over his legs, running off the disposable rubber suit he wore and leaving him feeling oddly detached from his surroundings. The concussion starting on his head might have helped with that part. The blood that trickled into his eye certainly helped with his difficulties in getting up.

He pushed himself up to his hands and knees, then squinted against the blood flow. His legs felt all wrong, like someone had taken the time to remove the bones and replace them with wet noodles.

He heard the janitor's scream, loud and shrill, in counterpoint to the sound of metal buckling and falling in on itself.

Nick Muller tried to turn his head too quickly and felt the axis of the world shift about forty-five degrees to the right. The next thing he knew he was on his side and looking at the janitor's legs.

And something behind the man's jeans. Something dark. Something big. He saw the writhing wave of dead flesh that came toward him and screamed. He was still screaming when it crushed him under its weight.

II

Jack Michaels was pretty sure he was dying. Even if he wasn't, it was starting to seem like a good idea. He'd spent the last day in a fever rough enough to keep him wrapped in blankets and shivering like there was no tomorrow.

And the damned fever brought along some funky-assed nightmares with it. Nightmares like he'd never experienced in his entire life. Just now he was going through a doozy.

There was a woman walking next to him, and while she was one of the most stunning women he'd ever seen, he also knew where it counted that she was pure trouble. She was naked, and so was he, and while he supposed he should have been embarrassed or aroused walking next to the beauty he was with, he felt nothing but calm. Like it was an everyday occurrence. Which it most definitely was not.

He wasn't walking in Serenity—and he was rather happy about that, because even though he wasn't embarrassed in the least, he felt it would be hard to keep the trust of the people he was supposed to protect and serve if they saw him walking around in his birthday suit—but the area seemed familiar. It was like he should have known where he was but couldn't quite find the right landmarks to make it all click. The sun was out, and it was warm enough that being in the buff wasn't completely uncomfortable.

"Why are you here, Jack?"

"Hell, I don't really know. I figure because I'm supposed to be here."

"No. No, you aren't supposed to be here. This is where people go when they die."

"This is Heaven?"

"I never said that. I said it's where people go when they die."

"Well if it isn't Heaven, what is it?"

"It's a place to wait."

"What are we supposed to wait for?"

She smiled at him, and he found her expression decidedly unsettling. "I already answered that."

"Is it Hell?"

"You've never believed in Hell, Jack. Why would you want to start now?"

"Well, if it isn't Heaven . . . That sort of limits the options left, doesn't it?"

She shook her head and smiled tolerantly. It was a much nicer smile, and he thought maybe she could be nice when she wanted to. But he doubted she wanted to very often. "There's more places than you can know, Jack. This one here is sort of a place to remember what happened to you and why you wound up dead in the first place."

"I don't think I'm dead yet."

"You're not, which is why I'm puzzled by you being here."

"Hey, I just wound up here. I figure this is all a dream, and I'll wake up soon."

"You might wake up, but this isn't a dream."

"You'd have to prove that to me. It's not every day I find myself walking through a nice forest with a beautiful woman." He looked over at her and felt himself stirring. She was finer than just about any woman he'd ever seen, and even if he was dead or this was a dream, certain parts of him liked what they saw.

She tsked at him and smiled knowingly. "None of that, Jack. I'm sure you're here for something else."

"Hey, a man's got needs." He thought about what he'd just said and *knew* it was a dream. He'd never used a line like that in his life, and he never would, at least not while he was sober.

"Everyone has needs, Jack. Sex is not a need. Not here at least."

"Really? Then what is a need around here?"

"Revenge." She said it quickly, like it was something she really didn't want to discuss. "We're here, and we're waiting for revenge."

"Against who?"

"Everyone who killed us."

"Well, if you're dead, how do you intend to get revenge?"

"We're being given the opportunity."

"How?"

She shook her head. "How isn't important."

"I wish you'd give me straight answers to my questions." If his voice was a little pissy, he couldn't help that. Pretty as she was, she was really starting to annoy him with all the cryptic comments.

"I'm not really here to answer questions, Jack." She moved toward him, her every gesture and step exuding sexuality. "I'm just here. Waiting, like everyone else."

"You're just talking in circles. What are you waiting for, damn it?"

She smiled again, that cruel, cold smile he'd seen hinted in her other facial expressions. "The right time."

"Okay, I'll bite. When's the right time?"

"Sooner than you think, Jack. Sooner than you'd ever be able to guess."

He was going to make another comment, try to get more information out of her, because somewhere deep inside he thought this dream might mean something.

But then he was dragged out of his fever dream and awakened by the sound of the phone ringing. Jack reached for the source of the shrill rings and missed. The room seemed to be tilting roughly, and he was having a damned hard time keeping up with it. After his third failed attempt to reach the receiver, he finally managed to grab it in his hand and pulled it to his face.

"Hello?" He barely recognized his own voice. He sounded like shit, which was fair, because he felt like shit, too.

"Jack? Are you all right?" He thought maybe it was only the fever that sent chills through him. The notion that Bethany could still get to him enough to make him feel that sort of chill at the sound of her voice was not one he wanted to dwell on.

"Hi, Bethany. No, not really, I think I got a fever going."

"I'll be right over."

"No that's all ri—" Before he could finish the comment he heard the sound of the phone disconnecting. "Shit . . . I don't need this . . ."

He tried to stand up. If Bethany was coming over, he had to make the place look a little better. He managed only to fall flat on his back on the bed. The way the room was spinning stayed mostly the same, but the speed of its rotation increased dramatically. He closed his eyes, figuring he'd just let himself recover for a minute. When he opened them again, Bethany and Terri Halloway were looking down at him with matching expressions of concern on their pretty faces.

Bethany's hand reached out and touched his brow. Her worried face changed a little, to worried and maybe just a smidge of happy to see him. "Jack, you should be in the hospital. You're running a nasty fever."

"I don't like hospitals." His voice was dry and raspy. Before he could say anything else, Bethany was holding his head up in her arm, and Terri was handing her a glass she made him sip from, cautioning him to go slowly. He didn't cough it all over her, for which he was grateful.

He closed his eyes again as Bethany was leaning in close to his face. Much as he wanted to see her, just even be in the same room with her, sleep forced its way into his mind again instead.

And dreams.

Dreams far, far different from his last. More erotic in nature, and involving Bethany. It was not what he expected, but he didn't actually mind. They were vivid, and he enjoyed the hell out of them.

When he woke up again, it was dark outside. The only light in the room came from his hallway, and he could hear the sound of the television in the living room. Canned laughter and someone named Kelly being called a slut by her brother. He thought he remembered the show, but everything felt fuzzy.

And everything was sore. Most of the muscles in his body ached as if he'd been exercising for hours. But his head felt clearer. Not 100 percent. But clearer.

His listened to the whispers from the other room, mother and daughter talking to avoid disturbing his sleep. For just a brief second he imagined the sounds came from his wife and child, not those of his long-ago best friend. *They should have been mine,* he thought. *They should have*

been mine, and Gene should have found his own girl. It was
stupid, really, the way that thought hurt so damned much,
but there was nothing he could do about that. It was a pain
that had never really healed. Twenty-odd years later, he
was still in love with the woman in his living room. Part of
him wanted to cry, but he ignored it the same as he had for
as long as he could remember. Tears were for weaklings; at
least that was what his father had always told him.

He sat up in bed, wondering just what the hell he'd done
to make him feel like he'd been gut punched a few dozen
times, and stifled the moan that wanted to escape him. Whatever bug had decided to make itself comfortable inside him
was not playing nicely, though he felt the worst of it was
probably over and done with.

He tossed his blanket aside and shivered in the sudden
cold. As he started to run his hands over his arms to warm
up, he realized for the first time that he was in the buff. His
face flushed red with embarrassment. He didn't remember
stripping down to his skivvies before he went to sleep, and
it wasn't his normal practice.

Despite the slight spinning of the room as he stood up,
Jack managed to get into his dresser and pull on a pair of
sweatpants and an old T-shirt without falling on his ass. He
walked into the hallway and down to the living room, wincing occasionally at the soreness in his muscles.

Mother and daughter looked at him with identical smiles
on their faces, smiles that said they were glad to see him up
and walking. Bethany rose from her seat, moving over to
him and helping him toward his favorite recliner. "How are
you feeling, Jack? You had us worried half to death."

"Better, I think." Her hand on his shoulder left tingles
running through his skin. It was stupid, juvenile even, but
just that small touch was enough to make his skin flush. "I
feel bad, the two of you coming over here and having to
play nursemaid for me."

"Nonsense, Jack. It was the least we could do."

"Well, it's not like you ladies are the reason I got the flu." He felt the blush again, a hot flash that made it all the way up to his ears. He wasn't used to the idea of anyone watching over him. More often it was the other way around, and that was what he was comfortable with.

Terri spoke up, her voice soft and pleasant if a little humbled. "If it hadn't been for you, I might never have been found, Officer Michaels." She looked at him for a second and then looked down, her face a little flushed in a way that was disturbingly fetching. "You saved my life."

"Oh, no, hey, that's my job, Terri . . ."

Bethany spoke up, breaking the tension that rose in the air. "Don't be silly, either of you. Of course it's your job, Jack, but we're still very grateful. Terri wanted to help. It's her way of saying thank you."

Jack nodded. "Well, you're more than welcome, Terri, I just wish I could have found you before—" Oh yeah, that one was easy to finish. *Before you were violated and left for dead,* or maybe *before your sick fuck boyfriend had his way with you.* Sure, those worked just fine.

"Well, anyway, it was the very least we could do." Terri said the words this time, her eyes looking into his in a way that seemed to communicate on a nearly sexual level. It left him feeling flustered all over again. The girl looked too much like her mother had at her age, back when she and Jack had been an item. It left him feeling uncomfortable and almost embarrassed.

"Well, thank you very much." He said the words as formally as he could, feeling it best not to even consider a smile at that point, in case the thoughts he was trying to shove aside should make themselves clear on his face. "I appreciate the TLC."

"That new constable of yours, Victor Barnes? He called, and we let him know you were under the weather, that you wouldn't be in until at least tomorrow." He started to protest, but she put two fingers over his lips and shushed him. "I know you don't feel right letting the rest of your men handle the work, but that's just the way it's going to be. You aren't leaving this house until I decide you're well enough." Terri giggled a little at that, and Jack blushed again but managed to nod. He resisted the urge to say, *Yes, mom* to her, but it wasn't easy.

"Terri made you some chicken soup, and you're going to sit here and eat it."

Jack nodded.

"I have to go home and feed Gene. He can't feed himself without possibly burning down the entire house, but as soon as I'm finished I'll be back over."

She surprised him then, giving him a quick peck on his cheek before she vanished through his front door.

Jack sat in awkward silence, not at all sure what to say to the girl left behind. She made it a little easier for him by going into the kitchen and coming back out with a bowl of chicken soup that was rich and tasty if a little oversalted for his personal tastes. She'd obviously taken some time with it, chopping all the veggies herself and such. It was probably a monumental effort for a teenage girl, and he made sure to let her know how much he enjoyed the soup and the effort.

He was still having trouble looking at her for very long. Nostalgia and a long, passionate love for a girl who got away were making him have bad thoughts. He made himself think of other things, like a few of the less pleasant car accidents he'd seen over the years, whenever his mind went too far in that direction.

After he'd finished eating, Terri took the bowl and spoon from him, walking back into the kitchen. He let himself relax a little after she'd left. Being around her was stressful and for all of the wrong reasons. He was almost certain he was getting signals from her, the sort he'd once gotten from her mother. Twenty years and the law made the idea of even considering those signals a dangerous proposition. But he was just as certain that anything he might be reading into her behavior was entirely in his imagination. A girl her age wouldn't be attracted to a man his age, first off, and second, she had recently experienced a truly unpleasant encounter with a boyfriend who couldn't take no for an answer. That wasn't really likely to make her suddenly feel randy.

He closed his eyes for a moment, just needing to rest again. He should have felt better than ever, but whatever the hell was working on him was not playing fair at all. He was more exhausted than ever.

He slowly faded from consciousness, with Terri Halloway watching him from the entrance into the kitchen. His mind drifted to the very ideas that he would not let himself think of while he was awake, and Terri watched him with eyes that were far older than any he'd ever paid attention to. Her mouth curled into a very slight smile as she moved toward him, preparing to finish the next step of what her master demanded.

III

Charlene Lyons put on her coat and zipped the thick down closed around her body. She was going over to the medical center to see Stan, because it suddenly dawned on her a few minutes earlier that she missed seeing his face.

She didn't really want to go to the center, she'd always hated anything that even resembled a hospital, or at least for as long as she could remember. She'd been to hospitals

three times in her life, and each and every time she went it
was to visit a family member. In all three cases, it was the
last time she saw a grandparent alive. Both of her grand-
mothers and her grandfather Simpson had died shortly after her visits. She was wise enough at the age of twelve to
know that her visiting them had nothing to do with their
deaths and young enough that the thought continued to
play with her mind from time to time.

Thinking about her grandparents made her realize for
the first time that every last one of them had been included
in the desecration at the cemetery. She'd understood that
on some level all along, but not on a truly conscious level.
It wasn't something Charlee wanted to know. The thought
of their bodies rotting away in some building with heavy
refrigeration didn't make her feel all warm and cozy inside. She made herself think of other things, like going to
see Stan. She hoped he was feeling better. She missed having him around to bug her with his comments in class and
his sometimes almost starstruck looks at her when he
didn't think she'd notice.

Stan was a nice guy. She mostly just missed him. She
was missing a lot of people lately. Jessie came immediately
to mind. Jessie was her best friend, and sometimes she was
annoying, sure, but she missed the hell out of Jess being
annoying. She still didn't know exactly why they weren't
talking. Well, okay, she did know, but she wasn't happy
about it. She'd been a bitch, and this time Jessie wasn't going to let her off the hook until she did the right thing and
apologized for it.

The weather outside was colder than she'd expected, despite having put on her coat. Only a few weeks ago she'd
been swimming with her friends, and just like that it
changed to bone chilling time. No chance of working on
her tan, no matter how subtly she tried to do it. She'd look
damned silly lying out in the sunlight when it was right

around freezing. Windburn, that was a possibility, especially with the wind going as hard as it was, but sunburn wouldn't happen in this weather. The sun was still there; it just wasn't doing much good.

None of the weather made any sense, either. The summer wasn't here yet and the trees were still green, but the air was as cold as winter, and she could see her breath in the air. Stupid. It was just stupid.

Charlee walked as quickly as she could manage, which meant about as fast as Dave on an average day. In only a few minutes she'd forgotten all about being cold and was seriously considering unzipping her coat. The fact that she could no longer feel her nose or her ears convinced her not to try it.

There was almost no one on the streets. It felt wrong. She knew it was all an illusion, there had certainly been plenty of people at school earlier, but that knowledge didn't take away the odd feeling of solitude.

Perhaps it was just the need to recover from walking so quickly, perhaps it was the fact that she was passing the cemetery where her grandparents' bodies had been until the desecration. Either way she opted not to study the impulse that made her decide to sit down on the edge of the graveyard's gate; she just did it. Charlee hopped up on the low stone wall and gasped slightly at the chill of the granite against her rump. She shifted until she was mostly comfortable and let her eyes go over the ruins of the final resting places for so many of Serenity's people.

Most of the headstones and statues had been uprighted again or replaced in many cases, and the numerous holes in the earth had tarps placed over them and secured with tent posts. It was safe enough, she supposed, but Charlee didn't really like the notion of trying to test the weight of the canvases over the emptied graves. The wind caught just so on a few of the holes, and the dense fabric over them rippled and fluttered with a sound like sails on the ocean. The arctic draft also managed to fill a few of the voids under the tarps and spill back out, emitting a low, mournful sound like a distant horn on a train.

She let herself get lost in her thoughts, mostly about her grandparents and their dead bodies—which were now waiting somewhere in an ice plant as she understood it—wondering if the dead felt anything, could understand what was going on in the world around them, or if they truly passed on to somewhere else, like Heaven, when they died.

Cheerful thoughts for an unnaturally cold late spring day.

With her eyes closed, Charlee could almost imagine the shaking rattle of the tarps over the empty graves was actually the sound of a train's wheels clacking hurriedly over the train tracks. Stan, she knew, would hear such sounds and dream of faraway places. But Charlee liked her home, liked the people she knew, even if she didn't show it as well as some people did. Was there something wrong with her? Some elemental part of her mind that simply didn't want to be close to anyone? Not that she knew of. She just never had seemed to need people as much as someone like Jessie did. She didn't know if that meant there was something wrong with her or not, but she was mostly content to live life one day at a time and not worry about companionship. There were exceptions, of course, like right now, when she could think of nothing she wanted more than to be with someone her own age and maybe crack a bad joke or two or just plain do nothing, so long as she had company while she was doing it.

She let her mind wander, her eyes closed to the bright glare that would soon fade as the sun started setting. The only sounds were the rush of an occasional car, the hiss of leaves skittering down the road carried by the breeze, and the rattle of fabric snapping over emptied graves that moaned as they saw fit. They built a rhythm that again made her think of a locomotive moving through the area.

She could almost see it, a dark iron serpent winding its way toward Serenity Falls, moving at a pace just slightly too fast to let a person run alongside it as it moved through the valley and between the trees on the edge of town. The low vibration of its weight rolling along the rails enough to set her teeth on edge, the great gouts of black woodsmoke— or maybe steam, but she knew it would be black—lifting above the tree line like a thundercloud being born from the bowels of Hell. She could almost smell the sulphurous plume as it spread over the entire area. The image both thrilled and frightened her.

In her mind's eye she watched the train coming closer, growing in size, every detail of its decayed, battered engine becoming more clearly defined. She wondered what a train like that would carry as cargo and shuddered lightly at the answer that came to mind. *The dead, of course. It would carry the dead, bringing them from wherever they'd gone and returning them to find out who had destroyed their life-less sleep by violating both their graves and their rotting bodies.* She'd been watching too many bad horror movies again. Her mom always told her to turn them off because they gave her nightmares, but Charlene had long since become something of a horror junkie. Not the crappy movies where everything was blood and decapitations, but the ones that actually left you guessing for a while, wondering just what the monster looked like and had actors smart enough not to split into smaller groups as soon as they re-alized that something had gone wrong.

Her teeth rattled against each other in the chill of the late afternoon, and Charlee crossed her arms over her nar-row torso for warmth, lost in the image that she had formed.

The sound of the train's whistle blasting through the cold air made Charlee jump. In all of her life she'd only ever heard train whistles in movies, and nothing she'd ever experienced prepared her for the sound of a real one cutting loose. The loud, grief-stricken wail moved through her body, vibrating through her and chilling her down to the marrow of her bones. A thousand people falling to their deaths might make that sound, she supposed, but only half as loudly.

Charlene Lyons opened her eyes and looked toward the impossibly clear banshee cry, almost certain that she had fallen asleep in the cold and was merely dreaming. Rising above the trees was a cloud of black, a serpentine stream of heated night that spilled over the edge of the woods where they came closest to the town. The rattling in her teeth didn't fade away as she clamped her jaws together; it merely changed to a different vibration.

Between the houses on the other side of the cemetery she saw something black and menacing moving over the remains of the old tracks for the quarry. Whatever it was, it was enormous. She caught faint glimpses of details in that darkness, hints of patterns in the cold surface looked all too much like faces frozen in screams.

Charlee finally rose from her perch of stone and shook her head as she looked on, watching the engine move past and counting the cars that followed the juggernaut. There were thirteen cars in all, and every one of them looked like it was forged from iron and patterned with the endless tortures of the damned.

Charlene Lyons was braver than the average twelve-year-old girl was. She might have managed to stay and watch the train go past without ever moving or running from what she saw, but for one sad fact.

She saw her grandparents' faces on the side of that dark train. Saw their mouths held open in silent agony, and saw the shadowy pits where their eyes should have been, looking directly at her, begging for mercy.

Charlee did the only sensible thing she could. She ran like hell, all thoughts of seeing Stan forgotten as she headed straight for home. Behind her, the train continued on its path, moving past the center of town and heading toward a farm where, once upon a time, a circus came to perform.

IV

The Pageant farm spreads over roughly seventy-seven acres of land. During most of the year at least three-quarters of that property is dedicated to apple orchards and pumpkin patches and a modern greenhouse that specializes in rare plants. Farming for produce is always a risky business, but rare houseplants tended to make it easier for the Pageants to pay the bills, regardless of what happened to the harvest.

The family had good business savvy, and they were smart enough to do their research when it came to the rare plants they grew. Most of them were almost impossible to grow in anything but a greenhouse environment. They were too delicate in their early stages or required temperatures that just didn't normally exist in New York. The greenhouse itself was broken into ten smaller compartments, each with environmental controls and special supplies for maintaining the proper pH in the soil. It wasn't all that difficult for anyone in the family to walk from an area where the weather was in the low seventies into an area that made Death Valley at noon seem mild. They did whatever it took to maintain the proper growing conditions.

The older members of the family took the brunt of the chores around the farm. They only left a few of the lighter tasks for the children, and a few of the younger adults, like Amber and Suzette, were immune to having to do anything at all around the farm because they had jobs that brought in much-needed cash. Suzette worked four days a week at the medical center, and three nights a week she attended classes on nursing. She was busy enough to earn her freedom from the farmwork as a result. Amber had recently managed to get a job at the bank, working as a teller. She, too, was exempt because her hours were long, and she was often stressed by the end of the day.

Tina and Ricky handled the care and feeding of the farm animals. There weren't enough chickens to actually produce eggs commercially, but there were plenty enough to make sure that the family seldom went without an omelet when the mood struck. For Tina the whole idea of farm life was already wearing thin at the age of nine. For Ricky it would likely never wear thin. He had all of the short-term memory of a five-year-old, and he fed the animals with the same sort of endless fascination that young children often possess. Ricky made the whole thing tolerable. He was over twice her age, but he was always so happy to see the animals that it was practically infectious.

Ricky was scattering seeds all over the place and watching the chickens when he heard the roar of the train coming their way. Tina was only a few yards off, tossing a bucket of slop to the four pigs the family owned when the loud whistle blew. Neither of them had any idea what made the sound, but they learned quickly enough.

Through the trees at the edge of the property, they saw the locomotive as it slowed to a halt near the edge of the farm. One look was all that Tina needed to know that something was decidedly wrong about the situation. She'd been on the land her entire life, leaving only for school and the occasional visit to the town proper. In that time she'd become very familiar with the area where the old railroad tracks lay in ruin. She'd played there with Dave on a dozen or more occasions as the years went past. She'd asked her big brother all about the tracks, and he'd described what they were for and why they weren't used. But, being Dave, he'd also explained that no train could possibly use those tracks again without extensive repairs.

She'd have seen men working on the tracks. Would have heard them. No one had done anything remotely like construction in that area in a very, very long time. The sight of the train coming to a halt just didn't fit any better than the idea of the full moon shining down on the farm at high noon. It didn't make any more sense than that, either.

Tina, being nine and therefore immune to such concepts as caution, promptly started walking toward the train where it hissed and waited. Though even her older brother would have called her fearless under most circumstances, Dave would have been truly, deeply stunned by the ease with which she walked toward the engine and the connecting cars that simply shouldn't have been there. Curiosity tended to make caution an endangered species where most of the Pageant clan was concerned, and Tina was a perfect example of that fact.

The train did not move any farther, but it was not still, either. It thrummed, idling with the force of a hurricane being contained in a bottle. Each step Tina made brought the sound closer. Finally she stood in front of the engine, looking up at it where it towered above her tiny form. Her brows knitted together as she examined the hulking thing, her mouth going into a pout of concentration. Tina walked around the locomotive engine, not quite touching it but getting close. She saw the faint patterns in the dark metal of the outer shell and pondered why it was they seemed to always make faces that looked like they were in pain.

From behind the engine, farther down the line, she thought she heard voices. They were faint, barely more than whispers, and the sounds they made were too small for her to actually comprehend. Whoever it was who was talking sounded angry. She backed away from the train, feeling the first hint of fear. Trains she didn't really fully understand, but angry voices were a different matter entirely.

There were a lot of people living on the farm and working together closely. Now and then tempers got out of control. She could still remember her grandfather driving her uncle off to the medical center after he'd made one too many comments about her mother not pulling her weight around the place. Daddy maybe wouldn't have minded that, but Uncle Harry called her a lard ass, and Daddy didn't take it so well. He used a broom handle to make his point known. There'd been a lot of angry voices that day and for several afterwards, too.

So she didn't want to take any chances with the ones she heard now. Tina backed away carefully, afraid of the voices and what might leave the train's compartments with them. When she felt she'd gone far enough to get a really good head start, Tina turned and ran for all she was worth. She made the farmhouse in only a few minutes, with her older brother in hot pursuit. Ricky might not really have known what was wrong, but he wasn't willing to stay there by himself.

Her father was in the den, his chores done for the day, when she bolted into the room and told him about the train. He listened, his rough face almost placid, and then he rose from his seat and called to his father.

Grandpa Pageant was still a big man, heavier in his shoulders than he was in his gut. She could see the resemblance to Dave in him and knew her brother would probably get to look a lot like the old man when he was past his prime. Though Tina understood about aging and dying as well as most nine-year-olds, she didn't much like to think about it, so she pushed the thought aside. He hunkered down in front of her and placed his weathered hands on her shoulders. "Did you touch the train, Tina?"

"No, Grampy, I didn't. It scared me."

The old man nodded his head, smiling in a way that didn't quite look right, like he was trying to smile but couldn't remember how. "That's a good girl. I want you and Ricky to go up to your rooms for a while, all right?"

She didn't want to go up to her room. She wanted to go along with her father and her grampy and look at the train again. It was scary, but she knew they'd protect her. Her father was still almost a god in her eyes, and her grandfather, well, everyone knew her grandfather was the toughest man on the planet. Heck, even her father deferred to him. But Tina knew better than to argue with him about it. She nodded and smiled and acquiesced.

She and Ricky were playing video games when the older Pageants left the house. The train was almost forgotten by then. Tina didn't really hold to anything for very long. Not unless it was something fun.

V

Jonathan Crowley heard the sound of the train as it pulled up to the Pageant farm, but not knowing the area he thought nothing of it. The air was already heavy with the fetor of the supernatural, and if the feeling that crawled through his skin and danced across his nerve endings grew a little stonger, he was too distracted to pay too much heed.

He was busy just then, looking for a murderer.

Mike Blake was learning that his initial feelings about Crowley were pretty much accurate. The man was trying to find his wife's killer, and for that he would always be grateful—if he in fact succeeded—but he still didn't like Crowley.

He had trouble liking anyone who constantly wore a shit-eating grin and always seemed on the edge of going postal. They'd left the house and driven to the center of town, where Crowley said he had some shopping to do. Once Amelia, Crowley, and Mike got there, they walked, with Crowley grilling him about his wife, her life and her death. It dragged painful memories to the foreground, but they weren't very far away from the front of his mind anyway, not after seeing—*Oh, God, she's suffering. I wanted to know she was in Heaven, away from the pain and instead she's suffering!*—Amy's ghost, or at least thinking he saw her.

"What was your wife like, Mike?" The question itself was innocent enough, but coming from the smirking stranger, it almost seemed like a taunt. Still, he looked into the eyes behind the rimless glasses and felt almost compelled to answer.

"She was my wife. I loved her. When I woke up in the morning, she was there and happy to see me, and when I came home at night, she was there and happy to see me. She made my whole world better with every breath she took."

"Yeah, okay, now tell me what she was like."

"She was perfect. Amy always had a smile for almost everyone. She was just about the perfect example of an optimist." He shut his mouth for a second, remembering the way her whole face seemed to join in on a smile. From the dimples at the corners of her mouth to the way her eyebrows lifted a little, like she was ready to laugh. Amy didn't have crow's feet around her eyes, but she had laugh lines. Her face had almost been designed for smiling, and the few times he'd seen her without a smile of some sort, she'd looked wrong, like something integral to her whole being was missing. "Amy was the sort of person who couldn't stand to see someone who wasn't happy. She needed to make everyone's day a little brighter, or she felt like she'd failed in some sort of sacred mission."

Crowley nodded, his eyes looking all around them. He focused on a middle-aged man getting out of his Audi, and Mike watched as he suddenly walked toward the portly stranger, his smile fading. Mike puzzled over the sudden change, looking to Amelia for a possible answer. She made an oh-shit-look-out face and pointed to the sign posted in front of where the luxury car was parked. Mike checked out the vehicle a second time after studying the sign, and understood.

Crowley walked to the driver's side door, his smile seeming to want to creep back in place. Seemed he always wanted to smile, like Amy, but for different reasons. "Excuse me, sir."

The man, not a local, or at least not one that Mike knew, looked toward Crowley, his facial expression making clear that he didn't want to be bothered. Crowley either didn't notice or didn't care. Mike would have bet on the latter. "Yes, young man, how can I help you?" His words were polite, but his tone said it had better be a damned good reason for keeping him.

"I was wondering, is it mental or physical?"

The man blinked, his fleshy face showing his confusion. "I beg your pardon?"

Crowley smiled broadly, leaning in closer until their faces were inches apart. "The handicap. Is it mental or physical?"

"What the devil are you talking about?"

"I'm talking about the handicapped parking space you're in. I don't see a sign anywhere on your car that says you have the right to park there."

Perhaps most people would have felt embarrassed to get

caught that way, but the businessman obviously found the
question as offensive as Crowley meant it to be. "I'll only
be here a minute, and frankly, I don't see as where I park is
any concern of yours." If he expected Crowley to back off,
he was disappointed.

"It's like this. I don't see a handicapped parking sticker
on your car." Crowley's smile grew broader, and that
schoolyard bully expression came across his face again,
which remained a strange paradox to Mike, who suspected
the man would have been more likely to be the victim than
the victimizer in his school days. "So you can move your
car and all will be well, or you can give me attitude, and I
can make sure that the next time you park in a handicapped
access spot, you'll need it."

The man scurried back into his car and moved a few
parking spaces down, his face as white as a sheet.

Crowley walked back over to them, his face showing
nothing but his usual smile. "So, tell me about the day Amy
died. What were you doing when you found out?"

Mike shook his head just a little, taken aback by the
abrupt change of subjects. He wanted to call the bastard on
his lack of anything resembling good taste while bringing
up one of the worst memories of his life, but he didn't. He
needed Crowley. Much as he didn't like the stranger with
the nasty grin, Amelia remained convinced that if anyone
could find out what had happened to his wife, it was
Jonathan Crowley.

He had his doubts, but after two years of waiting for
anything at all from the local police, he was willing to take
a long shot.

"I was at home. I wasn't feeling all that great, and she'd
gone off to the store for cough syrup and to pick up something light for dinner." He thought back, thought about the
feeling in his stomach as she left, the way the room
seemed to want to swim. He hadn't even told her he loved

her before she'd gone out. He'd been feeling too sick.
Sometimes, when he really wanted to torture himself, he
dwelled on that little fact and let it eat away at him. That,
and the fact that they'd had a tiff before she left. He
couldn't even remember what it had been about, just that it
had happened. "She was only supposed to be gone for a little while, but I never realized how long she was gone. I was
sleeping. I only woke up when the constable got there and
told me . . ." Oh yeah, he remembered the look on Tom
Norris's thin face. The pale, shaken expression. He remembered how miserable the constable looked when he told
him that they thought they'd found Amy. He'd wanted to
laugh, not because it was a funny joke, but because he had
always taken it for granted that if any constable ever came
to tell him about anyone being hurt it would be Jack
Michaels. Well, and the fever didn't make the whole thing
seem any more possible. All the way down to the morgue
he'd wanted to laugh because, really, he'd just known in his
heart it was all some sort of major league cock-up. There
was no way in hell that his Amy was dead. It couldn't possibly be true.

But it had been. It had all been true and worse than
true. Damned hard to make yourself believe it's all a
steaming crock of shit when you have to look down at the
body and see what happened to the most wonderful person you ever met.

If it had just been sex, he could have understood it. He
would never be able to forgive it, but he'd have been able
to understand it. Men are often aggressive, and some of
them, the unbalanced ones, sometimes took their aggres-
sions out in a sexual way. It happened; it shouldn't, but it
did. So he could have understood that. He'd resisted the
urge to force himself on a couple of women in his life, especially before he met Amy and realized that not every

woman on the planet was a heartless bitch. He'd resisted because he knew it was wrong and because he knew himself well enough to understand the guilt he'd have felt later. Guilt, he realized, was a truly important feeling to have. Without it, the world would have been fucked over a lot worse than it already was.

All he had to do was remember what he'd seen when they showed him Amy's body, and he remembered how important guilt was. Whoever it was had apparently needed to learn a few lessons about guilt and restraint.

It wasn't even sexual. Well, it was, but that couldn't have been all of it. It was just vile. Thinking back to the wounds that covered her body made him feel clammy and made breathing hard.

He told Crowley all about it, and then he got to the details on the body.

"The guy who killed her, he'd raped her and hurt her when she was alive. But Jack Michaels told me the worst of it was done after she was dead." He took a deep breath and looked down at the sidewalk as they kept walking. He didn't want to see Crowley, didn't want the man to see him when he felt like this. "They, he, whatever, they cut almost half her skin off. Peeled it back and just flayed her open. There was stuff rubbed all over her, dirt and plants and just all sorts of crap."

Crowley looked at him, really looked at him for the first time since he'd seen the man looming over him when he woke up. "Describe them."

"What?"

"Describe the wounds."

Amelia started to open her mouth, ready to protest, but one look from Crowley changed her mind about that. He heard her jaw shut with a click.

"What the fuck do the wounds have to do with anything?"

"They might have nothing to do with anything at all, Mikey. Or they might have everything to do with everything." Just like that, Crowley was in his face, the smile he wore almost radiating menace. Mike Blake backed up fast, honestly frightened of the man for the first time. "They might just be your average raping murderer's way of having fun, or they might be a clue to why he did what he did to your wife. Can you understand that?"

Mike looked at Crowley for a long time, not certain how to react. He must have taken too long, because Crowley turned away and started walking toward the Ketchum Pet Emporium, his face showing a look of contempt that made Mike feel like a kid caught masturbating in church.

"Where are you going?"

"Look, I don't really have the time to mess around with this. Either you give me answers, or I just take care of the main reason I'm here and call it a day. I'm just doing a favor for Amelia. You don't want my help, that's fine with me." He kept walking, dismissing Mike with a simple wave of his hand.

And Mike Blake watched him walking away with a sinking feeling deep in the pit of his stomach.

"Wait! Come back, please!"

Crowley turned and looked at him with one eyebrow raised. He said nothing, merely asked his question with his eyes.

"I—" Mike closed his eyes and made himself breathe deeply. He focused himself and did all he could to remember the atrocities without letting his emotions crush him. "The skin on her legs was peeled away on the front and back, from her ankles all the way to her privates. They . . . they twisted the flesh around on itself, like they were making rat's tails out of towels. And it was sort of knotted around her knees."

Crowley came back, his brown eyes alert behind his

glasses, focusing solely on Mike. His smile was gone. "Go on . . ."

"Her hands . . . They took the skin off her hands. It was just gone. There was meat and bone . . ." He felt his breath catching, felt the way he wanted to start hyperventilating, and made himself take another deep breath. "They cut it all away and took her skin like it was gloves, I guess. And her belly . . . they gutted her like she was a fish."

Crowley just looked at him. Amelia's voice came to him, words of consolation, maybe, but he couldn't really hear them through the ringing in his ears. He wanted to be sick. Could feel the sour spittle in his mouth that told him puking seemed like a good response to the images he was dredging up from the back of his memories.

Before he could go on, Crowley interrupted. "Think back, look very, very carefully. Were there any markings on her?"

"Fuck all, man, I just told you she was gutted like a fucking fish! I think that qualifies as a marking."

Crowley smiled thinly. "Markings, Mikey. Writing, symbols, strange things that weren't on her body before she was gutted and half skinned."

Oh, God, how he wanted to swing at the bastard. He wanted to break out teeth, make him bleed and beg for mercy! But he couldn't. Crowley was his only real hope left of finding out anything.

And I'm scared, goddamn it. There it was, like an admission of guilt for some crime that had haunted him for a long time. *I'm really honestly scared of this freaky bastard.*

"I think there were. I couldn't tell through all of the stuff on her body. They'd practically covered her with dirt and everything . . ."

Crowley looked at him, making him feel smaller and more uncomfortable than he would have thought possible. "Good enough."

He then turned and walked into the pet shop, not waiting to see if they would follow. They did.

The place smelled like damned near every pet store on the planet smells. It was musky and had an undercurrent of puppy breath. Jack Ketchum was a cat lover, and was a regular at the bank where, once upon a time, Mike had been somebody. He spared a warm smile that helped ease a little of the tension in Mike's body. And they exchanged pleasantries for a few minutes.

Crowley came up to the counter with a kitten and a rat and carrying cages for both. He brought up several cans of food and a box of hamster pellets. Amelia paid for everything.

After that they went back to Havenwood, where Crowley gave both animals to Amelia to care for. He did not give them to her to keep, but merely because he claimed he didn't have room for them where he was staying, wherever the hell that might have been.

Five minutes after that he was gone.

Mike sat in the living room and held his head in his hands, drained by the entire experience. There were things he never wanted to think of in his life, and right at the top was everything that had been done to Amy.

Sometime later, after he'd had a while to himself, Amelia came to him and soothed his soul by way of his body. He wasn't truly sure if he loved her, but he believed that he could in time.

It helped. Despite the guilt he felt, the way his mind kept gnawing at itself whenever he thought of Amy while he was with Amelia, it helped.

VI

Jacob Parsons sat in the rental car, the engine idling, while he waited for Mary. She'd gone inside on some errand or other for Jonathan Crowley—much as he wanted to think that they'd come to a mutually beneficial arrangement, Jake wasn't quite willing to let himself think of the research as anything but an errand—and he wasn't quite up to heading in himself. He hadn't been feeling quite right since—*You're gonna be joining them in the darkness before this week is over, Jacob Parsons. You'll die and leave poor Mary all alone.*—Stan Long had made his unpleasant proclamation at the hospital. Jake had been doing psychic research for almost a decade now, and while he tended to be a little more skeptical than his wife, he also was, for better or worse, a believer in the occult. Though little of what he'd seen had ever managed to manifest itself in the form of physical evidence, he didn't really have a lot of room in his life right now for doubt, much as he desperately wished that he did.

It hadn't been the kid talking. He knew that. He knew it as surely as he knew he loved Mary. That was the part that bothered him. He'd run across plenty of fakes over the years, and all they ever managed to do was make it clearer than ever when he saw the real thing.

You're gonna be joining them in the darkness before this week is over, Jacob Parsons. You'll die and leave poor Mary all alone.

Which really sucked when he considered the things that came out of the boy's mouth at the hospital. Jake was scared. He'd always been the one in control—or at least he liked to tell himself that—but he had doubts about that this time around.

You're gonna be joining them in the darkness before this

*week is over, Jacob Parsons. You'll die and leave poor
Mary all alone.*

Here he was, on a mission, and the only thing he was actually doing this time around was playing chauffeur while
Mary all but offered herself to Jonathan Crowley as a personal secretary and possibly more. Good Christ, she was
practically gushing whenever she saw him. She was known
to flirt from time to time, especially if it meant getting
down to the nitty-gritty of a case, but this, this felt different.

Or maybe he was just imagining things. Maybe he was
just picking up on signals that he was afraid he might see.
Mary was a fine-looking woman, and he'd always felt she
could have done better than him. Known it, really.

He lit a cigarette, looking out at the street in front of the
local excuse for a newspaper. Crowley wanted details on
an old case, some local girl who'd been killed a few years
back and who, he believed, was somehow connected with
what was happening to Stan Long. The man was over at
the police station, looking in on what he could possibly
find out about the case from the actual officers who'd been
involved.

*Like he'd have any chance in hell of getting information
on an unsolved case.* Jake snorted smoke from his nostrils
in what came close to a laugh. The man was creepy, might
be able to intimidate a little kid like Stan Long, but cops
were a different story altogether.

Cops didn't like to share information on unsolved murders. Jake knew that well enough. He'd tried bribing quite
a few of them and almost never got good results.

He watched a young woman walking toward the car,
her hair blowing in the chilling wind. She smiled at him—
the sort of smile that made him forget, just for an instant,
that he was married—and continued on her way. Parsons
looked out the rearview mirror of the car, his eyes tracking
the girl who was just possibly at the age of consent and

enjoying the way she walked. Mary was the only woman for him, but there was nothing wrong with looking now and then.

He was still watching her when the teenagers came around the side of the small brick building his wife was inside. There were three of them in all; none of whom looked like the sort the girl would hang around with. She was dressed in jeans and a thick jacket to fight off the cold. And while all three of the boys wore jackets and jeans, they wore theirs like they were uniforms and created their own insignias as they went along. One had patches all over a jacket that was far too thin for the weather, another had attacked his coat with pens, drawing the logos of a half-dozen or more rap bands on the light blue fabric. The last fairly jingled when he walked, a side effect of the slogan-covered buttons that adorned every spot where he could fit them. Any one of the three would have made him nervous, but all three of them together were not an idea he liked to think about.

He watched as they moved after the girl, their faces set and their body language making it very clear that they were looking to get to know the girl, whether she liked it or not. He wanted to call out to her, wanted to warn her about what was following after her, but—*You're gonna be joining them in the darkness before this week is over, Jacob Parsons. You'll die and leave poor Mary all alone.*—he really didn't think the odds were in his favor. They were all young and in shape. He was getting older every day and had never been a very physical man. His stomach was filled with nerves that refused to stay quiet about his chances of doing anything but getting himself hurt badly; no, the odds were not in his favor, at least according to the fluttery feeling that kept working him over.

He cast his eyes around the area quickly, hoping that someone there would be able to help the girl, help him avoid getting involved in the entire affair. *What do I know? Maybe they're her friends, and they're just playing games.* But he didn't believe it, not even as he thought up the possibility. It just didn't ring true to him. They were years younger than the girl. Not a one of them could have been older than fifteen or sixteen, and he didn't like the way they were looking at her. No one was on the street, except for him, the three boys, and the figure of the girl who was ready to move around another building and out of sight.

Jacob opened the door of the car and climbed out, not letting himself think about what he was doing. Thinking meant he'd sit his ass back down and leave the girl to her own fate. She turned the corner at the next street, heading away from him and going who knew where. It seemed important to him that she get there unmolested.

Once, long before he'd met Mary, Jake had been in a similar position. He'd been at a college party at the fraternity house of one of his best friends, Chris Benfield. Chris was everything that Jake was not, including popular and wealthy. He was also a good enough friend to drag Jake along with him whenever there was a good party for meeting girls.

He'd met several that night, and one of them had been quite a looker. Looking back on the situation, if he'd been a little braver he might have managed to get together with her for the evening, and she might still be alive.

It was the sort of party where damn near anyone could show up, and a lot of the people who dropped in were looking for nothing more than a heavy bout of carnal knowledge. Not, mind you, that he found anything wrong with that notion. It just wasn't something he ever managed to achieve in those days without months of dating or the use of a magazine and his right hand. That was more Chris's area of expertise.

He couldn't remember her name, and that bothered him.

But he could remember the way she looked. She had sandy hair and blue eyes that he could have stared at for a hundred years or more. Her smile was bright, with dimples that seemed to multiply in the nicest way. And her body was enough to make him want to grovel before her.

And she liked him, that was obvious even to him, but he couldn't get the nerve up to take their meeting beyond the level of pleasant conversation and very, very mild flirting. When her signals weren't returned, she politely broke away from him and left Jake mentally kicking himself for his cowardice.

Fifteen minutes later he saw the same girl, the one he could have been with if he'd had even the slightest hint of a spine, laughing and flirting with another guy. One of Chris's frat brothers to be exact. Burt Madison was considered quite the party animal by his friends, and there were rumors that he could get rough when a girl said no. But there had never been anyone who really complained about it. No one he'd ever run across could actually say that the jock had truly forced himself on a girl. Jake thought about going over and warning her about his reputation but decided against it in the end. It would seem far too much like sour grapes, and he didn't need a reputation as a whiner to add on to his rep as a loser. Ten minutes after that, he saw the girl and Madison leave the party to go for a walk, and Jake got depressed and drunk enough to make an ass of himself.

Three days later they found the girl's body. She was new to town, and no one really paid much attention when she didn't show up for class. They paid attention when she was found though. Everyone who'd attended the party was questioned by the police, and Jacob's words about seeing her leave with Burt Madison eventually led to him being first the primary suspect and, later, the man convicted of her rape and murder.

The girl rounding the corner looked a little like the one he'd let get away. The one who'd been used and discarded by a jock with a dick he felt needed affection whether or not the ladies were willing.

He remembered that party as he started following the boys. His hands balled into fists, and his eyes narrowed. The fear was still there, but he was damned if he'd let it happen a second time.

He watched the boys following the girl who'd smiled at him, and he tailed them. Deep in the reptilian center of his brain there was a little voice doing its best to remind him that he wasn't a cop, a hero, or even a badass. It kept whispering about the odds of an old fart taking out three young bucks and pointing out that he had a lovely wife who would soon be wondering where he was.

You're gonna be joining them in the darkness before this week is over, Jacob Parsons. You'll die and leave poor Mary all alone.

And he just ignored it. He kept following the punks, despite the sweat on his palms and the way his heart was pounding. Because he kept remembering a pretty girl he could have fallen for and what had been done to her when he let himself listen to that voice so many years ago.

The boys vanished around the corner, all of them wearing smirks that said they were looking forward to a whole lot of fun at someone's expense. He watched them cut fast around the edge of the building and sped up, fearing they would get to her before he could stop them. Jake turned into the alley between the two brick buildings, the wind channeled between them cutting across his exposed skin like a knife.

He spotted the three boys immediately. They were moving down the narrow passageway like cats stalking tender prey. Said prey was up ahead, unaware of what was going on behind her.

"Hey," he called, his voice stronger than he'd expected. All four of them turned to face him, each with an expression of surprise. "I don't know what you think you're doing, boys, but I think you ought to leave her alone."

The three kids looked at him, and he looked back. They didn't say a word, which he found very unsettling. Instead, the one closest to him started walking back his way, his right hand slipping into his back pocket. Far off behind the kid, the girl looked at him, her face almost expressionless.

Jacob Parsons walked toward the boy, his hands held out in front of him, as if to ward off whatever the kid might decide to do. The boy had dark, curly hair and green eyes. He was almost model handsome, but the look on his face was not one that said he cared in the least if he was good looking. It was an expression of annoyance and maybe even a little disgust. "You know what the problem with you is?"

Jake shook his head, frowning slightly. He was an adult, and as such was supposed to have authority over kids like this one.

"The problem with you is that I've about had it with everyone telling me what I can do and what I can't do." He pulled out whatever prize he'd been looking for and started toward Jacob with a nasty smile on his face. "That means I'm gonna fuck you up, old man."

"Look, I don't want any trouble, I just don't think you should touch that girl." His voice wasn't sounding so calm anymore. Actually, it was starting to sound a lot like that part of his brain he'd been trying to ignore. The kid kept coming, apparently having decided that he was done with talking. Jake tried to back up, but his legs didn't seem to want to move.

"Now ask me if I fucking care what you think."

Down the alleyway, the girl shook her head, moving back toward them. He looked at her and shook his head back, his eyes meeting hers over the tops of the other two boys' heads. She might have said something to him. Her lips were moving, but he couldn't make out the words. He couldn't do much of anything at all but stare at her as the pain started in his chest and radiated out through the rest of him.

Jacob looked down, puzzled and startled by the sudden pain. The kid's hand was against his chest, and the knife hilt in the boy's hand pressed tightly to his sternum. Blood started running out of the wound where the blade of the knife was buried deep inside him as the punk started pulling his weapon back. Jake looked in his attacker's eyes and saw only dark hatred in them.

His arms wouldn't move. He felt like someone had tied them at his sides, and no matter how hard he tried to get them to move, it just wasn't going to happen. His legs were already stuck firmly in place, and he realized that he was about to die. *Hell, I'm probably already dying. That much blood doesn't come out of a flesh wound.* He looked at the boy's hand as it came back around for another strike and felt the impact of the blade going into him. *It should hurt more than that, I think. I barely even felt it.*

Jacob Parsons looked toward the girl, who was still looking back at him, and thought of Mary. He didn't want to die. Not this way, not without telling her he loved her. Somehow the world shifted, and he stayed where he was. That, or it was the other way around. His eyes were looking toward the sky and the face of the boy who'd murdered him. The kid looked terrified for around half a second, then he grinned again.

What do you know, that boy Stan was right after all.

The universe went black.

And then things got interesting.

VII

Dave and Jessie were waiting at his house when Stan got home. They smiled and waited politely while his father helped him from the car and he walked into the house, moving like an old man. Stan smiled back, glad to see Dave and even Jessie. He just felt a little weirded out around her at the present time, because he could see that she and Dave were getting close. It was a strange sight, but one that he knew he'd get used to. Well, one he hoped to get used to at any rate. He had no idea how long he'd manage to avoid being in the hospital this time.

If you'd asked Stan just what he thought of Jonathan Crowley, he'd have looked at you with a blank expression. He had no memory of meeting the man. He didn't understand that something had been done to him. He just knew that he wasn't having seizures anymore. It was enough to make him happy.

Well, a little happy. The chill between his parents was a hundred times worse than he'd felt before. He wasn't exactly ready to sing and dance about it. And then there was Beau, who'd been torn apart by a pack of wild dogs. He'd had a good cry earlier, when they told him about Beau, he wasn't feeling much better about losing his best friend in the whole world, either.

Okay, all in all it was a pretty shitty day, but at least he was out of the hospital, and that was a plus of sorts. He sighed. By now Beau should have been going crazy, barking up a storm and shaking all over with anticipation. Even when he just came home from school the Saint Bernard was ready to have fits.

April opened the door to the house, smiling as brightly as she could. He smiled back, glad to see her. At least *she* hadn't changed. At least one person in his life wasn't

freaking out and falling away from him. He was grateful
for that.

Stan moved into the house with about as much energy
as a ninety-year-old man. He felt like he imagined an old
man would feel: stiff jointed and weak. Most of his muscles still felt like someone had stretched them over a rock
and tried to tenderize them with a hammer. He sat on the
overstuffed couch in the living room and reached out a
hand, waiting for Beau to show up for a second before real-
izing that Beau would not be with him.

His parents were trying to be good about not fighting.
They weren't succeeding, but they were trying. Mom was
smiling and sweet enough to make June Cleaver seem
downright nasty, and Dad was smiling like a politician as
he carried all of his stuff in from the medical center.

I'm giving it a week before they split up for good. Even
that thought didn't seem all that depressing, not when he
thought about Beau. Somehow their separation didn't seem
like the worst thing that could happen anymore. *Beau's
dead. He won't be back. He won't come begging for my
food, and he won't ever come barking at me when I come
home again.*

Stan sighed, heard the watery tremble in his breath, and
did his best not to let the miserable feeling in his chest
grow any bigger. Dave sat down next to him on the couch,
and Stan looked over at him. Dave smiled, that same old
bland, Dave smile of his, and wrapped an arm over his
shoulders. Mom and April vanished, leaving him alone
with Dave and with Jessie.

Jessie smiled softly, sadly, and moved over to him. She
put her thin arms around his neck and hugged him with
more strength than he would have expected. He hugged
back, glad for the contact but in a distant way.

They didn't talk. Not really. They might have said a few
words, but neither of his friends talked much before they

left. After they were gone he was alone, and he made it slowly up the stairs to his room. Then he crawled into his bed—a real bed, not one of those damned electronic wonder beds they had at the medical center—and drifted to sleep.

In his dreams he knew who Jonathan Crowley was. He knew, and he was frightened.

VIII

Nancy Lyons did not die easily. She died bit by little bit, her mind being the first part they let expire. The woods were almost quiet now that the screaming had stopped. There was just the sound of the falls off in the distance, a constant shushing noise, and the occasional animal making its presence known.

Then they took turns working on her body. It was a slow process but very, very satisfying. She was pretty much a drooling receptacle by the time they'd finished. Marco De-Millio looked at what was left of her under the blood that was drying on her remains and smiled thinly as he blew cigarette smoke from his nostrils. His muscles ached, but in a good way. Not far away, Andy was still in a stupor, the thick cast on his arm was already covered with signatures and graffiti. Now it had a thin veneer of blood on part of it. Perry was in the hospital, and the chances of him making it weren't the best. That freak had used him as a shield when Alden Waters tried to kill him. Andy'd kept himself busy with Nancy long after everyone else was finished. He said he was doing her for Perry, too. Butch Carmichael was studying the blade of his knife and licking flecks of crimson from his lips. *Never realized how sick a mind he has.*

Ol' Butch is . . . inventive. Marty Hardwick was drinking a beer, grimacing at the taste. He'd said himself he couldn't stand the flavor, but there he was, doing his best not to gag as he forced it down his throat like some sort of penance for what he'd done to Nancy. And then there was Derrick. Derrick was satisfied but still had that look on his face that said he wanted more. Derrick wanted a lot more. And maybe no one else had noticed, but Marco felt a smile creep over his face when he thought back on how the lanky bastard kept calling Charlene's name whenever he finished his business with Nancy.

It didn't take a genius to figure out that Derrick wanted Charlee as their next date.

What the hell? He thought. *It won't be that hard to arrange.*

Marco crushed out his cigarette and stood up, stretching until he felt a few vertebrae pop themselves back into place. The cold air was starting to work on him, and he shivered. His eyes ran over Nancy's body, and he felt himself stir in recollection of what they'd done. He made a mental note to look in on the Lyons house soon. Charlee was sounding better and better by the minute. He wondered if she'd scream as much as Nancy. He hoped she would.

The sounds of the train whistle blowing sent a pleasant tingle through his body and made the smile playing around his lips grow eager. "Come on, boys. Train's pulling into the station soon, and I figure we better be there if we want to keep having fun."

Nice of Karstens to take care of them. Nice of him to pick Marco to speak to in the darkness, and to let in on his secrets, like the fact that he wasn't nearly as dead as some people maybe would have wanted him to be. Karstens gave orders and he listened. That was why he called in Andy and Butch after they'd grabbed Nancy. He wasn't going to disobey Karstens. Not ever.

He started walking, heading toward the source of the
engine where it rattled and thrummed its way down to the
Pageant farm. He dug in his pocket until he found the keys
to Nancy's car. It wasn't like she was going to need it any-
time soon.

He hadn't understood all of Karstens's instructions, but
he understood enough. He knew they had to meet with the
train if they wanted to keep his blessing, and that there was
something in the train that the constable wanted. He just
didn't yet know what it was.

But Karstens would fix that when the time was right. He
knew the dead man could handle almost any problem that
came up. Karstens had told him as much when he came to
him in the jail cell, while he was sleeping, and laid out the
rules for him. The rules were easy to follow, too. *Just do
whatever you want, and use a little caution, and be ready to
do what I tell you to do when the time is right.* How much
easier could it get? In exchange for following those simple
directives, Marco and the boys had been promised immu-
nity to getting caught and hurt again. So far it was working, too.

Of course, Nancy was only their first real attempt, and
Marco didn't know if they could really trust what Karstens
had said until they tried a few more times. It only took a
few seconds to get the car started, but it took almost a full
minute to figure out the gearshift. Drivers' education had
been great for figuring out turn signals but didn't do crap
for trying his luck at a manual transmission for the first
time. The car stalled twice and then did a series of rabbit
jumps before he started to get the hang of what he was doing. Under other circumstances the rest of the guys might
have teased him, but right now they were probably all feeling as mellow as he was.

Marco turned up the radio and found a station playing
classic rock and roll. None of the top forty crap here, boys,

thanks very much. Real music, AC/DC and a little Black Sabbath to set the blood boiling.

"Hey, Andy!" He shouted so the taller of the Hamilton brothers could hear him over the music blaring through the stereo.

"Yeah, Marco?"

"Doesn't that faggot Dave have a couple of older sisters?"

"Shit yeah, man, he's got some fine looking bitches at his place!" Andy's grin was almost rabid. Marco knew just how he felt.

"Well, I guess we ought to get ready for them, don't you?" The suggestion was met with a chorus of lewd comments. "Yeah, boys, I think we're gonna keep it nice and slow for now. Maybe even pull over and walk the last little bit."

"Why you wanna walk, Marco? Didn't he say we'd be safe?"

"Yeah, Butch, he did. He also said we should be discreet. No reason to ruin the fun before it's begun, old buddy." Marco made himself scowl, pretending for a second that he was disappointed in the reaction. "You really want to test how safe it is? Do you really think we'll get off with another warning?"

Andy piped up, "Perry sure wasn't bulletproof, man. I don't want to test it."

Everyone soured for a few seconds thinking about Perry and what he was going through. The bullet that pulped his insides had torn through both intestines, and there was a whole mess of infections doing their best to kill him. He hadn't even regained consciousness, and no one but his family was allowed to visit him. Mostly that meant Andy dropping in to see how he was doing.

Marco pulled the stolen car off to the side of the road, then, thinking about it, drove it behind a cluster of trees. No reason to advertise that the dead girl's car was around, just in case anyone found her out in the woods.

The whole gang, minus Perry, started walking away from the road, cutting across the edge of the Pageant property and heading toward the far end of the farm. What they were looking for was there, hidden from their view at the moment, but not for much longer.

None of them spoke. They really didn't have anything to say. But they communicated anyway, in the same way many longtime companions can make their meaning known with little more than a gesture or a facial expression.

The hills the farm was built on were gentle and sloping, worn down by generations of farmers who'd made their livings there. The fields themselves were practically buried in young growth, pumpkin patches and corn rows and a little of everything a person could possibly want to eat— provided it would grow in the area. Strange that the air should feel so cold and the plants on the farm should be doing just fine.

They were careful, but Marco knew they'd be spotted as they got closer to the place where the train could be seen. As they crested another of the small hills, he got his first sight of the engine where it crouched blackly at the edge of the farm. Karstens could promise anything he wanted. The damned thing still made Marco's skin crawl. And he could tell by the looks on the others' faces that they felt the same thing. Whatever it was down there that took the form of a train, it wasn't natural, and it wasn't right.

"We're supposed to go into that thing?" Derrick voiced the doubt they all shared. It was one thing to grab a girl and have a party—although even a few weeks ago none of them would have seriously considered rape and murder as a viable option in their lives—but this didn't look like it would be fun or rewarding in any way, shape, or form.

"You like what we did earlier to Nancy Lyons, Derrick?"

"Yeah, Marco but that thing—"

"That thing is what we have to deal with if we want to stay on Karstens's good side."

"Yeah, well, maybe we don't need him. Maybe we can do it on our own . . ." Butch didn't normally like to assert himself. He much preferred staying in the background and letting other people do his thinking for him. It was one of the things Marco liked best about the fat kid. But there were times when he felt the need to voice his opinion. Like now.

Marco didn't much like it when any of his merry men got uppity. So now and then he decided it was time to make an example. This was one of those times.

Before Karstens came around and—*What did he do to us? Why are we different now?*—made his little changes in the gang, Marco's idea of teaching someone a lesson might have gotten as bad as actually pushing a person to the ground and making a lot of threatening gestures. He wasn't really very good at violence, and he had just enough of a conscience to avoid getting into serious trouble.

That was before Karstens.

Marco lashed out. His fingers wrapped into Butch Carmichael's hair and pulled hard. Butch wasn't expecting any sort of retribution for his offhand comment. At worst he figured he'd be called an asshole, and he got much worse than that from the old man. He let out a squeal and fell to his knees as Marco pulled hard enough to feel half of the hair tear away from the scalp.

Marco dropped over the redhead, his eyes burning and his teeth bared. "Are you fucking stupid, Butch? Do you really want to prove it by keeping up that kind of talk?" He twisted the hair some more, and Butch moved his head to compensate, his flabby face going paler as tears started in his eyes. Marco's voice became a hiss as he continued talking. "We were caught trying to break into a house and rape the bitch living there. We should be rotting in jail right fucking now . . . But we aren't. That's because Karstens wanted us free. We just finished turning Nancy Lyons into a shredded sperm bank. All of us, you too, so don't think you'll get off easy if we get busted. And we *will* get busted, Butch. Unless we do what Karstens says."

Butch was crying, blinking his eyes rapidly to try to hold the tears back and failing. Marco let go of his hair and leaned in closer. "Do you get me?"

Butch nodded and pushed Marco back, his doughy face trying to look mean and looking pouty instead. "Yeah . . . Yeah, I got you, Marco."

"Good. Then get the fuck up and let's get this shit done. I don't want to do it either, but I sure as hell don't want to go to jail. So suck it up, Butchie. We have work to do."

Butch stood up and dusted his clothes off with as much dignity as he could muster. Then he looked down at the train in the distance where it sat, unmoving, but looking like it was ready to spring forward and attack whatever struck its fancy. He started walking again, and Marco slapped him on the shoulder to let him know there were no hard feelings.

They'd have gotten all the way to the train without problems, if it hadn't been for the constables showing up. They'd cleared the houses without incident and were on their way past the barn when they heard the sirens. Marco hissed and pointed, and they did the only thing they figured they could do and bolted into the two-story structure where the Pageants kept their tractor and their supplies.

It was hardly exceptional as barns go. There was dirt and hay and a second level where they kept still more hay to prevent the horses from eating too much at any time, Marco supposed. There was also a ladder up to the hayloft, and they took full advantage of it, scurrying up and away from easy sighting. The left door on the second level was open a bit and faced in the right direction. Marco watched the cops pull up into the dirt area in front of the main farmhouse and climb out of their cars. The giant who almost always seemed to be on duty was there, and so was Tom Norris. Norris was a bastard, and he really liked messing with Marco and all the others. If he'd been alone, they might have even done something about him.

But the big guy made all the difference. Marco had doubts a gun would take him down. As if they had a gun. Perry had a .22, but it was a piece of shit, and he didn't have any bullets for it. Besides, Perry was in the hospital. That tended to make the whole point kind of a waste.

So they settled in, and they waited instead. They had all the time in the world. Besides, there was always the chance that Dave's sisters would show up. Any of them would do. Even the little one who was in the third grade.

Marco wasn't really all that picky. He just wanted to have fun.

IX

Greg Randers was at his apartment, sitting in front of the television and watching the shows for a few seconds before switching channels. Nothing was drawing his attention. Nothing on the TV seemed capable of making any sense. Not much did anymore.

Nona was acting strangely, and that in turn left him both angry and confused. Angry, because she wasn't returning his calls and had said, "*Greg, please understand . . . Carl's dead, we killed him, and as much as it hurts me to say it, I loved him. It—it's something I have to deal with. I'm in mourning. And then there's the police . . . until they find him, we can't afford to be seen together.*"

She asked him to be patient, to give her some time to

work everything out. And he'd agreed, of course, because he loved her and he wanted to make her happy. Confused, because he couldn't understand how, after everything the man had done to her, she could even consider feeling bad about it.

She still wouldn't say that she loved him, Greg, but she'd just confessed the other day to loving the man who beat her and made her life a living hell. He pushed a button on the remote and surfed past an old episode of *McHale's Navy*. Ernest Borgnine was a creepy looking man, and that was all there was to it, but Tim Conway was pretty cool. Next up was a repeat of *Three's Company*. He admired the girls for all of five seconds and then changed the channel again.

It was at times like these that he could admit he was whipped. He couldn't have been more neatly wrapped around Nona's finger if he was actually her wedding ring. The one Carl had given her, not the one he hoped to give her himself someday. He hated himself when he thought about it. Because he couldn't decide if he really, truly loved Nona, or just the sex between them. There was almost nothing she wouldn't do in bed, and she was damned inventive. She'd done several things to him and had him do several to her that he had never even considered. Just thinking about it got his loins in an uproar. And that, friends and neighbors, was the last damned thing he needed right now.

Outside the wind was blowing hard enough to rattle his windows. The sort of cold wind that he knew instinctively would crawl up his clothes to touch his skin and freeze whatever it could touch. The very thought of it was chilling, almost as chilling as—*They haven't found the body yet.*—remembering what had happened to Carl, what they'd done to him. Bad enough that the man was dead, but what they'd done to hide the fact that it was murder was worse.

They haven't found the body yet.

And he figured maybe that was a big part of Nona's attitude. Carl was—*okay, used to be*—a pig of a man, and he
was controlling and brutal to her, but she wasn't really very
keen on what they'd done afterwards, or on the fact that no
one had found him. *Well,* he thought, *it isn't exactly like
they can go looking for him with bloodhounds, and we put
him pretty far from the beaten path.* He should have taken
comfort from the thought, but he didn't.

Greg stood up and stretched, feeling restless and wanting desperately to do something other than sit around hoping that Nona would call. Maybe a walk would do the job,
let him unwind enough to actually think straight again. He
hadn't been thinking straight since—*since I left his body in
the woods. They haven't found the body yet.*—the last time
he'd spoken to Nona. If it took too much longer for them to
get together again, he was pretty damned sure he'd just go
insane. He slipped on his running shoes and grabbed his
coat. It was cold out, and the idea of freezing to death really wasn't very appealing just at the moment.

He opened the door to the world outside his apartment
and felt the earth tilt hard to the left, away from where it
should have been and straight into the twilight zone. The
only thing missing was Rod Serling's voice telling the moral
of the story. The problem being, of course, that the moral of
this particular tale was probably something like: Make sure
the man you murder is really dead before you leave him
in the woods.

No Serling, but Carl Bradford made up for it in spades.

Carl had looked better, to be sure, but he was much im-
proved from the mutilated corpse he'd been the last time
Greg had seen him. Every wound that had been left open
on his body was now closed, but it looked like some ma-
niac with a hot glue gun had done the patch job while
slightly drunk and desperately behind schedule. Thick,

heavy scars wrapped over his arms, face, and neck, livid,
angry marks that looked like they could split open if Carl
even so much as sneezed. And, oh, Greg desperately wanted
to see an allergic reaction. Carl looked down at Greg Randers with one good eye and one that, like his flesh, looked
like it had been hastily glued back together. He seemed to
have around three pupils in his fractured right iris, each a
different shape and size. His clothes were wrong though;
they should have been all torn up and bloody, and instead
they were nice and neat and clean. They were different
clothes, too, which meant that somewhere along the way
either the Carlenstein Monster had gone shopping or he'd
gone home and switched into something a little less dis-
gusting than what he died in. Which would mean that he'd
seen Nona.

Greg would have been hard-pressed to actually say
which was more terrifying: the certain knowledge that Carl
was about to destroy him, or the thought that he might have
already gotten his hands on Nona. The two together made
his testicles shrink into his belly.

"C-Carl?"

"Yep." Carl punctuated his answer with a punch to Greg's
already broken nose. Greg fell back with both hands moving
toward his face and the taste of blood spilling into his mouth.
Carl caught him before he could actually fall very far. Greg
immediately wished he'd let him go. Sadly, Carl didn't seem
to much feel like granting him any of his wishes just then.
He seemed more inclined to hand him a few heaping nightmares instead.

The man he'd killed reached down and planted a hand
between Greg's thighs, then made a fist. Greg had just
enough time to realize what he was doing before the pain
hit him like a freight train. He managed a faint squeaking
noise before he collapsed; the pain in his face dwarfed by
the wave of nausea that flowed through his entire body.

"I figure I owe you that for starters." Carl's voice sounded wet and phlegmy but filled with good cheer. "I haven't found Nona yet, but I will. Until then, I guess you and me ought to talk about what's right and what's wrong in this world."

Greg would have protested if he'd had the breath. Not, mind you, that he thought it would have done any good.

Carl kept that hand on his testes and reached out with his other hand, grabbing the front of Greg's shirt, which promptly tore under the unexpected pressure. Then the world wobbled madly for a few seconds until Greg realized he was being carried over the man's broad shoulders.

Up close, Carl was rank under the fresh clothes. He smelled like something that had died and been left in the woods. Greg felt his stomach churn at the scent and promptly vomited. Carl had good reflexes; he managed to get out from under the stream of puke and drop Greg on his head in the process. After that, Greg didn't know anything for a while.

When he finally managed to come back to something akin to consciousness, there wasn't a part of his body that didn't seem to hurt. He opened his eyes and looked around as his vision blurred and shifted again and again. Something up in his head apparently hadn't liked being dropped, because it was damned hard to focus on anything at all. He turned his head and groaned as the world spun far too quickly. His stomach was threatening another rebellion, and there wasn't much he could do about it, should the threat become a reality.

Carl grabbed his shoulder and spun him in a half circle. Yep, that did it. Stomach acids and bile shot out of his mouth and dribbled across his clothes. The dead man in front of him looked down with disgust and stepped back a bit. *I guess being a zombie doesn't mean you have to like the smell of puke.* The thought almost managed to be funny but fell short of actually getting a laugh. It would have taken a lot more than a little accidental zombie humor to evoke even a chuckle right then.

"You're a pig, Randers. I don't get what Nona sees in you." Carl leaned in close, his nose wrinkling at the stench, and looked at him with his cold eyes. "We're gonna wait here for a while, buddy. I want to see you and Nona together."

Greg looked around the house, Nona's house, the one he'd never, ever seen the inside of, and moaned. He wanted to protest, but it just wasn't in him. Carl moved away from him and drew back the curtains, revealing that the sun was setting.

They sat alone, with no words to say that the other wanted to hear. Nona would come home soon, and Greg knew his life was over as soon as she did.

X

Some things were not supposed to be. Victor Barnes accepted that as a fact of life. One of the things that wasn't supposed to be, however, was five feet in front of him and twice the size of anything he'd ever seen before.

"It doesn't much look like a train is supposed to look, does it?" Norris's voice was a pleasant reassurance that not everything in the world had gone off on a tangent. He didn't really know a whole lot of people in town, but he knew Norris, and that helped.

The damned thing almost managed to look like a train. Hell, from twenty feet away, the illusion was close to perfect. But when you were right up on the engine, when you looked closely, you could tell it wasn't metal. You could

see that what looked like seams were actually folds in
whatever the hell it was made of. The surface was almost
oily, like leather that had been buffed to a high gloss. And
it stank. When he was younger, living on the farm in Penn-
sylvania, his father used to slaughter the occasional pig or
even, once, cow. Most of the animal was used quickly,
carved up properly and either frozen, sold, or given away
to neighbors. That much meat would go bad if left out.
There was one time, when his father was finished killing a
cow, that a family emergency came up. His sister had been
in a bad incident with the man she'd once planned to
marry. He left her and moved up north, and never came
back. Maybe she'd just lost control like she claimed, and
maybe the car she was driving was aimed by her own
hands at the old oak tree at the edge of the farm property.
Either way, the family suddenly found out that some things
are more important than a side of beef. They were, all of
them, several days at the hospital in Allentown, waiting for
her to recover from what had happened. By the time they
got back, the beef they'd been planning to sell was well beyond edible and working toward its second season as a
home to maggots. The smell was enough to make him gag,
and that was the exact same scent he was getting off of the
imitation locomotive he was looking at.

Victor Barnes held his hand out toward the engine without actually touching it and felt the cold that seemed to ra-
diate from the dark shape. It was cold enough that the air
was steaming. That only added to the illusion that what he
was looking at was a real engine. Only instead of hot
clouds of steam, he was looking at the moisture in the air
as it froze.

"Norris, I don't know what the hell this thing is, but I
don't like it."

"Can't say as it's doing much for me, either." Norris
spat on the ground and crossed himself. He then spent

several minutes walking around the train again, as if he might suddenly find something that he had missed before. "There's not enough left of the old train tracks to get something that size out here, and there aren't even signs that the ground's been disturbed. What the hell are we supposed to do about this?"

"How the hell should I know?" He shrugged. "What? Do we give it a ticket for illegal parking? I mean, seriously, what are we supposed to do?"

"I got no idea, Barnes. No idea at all."

"Any word from Michaels as to when he'll actually be back at work?"

Norris actually blushed and looked away, which was, frankly, not what he'd expected. "Umm. I don't think he's gonna make it in today."

"What aren't you telling me?"

"What do you mean?"

"I mean I want to know why you're suddenly looking guilty about something. What are you holding back?"

"It wasn't Michaels that called in. It was a woman." God above, the man was actually blushing even more.

"So?"

"Jack isn't seeing anyone that I know of. Or if he is, he's being very secretive."

"Ah."

"Yeah."

"So you figure he's scoring and maybe playing hooky?"

Norris blushed so hard his ears looked ready to actually catch fire. "Something like that."

"Don't you think he could pick a better time? I mean, shit, Norris, we're a bit understaffed just now."

"Look, maybe he's just taking it badly that he had to shoot Karstens."

"Yeah, well, I can see where that would be an issue, but I'm getting a little tired of the sixteen-hour days around here." Vic leaned back against his truck and rubbed at the bandages over his forearm. The place where the dog had munched on him was feeling swollen and pissy. He figured if it started itching much more, he might just have to get it looked at by an actual doctor, and that was not something he liked the idea of having to do. He hated doctors. Still, infection was a risk, and he liked the idea of losing an arm even less than the idea of going to the medical center.

"I know what you mean. I didn't exactly plan on any of this crap, either."

"Yeah. Well, I think I'm gonna have to pay Jack a visit before it's all said and done. If he isn't puking his guts out, I'm thinking maybe he can get his ass back to work, or he can have one less constable. I don't mind doing my part, but this is bullshit."

Norris didn't say anything; he just got a hangdog look on his face and stared at the ground.

"Meanwhile, let's try to figure out if this train thing over here is violating any town ordinances."

Norris opened his mouth, prepared to respond to Vic's last comment, when the train suddenly cut loose with a massive shriek. The sheer volume of the sound would have been enough to make Vic half jump out of his skin, but the odd wailing note was enough to make him want to run home to his mother and hide under the covers. It wasn't natural that a train whistle could sound so hopeless, but then again, it wasn't exactly a natural train.

Victor Barnes looked over at the locomotive and shivered. The thing surged forward like a monster on a leash, pushing into the ground not five feet in front of him, shoving grass and topsoil aside with ease. He felt the earth shudder beneath his feet and backpedaled quickly, giving himself another dozen yards between him and the engine that howled and moaned as it shoved forward. Norris did the same thing, backing hastily away and actually drawing

his revolver as if it could hope to do anything against the
monster before them.

Victor was not a man who was used to the idea of being
pushed aside. He weighed as much as any professional
wrestler and stood a solid six feet nine inches in height. He
was, frankly, used to doing the pushing. The locomotive
couldn't have cared less. It shoved forward again, cutting
deep into the ground and knocking the constable on his ass
with about as much difficulty as Victor himself would have
had with the average toddler. He rolled twice before coming to a stop and shook his head hard as he tried to regain
his composure. It hadn't really hurt, but it was damned
embarrassing.

He forgot all about the humiliation factor when he looked
at the source of his latest dilemma. The train was sort of
melting, slithering forward with almost serpentine grace
and liquefying before his eyes. Across from the odd sight,
Norris was shaking his head and looking at the black, oily
substance as it spilled into the ground with a hissing noise
like escaping steam. He pointed his revolver at it and almost squeezed the trigger before stopping himself. The
look on his face matched exactly what Vic was thinking:
*What if he gets its attention? What the hell will we do if it
turns around and comes back up?*

Half a minute later it was gone. The huge train engine
and the cars behind it were just plain gone, almost like
they'd never been. The only proof that they'd ever been
there showed itself in the form of the hole now cut into the
edge of the Pageant farm field. Not far away, the older men
among the Pageants were looking at Vic as if he should,
somehow, have an answer to what had just occurred.

He looked at Norris, and the constable looked back with
wide, dazed eyes.

Norris spoke first. "Would somebody tell me what the
hell is going on around here? Please?!?"

Vic didn't respond. He had no idea in hell, but he was pretty damned sure he wouldn't like the answer when it came around. Whatever that thing had been, he suspected it wasn't finished with the surprises just yet.

The radio receiver strapped to his shoulder epaulet squawked out static, and then he heard the sound of Jack Michaels's voice sounding in his ear. "This is Michaels, is anyone there?"

"Affirmative, Jack, this is Barnes. You feeling good enough to be at work?"

Michaels made a sound that could have been a weak laugh or a regurgitation. "No. No, I'm not. But I figured someone has to take over for Steinman. He's got whatever the hell I have, and I'm feeling less like puking than before."

"Glad to hear it. Look, we've got a situation out at the Pageant farm. I don't know what just happened, but it's a little screwy."

"Does it involve a body?"

Victor frowned and looked over at Norris. Norris looked back and shook his head. "Not that we can figure."

"Then it can wait. Right now we have a murder to look into."

"What? Who the hell got murdered?"

"One of those parapsychologists got himself stabbed. Right now, I'm about to go see if I can find his wife and let her know."

"We're on our way, just as soon as you tell us where we're going." He was calm enough on the outside, but part of Victor Barnes—the part he did his best never to show— was ready to have a tantrum. He was tired, sore, and hungry. The last thing he wanted was something else to have to look into.

Norris dusted himself off and stood up again, his face pale and sweaty, despite the cold. "So, we're leaving here?"

"Yeah, looks like there was a murder . . ."

"Good. Let's go."

"You're glad there was a murder?"

"No," Norris replied, a faint hint of a smile showing on his face. "But I heard Jack say something about a stabbing. Stabbings I can deal with. Disappearing trains and dead dogs that bite are a bit out of my league."

Vic nodded and started toward the truck after promising they'd be back later. Stabbings, he figured, were at least within the realm of the possible. Any more weird crap happened in the town, it'd be time to find greener pastures.

XI

Dave and Jessie left Stan's house feeling sorrier for him than they did when they visited him at the hospital. Dave especially felt for Stan, because in addition to being his best friend, he knew and loved that stupid old dog almost as much.

"Do you think he'll be okay, Dave?"

His looked over at Jessie, her big brown eyes almost as round as saucers behind her eyeglasses, and nodded slowly. "Yeah. He'll get through it."

"What happened? At the hospital I mean. Who was the guy who went into Stan's room?"

Dave stopped walking and felt the cold air whip across his scalp, lifting his fine hair into a wave that shivered with the wind. "I don't know. I know I've seen him before, but I don't know where."

"I didn't like him. He was creepy."

"Yeah, but you can't let him know that sort of thing, Jessie. You have to hide it when someone creeps you out. Especially someone like him."

She got a sort of puzzled, pouty look on her face that made him want to kiss her. He resisted the urge. It was a little too early on to be sneaking in smooches whenever he felt like it. But it wasn't easy. Kissing Jessie was right up there on the list of his favorite things to do. Also, much as he liked the kissing part, he didn't like it so much that he was willing to ignore what Jessie wanted. Right now it was talk, so he talked.

"Why someone like him? What makes him special?"

"I think he's the sort of person who looks for weaknesses and then sort of attacks them."

"Why? I mean, why would anyone do that?"

Dave shrugged, trying to find the proper way to explain it. "I don't know, Jessie. I just sort of get that feeling off him."

"Well, it looks like he helped Stan, so I guess he can't be all bad . . ."

"Well, I wouldn't trust him anyway."

Jessie glanced at her watch and got a wild-eyed sort of look on her face.

Rabbit in headlights, he thought. *But a really, really cute rabbit.*

"I have to go, Dave! I have to get home in time for dinner, or my mom'll have a cow."

Dave reached out and squeezed her hand in his for a second, wishing he could freeze time. "Okay. See you tomorrow."

She looked at him with those brown eyes focused on his, and he leaned forward, giving her a soft kiss. It was even better than the last one, but still he wanted more. He sighed when they broke the kiss. She sighed, too, and smiled at him.

Dave watched Jessie walk away, then turned to head back to the farm. It was almost dinnertime at his place, too, and if he missed it, he'd be stuck with leftovers. It was never as good the next day, except when it was spaghetti.

He'd almost made it all the way back home—a hike of nearly two miles, though he never really let it bother him as he was used to it—when he heard the sirens heading away from the farm. Despite his normally placid exterior, Dave was just as capable of feeling emotion as the next preteen boy. He ran as hard and fast as he could, his heart beating in his temples as he covered the distance.

It could be anything, anything at all, but police did not use sirens without a reason. Dave's mind ran through the possibilities as he moved. Tina could have fallen off one of the fence rails she was always told to stop climbing and walking. Ricky could have fallen into the pond and drowned. One of Amber's boyfriends could have decided to go past where she was willing to go physically; his father could have worked on that damned thresher that was never working and gotten his arm caught. Dave ran faster, heading across the long field to the farm instead of just walking down the road like he normally did. He needed to know that everyone was all right, and he needed to know now.

Maybe if he hadn't already been winded, the fist to his solar plexus wouldn't have dropped him as quickly. One second he was running hard toward the edge of the barn, and the next he felt Marco DeMillio's fist in his guts even as he saw the face of the older boy swing into view around the corner he was just getting ready to pass. Dave left the ground completely, his midsection wrapped around Marco's forearm, and then he hit the ground like a rag doll. His glasses went their own way as soon as he landed.

It's hard to be shocked when you can't remember how to breathe, but Dave managed as best he could. He looked up and blinked dazedly as Marco stepped in closer. "Where you running to so fast, Davey?"

"Unh." It wasn't much, but it was the best he could manage at the time. He tried to push himself up but only made it as far as his knees. Marco and the rest of his buddies moved in. Dave winced, knowing he wasn't going to have a chance in hell against them. Even the tall skinny one could kick his ass. He balled his hands up in the soil and prepared to get the shit beat out of him.

And he kept waiting. No blows came down, though he'd been ready for them.

Finally, Dave looked up and saw Marco looking down. The expression on Dave's face must have been funny, because Marco was chuckling, and so were his butt buddies. "What? You thought I wanted to beat your ass? Hell, Davey, I can do that at school." He didn't like the sound of Marco's voice. It was malicious and filled with pleasure. On the other hand, it was much better than the feeling of one of those biker boots of his across the side of the head would have been.

"So . . . What do you want?"

"We want to know what the cops were doing here. What was that thing they were messing with?"

"I don't know. I was sort of trying to find out when you hit me."

"Yeah, well, that was just to let you know that I'm not kidding. I want you to find out." Marco squatted next to him, his face closer to Dave's than the younger boy was comfortable with. "When you do find out, you tell me. Because otherwise . . ." Dave fell backwards as Marco's hand materialized between them. A silvery flash sprang out in the older boy's hand and showed itself as a blade. "I might have to change your looks. You get what I'm saying?"

Dave nodded solemnly, his eyes wide. "Got it. But I have to eat dinner before I come back, or I won't be allowed out of the house."

"We can wait. And Dave, don't try telling on us, because

if we even think there's a chance the cops will show up, I promise you your whole family will regret it." Marco licked his lips, his eyes looking almost like marbles in his head. "Especially your sisters."

Dave shook his head. "I won't tell anyone about it, Marco. I promise."

Marco backed away, putting the blade back in his rear pocket. "Good. You have twenty minutes, Davey. Any longer than that, and we'll be gone. But we'll be back."

Dave nodded his head, wide-eyed, and then he ran as fast as he could toward the farmhouse, stopping only long enough to retrieve his glasses. Marco aside, he had to know what was going on.

He made it to the farm in under a minute, but he was panting heavily when he got there. The family was at the dinner table, eating in stony silence. He suspected there would be hell to pay for being late. There were very few fast and steady rules around the farm. Do your chores every day, don't lie, don't steal, don't embarrass the rest of us: those were effectively written in stone. The only other one that mattered was don't disobey us. Parents got to make the rules. They also got to mete out the punishments. Normally his missing a meal wasn't a problem, but whatever had happened earlier looked to have put the whole family in a bad mood. Still, he'd take the whupping if it came his way. Right now he had other things to worry about.

Like the dumb son of a bitch hiding out at the barn, and all of his friends.

What they failed to understand about Dave was that he wasn't exactly like other twelve-year-olds. He was raised to be independent and to handle his own problems. No one at the Pageant farm, excepting only Ricky, who was not capable of being on his own and unattended, was raised to be anything but a free thinker. They came in for advice, they asked questions of their elders, and they were punished for being stupid, but they were also left to their own devices more often than not.

At the age of nine, when Mike Bertucci was going through an I'll-prove-I'm-the-toughest-by-beating-on-everyone phase, Dave came home four consecutive days in a row with new bruises and scrapes on his body and face. He cried all the way home each time. His father was sympathetic, but, unlike most parents, did not interfere until Dave asked him to. Even then, he didn't pick up the phone and call the school principal or Bertucci's parents. What he did instead was give Dave a baseball bat. "Handle it, son. Make him know never to beat on you again."

Dave handled it. He only had to hit Mike twice to settle the matter. After getting his fifth beating in a row, he reached into the shrubs where he'd placed his bat earlier and pulled it out. The first shot he took was across Mike's stomach, to slow him down. Mike fell to his knees and gasped and turned red and coughed a lot. The second blow was across both of Mike's shins. Mike screamed with that one. Dave looked him in the face and told him if he ever even thought Mike was thinking about hitting him again, he'd use the bat across his head and his nuts. Mike calmed down a lot after that.

Dave got three days of suspension for that one. That was the first time he'd ever had to deal with a principal in a disciplinary fashion. His father didn't beat him. His father didn't punish him. Instead, he gave him a few more chores to do, simply because Dave had the time.

And now Dave figured it was time to teach a lesson to Marco. Of course, Marco wasn't exactly playing fair. He'd threatened the family and made a few crude suggestions about his sisters. Dave wasn't stupid. He had the same sorts of thoughts about girls. He just knew better than to think them out loud.

He grabbed the shotgun in one hand and pulled the shells from the cabinet with the other.

As he passed the dining room table, his father caught his eye. "Back in a few minutes, Pa."

"What are you planning to hunt, boy?"

"Got me a bigger Bertucci to handle."

His father nodded solemnly, ignoring the looks from the rest of the family. "What color shells you got there?"

Dave blinked. "Green, of course."

His father nodded. "Aim low. Don't get 'em in the eyes."

"Yessir."

"Dave?"

"Yeah, Pa?"

"We'll talk about this when you're finished. Understand me?"

"Yessir."

His father nodded once and went back to eating. It looked like spaghetti. With luck there would be some left. He was hungry. As he left through the side of the house that faced away from the barn, he loaded the shells into the shotgun.

There are advantages to knowing the lay of the land. Dave knew the farm as well as anyone who'd lived there all their lives could. He knew the area around the barn especially well, and he knew that, from certain angles, it was impossible to see into the wash that surrounded the whole place. He moved through the long trench with practiced ease, maneuvering over most of the obstacles by sheer memory as the sun set. When he came to the barn, he came from the side that faced away from the farm.

Marco and company were still there, but they were looking antsy. The cherries on their cigarettes were the main source of light now, save for the glow from the farmhouse. They were talking low, and Andy Hamilton was looking around toward the farm, his cigarette bobbing in the air. "I don't think the little fucker's coming back."

Dave pumped the action on the shotgun and lowered it toward the legs of Marco DeMillio. "Think again, dumb ass." They had just about enough time to look stupid before he squeezed the trigger. Thunder exploded through the darkening night. The noise repeated five more times, over the sounds of screams.

CHAPTER 2

I

Life in a small town, well, really, any town of any size, is often an endless series of repetitions. Wake in the morning, go to work, come home, relax—possibly going out of the home again to manage that last part—repeat. There had been changes in Serenity Falls, and some lives had been altered or even lost of late, but by and large, the city remained on the same course it had been following before. Rise, work, relax, repeat.

Despite attacks by wild dogs and a murder or two, life continued on in the same way. It takes more than a few deaths to alter that sort of routine. If it didn't take more than that, most of the world would be a far more chaotic place than it currently is.

The largest change that was truly noticeable to most of the people in Serenity Falls was simply that the quarry had been acquired and a lot of families that had been on the edge of destitute suddenly weren't. Families that had been on the last rung on their financial ladder were able to start crawling out of mounting debts and begin paying off the bank, which had been in financial straits as well, simply because the bank manager, Rich Waters, was a nicer man than he should have been. He'd risked his neck on a few occasions with his generosity, and now he could feel vindicated.

The cemetery was put back in some semblance of order. The headstones that were destroyed outright were replaced—partially by a very generous donation from the Dunlow Natural Resources Corporation—and the ground was merely waiting to accept the bodies that were being sorted by a forensic team. While a lot of people were still upset by the entire incident, they were no longer outraged. Time heals all wounds, or at least numbs them enough to let life go on.

Though actual production hadn't started at the quarry, there was work aplenty to go around. Most of the equipment that was stored near the site had to be cleaned and checked before it could be used again. It was, frankly, easier to let the men who'd used it originally get it back in shape. That might sound easy, but there are rules and regulations, and most of the workers needed to be recertified to handle the equipment that had been gathering dust for so long. The new owners were spending a large sum to get things back in order, and they were anticipating an even larger return on their investments.

The people who weren't actually handling the heavy equipment still had plenty of work to keep them occupied. There was granite to be gathered, true, but before that could happen the land had to be surveyed, the path cleared for the track that would be laid in order to expedite moving what was gathered. There might be more efficient ways to move the granite, but the old method of using rails and carts would do for a start. Too much money was going into reopening without adding in the cost of new cranes.

The economy in Serenity was feeling the boom from the quarry's reopening. The bars were doing more business than their owners had thought possible, and that in turn meant they had to hire a few extra hands to manage the increase. People who'd been doing without for longer than they wanted to remember were spending a little more, too. From the grocery stores to the McDonald's on Fairmont, everyone was feeling the added income in one form or another.

And entertainment was also doing better. From the family pleasures, like a good movie or a dinner out, to the illicit drug trade and prostitution. Money was good, and it was being shared, even when most were still recovering from the lean times.

Life was going on in Serenity Falls, and for the most part, it was good.

At least on the surface.

There were still troubles to be found, and one didn't have to look too deeply to locate them. The constable's offices were down one man, thanks to Bill Karstens's going off the deep end. The crime rate in general was rising, though few would have believed it unless they worked within law enforcement. Though there were normally six constables all told, the number would have to increase soon. There was no argument from the honorable Matthew Waters—father of the esteemed bank manager—because he was sensible enough to understand the need. The town's coffers were hardly overflowing, but they were doing well enough to allow two more officers without too much pain. That meant a total of three positions opening up within the town.

So far, there weren't that many who were eager to be constables, qualified for the job, and in good enough legal standing that they could be hired. There were many who were willing to learn as they went, but that just wasn't the way it was done. There was one exception made, for Tom Lassiter. He was a good kid, and as far as Constable Michaels was concerned, he'd proved himself when he helped out with the vandalism at the cemetery. He was hired on the spot and made the new dispatcher. In the meantime, a couple of the Melmouth County sheriffs would be assisting them, working effectively as temporary constables when they weren't working in their actual capacity as sheriffs.

So yes, it was fair to say that the people in Serenity Falls were aware of changes going on in their lives, but it was just as fair to say that most of them remained only marginally affected by those changes. Their day-to-day lives were not altered or shattered or in any substantial way not devastated by what had taken place.

Nothing lasts forever.

II

Marco knew he'd live through it; intellectually, he knew the pain would go away. Emotionally, he was pretty certain he was dying. Small blazes seared under his skin, and he clamped his jaws together and winced as he pulled his shirt off. His pants followed a few seconds later, amid a chorus of whimpering noises and hissed profanities. All of them joined in, the whole merry gang, as they, too, were in agony and forcing themselves to move.

Stripped down to their underwear and bleeding lightly in what felt like around a million spots along their bodies, they hobbled over to the water in the quarry and jumped in, seeking releif from the burning pain.

The water was just above freezing, and any pain they might have been experiencing was replaced quickly by the numbing shock of going into the late springtime swimming hole. It was just starting to be summer, but the weather could have never proved that fact. Marco gasped and would have screamed if he could have managed it. Working as quickly as he could—he could already feel his muscles protesting the sudden change in temperature as his blood flowed toward his most vital areas in an effort to preserve them from the harsh environment—he moved his hands over the parts of his body where the pain was the worst.

He didn't know if he should laugh at Dave's audacity or just curl up and die. *Rock salt in the fucking shotgun, like I shouldn't have realized a family of fucking farmers would have weapons.* Either way, he was going to make Dave pay for the wounds to his body and his pride.

Two minutes later, he crawled out of the water, shivering violently. The worst of the pain in his skin had lessened to almost tolerable levels, but now the cold was setting in properly. He thought about the story he'd seen on TV once about men in a group who called themselves the Polar Bear Club, who actually went swimming in the worst parts of winter, and decided they were all certifiable. His teeth where chattering away without his control, his testicles had pulled themselves up into his belly seeking warmth, and all in all, he felt like he was carved from ice.

On the bright side, the salt wasn't really screaming into his nerve endings anymore. He was more uncomfortable than in pain. The wind blew and made his body want to spasm from the chill. Marco stood up and grabbed his pants, pulling them on over his wet underwear. The weather had sapped any remaining warmth from the jeans, and he got little comfort from them save the wind resistance. The others followed his lead, crawling from the water like primordial amphibians from the sea, shaking in the harsh, bitter cold.

Marty managed to put his pants on in one motion, smooth as silk despite the tremors in his body. His face was dark with rage. "I'm gonna gut that little shit like a fish, I swear I am!" His words were almost stuttery from the clicking of his teeth. He slapped at his arms to get blood flowing again.

Butch Carmichael was quiet, his fleshy face paler than usual. A lot of people might have thought he was freezing to death or that he was shocky. Marco knew better. Butch always got paler when he got really, truly pissed off. "You're gonna have help. I'm gonna burn that prick alive." Butch was fairly short and round, with reddish hair that looked like it belonged on a clown instead of a teenager. He was also one of the meanest bastards alive when you got him riled. Marco allowed himself a smile at the thought of what Butch would do to Dave.

Andy wasn't talking at all. Not that Marco was surprised by that. Andy almost never talked when he was thinking. You could almost see the gears in his head working feverishly. Whatever he was contemplating, Marco knew somebody would be on the receiving end of a bad scene. He wondered, more curious than concerned, what would happen to the cast on Andy's arm.

Derrick Brickman was just cursing under his breath a lot. He was mostly bluff and bluster unless he was getting help from someone else. He was a follower, not a leader, but he was very good at following. He'd do anything at all if you told him to do it. Thinking about the things he'd done to Nancy earlier made Marco smile, and made a part of him, a small, faint voice, wonder when he'd started getting off on that sort of sick shit.

And Marty? Well, Marty was a Hardwick. The Hardwicks had a long reputation in town for doing what they

wanted and getting away with it. Hell, the Hardwicks sometimes seemed to run Serenity—not in an official capacity,
but as a sort of pulse of the town. Normally when the Hardwicks wanted something done, well, they just found people
who agreed with them on how to do it.

They dressed and then they moved, heading away from
the quarry and toward the house where the freaky guy had
put a hurt on them. He wanted to get that guy at least as
much as he wanted to get Dave Pageant. But one target at a
time. That was the best way, and if he was going after the
man with the funky grin, he was going to have to have a
weapon on his side. Like, maybe a shotgun. Only he
wouldn't use salt to handle the matter. He'd use lead.

"So where are we going, Marco?" Derrick's eyes said
he wanted to hurt something, maybe get a little payback,
with interest. Much as Marco wanted the same thing, he
knew better.

"Home. Go home and get some sleep." Derrick blinked
slowly, a sure sign that he was actually trying to think again.
Marco had mercy on him and explained. "Right now we're
all tired, cold, and sore. Get some sleep. Then we meet back
at the Quik-Mart just after midnight."

"But my folks don't let me go out that late . . ."

"Sneak out, you moron. Don't tell 'em where you're going or that you're going at all, just sneak out." Just sometimes, he wanted to hit Derrick in the head with a shovel.
Most times he actually sort of liked the kid.

They each went their own ways when they hit the
main road. There would be time for getting back at Dave—
and they would get back at him—but first Marco had a few
things he wanted to get done. His old man had been something of a hunting buff. Being as he was dead, he didn't
really do much hunting anymore. But he had left behind
some great crap that he'd picked up over the years. In particular, he had all sorts of traps. Some of them had teeth.

III

It just might be fair to say that the hardest task an officer of the law has to deal with is passing on the news to a family member that a loved one has died. Jack Michaels prepared himself for that unpleasantness as best he could.

Then fate stepped in and made his job a little easier. Despite the urgent calls that had the man listed as dead, Jacob Parsons was alive. Barely, but he was alive. Mary Parsons was with her husband in the hospital, her face red from crying, her eyes bleary and swollen from the tears. It was true, even by her own reckoning, that she sometimes forgot how much she loved him. He was not handsome—his receding hairline was one of those disasters that looked like a scorched earth policy in action, his nose was too big, his mouth looked like it belonged on a fish, and his eyes, while expressive, were rather a dull shade of brown—and he would never win any Mr. Universe pageants, but he was kind, warm, and had a good sense of humor. He was also genuinely one of the nicest men she'd ever met. All of which was nothing compared to what he did to her heart. He made her feel like she was special, even when she was being a bitch, which was more often than she liked to think about.

And at the present time, he was barely alive. *Coma* is an ugly word, made uglier by the fact that it simply didn't say the truth of the matter well enough. *Coma* in this case meant not responding to treatment and possibly dying. He'd lost a lot of blood and had seemed dead when they found him. It wasn't until the constables showed up that the big one—she couldn't remember his name and didn't really have the energy to dwell on it—had noticed that he had a pulse. He hadn't waited for an ambulance but had scooped her husband up and driven him straight over to the medical center.

If he hadn't figured it out, Jake might well be dead now. The thought made her shiver. She needed Jacob. He was the single thing in her life that made her feel sane from day to day.

She'd come out of the library and found the car without him in it. At the time, that really didn't surprise her very much. Jake liked to take walks, and he knew she could be hours and hours on her research. What did surprise her was that he didn't show up by the time the sun set. Normally he'd have snuck into the library at some point and asked her what she'd like for dinner. It wouldn't matter that she wasn't hungry, he'd have done it anyway, because he was constantly worrying about her. It was just the way he was. Jake wouldn't forget something like that. He wasn't capable of it. So when sunset came and went and he hadn't returned, she got a little worried.

Gooseflesh crept across Mary's neck and ran down her arms when she remembered what Stan Long had said to her husband in a voice that was decades too old to have come from his adolescent mouth. *You're gonna be joining them in the darkness before this week is over, Jacob Parsons. You'll die and leave poor Mary all alone.* She closed her eyes and prayed that the words were only words. She loathed the idea that Jake might be dying and the thought that she would be left all alone. Jacob was really all she had in her life. There were friends, to be sure, but none who were truly close, none who meant anything at all when compared to her husband.

Beside her, his cold hand held in hers, Jacob Parsons lay in a state as close to death as he could possibly get without actually being dead. His breaths were forced by pumps and tubes. His heart was running on its own but at a level that was weaker than it should have been. His eyes did not move behind their lids, and his hands—usually so warm and oddly soft for a man who worked with them constantly—felt like wax sculptures.

Mary Parsons closed her eyes and cried silently, unaware of the changes taking place in her husband—just as she was ignorant of the fact that Jack Michaels was the one who found him first and left him in the alley. Just as she knew nothing of the fact that he'd been dead—truly dead, not only nearly so—when the constable stumbled across him.

Jack Michaels had made a few alterations to the fiber of Jacob Parsons's earthly shell, just as Terri Halloway had remade the officer while he tossed in a feverish dream near the edge of death himself.

The transformations were not accidental. They were deliberate. There was no contagion responsible for the metamorphosis taking place and no risk that the agent responsible could be transmitted accidentally. Make no mistake about that. There was an agenda being followed, and it had been planned a long time in the past.

IV

To say Nona was startled to find Carl and Greg in the living room of the house would be an understatement. Greg, because she'd asked him to let her think, and he was normally good about that sort of thing. Carl, because Carl was dead, or at least he was supposed to be. Somewhere along the way, he seemed to have forgotten that part of the scenario.

Everything was going fine until she opened the door. She'd been working, then she'd gone shopping for groceries,

and, because she had the free time, she'd gone off to see the
latest Adam Sandler movie. He wasn't good-looking, and
his humor was often crass, but she liked to watch him on the
big screen. She was still chuckling over the stunts and gags
planted throughout the movie—probably his best since
Happy Gilmore in her opinion—when she opened the door
and saw her dead husband sitting on top of her lover's bound
form. Greg looked like he'd been dragged over a few hundred yards of bad road and then had a car parked on him. His
face was bloodied and battered, his body doing little better.

The source of all Greg's wounds was using her lover's
body as a place to rest his posterior, and he was smiling
past the blood spatters on his face. He looked almost like a
clown with the red around his mouth; most of which, she
suspected, had been on his hands at one point or another as
they, too, looked like they'd been painted. Judging by the
way the pigment was turning rust colored and flaking
around the edges, she was pretty sure he wasn't using anything created by Revlon.

Her eyes took in the sight before her within seconds, but
her mind just wasn't quite ready to accept it. Three bags'
worth of groceries and her purse fell from numbed fingers
as she thought about it. Greg should be at work right now,
and Carl—well, Carl should be rotting in the woods. Nona
stepped halfway through the door and then caught herself.
No sir, not gonna do it. I am not *going through that door
and into that room. Carl looks a little too happy to see me,
and when Carl looks happy that way, I'm in for a scream
or two.*

She stepped back from the threshold as her blood pressure did a few belly flops and her skin turned wet with perspiration. The cold outside seemed eager to freeze the sweat
to her body, but that was A-okay. Much better than dealing
with Carl really.

She was reaching for the doorknob to slam the damned

door closed when she heard the wet sound of Carl's voice. "Nona," he said calmly—the same calm he normally had going before he took off his belt to put her back in her place—"If I have to come after you, it's gonna be a whole helluva lot worse. You know that, don't you?" His voice was wrong, distorted and filled with the sort of bubbling sounds that surely meant pneumonia or worse, but underlying that was the same silken purr his words always took when things were about to get ugly.

In The World According to Carl, he could not actually rape his wife. She was his spouse, and anything he did was within his rights as her husband. Nona knew better. She knew that what he'd done to her on several occasions was no less than a violation of her body and an attempt to break her spirit. She knew that the marks he'd left on her with his hands and with his teeth weren't from passion but were a way to remind her that she belonged to him.

Her mind flashed back to when they'd first been married, when they'd actually been happy, and he had been a caring, loving man. She knew all too well that the change he'd gone through had been brought on by her infidelity. She'd had a one-night stand with Stephen Wilkins, had been seduced by a man who could charm a nun out of her habit, thank you very much. After that, after Carl found out, that was when things went sour fast.

Was she to blame for him becoming an abusive bastard? Maybe, but nothing she'd done had warranted the repeated beatings. Fear alone had kept her his prisoner in the past, and she'd only ever managed to defy him once; the same night she'd helped kill him.

Only Carl wasn't dead. And that was the part that just kept spinning like tires stuck in a thick pool of mud. She couldn't get around it or drive through it; it was messing with her too severely. She wanted nothing more than to run for all she was worth. But his voice, damn him to hell, his

voice with that soft, almost teasing quality, she was like
Pavlov's dog responding to the dinner bell. Only instead of
salivating, that voice made her need to obey him. Failure to
obey, after all, brought even greater punishments.

"Come on, sugar. Don't make me have to lose my temper. You know I don't want to have to do that."

She looked back into the living room of her house,
where Carl and Greg were both waiting for her. Carl was
smiling, his face distorted by a series of scars that made
him look like he'd been broken and poorly mended. Greg
wasn't smiling. Greg's eyes pleaded with her to just run,
just get the hell out of there before it was too late.

Greg started to say something to her, his busted lips moving awkwardly as he formed words. "Ruhn, Nona. Get out of
here." His voice was so weak, so wasted and pale in comparison to what it normally was. He might have wanted to say
more, but Carl's hand moved down from its perch on his
knees and down to Greg's shoulder. She saw the thumb of
his bloodied hand disappear up to the first joint inside of the
bared flesh on her lover's body and heard the sound change
from an attempt to make her see reason into a squeal worthy
of a piglet caught in a bear trap. He couldn't have jumped
any harder if someone had stuck electrodes into his eyes.
Greg screamed and in the end, that was enough to get her
going.

Nona turned on her heel and took to the proverbial high-
way with a speed that would have shamed the Roadrunner.
Nona was not, as a rule, an athletic woman, but she was
still in good shape. She could run like a greyhound when
she had to.

"Nona! You get back here, you bitch!" Oh, that wasn't
good at all, he sounded angry enough to get positively vicious as opposed to merely brutal. Nona's heart did a few
extra hard thumps in her chest, and she moved even faster
than before, goosed into high gear by the thought of what

he'd do if he caught up with her. She heard another weak, almost kittenish mew come from Greg and knew, just *knew,* by God, that Carl was up and coming after her.

She left the driveway, never even giving serious thought to trying for the car. By the time she could get in and lock the doors, Carl would be there, ready to punch his way through the glass, the metal, anything at all to reach her. Besides which, her keys where in her purse, which she'd just left behind. Nona was terrified, horrified, really, about what was happening in her life. But at least she'd gone casual today. At least she was wearing shoes she could run in as opposed to the high heels she often wore. The road was dry, but she knew good and well how hard it was to get any worthwhile traction in heels.

Carl's beefy hand grazed her back, just missing a handful of blouse that would have cost her everything. Her skirt, designed to enhance her assets, not her running speed, was a hindrance, and it was costing her speed. She reached down with one hand and hiked the skirt high up her thighs, freeing her to make a longer stride in her run. And despite the fact that her dead—well, maybe undead—husband was running after her, despite the fact that he would surely make her into so much hamburger if he caught her, she hoped no one saw her practically flashing the neighborhood as she moved.

"Nona, don't make it worse than it already is! Get your ass over here!"

Don't let me fall, please, God, don't let me fall. I'm sorry for everything I've ever done wrong, but please, God, don't let me fall and don't let him catch me. She forced herself to move faster still, her breaths coming faster and faster as she devoured oxygen and tried to keep ahead of Carl.

Maybe, just maybe, sometimes the powers that be listen. Nona managed not to become a cliché in a bad horror

movie. She managed to keep her feet. Carl was not so
lucky. Carl's left foot just didn't do what it was supposed to
and gave out under him. He fell hard and slammed into
the ground, his fingers once again grazing her skin before
she outdistanced him. Nona didn't look back; she didn't
dare look back. She merely gave her silent thanks to God
and pumped her legs, looking for a way out of the hell her
world was fragmenting into.

V

While Nona Bradford was running from her dead husband,
a handful of the local high school kids were finishing their
own special tasks. Eva Spinelli and Chris Parker were
among them, smiling to each other and as in love as they
had ever been. There had been a few tense days after the
dog attack—Chris was rather offended that Eva had left
him to die, but, in hindsight, decided to forgive her—but
that was all in the past. They and several of the others
who'd been victims of the pack's savagery were moving
through Serenity Falls with sheaves of fliers to pass out and
post on every available space large enough to accommo-
date them. The fliers were given to them by an old man
who promised them monetary compensation for seeing
that they were spread throughout the town.

Down at Kelsey's Drugs, they covered the wall just past
the massive bay window with over twenty of the garish
color prints. The Kinkos where they met the old man and
received the first half of their payment was practically wall-
papered with the high-gloss advertisement. Cars that were
parked on the road soon became nests for the ad, often

folded under a windshield wiper or slipped through cracks in the windows. If there was a spot missed by the teens, it wasn't for lack of trying to find it.

For a lot of the people in town, those too young to remember the last time the advertisement had shown itself in Serenity, there was a pleasant sense of nostalgia to the flyers. A few of them thought it a joke, but others picked it up and smiled, thinking it might be fun to take their girlfriends, their wives, their families. For others in town, those whose lives spanned back far enough, the picture sent chills, or, worse, brought back a deep, cold hatred.

Eventually, their work finished, the teens went on their way. What they left behind were hundreds of small, full-color posters.

If they had known anything at all about the history and violence that took place on the Pageant farm almost fifty years earlier, Marco DeMillio and his cohorts would never have thought to set foot on the property. They would have done any and everything to avoid getting anywhere near the place. They did not know. They were not told. Few people will willingly admit that they murdered innocent people, and fewer still would consider telling their children.

The fact of the matter is, Marco and his goons did not know about the murders. They didn't know, and they didn't care. They had plans of their own. Most of those plans involved putting a serious hurt on Dave Pageant, whose rock salt was still leaving a few of them with lingering pains in their legs and asses.

Just behind him, Marco heard the sounds of Marty Hardwick panting under the weight of the package they planned to use on good ol' Davey. Wrapped in a thick wool blanket were four well-oiled iron bear traps. Each of them was old enough that it probably should have been in a museum somewhere, but Marco didn't care about that. What he cared about was the warning his Uncle Bruno had given him when he was still in grade school. Bruno—who lived with the family for a few years—had taken him out to what in its heyday had probably been a nice barn and showed him what he referred to as his "museum of hunting tools." What it amounted to was a collection of old junk, most of which hadn't been used in the last fifty years. But in a corner of the area was a small pile of the most lethal looking traps Marco had ever seen. His uncle took great delight in showing him how they worked, and demonstrated their strength with the wooden handle of a rake that had long ago lost most of its tines. The trap snapped the inch and a half thick wood with the greatest of ease.

Thinking about what the traps would do to Dave's hands and face was almost enough to make him shiver with pleasure.

Marty got stuck carrying the traps because he still owed Marco around twenty dollars for all the mooching he'd done. You'd have thought he was carrying a car slung over his shoulder the way he was panting and moaning. Marty loved to whine about his miserable lot in life but seldom remembered how he got stuck with the extra workload. It was one of the many things Marco liked about the guy. That, and Marty was really, really twisted in the head.

The group had made it back to the farm, moving as quietly as they could—give or take the whining of their mule Marty—and Marco's pulse was growing faster. He didn't know which idea pleased him more, nailing Dave to the ground or just plain nailing the little shit's sisters. The twins were hot.

He was still contemplating which of the several females at the farm he wanted to do first when the circus came back to town.

Marco died screaming. So did all of his buddies.

And Dave Pageant watched it all.

VI

They were most of the way to the homicide site when they saw the running woman fall. Vic had no idea who she was, but thought she might be attractive under better circumstances. Tom Norris knew exactly who she was, and he said so. "That's Nona Bradford. I don't know what she's running from, but we better do what we can to help her."

"Yeah, well, the corpse isn't gonna go anywhere, right?" Norris chuckled at that and then hit the flashers. The woman—her eyes as wide saucers—stumbled and fell to the ground. Norris was halfway out of the truck before Vic could come to a complete halt.

Even as he followed, he saw Tom pulling his nightstick and heading toward a man who looked ready to stomp Nona Bradford into the concrete. "Carl," Tom warned as he moved to intercept the larger man. "You don't want to do anything that's going to get you arrested. You just want to calm yourself down right now."

The sun was well on its way to set, and through the dusk, Victor could just barely make out that there was something wrong with the man Tom was speaking to. He moved faster, ready to back up his partner.

Carl Bradford apparently didn't feel like waiting that long. He took the liberty of swinging on Tom without so much as blinking. His fist hit Norris's head, and Norris's feet left the asphalt. His ass hit the ground a moment later. Norris slumped backwards and didn't get back up.

Victor Barnes was used, frankly, to having people see him coming and blanch. He knew he was a big man, physically, and that he was intimidating to almost everyone he saw. He also knew about a dozen ways to break the bones of his opponents without really trying very hard. He'd done far too many things in his life to walk away without that sort of knowledge. He was not fearless, but he was certainly hard to intimidate.

One look at Carl Bradford up close was enough to make him hesitate.

Carl didn't feel the same worries. He took a swing at Barnes and almost connected before the giant ducked the blow. Carl Bradford also knew many, many ways to hurt a man. And though he didn't bother to let it show on what was left of his face, he had doubts about being able to take down the constable. Carl was used to being the biggest kid in the playground as it were, but Victor Barnes made him feel like a preschooler trying to go up against a high school senior.

It didn't take Vic long to get over his shock at the man's physical appearance. Something about Carl trying to knock his head off his shoulders helped him snap out of his daze in record time. There were parts of Vic's life that he was not overly proud of—and really, who among us can't say the same—but it was those chapters he did his best to avoid thinking about that were also responsible for his quick reaction time. He hoisted one knee into Carl's crotch while feinting a punch to the man's face at the same time. Victor was big enough and strong enough that he practically threw his opponent backwards with the blow.

Carl grunted and dropped, falling to the ground on his hands and knees. His whole body trembled as he started rising. Vic was surprised to see the man rising at all, but not so shocked this time that he couldn't react. He shot a foot into Bradford's ribs and sent him rolling over. He was almost certain he heard something crack over the sound of the man grunting. Behind him, the woman who'd been chased by scarface was screaming something incoherent again and again. She was hysterical, and he couldn't really say that he blamed her. The man he'd just done his best to knock senseless was rolling over and standing up again.

Fair to say that there had been a few men along the way who were tough enough to give Victor Barnes a run for his money. Most of them were hard, vicious, and hopped up on enough cocaine that a few bullets through their heads wouldn't have stopped them for a while. But even they normally slowed down after he'd broken a few bones. Carl Bradford apparently didn't believe in lying down on the job. He finished his roll over to his feet and came up like a coiled snake. His fist met with Victor's privates and landed like a sledgehammer.

Vic let out a roar that would have made most grizzly bears head for higher ground and brought both of his fists down on the man's head as hard as he could. The force of the blow rattled through his arms almost as much as if he were gripping an active jackhammer. This time he knew he heard something break, and felt a cold dread run through him that he might just have committed murder inadvertently. Bradford dropped for the second time, his head slamming into the concrete between Victor's shoes with an audible crunch. He wasn't moving.

Under most circumstances, Victor would have been checking for vitals right about then. Instead, he doubled over, looking down at the body of his victim, as the blow he'd taken to the balls finally caught up with him. His stomach was turning almost as much as it had at the Pageant place earlier, and his vision blurred a bit. He gulped air as best he could and closed his eyes to stop everything from swimming. Very few people had ever hit him in his testicles, and none of them had ever hit him as hard as the man lying on the ground beneath him. He felt a strong need to vomit and was tempted to let it happen. The freak on the concrete just about deserved it. On the other hand, he was the one who'd get stuck cleaning it up afterwards. He opened his eyes again. Everything was a little more stable.

The woman moved over his way a bit, and he looked at her, his head cocked almost sideways. She was pretty, and she was terrified. "Are you okay, miss?"

She looked at him, about to speak, and then her eyes went wide, and she backed away again, shaking her head almost fast enough to blur her features. He looked down just in time to feel the teeth cutting into his calf through the fabric of his pants. Victor Barnes screamed again, this time in pain, not in rage. The bastard didn't just bite down with his teeth, he was grinding as hard as he could. He felt his leg give out, felt himself falling, and couldn't stop it from happening. What he could do, what he did do, was make sure he fell in a way that was beneficial to him. He did a drop directly down on Carl Bradford that would have made Hulk Hogan proud, his elbow driving hard into the man's lower back, around the kidney region. He landed hard, his leg bent at an excruciating angle, and he felt hot lightning flashes rip through his nerves around where Bradford was biting down.

Bradford made a loud barking sound and let go with his teeth. Vic rolled to his side and tried standing up, but his right leg, complete with the new bleeding wound, didn't feel much like playing. Add on the way his testicles were protesting their abuse a few seconds earlier, and it becomes easy to see where the constable was feeling a bit challenged at the moment. He pushed up with his left leg, balanced himself for all of three seconds, and then dropped back down on his right knee in a half crouch. Standing wasn't going to be an option, and that limited what he could do.

Carl Bradford didn't seem to be having the same difficulties. He hopped right on back to both feet, barely even breathing hard. Of course he was having a few problems of his own, like the broken neck that wasn't letting him lift his head up very high. His face, already wrecked and poorly reassembled by the look of it, was busted open across his lips, and his nose had been smashed sideways when Vic hit the back of his head.

Carl Bradford grinned, a sight that was never really pleasant to begin with and was now absolutely unsettling, and spoke. "Sucks to be you, doesn't it?"

Victor Barnes, who had little difficulty dealing with a pack of dogs that wouldn't stay dead, was having a great deal more trouble believing what his eyes insisted on showing him. Wounded animals were one thing, but men with broken necks didn't just stand up and smile at you while cracking wise. It wasn't physically possible.

It's decidedly conceivable that a more adept officer of the law would have reached for his handgun. But Victor Barnes hadn't been carrying a weapon for years. Frankly, he didn't need to. So instead, he swung his fist around in a wide arc and hit the freak in front of him with every ounce of strength he could muster. Carl didn't quite make orbit, but it wasn't for lack of trying. He left the ground completely, and something hot snapped inside Vic's hand at the same moment.

And then the bastard got up again. His head lolling worse than before, Carl Bradford rose from the street where he'd landed and started moving toward him with a scowl across his twisted features. The wound in Vic's leg was starting to throb a bit—adrenaline keeping the worst of it down to a dull ache—and he felt a strong flow of warmth running over his calf. He could guess what it was but didn't have time to do anything about it. Right now that big dead guy was heading over his way again, and this time he looked intent on getting nasty.

Bradford's head took that moment to explode. That was really what it came down to, an explosion of viscera and bone fragments. The man took a step forward, and then his head just went splat and rained down across Victor's chest

and face. Any doubt he'd had that the man was already
dead disappeared the instant the smell of the waste tickling
down his body hit his nose. Constable Victor Barnes managed not to vomit a second time, though it was a close
thing.

He might have had an easier time of it if the dead man
hadn't kept walking in his direction. Vic managed to get
himself motivated enough to crawl backwards away from
the headless dead thing, his stomach still threatening rebellion and his leg bleeding all over the place from the bite
taken from his calf. He saw Tom Norris standing behind
the shambling thing; saw the blood streaming from his broken nose and the look of absolute disgust on the man's
face. Norris pulled the trigger again, this time blowing out
a portion of Bradford's back and a few vertebrae besides.
The body stopped moving forward and dropped to its knees,
swaying like a tree in a hurricane.

Norris unloaded the rest of his pistol's rounds into the
body. Vic thought very seriously about passing out, his vision graying and then coming back into focus several times.
In the end, he just lay back on the ground and stared up at
the darkening sky. He heard Tom talking, heard the woman
making wheezing, crying noises, and decided they could
wait. He closed his eyes and let the gray overwhelm him.

VII

She waited as calmly as she could while the sun went
down. Somewhere out there, her little boy was alone in the
cold, and it was enough to make Penny Grey want to
scream. He was such a sickly boy, so small for his age, and
always so terribly sad. Oh she knew part of that was caused

by her being too worried about him, too protective of him, but that didn't make it any easier for her to deal with.

Lawrence was her life, had been for a very long time. Her sister, Lois, might think she was overly protective, and just maybe she was, but Lawrence was all she had left. Lawrence, who was supposed to be cursed, if her dead ex-husband could be believed. Daniel was always filled with the strangest flights of fancy. But the thought that Lawrence could ever do anyone harm was definitely one of his stranger ones.

But now he was gone. She'd left to pick him up from school at the same time as always, fully prepared to find him waiting at the sidewalk or moving toward her with his little face aimed at the ground, and he hadn't shown up. She'd waited a full fifteen minutes for him, and then she'd gone into the school, prepared to tear the place apart if she couldn't find him. And then she got nervous. Mr. Wortham and both of the custodians helped her look for Lawrence, but to no avail. Finally, unhappily, she'd had to accept that he wasn't in the school. A check with his last teacher of the day confirmed that he'd been in class, but beyond that there was no sign of her son.

So for the last few hours she'd been making calls to the constables and pacing nervously, worrying about what had happened to poor, frail Lawrence. She'd made all of the phone calls to family and friends, but no one had seen him. Lois, God love her, was almost as distraught as she was. She'd promised to come over as soon as she could.

And Penny needed that. She needed the comfort of a family member like she never had in her entire life.

There was a time when she'd been stronger, more capable of being on her own, but that was in the past. These days she didn't seem capable of being strong unless there was something to help give her focus, to direct her. Like the love of her son. She could be strong for him.

Penny moved into the kitchen and thought about preparing dinner. It was getting dark, and he'd be hungry. Her hands flew around uselessly, unable to figure out what to do with themselves, and she walked away from the kitchen again, deciding that when her Lawrence came home she would take him out for a treat to help soothe the fears from him. There was a voice in the back of her mind that railed at her for even considering the idea. She'd been too soft with him, not nearly strict enough, and he didn't need comforting, he needed a good ass blistering to remind him why there were rules. But that voice was crushed almost as soon as it rose. She just wanted him home, safe and in her arms where he belonged. Everything else was secondary, and he didn't need to be punished, he needed to be protected.

And miracle of miracles, there he was, walking through the front door as if he'd just gone to check the mail. His clothes were a little messy, his thin hair was wild and windblown, but he looked whole and alive.

"Lawrence!" She moved toward him, intent on putting her arms around his delicate body and hugging him as fiercely as she could. "Oh, thank God you're all right!" She scarcely even noticed the tremble in her voice, the desperate release of tensions that came with it.

Lawrence looked at her and stepped to the side, gracefully dodging under her embracing arms. "Don't touch me, Mother."

He couldn't have stopped her any better if he'd dropped a stone wall between them. The tone in his voice wasn't one she was used to. It was . . . well, it was defiant.

"What do you mean? How dare you tell me that I can't touch my own son."

"I don't want you to touch me. I don't want anything to do with you." The look in his dark eyes was enough to make her weak in the knees.

"What?" She moved forward, determined to put her

arms around him and hug away the ridiculous attitude he
was shooting her way. That deep voice, the one she always
did her best to ignore, was roaring now, ready to knock
some sense into him. Where did he get off speaking to
her—*to her*!—that way, as if all of her sacrifices over the
years meant nothing at all.

He dodged under her a second time, sliding past her
and into the living room just past the foyer. "I said don't
touch me!"

His words were a slap, an assault on her senses. She
rose up, more shocked yet than wounded, and looked down
at her son. That little voice, her secret voice, getting out
just a little bit at that moment. "How dare you?"

"It's easy, Mother. I hate the idea of you ever touching
me again." He was so calm, so cool as he said the words,
and his dark eyes looked at her with a hatred that felt almost like it would burn her skin. Lawrence backed away
from her, not out of fear but out of disgust.

"Lawrence, what's gotten into you?" There, that sounded
authoritative, certainly better than any attempts to cajole
him back into her arms would. She'd have to be stern, have
to get him to understand that what she was doing was for
his best. "Do you understand that I had to call the police
on you, Lawrence? Do you realize what you've put me
through?"

"I don't care. I don't care about the police, or about you,
or about this miserable, shitty little house."

Lawrence never used profanity. Never. It was unheard
of. His use of it now made the world grow a bit fuzzy, but
she bit the inside of her lip, and everything snapped back
into focus. Now she was angry, not shocked. She could feel
her blood pounding in her temples and knew for the first
time in a very long time what it meant to feel something
other than fear for her son's safety.

"That's enough out of you, young man!"

"That's not enough of anything, Mommy." And the tone of voice that he used was bitingly sarcastic. As if the thought that she was his mother was some sort of joke that he'd grown tired of. "That's not enough of any damned thing."

He spun and started toward his room upstairs, and she followed, her blood pressure escalating at a steady pace. "You get back here, Lawrence! You get back here right now!"

And he laughed at her, laughed, as if whatever was on her mind was the least significant aspect of his world. "I'm busy! I have things to do."

"You don't have a damned thing to do but turn around and listen to me!" She reached out her hand and grabbed his shoulder. Enough was enough; she wouldn't tolerate this sort of behavior for a moment longer.

"GET YOUR FUCKING HANDS OFFA ME!" His voice came out as a roar, and his hand when it slapped hers away felt like a hammer blow. Penny reeled back, as shocked by his scream as she was by his violent reaction to her touch. His face was red, livid as he turned and started down the stairs, teeth bared and eyes blazing. For an instant she flashed back in time, saw in her son the face of her dead husband, the rage and the barely contained hatred so often shown on Daniel's face so many years ago. Lawrence moved down the stairs, his fists balled up and his jaw set. "You don't touch me, woman, or I swear I'll kill you myself!"

Penny wanted to protest. She wanted to rear up and knock a few of his teeth loose for daring to speak to her that way, but all of the impulses in her brain were failing to reach any of their destinations. She hadn't felt shock like that in over a decade. He came forward until he was looking into her face, his own separated only by the fact that he was still shorter than she was, and spoke softly. "It stops now, Mother. I'm not going to stay locked away in this

shithole anymore. I'm going out. I have things to do. Deal
with it."

And then she did it. Her hand finally managed to get the
signal from her head, and she slapped her only son across
the face hard enough to knock him on his ass. It would
have been hard to say which of them was more surprised,
Penny or Lawrence.

Oh, how she wanted to reach out for him, to apologize
for ever, ever hitting him. And, oh, how she wanted to do it
again. "Get up to your room, Lawrence. Get up to your
room and stay there."

He sat sprawled across four stairs, looking murder at her,
his face pale and his skin pasty, wet with perspiration. "No.
Not this time. This time I'm standing up, and I'm going
down the stairs and out the door. And you won't stop me."

"Oh you don't think so?" She was feeling a little more
in control, freed by the act of striking him, no matter how
much it had hurt her to do it. Her hands reached down, pinning his skinny shoulders to the stairs, and her mind—still
halfway lost in the impossibility of her world spinning out
of its usual orbit—tried to focus on what exactly was going
on. She'd had her moments of defiance when she lived on
the farm with everyone else. She'd been raised as a free
thinker, but that didn't mean she'd always met with the ap-
proval of her parents. They hadn't liked the idea of her
marrying Daniel Grey in the least, but she'd done it just the
same. That they had been right in that case wasn't significant at the moment, she'd made her choice and lived with
it. Now her son was feeling the need to spread his wings,
and that was okay to an extent, but not the way he was going about it. She'd be damned before she'd let him get
physical with her. "You get your little ass up the stairs,
Lawrence, before I have to show you who wears the pants
around here."

He sighed, one hand moving to pinch the bridge of his

nose. His eyes were closed as if to show how hard it was
for him to be patient. She knew the look well enough; it
was a gesture she'd used a few times with him in the past.
"You know, Lawrence loves you, for reasons I personally
can't understand. So I've tried to be patient about all of
this." The voice was all wrong, deeper and much stronger
than ever came out of her son. "But as much as your baby
boy might care for you, I just find you annoying."

He didn't stand up. He just sort of rose from the ground
and was suddenly upright. Her hands on his shoulders were
pushed back as he repositioned himself, and Penny was
flung backwards until her backside was stopped by the wall
of the stairwell. Lawrence, her precious little boy, looked
at her with eyes half lidded and his mouth pulled down in a
nasty scowl. "I've been trying my best to play this out
slowly, but I've got to say, I really don't feel like it anymore. I've been stopped half a dozen times by that miserable prick, Crowley, and I've been held back by having to
wait for the right time."

"What are you talking about?" Penny looked at her boy
as he stood there, his hands moving around and dusting
imaginary debris from his school clothes.

"Shut up. I'm not finished with my rant. Everything is
in place now. I don't have to be nice anymore, so, Penelope
Grey, I won't be." And Lawrence, her sweet, wonderful,
loving, obedient boy, reached out with his hand and tore
through her chest, his fingers breaking through bone as if
merely pushing past toothpicks. His fingers crushed the
meat of her heart as surely as his actions shattered the fig-
urative heart within her soul. Hard to say which hurt her
worse, which made her scream in her last minutes of life.

Lawrence Grey licked his fingers clean and then took
the time to change clothes before leaving the house for the
last time. Appearance was everything, after all, and he had
a show to attend.

VIII

Stan sat outside on his back porch and looked at the spot where they'd buried Beau. The night air was nearly frigid, but the thick down coat he wore kept him warm enough, and warmer by far than he felt in his soul. He looked without seeing as his mind was lost in the past. Beau was dead. And much as he might want to get past that sad fact, it kept wrapping around him and pulling him away from his own thoughts. One second he'd be thinking about his dad— *Funny how that face never smiled anymore.*—or his mom—*And I'd never noticed the lines on her face until just recently. She'd always seemed younger than the mothers of my friends, but that's gone now.*—Or even April, who had moved on to be as sad and almost painfully bitter as his parents since Beau was killed.

And just like that, the realization that his best friend was dead came back to bite him in the ass. And it was getting harder and harder to remember if he'd ever been happy. Dave and Jessie had been by earlier, doing their best not to advertise that they were falling for each other and failing, and even that hadn't been enough to slow down the thoughts of Beau.

He blinked a few times, fighting back the tears that wanted to fall, and succeeding for the moment.

Stan let out a long, slow sigh and heard it mimicked not four feet away from him.

"Hi, kid." He turned and looked at the man from the hospital, the one who had made the seizures go away. He hadn't even remembered seeing the man until just that moment, as if someone had flipped a switch inside his brain. The stranger looked at him and smiled softly in the near darkness. "I heard about your dog. I'm sorry."

Stan had nothing to say to that, so he nodded, hoping it was enough.

"You haven't been having a good time lately, have you Stan?"

"Not hardly."

"Had any more problems with the voices?"

"No. Thanks for that."

"Not at all a problem, I assure you."

"You're not here to talk to me about my problems, are you?"

"Maybe partially. Mostly, I need to know where one of your friends lives."

"Which one?"

"Joey Whitman."

"What did Joey do?"

"Well . . . let's just say we had a disagreement."

"Oh." Stan looked away for a minute, his eyes going back to where Beau was buried. "Are you going to hurt him?"

"Joey? No. No, I want to help him."

"Like you did me?"

"Sort of. It's a little different, but the same basic idea."

"What's wrong with him?"

"Well, you know how you had all the voices going off?"

"Yeah."

"He's only got one voice. But it's really, really loud, and it's making him do things."

"So, he's possessed?"

"Pretty much." Crowley made a sour face. "When did kids start getting intelligent at your age? When I was your age, no one knew what the hell a possession was."

"*Exorcist*. I saw it when I was nine."

"Your parents let you watch that when you were nine?"

"They didn't know."

"Ah." The man pushed his glasses back up his face with

one finger, his eyes looking over at the spot where Stan had
been staring. Stan realized he was out in the cold with only
a thin windbreaker but decided not to ask about it. "The
thing is, whatever has Joey in its grip is actually something
that's been trying to get my attention. I figure the sooner
I deal with it, the better for Joey."

"Are you sure you're not gonna hurt him? 'Cause Joey's
a pretty cool guy. He helped save my life when the whole
drowning thing happened."

"Well . . . I could lie to you and swear that I won't hurt
him, but I really don't want to do that. I can promise that
I'll do my best to avoid hurting him, if that helps."

Stan looked at the man dubiously. On the one hand, he
had helped Stan a lot. Without his help, he figured he'd either still be in the hospital or he'd be dead. There was no
two ways about it; the seizures had only been getting worse
before Crowley stepped in. On the other hand, he was still
a creepy guy. He looked normal enough, he talked like a
real person—even if he did talk down just a little bit—but
he was damned scary. Finally he decided to tell him. He
gave the address and looked over at Beau's grave, a small
patch of brown soil near a small tree at the edge of a small
hill in his small world. Somehow everything seemed di-
minished with Beauregard gone. He couldn't have said exactly how, but there it was. Everything was pale and faded
and worn beyond the point he wanted to think about. His
family was falling apart, and even that didn't seem to matter much.

Crowley left him in the cold night after placing a hand
on his shoulder briefly. The scary man didn't say a word,
but Stan found the touch oddly comforting just the same.
He knew that somewhere along the way the stranger had
felt the same sort of pain and understood his grief. It was
enough for the moment.

IX

Somewhere in the back of her mind, lost to the rest of the world, Becky Glass was having dinner with her mother and father. She was glad she'd gone into the woods with Joey, glad that she'd taken the risk and dealt with the witch in the woods, and eternally grateful that the witch really was more than a legend. She'd had her doubts, but she'd had to try, and for once, thank God, just for this once, it was worth it.

Her father didn't talk much, but that was hardly unusual. Her mother chatted a lot and that, too, was part of the daily routine. Her mother, ever experimental, had served them up a homemade beef potpie that was much better than she'd expected.

And in the world beyond the pleasant pipe dream she was experiencing, her body was walking through town, run by a sentience that couldn't have cared less about the fact that her father was mincemeat. That sentience was broken just now, fractured deliberately into three separate parts and doing what it could to handle several tasks simultaneously.

That sentience was also not having a very good time of achieving any of its goals. Maintaining cohesion—mentally speaking, not physically, thanks very much—was proving a lot more difficult than it had imagined. It was all a lot easier when Karstens was still around. Karstens was an easy pawn to use, not exactly the brightest lightbulb in the chandelier as it were. But the three children, the youngsters it inhabited now, were proving to be a bit frustrating. The Lawrence Grey body was pretty much doing its own thing, and as of half an hour earlier, that included matricide with a side order of cannibalism. Not that it had ever minded a little raw human flesh, but there was a time and a place.

This body, the girl, was proving to be troublesome for entirely different reasons. Puberty, it seemed, was not only a serious issue but also a good excuse for the body of Rebecca Glass to start feeling seriously frustrated. It wasn't exactly the end of the world, nor even remotely close to the end of its plans for the Hunter, but it was damned distracting. It had to fight constantly to stop the girl's body from sending out the sort of signals that made males of the species decidedly randy. Under other circumstances it might have been tempted to play for a while, but right now it had to focus on other things.

Like the damned curse sitting smack on top of the town of Serenity Falls. Unlike the Hunter, the thing inhabiting Becky Glass had been in town long enough to study the curse and was stunned by the complexities woven into the damnation of Serenity. Layers upon layers of spell casting the likes of which it had never run across went into that curse, and now, when it had finally managed to claw its way up to this reality again—a task that was daunting under the best of circumstances—something had triggered the curse into its final phases. Oh, it suspected it knew what that something was, suspected, in fact, that its presence was the primary cause of the dilemma. But that didn't mean it had to be happy about the entire sordid situation.

The basic tenet of the curse was simplicity itself. Every person who lived in the town of Serenity Falls—most especially those whose families had their roots in the origin of the town—was to suffer in one way or another. Most of them met with untimely deaths or simply went a little crazy, but there was a special focus on murder and lust. It was a subtle curse, not meant to be blatant at all until the final stages. As curses went it seemed mild until the implications came around. The primary focus of the curse was simply that it made temptations seem more promising than they should have under normal circumstances. Coveting thy neighbor's wife? Well, by all means, have a good time. Consequences for actions didn't seem as significant to the people in Serenity as they did elsewhere, because the humans living in the area were numbed to worrying about that sort of thing. They gave in to temptation a lot more than they should have, because that was what the curse told them to do.

More importantly, they gave in to their fears more often. Their fears and their hatreds. Lust was easy. Given a few drinks or enough time, most of the humans it had encountered over the centuries would succumb to lust. But fears were a different beast entirely. Fears could be countered by other fears. It was one thing to worry about whether or not your children would be safe with the occasional stranger, but under most circumstances, fear of being wrong, fear of being caught in whatever actions a person might take would counter the initial fear.

It would have been a lie to say it understood all of the reasons behind the curse, but it most certainly could appreciate the end results. Rape, murder, mob justice, matricide, a few more rapes and murders . . . Pleasant distractions for the most part.

In her mind, Becky went about the evening with her family. In the world beyond her pleasant fantasy, she left the house, unnoticed by her mother who was still miserable with grief, heading toward the Pageant farm. What moved her body wanted to see what was coming, wanted to know what it needed to do in order to use the forces it felt building to its best advantage.

X

Sometimes wishes do come true, but almost never in quite the way they were wished for. Dave Pageant had spent the latter part of his early evening explaining to his father why he'd felt it necessary to unload a half-dozen shotguns shells' worth of rock salt into the asses of his enemies. His father was very understanding, but only because of the threats to Dave's sisters. Now, after dinner and finishing his homework, Dave sat outside in the shadows of the barn and watched the different points of access to the farm. He figured they'd be back, and if they came at night, someone had to watch for them.

And he wished with all his might that if they came back, he wouldn't have to hurt them. That they could hurt him never really crossed his mind. It wasn't the way Dave thought. He just wasn't programmed for those sorts of notions.

The air was still damned cold outside, and Dave reached over to his thermos full of hot cocoa and poured himself another cupful. It was still hot and still tasted just right going down. Wisps of steam ran up and glazed his spectacles lightly with a fog that faded as soon as it appeared.

He'd just finished the hot chocolate when he heard the sounds of the older boys heading his way. They were doing their best to be quiet, and probably succeeding pretty well, but Dave had been sitting outside on the isolated farm for well over two hours, and he knew what to listen for. Cows do not whisper, or if they do, he'd never heard it happen. He calmly shook his hands out and peeled the mittens from them. The cold air running across his sweating fingers was almost enough to make him gasp. He rolled over in the soft grass and pushed himself up into a kneeling position, then rose all the way up until he was standing.

There was a part of him that truly wished this hadn't happened, but as usual, he pushed that aside and got on to what he had to do. This time, it wasn't rock salt in the shotgun. They'd had their warning, and he was ready to take care of things once and for all.

Dave hid in the shadows of the barn and listened as they came closer. He took very small breaths and made sure they couldn't see the warm air escaping when he exhaled. They had weapons this time, but nothing as sophisticated as a shotgun. Oh, no, they had bear traps. Dave closed his eyes, imagining what they might use them for and seeing his sisters pinned to the ground while the pigs moving his way raped them. He could just imagine Marco getting off on the idea of forcing himself on a girl who was nailed to the ground by bear traps on her hands and feet.

Dave took careful aim with the weapon in his hands. Biggest difference between what he had and what they had was range, serious range. The first two shells were pellets, birdshot to make sure they understood how serious he was about keeping his family safe. The rest of the shells were the slugs his dad used for deer hunting. Two warnings were all he was willing to risk when it came to the number of bullies who were making threats.

They weren't quite in range yet, so Dave waited. He would wait as long as it took.

They never made it into the proper distance for making his point clear.

Something else happened instead.

One second they were moving in a line toward where Dave waited, and the next the ground just sort of exploded all around them. The sun was a distant memory, and the lights from the street leading past the farm really didn't reach nearly far enough to let him make out the details clearly. Despite his time adjusting to the darkness, Dave couldn't see exactly what came out of the ground and wrapped around Marco and his friends. All he could see was the way their bodies jerked hard—like fish caught on hooks and yanked savagely toward the boat—and the way they didn't so much hit the ground as sink into it. Marco had just enough time to scream before whatever it was that was wrapping around him like ivy reached up to his mouth and shot into it and then down deep, like watching someone puke up a few hundred pounds of spinach, only in reverse.

Marty looked like the one who might get away for a few seconds there. His scrawny frame was whipped around like a willow in strong winds, and the bear traps he was shouldering fell from his body in a rattling rain of metal. He let out a sound like a barking dog suddenly getting the hiccups and then disappeared from sight. By the time he was gone, the rest of the crew had been hauled beneath the grass as well.

Dave didn't even have time to set the shotgun down before it was all over. The boys he'd been waiting for were just gone, swallowed by the farm where he'd grown up. He reengaged the safety on the weapon and set it against the side of the barn, his eyes staring at the spot where they'd been.

And then he just stood there for a while, trying to make sense of the whole thing. After about ten minutes he gave up. Dave very slowly and meticulously gathered everything he'd taken with him when he left the house and headed for home.

Most everyone was asleep when he slid back through his bedroom window. He could have used the front door, but didn't feel like answering any questions. Amber was in her bedroom next to his own, and he could hear her talking in low, seductive tones through the wall. Normally he would have listened in and done a little fantasizing over what she said, but right then he couldn't have cared less.

Dave went to sleep with the smell of cotton candy in his nostrils and the sound of calliope music playing in his

head. The smell was exactly the same as when the whatever-
the-hell-they-were-or-it-was had attacked Marco and the
rest. The sound, well, that was the sound he sometimes
heard out in that field late at night. Normally the cheerful
piped music made him feel better. Not this time. This time
he thought of the thing under the ground and wondered
what it was and why it existed.

He had no idea and was pretty sure he wanted to stay
ignorant.

He managed all the way until the next morning before
he saw what bloomed in the field overnight.

Then he knew he wanted to stay ignorant, but of course
by then it was too late.

XI

Marco had, for most of his young life, considered himself
to be unique in his philosophies. In his way of thinking, the
world he lived in was hell, and it really couldn't get much
worse. From an early age he was ridiculed because he was
from that place euphemistically called the wrong side of
the tracks, and he was often accused of crimes he had
never considered committing, based solely on the fact that
he was his father's son. His father, who'd left town before
he was even born, had left behind a stain that painted
Marco's entire world.

His mother was often abusive, and when she wasn't,
you could bet she was doing her abject best to avoid dealing with the issues that her children brought into her world.
She was, in short, not exactly an ideal role model. Marco
learned from her as best he could.

And he took what she taught him and incorporated it

into the Gospel According to Marco. Part of that gospel simply stated that since he was already in hell, he had to make the most of it. That meant that he could do as he pleased as long as he wasn't caught, and damn the beliefs of those too blind to understand his reasoning. That was what had made dealing with Karstens such a pleasure. Karstens understood where Marco was coming from, and he sympathized.

Karstens promised to help Marco and his buddies realize the pleasures that were theirs for the taking, and he made it clear that they would not suffer any punishments for their actions, so long as they did his bidding in exchange.

He thought they had a deal. He thought he could trust the man, because, really, except for a few small injuries, they'd gotten away with a lot just lately, including rape, murder, attempted murder and attempted rape, several random acts of violence, and even grand theft auto. Not a bad run for a starting point. It seemed like a good way to get a better seat in hell if he was forced to stay there anyway.

The only things he hadn't counted on were that Karstens might have lied—as evidenced by his present situation—and that his philosophy might have been very, very wrong indeed. He'd thought he was in hell before. Now he knew better. Nothing like the real thing to make a myth out of the delusion.

The thing that pulled him into the darkness under the Pageant farm shattered any thoughts Marco might have had about being creative in his earlier tortures on Nancy Lyons. He'd gotten off on making her scream and cry when he was raping her. He'd had the best time of his life in those few short hours. Even watching the other guys go at her was exciting, because it was dangerous and because he finally had a chance to make one of the bitches—in this case defined as any woman who wouldn't give him the time of day—pay for the privilege of being a bitch.

And now something bigger and badder was returning the favor. Now he was the bitch, and there wasn't a damned thing he could do about it. He didn't even have the luxury of screaming, because, of course, his vocal chords were gone. His teeth were gone, his eyes were gone, his skin was fading away in a suspended level of pain he would never have thought possible. Oh, and that lovely instrument of torture he'd used on Nancy Lyons? The very tool he'd derived so much pleasure from earlier in the day? That was gone, too. He'd felt his manhood torn away almost as soon as he was dragged beneath the turf.

And it just kept getting worse.

It took forever or so for him to realize that he wasn't alone in the darkness. Some time after that revelation he heard the noise of a single voice speaking to him softly, almost lovingly. Marco whimpered at the notion that here, at last, was someone who could make his pain go away. Here was someone—God maybe?—who could bring him back to something akin to a normal level of discomfort and maybe even make him whole again. He could sense the power of the thing that moved with him through the endless night of his new universe. He knew it could make him whole again if it wanted.

Without a voice, Marco begged the entity to help him. He received nothing but laughter in return. And then he felt that presence reach into him, past his flesh and bone and into the very essence of him, tearing and devouring as it moved.

He'd been wrong again, as he had about so many things. Karstens couldn't help him, his life before had not been hell, and the presence he knew could rebuild him was instead rebuilding itself by consuming him.

Marco DeMillio died as he'd lived. And he kept dying long after his body was remade.

XII

There was a desire to put itself completely back together that was almost overwhelming when it let itself contemplate the idea. Being broken into three parts wasn't exactly the easiest way to stay focused. Joey, for example, was determined to stay not only aroused, but painfully so, to the point where concentration was almost impossible. Worse still, the boy's mind was constantly turning back to Becky. Some part of the boy was mixing the need to comfort the girl's mourning with the realization that she was a girl in the first blooms of puberty. Or, translated, he wanted to mate with her.

It idly wondered if letting the boy have his way would be masturbation or something else. The boy's parents were watching television, leaving him alone to contemplate what to do next. Something had just happened, it could feel what the Joey-aspect kept referring to as a "disturbance in the Force." The curse, it appeared, was finally doing something.

The Joey-form, in addition to having hormonal surges of lust, apparently had a small bladder. It stood up, annoyed by the inconvenience, and walked across the hallway to the bathroom. And right into Jonathan Crowley's waiting grasp.

"You aren't very observant tonight, are you, sweet pea?" He reached out and grabbed the thing in Joey's body with hands that struck like cobras and hauled him into the bathroom. It started to react, but before it could do more than ball the fists on the boy's body, Crowley had covered its face with his hand, preventing even a single sound from leaving Joey's mouth. "No talking . . . Talking is for later."

The thing in Joey's body started drawing forth its power, ready to finally get down to business with the Hunter. But then Crowley spoke again, softly whispered words that sent a violent wave of pain screaming through every nerve ending in the body it possessed and it lost all control over the host form. The eyes closed, the muscles twitched and spasmed, and the mind that so wanted revenge for past sins was seared into a stupor.

When the pain faded again, its surroundings had changed. It was outside, in the woods, the biting cold of the night sending shivers through Joey's being. It was also bound, hands and feet stretched away from the body and tied to various anchors, a rock on the left ankle, a tree for the right arm, the other limbs apparently staked to the ground by tent posts. Crowley squatted next to him, seemingly unaffected by the chill weather. He was carving something from a piece of wood he'd found, and though he didn't seem to be paying the least bit of attention to the creature inhabiting Joey, it knew from past experience that the lack of interest was a sham. It did not speak but merely looked at Jonathan Crowley.

"Thing is, I still haven't figured out what you are."

It chose not to answer.

"The other thing is, I don't really care." Crowley set down the piece of wood and put the small knife back in his pocket. "I'm just sick of you." He rested his hand on its chest and smiled. "So I'm getting rid of you."

"Let's not be hasty."

Crowley raised an eyebrow and looked at it.

"I have information you want, Hunter, about what is going on in this town."

"I can find out all by myself when the time is right. I don't really need to barter with you." Crowley dug around in his pants pocket for a moment and then pulled out a small amount of powder. "In fact, I don't really think I want to barter, not when I can make you scream like a little girl instead."

Crowley lifted the thin T-shirt over Joey's chest and spilled the dusty gray powder over where the heart beat beneath. And it roared with agony, arching its back to escape the pain. Crowley watched on, his face almost showing affection past the toothy grin. Then he frowned, a mocking, petulant pout that was roughly as sincere as an apology from Genghis Khan might have been. "No screams? Pity." He shrugged. "Oh well, I can always do it again."

"Hurt me again, and I will kill this body. I have that power."

"And this is supposed to make me hesitate because . . . ?"

"You have always protected the innocent."

"Not really heavy on my list of priorities these days."

"Since when?" It almost snorted laughter when it spoke. The last thing it had expected was a comment like that from the Hunter. "You've always been out to protect your precious humans from harm."

"Well, let's be honest here, shall we? You and I both know the best way for something like you to get inside someone is to be invited. The second best way is to find someone who is willing to accept you in, even if they aren't conscious of that action, and the last best way is to just get someone who is weak or dead. So the way I figure it, the little shit probably had it coming to him, and even if he didn't, it'll be a mercy killing. Anyone that weak would never be happy in this world."

"Well, that's rather mercenary, isn't it?"

"If you say so." Crowley poured more of the powder onto Joey's chest, and this time he grabbed the boy's head between his hands and started speaking as the entity in the boy's flesh started screaming. It railed and tried its best to escape the pain until, finally, it had no choice but to flee. No matter. This way it could reunite with one of the other parts of itself and be stronger, more prepared to destroy the Hunter.

So it pushed, forcing itself out of Joey by way of his mouth, spilling force on the boy's breath and flowing quickly toward the ground where it would be able to hide until the time came to remerge with itself. Less than a second passed before it realized something had gone very wrong.

It thrashed, pushed, and tried desperately to break free, but to no avail. And shortly after it realized it couldn't escape from wherever it was, it expanded its senses to allow it to see beyond the normal range.

And realized that the Hunter had won.

Jonathan Crowley looked down at the unconscious boy and smiled softly. Then he turned his attention to the wooden carving he'd made and looked more carefully as it looked back, studying him with an odd turn of its head.

"Found a place with lots of little dollies, and each and every one of them has something that most dolls don't." Crowley picked up the wooden carving and studied it for several moments before speaking again. "I wasn't really sure if that would work, but there it is, and here you are."

His hand grabbed the carved wooden statue, and he held it close to his side, mildly repulsed by the way it tried to squirm against his palm. He held it tightly and shifted his attention to the boy. Crowley got comfortable in the darkness and waited. It was time to talk with the boy and find out what he remembered of his . . . cohabitation. He could be patient. He had what he wanted, for now at least.

CHAPTER 3

I

Morning came fitfully to Serenity Falls. The clouds in the sky were as bruised and swollen as the victim of a violent mugging and seemed about as cheerful in their disposition. The air was biting cold in a time when it should have been getting positively sultry. The last week of school was mostly over and the world of summer break was upon the youths in town, but most of them didn't seem overly excited about it. Most of them were trying to understand just what, exactly, was going on in their town.

The day should have been almost sedate, excepting the anticipation of the kids to finally be free from the daily grind of higher education, and it was, but not in a good way. There was a tension in the air that was palpable; a certain feeling like most of the world must surely be holding its breath. Oh, people were still getting out of bed and getting ready for their day, and a few poor souls were up well before the sun to take care of work, but by and large, there were no smiles on the faces of the townsfolk, and there were few who could be said to walk with a spring in their step.

The Long family woke up and dressed and went their separate ways with only a few words spoken. Both Stan and April looked ready to cry, and their father looked like he could have used a few hundred hours of sleep. As for their mother, well, she looked like the idea of taking an ax to her husband didn't seem like a bad notion. While the others all did their best to avoid eye contact—almost like they felt it best to just ignore their problems in the hopes that they would go away—Addy Long seemed to want a serious fight to break out. More importantly, she seemed ready to start it. Her family left en masse, and she in turn stayed home, brooding.

She had made her decision, and it was easier to leave in anger than to leave in simple silence. By ten in the morning she had packed her bags and loaded the station wagon with enough clothes to see her through the next few weeks.

Greg Randers lay in his hospital bed, heavily sedated and in a great deal of pain despite his unconscious state. Good old Carl Bradford had not played nicely with him, and in addition to the seventy-three stitches that sewed up the wounds he'd had dealt to him by a dead man, the doctors had determined that exploratory surgery was necessary to make certain he wasn't severely injured and bleeding internally. He was, actually, and now that the problems had been found and mended as best modern medicine could manage, he was going to be a while in recovery. On the brighter side, the doctors didn't feel he'd need extensive physical therapy.

Nona Bradford was in much better shape physically, but mentally she was having a little trouble with her husband's resurrection. She couldn't help but wonder if he'd manage it a second time, and the very notion had her as fragile as the finest crystalline goblet.

Another new attendee at the medical center was Victor Barnes, who had finally decided to actually see someone about his numerous injuries right around the same time the wound in his arm swelled and started seeping a clear and foul-smelling fluid. A little alcohol wasn't going to take care of it, and though he was loath to actually trust a doctor after several of his past experiences, he was not foolish enough to want to risk blood poisoning. Most of his most recent injuries were the result of bite wounds, after all, and he'd heard there were too many germs in the human mouth alone to easily count.

But he didn't have to like it, and he could easily attest to the fact that it was annoying and inconvenient to say the least. Though he wasn't at all sure that he wanted to settle down in Serenity for the rest of his life anymore, he was loath to just sit idly by when there was so damned much going on in the town. The number of able-bodied constables was fast dwindling, and he hated to add his own name to the list of those who couldn't be counted on for the present.

He took the antibiotics prescribed and agreed to stay the night for observation, but he refused the pain pills and sedatives, just in case he might have to go back to work. Too much weirdness was going around for him to believe he'd actually get a chance to rest properly.

The mortal remains of Carl Bradford were set aside for a proper autopsy.

Though it was, indeed, the last week of school and there were finals to be taken, several students were missing from the fifth grade classes that day. Lawrence Grey was absent for the first time in three years, marring his nearly perfect attendance record. Had his mother been alive, she would have fretted over that fact. Penelope Grey was always worried about her son before she shed the mortal coil. Dave

Pageant was not in school, and that was almost unheard of. Still, there was no real concern on anyone's part. Dave was a Pageant, and they were known to be an odd sort. Joey Whitman was not in class, either, though that was hardly unusual. He normally managed to miss at least one day out of every fifteen in school.

Several of the more rambunctious teens—the older kids who had recently developed a far worse attitude than they'd managed in the past—were also absent that day. Most of their teachers merely marked that as a reason to celebrate.

In his cell, Terry Palance did what he'd been doing ever since he'd been arrested. He worked out, doing every exercise he could think of that didn't require heavy weights or running. Mentally he continued to consider how miserable he was and how unfair his fate in the world and in Serenity. He had been a prick, true enough, but he hadn't touched Terri, and he didn't deserve to spend time in even the town's cell for what had happened. His mother still refused to post his bail, and he had to accept it, but he didn't have to enjoy it.

Some people might wallow in their miseries, but not Terry. Instead he just kept getting angrier and angrier. He didn't let it show though. He just let it seep into his soul, that dark anger, and reveled in it. What little guilt he'd once felt was gone. What little that remained of his willingness to forgive was crushed under the constant onslaught of his anger.

Terri Halloway, on the other hand, was one of those few who seemed genuinely to be thriving. She seemed happier than she had in a long while, and she was glad to let April know that she had a new boyfriend, who was, as far as she was concerned, a fabulous lover. She would not say what his name was, merely that he was older, and that April knew him. The information did not sit well with April, but

she kept her own counsel on the matter. She was hardly one
to judge.

Mike Blake woke up next to Amelia and watched her
sleep, almost hypnotized by the soft sound of her breathing
and the movement of her eyes beneath closed lids. Several
times he almost touched her, but then decided not to for
fear she might fade away into nothing more than a dream.
He knew the steady dread he felt when lying next to her
was all in his mind, but that didn't make it any easier for
him to deal with it. She was real, she proved that only a few
hours earlier after he'd recovered from his latest fainting
spell—and kids, he knew there was something seriously
wrong with that, too—but the feeling stayed there just the
same. Every time he watched her sleep, he feared she
would simply vanish if he tried to touch her. She'd pull an
Amy and die, or just evaporate into a pale mist and then
blow away on the winds of fate. She was still sleeping
when he went off to take his morning shower.

Jack Michaels woke up to the same sort of day he normally managed. He turned off the alarm clock, thought
about it for five or so seconds, reset it for another fifteen
minutes, then closed his eyes and let himself drift for a
while. The second time he shut off the alarm he got out of
bed and climbed into the shower. A quick breakfast of cereal
and coffee—a change since he'd arrested Terry Palance—
and he was on his way to work. He knew there was something different about him, and when he concentrated very
hard, he understood that Terri Halloway had done something to him, but he didn't want to think about it, didn't
want to remember. He was very good at avoiding the entire
memory when he set his mind to it.

He went through his day meticulously, setting up ap-
pointments for the few applicants he'd run into for the
openings on the force and going through the paperwork

that had to be done. It was work, and he went at it with
gusto. He hardly seemed different at all.

Looks could be deceiving.

The folks at the Pageant farm definitely didn't have a
usual morning, however. Not by a long shot. While most of
the town was getting on with the daily grind, the Pageants
were looking over the ground where the murderous boys
had come to pay a visit the night before.

Things had changed.

The ground that had been left untouched for years had
suddenly bloomed in the night. But the crop didn't exactly
make sense. There were three massive pillars rising from
the ground and streamers dropping down from them almost like offshoots from spider plants. The lines ran from
the top of the thick, black columns and trailed lazily down
in almost perfect symmetry. Dave hadn't the vaguest clue
what the hell they were, but he knew they stank like a
slaughterhouse in August and seemed to be growing straight
out of the ground like diseased trees that were just a little
too perfectly straight.

The twins were next to him, dressed in their pj's same as
he was, and all three of them just stared for a while. Maybe
it would have been best to wake the folks, but none of them
really gave the idea any serious consideration. Sometimes
you just needed to look things over for yourself for a while
before making up your mind.

Amber scratched idly at her hip, and Dave watched her
long fingers on their trek back and forth. He wondered
when she was going to actually settle down and start be-
having like he figured a girl should, but kept his mouth
shut. He wasn't really fond of just giving advice or suggestions that hadn't been asked for. Suzette looked his way
and squinted one eye half shut in an expression that looked
like she was trying to avoid the glare of the sun but that he

knew was just the way she looked when she asked a question. "Think we should wake Dad?"

"Dunno. I figure he'll be up soon anyway."

"I'm thinking he ain't gonna like it much." Suzette and Amber said the same thing at the exact same time. Stan always freaked out when they did that, but Dave was used to it.

Tina poked her head out the door and looked at what they were watching. She disappeared half a second later, and Dave smiled. "See? He'll wake up any second now. Tina'll take care of it."

Amber finally stopped scratching and yawned. "I need coffee." She looked directly at Dave, and he sighed. He knew Amber was asking him to make it, and he figured it might be a little more interesting to stay around for when his father saw the things growing in the field, but it might be calmer if he was watching the hot brew percolate. He nodded to his older sister and went inside. He was just pouring the first few cups—there were going to be plenty of people who wanted coffee inside of five minutes by his reckoning—when he heard his father and his grandfather start talking about what was out there. Both of the men lit up cigarettes and shivered a bit in the cold. From where he was in the kitchen, he could see his sisters—including Tina—and his father and grandfather.

He was a little curious as to what they were saying, but not enough to want to go out there. His dad wasn't exactly looking happy about anything. Dave looked out past his family and over at the field again. Some of the stringy webs stretching down to the ground seemed to be growing wings.

He thought about telling his father what had happened the night before and then decided against it. He might not have actually done anything to Marco and his buddies, but there was no guarantee his father wouldn't blame him anyway.

Caution was always good when treading in new territories. The situation needed to be studied for a while. Dave opened the refrigerator and started cracking eggs into a large mixing bowl. The smell wasn't even noticeable from here, and he was starting to get hungry. First in the kitchen meant he could decide what he wanted for breakfast. He wanted an omelet, and figured he'd make enough for everyone.

And so the morning came to Serenity Falls, the sun rose as it always did, even if it was hidden that particular day. People went about their business with varying degrees of success. Some of them were bored, some were happy, and some were ready to call it a day before they even got out of bed.

And Jonathan Crowley? Well, he and his new friend Joey went into the woods, and while Crowley did little talking, he listened to a great deal of news. And the longer he walked, the broader his smile grew.

II

The woods were darker than he might have supposed, but that probably had something to do with the overcast sky. The air was cold enough to make his nose want to run, and that was a little weird. It had been a long, long time since Jonathan Crowley had actually lived full time on the East Coast, but not so long that he couldn't remember the summers being a great deal warmer. And did he have a nice winter coat? No. Did he have any coats at all? Yes, but

they were all at home. The one exception he'd brought with
him didn't survive the car blowing up. So he was cold. Looking at the bloated clouds scudding their way across the sky,
he figured he could probably add wet to that soon enough.

He looked over at the boy next to him, and his grin
spread a little wider. The kid was doing his best not to be
scared, but his face seemed designed to be as readable as a
good book. He was terrified. He had no desire to be in the
woods and less desire to be in the woods with a man who
he'd sent a pack of dogs after while he was possessed.
Crowley liked that Joey was scared. It made controlling
him much easier. More importantly, it might stop him from
doing stupid crap in the future.

"I think it's right over here, sir." The kid's voice cracked
nervously.

"You think it's over here? What? You weren't here the
last time you came this way?"

"Becky led the way. I just sort of followed."

Crowley chuckled at the way the kid blushed. But for a
change of pace he didn't say anything too harsh. He'd been
young once and understood the appeal of watching the opposite sex instead of the trail. Despite his natural tendency
to want to add a little insult to any injury, he shut up on
making any snide comments.

They crested a small hill on the path, and Jonathan Crowley soaked in the appearance of the house he looked at. Not
exactly a mansion. The structure was solid and most likely
functional, but it wasn't going to grace the pages of *Better
Homes & Gardens* any time in the near future.

"This is the right place."

Crowley looked over at his tour guide and smiled. "You
sure you shouldn't have been looking for the witch right
here, Hansel?" It took the kid a few seconds to catch his
reference, and then he cracked a small smile before trying
to decide if he'd been insulted.

"Why?"

He shrugged as he started moving toward the cabin. "The only thing missing from this place is the giant candy canes on the sides and maybe a few layers of frosting. I don't trust it at all."

"You don't trust a house?" Joey looked at him like he was maybe a little crazy, which he was, but that wasn't the issue here.

"More like I don't trust whoever built it. And I don't trust that what we're seeing is real."

"What else would it be?"

"An illusion to make it look less like a trap."

"Why would anyone want to make a trap out here?"

"To lure stupid kids looking for miracles into doing their dirty work." He smiled. It was the sort of smirk normally employed by traveling ministers and used car salesmen.

"I'm not stupid. And I still don't see why anyone would change the way a house looks."

"Yes, you are. But not super stupid. I'd have done the same thing at your age, especially if there had been a girl involved. As to the house, why do girls put on makeup? Why do chameleons change the color of their skin? They just do. Sometimes to make themselves look better and sometimes to make themselves look more intimidating. Either way, it's just an illusion. It's a way of hiding the truth."

"Seems sort of stupid to me . . ." The comment wasn't meant to be heard, but that had never stopped Crowley from responding in the past.

"Well, is it any dumber than coming into the woods to find a way to resurrect a dead man?"

"I told you, I was just along to see that Becky didn't get hurt any worse."

"And I told you, next time you get that sort of idea in your head, don't go with it. It's right up there with chewing on power cords for what it can do to you."

"I kind of got that part . . ."

"Good. Make sure it stays got."

The two of them stopped in front of the house, and Crowley closed his eyes, breathing in the cool air and feeling the subtle changes in the wind as it moved around the building. Whatever the kid had seen had been fake. What they looked at now was the reality. Crowley knocked on the door politely and stood smiling at the faded wood on the entrance into the house. He waited politely for a full minute and then knocked again while Joey fidgeted near his left side. He tried one more time, and then he twisted the doorknob. The door opened easily.

The interior of the cabin was much like the outside: a meager collection of furniture and supplies went along with a general air of neglect. There were only a few knick-knacks or extras anywhere. The place was almost barren, and though there were no boxes, it seemed to have the air of a place that was about to be left behind. Like someone had moved out everything important and was just waiting for the right time to close the door. The wood used to build the place was a little warped and could have used a few coats of furniture oil if nothing else.

"Gotta be honest with you, kid, I'm not really impressed by your friend's use of space or decor."

Simon MacGruder took the liberty of answering in Joey's stead. "I'm not overly impressed by his choice of hiking companions, either, but it's his choice, of course, not mine." The voice was pleasant, and the demeanor was equally disarming. Crowley didn't trust him for a second. The man was stocky but not overly tall, with a short crew cut that was more silver and gray than anything else. His eyes were almost the same color as his hair. His face was lined, but in a way that was a complement to his broad face, rather than a deterrent. His face had character, not age. He could have been an old forty or a young seventy. His clothes—well worn Levi's and a flannel shirt—gave him a homey appearance that didn't really fit with the vibe Crowley got off of him.

"Sorry, I was just expecting a rather different place from the way Joey was talking."

"What do you mean?"

"Well. The way he was talking about you, I sort of figured you'd live in a giant emerald palace with guards and just oodles of smiling, happy little people."

"I'm hardly the Wonderful Wizard of Oz."

"I noticed." Crowley extended his hand. "My name is Jonathan Crowley, Mr. MacGruder. I'm sorry to bother you, but I wonder if you could fill me in on this witch of the woods Joey and his little girlfriend went off to see."

MacGruder chuckled and shook his head. "You don't mean to tell me you need to find a witch, do you, Mr. Crowley?"

"You never can tell. Maybe I need a love spell cast on someone."

"If you're here with Joey, I imagine he could tell you everything you need to know. I just told the kids where I would go if I was looking for the witch."

"Are you saying there is a witch in the woods?" Crowley looked at the man, and their eyes met. Whoever he was dealing with, the man had a strong will. Most people tended to get very nervous when looking him in the eyes for too long. That he was smiling didn't make it any easier for the average person to keep on facing off against him. He could see Joey out of the corner of his eye, looking from MacGruder to him and watching the interplay of words. He made a note to himself to remember that kids could be sharper than they looked. He knew the tension was there, and MacGruder knew it, but the boy was watching them and understood that the pleasant tones they were using with each other were a sham. The tension was thick enough to cut with a knife.

"I tend to think there must be some level of truth to the legends, Mr. Crowley. There almost always is."

"Not in my experience. I've made a habit of looking into claims of witches and all sorts of other things. Most of the time, what I've found was either not what was expected or just a lot of hocus-pocus."

"Really? How unusual. I would have expected a more open-minded attitude from a parapsychologist."

Crowley laughed. "I haven't actually studied that sort of thing in years."

"True, but I've heard about you over the years, and I saw your work with Kirlian photography. I have to say, I was rather impressed."

Crowley nodded his head, his eyes still locked with the gray eyes before him. "Thanks for that. Is it a hobby for you? The studies I mean, or are you interested for other reasons?"

"Oh, more like a passing interest while I go about my day." The voice was so casual, so almost indifferent, and at the same time he could hear the undercurrent of threat in the tone of MacGruder's voice.

"Really? What do you do out here all day long? Are you a writer or just a recluse?"

"I'm just a hobbyist with a penchant for the unusual. Mostly I'm retired these days."

"What did you used to do?"

"I made money hand over fist, and I spent a lot of time moving around. I guess you could say I was more of a philosopher than anything else."

"I can relate to that. I spent a lot of time doing nothing much more than that. These days, I tend to think of myself more as a troubleshooter than anything else."

"Really? What a strange change in vocations from parapsychologist to troubleshooter."

"Not that much of a stretch when you get down to it. I just tend to think a lot of the emotional scars people deal with come from sources beyond their control. But they aren't always beyond mine."

MacGruder looked away from him then, smiling at Joey. "How's everything going with you and Becky, son?"

"Umm. Well, we found something in the woods, right where you said we should look, but I don't know what it was. Since then, I don't remember too much. I was sort of . . ." He stopped, at a loss for words.

"He was sort of possessed by something. I took care of it." Crowley's smile broadened as MacGruder looked back at him. "Like I said, same sort of problem, but these days I go for the source of the trouble rather than dealing with the symptoms."

"Is that what you think I am, Mr. Crowley? The source of what happened to Joey?"

"Well, that's what I'm here to find out, isn't it?"

"How absolutely flattering, to think that I could cause that sort of problem." He smiled like a grandfather discovering he'd had a profound impact on his grandson, his eyes positively beaming with pride when he looked at Joey again.

"I can feel it, you know. You aren't what you claim to be."

"Neither are you."

"Nonsense, Mr. MacGruder. I claimed to be nothing more than a troubleshooter."

"True. But I suppose it depends on the definition of trouble that one uses."

"Good point." Crowley ruffled Joey's short blond hair, ignoring the look of annoyance the kid shot him. "From my perspective, anything that would take a relative innocent like Joey here and try to convert him into a new home for something unnatural and malevolent is generally considered trouble."

"I am guilty of nothing more than giving a couple of youngsters advice and hot cocoa."

"That may be, but at the very least the advice was poor."

"None of us is perfect, Mr. Crowley."

"No argument there. Listen, what exactly is the witch of the woods? Can you tell me that much?"

"She's a myth. A side effect of the town's own history."

"The one witch burned here back before the Revolutionary War? Seems like a pretty long time for a myth to stick around unless it was fed somewhere along the way."

"Look how long the Folk have been considered a possibility."

Crowley looked at MacGruder sharply and saw the gloating smile that was starting to form on the man's face. "The Fae? Not really all that hard to figure out. Disney alone has made millions on the idea of little girls with wings and magic fairy dust."

"Come now, Mr. Crowley, you and I both know there's more to this than an occasional cartoon."

"Very true. But that's my point. Myths don't tend to stay around unless there's a reason. What has this witch been up to that lets her keep the attention of so many kids for over three centuries?"

"I think she's been dead. Maybe it's her ghost that they see. Some little echo of her spirit that insists on lingering around because her death was unjust, and she hasn't yet been avenged."

"It would take a very powerful spirit to last for that long without some sort of fuel for the fire."

"Maybe she's had fuel. Maybe she's been fed regularly by someone who cares for her."

"Why?"

"Maybe someone longed enough for her and her soul to risk everything to see her avenged."

"Really a bit obsessive, don't you think? Hold on for

three hundred–plus years and feed an angry spirit enough energy to keep it going? To what end?"

"You're an educated man, Mr. Crowley. And I'd wager you've had a few loved ones in your life. Have you ever had them taken from you by force?"

Crowley didn't answer. He simply stared at the man and did his best not to think about the past.

MacGruder came closer, until they were only inches apart. "Are you telling me there's nothing you wouldn't do to make sure that your wife was at peace if she was raped, tortured, and murdered?"

"I think I'd take it out on the guilty parties, not on the people around the guilty parties."

"How can you be sure there is a difference?"

"I've never followed with the sins of the father philosophy." He shrugged and grinned. "Besides, I believe in immediate gratification. Why would I want to wait three hundred years to see justice served?"

"There's always the possibility that the revenge would be worth the wait. Then there's the possibility that you might not be prepared initially."

"Nonsense. I can use my hands. If I had been the husband of the unfortunate woman, I would have just wrung the neck of Niles Wilcox and called it done."

MacGruder looked ready to make a rebuttal, but, frankly, Crowley was sick of hearing him preach.

"Or maybe I'd consider that my wife got lonely being all by herself and decided to have an orgy or two. Hell, maybe she was really a witch and used her wanton magics to make Wilcox into her love slave."

MacGruder's smile faded instantly.

Crowley leaned in just a fraction of an inch closer, smiling broader than before. "Maybe I'd be worried about not having been enough to satisfy her needs." He looked at the face of the man before him as it suddenly lost all hints of emotion. The character lines on the kind face were still there, but now they looked like what they were, signs of repressed anger. "Maybe I'd worry about why I waited three hundred years. Do you suppose, hypothetically speaking, naturally, that if her husband were still around, he would even remember what it felt like to touch her? To feel her presence and smell her scent when he woke up in the mornings? Or do you think that whatever he did these days would be more akin to slowly torturing his deceased wife's spirit?"

Crowley leaned back away from the man in front of him and waved a hand as if to dismiss the matter. "At any rate, I don't think one life would ever justify placing a curse on an entire town."

"What makes you think there would be a curse involved?"

"Well, it would hardly be likely that a man who would let his wife's spirit endure three centuries of misery would be around to continue feeding the poor, wretched soul energies without having another reason."

"Maybe he just likes the area?" MacGruder's eyes shone with amusement again, now that Crowley had backed off the subject of motives.

"Or maybe he just comes back from time to time and looks in on things, sees how his pet project is cooking."

"Or maybe," MacGruder put an arm on Joey's shoulder, gently turning him and leading him toward the door. "Maybe he's just coming back around because the time has come for everything to be finished."

"So, hypothetically speaking, what would someone do to get revenge?"

"Oh, I wouldn't presume to know, Mr. Crowley. But I suspect it would be big."

Crowley turned and walked toward the door, following behind MacGruder and Joey. Joey, for his part, was looking extremely confused. That suited Crowley just fine, and he

suspected it pleased his host as well. "Well, if I were to find
out about a curse of that magnitude, I imagine I'd have to try
to stop it from reaching its culmination. Nothing against the
dead woman's husband, naturally, but I'd feel obligated to
help the local citizens if I could."

MacGruder ushered Joey through the threshold and
turned to look at Crowley. "I can understand that. Or course,
it's possible the husband would be prepared for interlopers.
He might have arranged a few things to keep a person like
you too busy to really make a difference."

"You think so?" Crowley's voice reflected his amusement.

"It's just a matter of knowing who might interfere, really. Say a person had made calculations about the possibilities of someone in a very, very limited field trying
to stop what was set in motion." He looked at Crowley
and shoved his hands into his jeans pockets with a smile.
"Knowing that there are only a handful of people in that
particular field who might be strong enough to do something about a plan that took three hundred years to finish,
he might arrange for someone close to the troubleshooter
to be placed in extreme danger." He flashed the sort of grin
that Crowley knew from looking in the mirror. "Not a wife,
of course, because a proper troubleshooter would never be
stupid enough to actually have a wife. Or if he did, she'd
probably have already been violently murdered because of
his chosen field of expertise. But maybe someone who
could have been important in his life if he hadn't decided
to become a troubleshooter, or maybe someone who was
almost like a daughter to him. And maybe the creator of
the curse would arrange for an old, long-forgotten enemy
to come back onto the scene and create a little havoc. The
sort of chaos that can lead to distraction."

"So, assuming that the engineer of such a curse had the
foresight to find out about a troubleshooter, how close

would he put the troubles together?" He was holding his breath. Some freak in rustic clothes was making him worry when he really didn't have the time or the patience to worry. His pulse was starting to go faster, and he could feel his skin wanting to break into a sweat.

MacGruder lifted his left arm and pulled back the sleeve of his red flannel shirt. His face was so casual, so calm, that Crowley could have done no more than ask him for the time. "If I were the one responsible, knowing that the troubleshooter had really done nothing to me, I might arrange everything to start just around sunset. And I would probably set things up so that the distractions were close together but not in danger of overlapping unless, say, the troubleshooter was distracted by frivolous hunts through the woods for myths that don't really exist."

"Has it already started?" Crowley felt his smile come back. Whether it was fear, excitement over a challenge, or elation that it would all be over, he couldn't have said just then. Maybe it was a little of all of those things blended together.

"I'd say it would be starting right about now. And I'd think that if the troubleshooter were foolish enough to, say, try to punish the party responsible, he'd be too late to make much of a difference. And I might even tell him to look for the boy who had so many uninvited guests, because, if I were the one orchestrating this, I might start there."

Crowley turned from the man and passed through the threshold of the house. "This isn't finished, Mr. MacGruder."

Simon MacGruder got a brief look of amused shock on his face. "My good man, I'd be surprised if it was."

"Do you feel anything at all for the people you're about to hurt?"

"Yes. I feel absolute, undiluted hatred for every last one of them."

"Why?"

"They still have the capacity for happiness. I couldn't quite take that away from them."

MacGruder closed the door. Crowley wasn't overly surprised to see that the gingerbread house was little more than a battered old shack, after all.

III

Stan looked at the test in front of him, thought carefully, and watched his hand move across the paper, writing out his answer in longhand. He knew it, sensed it, really, that his family was over. The tensions this morning were far, far worse than they had been, and he wondered what his mother and father had said to each other the night before, when they spoke instead of whisper-hissed for the first time in what seemed like forever. He had no delusions about them staying together, not anymore. And really, it was almost liberating knowing what was going to happen.

He looked away from the test in front of him and smiled at Charlee Lyons. She smiled back, a little shyly, and he figured that was because she thought he was angry at her for not visiting the medical center when he was in there. He hadn't been angry, of course, but it would be harder to explain that properly than to just let it go.

Becky Glass was sitting not far away, but he didn't want to look at her. There was something about her lately that made him both nervous and excited whenever she was around. She had become someone else, and while he couldn't truly say he knew her well, he thought maybe the new Becky was a little dangerous. Well, okay, and a little sexy, which was an enigma in and of itself. Whenever he looked at her he wanted to run his hands over her body, and he wanted to run away at the same time.

His hand moved across the paper in strong, confident strokes, as he lost himself in thought for a second. And he felt it coming, the gradual buildup of something bad. Behind his closed eyes, he saw the cold waters of the quarry filling his memories and wondered if maybe he was supposed to die there. Maybe it would have been better, really, because just lately his life hadn't been meeting up with the minimum daily requirements of decency. His life had gone to shit in a handbasket ever since that day when Becky Glass pulled him out of the waters, and she and Joey brought him back from the cool, soothing balm of drowning.

Stan was halfway through his final exam in his math class when the seizure nailed him. It hit him harder than the worst of the ones he'd gone through before, and his body slammed backwards into the seat of his desk hard enough to break the formed wood. His feet slammed against the floor and forced the desk back into Burt Cavandish's desk. Burt started to protest but stopped when he saw the way Stan's head pulled back, saw the whites of his eyes as the capillaries that normally hid just under the surface began to rupture, spreading a wave of blood over the wet surface and changing their color to a bright crimson stain.

Burt let out a scream, and several others joined in as Stan continued to arch back against the seat, bending the metal frame with the force of his convulsion. His teeth were clenched, and Burt could actually hear the sound of the enamel on his molars and bicuspids breaking.

Mr. LeMarrs, despite his ponderous size, moved quickly toward Stan, pushing between desks that were too close together and almost knocking Charlee out of her seat. She watched as the man reached Stan, trying to calm her friend down.

LeMarrs barely even touched Stan before he was attacked. Stan's mouth opened, stretching wider than it should have. She could see the skin on his lips split on both sides, see the raw flesh and the dark blood that immediately fell like a madman's demented milk mustache, running over Stan's turtleneck and down onto his narrow chest in a rapidly spreading stain.

Charlee let loose a shriek like breaking glass as something spilled from Stan's mouth. A hurricane force of lightning-bright energies erupted past his shredded lips, burning his own flesh and then striking LeMarrs square in his heavy chest. The math teacher—hardly a lightweight at almost 350 pounds—didn't so much fly through the air as catapult into the wall and ceiling, his skin blackening and breaking like a rotted fruit as he went. He didn't so much hit the wall as explode against it, a scream just starting to build in his lungs.

Stan Long stood up, bursting through the top of his desk, scattering fragments of wood, notebook paper, and his number-two pencil in the process. His face was just gone, replaced by rows of teeth and a jawbone that glowed with the power that still spilled from somewhere inside him. His eyes looked toward Charlee, and she knew in that instant that he was feeling everything that was happening, feeling it and hating it and dying from it. His eyes—bleeding openly and barely recognizable—still told her that he felt cheated. Somewhere along the way he had figured to have the same chances as everyone else, and it didn't work out that way. He screamed, and rather than the sound being muted by the roaring energies vomiting from him, the sound was amplified. Charlee clutched at her ears and closed her eyes, the noise overwhelming her and making her wish for little more than continued existence.

It took longer than she would have ever thought possible for him to stop screaming.

The heat that seemed to burn Stan did not reach beyond him. Instead the air became bitterly cold, and Charlee could feel the moisture in her eyes evaporate as surely as if she'd walked out into a February morning. She felt like her eyelashes would seal together if she kept her eyes closed an instant longer.

Charlee opened her eyes just in time to see him move. Stan's hand reached for her, a silent plea for help, but she could only push away from him and from everything going wrong in his world. Charlee backed away from Stan, and so did everyone around her as he tried to reach her. And then he stopped, his whole body shivering in a wind that emanated not so much from his mouth but from somewhere deep inside his being, before he fell face forward to the floor. Whatever had been blasting out of his body continued to the very last, only stopping when he hit the linoleum.

Next to him was his final exam paper. Charlee looked at what he'd written there and sank to her knees, unable to feel or think or even breathe. The simple words "EVERY SOUL WILL SCREAM" covered all the spots where his answers should have been.

IV

While her brother was spontaneously combusting, April Long was grabbing a cigarette at the side of the school, waiting for Terri Halloway to show up. Terri said they needed to talk, like, right now, and asked her to meet at the smoke hole as most of the kids called the small, sheltered spot.

She'd just ground out her second coffin nail and was lighting a third when Terri made her appearance. "Hi, April."

"Hi. What's up?"

"I wanted you to meet someone. I can't keep it a secret anymore. I had to let someone know about my new boyfriend." Terri's brown eyes looked almost feverish in the pale light. The clouds above were growing darker, and April was pretty sure that the temperature had dropped even more while she'd been out here.

She wanted to scream. Terri knew better than to pull this sort of crap. They were supposed to be doing finals, and even though she wasn't actually taking a test this period, even though she knew she would ace the class, she didn't like the idea of being yanked outside to meet some guy that she couldn't even tell anyone about.

But when Stephen Wilkins walked around the corner of the building, smiling that same perfect smile he'd once had just for her—Stephen, who had taken her virginity and been her entire world for a few sweet months, who had become the source of much grief in the Long household and had abandoned her and later killed himself—she felt all the power to operate her vocal chords fade away.

"April, this is Steve. He's the guy who makes my heart beat faster." Terri's voice was light and cheerful, just like it should be. Just like hers was once upon a time, when he used to hold her in his arms.

April backed away as Steve came forward, his hand out to shake her own. She shook her head and tried to think of how to speak, how to tell him to get the hell away from her. He'd already killed her heart once, and she wanted nothing more to do with him or his lies. She closed her eyes and tried to calm herself.

And when she opened them again, Terri was looking at her with the strangest expression. "April? What's wrong?"

She looked at the man in front of her and realized that she'd made a mistake. He was almost as tall as her Steve had been, but that was about all they had in common. This man was several years younger and looked nothing like Stephen Wilkins. He was cute, but he was also not at all her type. At the moment he was looking at her quizzically, trying to figure out why she'd almost jumped out of her skin when she saw him.

"I'm sorry. I just thought I saw a ghost."

Terri laughed. "What? You mean Steve Wilkins? Oh please, he's old news." She waved her hand between the two of them, a gesture to wipe away a bad scent in the air. "I was finished with him before he even considered fucking you."

"What?" Icy terror. She'd heard the phrase a few times but never really thought it was a term she could use to describe her own feelings. Even finding out that her father knew about Wilkins didn't freeze her veins this way. "What did you say?"

"Wilkins, Steve Wilkins? That *is* who you were thinking of, isn't it? It's not exactly a secret about you two."

"What are you saying?" Yep, that was a good counterargument. April's mind felt as cold as the air outside. She couldn't quite get a coherent thought to come out. "I don't know what you're talking about."

"Of course you do, April. You and Wilkins doing the nasty. Screwing like bunnies. We talked about it a lot."

"I never said anything like that to you . . ."

"No, not you, silly. Steve. He called me on the phone after he took your cherry."

"What the fuck are you saying, Terri?" There, that almost sounded like a real comeback. A few more seconds, and she was sure she would be up to a proper rebuttal. She couldn't get over this. Terri was her best friend, they'd always shared secrets with each other, but she'd never ever told Terri about Steve, because they were supposed to be a secret. She couldn't believe that somewhere along the way Steve had decided everything between them was public information. "You're so full of shit."

"Oh please, April." Terri was *laughing* at her now. Laughing, like it was all a big funny. And why the hell was she being so cold and cruel? "He told me all about how you were and what you liked and what you wouldn't let him do. And he told me how you kept coming around after it was done, like you and he were supposed to be married or something."

April's legs got that weird rubbery feeling, and she slid down the cold brick wall, looking up at Terri and trying to find some sort of rebuttal. "I don't . . ."

"Yeah, I know what you don't do. He told me, remember?" Terri winked at her, an expression that was both lewd and insulting, made more alien by the fact that it was on Terri's pretty face. "But I figured, what the hell, you like older guys, and you could use some cheering up, what with your family falling all apart. So I decided you could share my Steve with me."

April blinked, looked away from Terri and back toward the man she'd brought with her. The very notion of being with him made her want to gag. He looked like a loser, and he couldn't hope to compare with the memories—no matter how tainted—of the one man she'd loved. "Get the hell away from me, Terri." Her voice sounded so small, so weak. Maybe it was that whole problem of not being able to get a decent breath coming back to get her.

"Geez, don't have a cow, April. I was just trying to be nice."

"Get away from me."

"What's gotten into you, April? You used to like sharing

things with me. I thought maybe you'd like having a little fun."

"Get away from me!" That was a little better. More authoritative, more in control. She didn't want life to slap her down with any more surprises, thanks just the same. At least a little stability would be nice. It felt so good, she said it again. "Get away from me!"

"Whatever." Terri looked down on her, her pretty face disgusted by what she saw. "You try to be nice to the local loser and what do you get? Attitude. Come on Steve, maybe her mom will like you better."

"What?"

Terri smirked. "Well, let's just say you aren't the only Long girl Steve had fun with. He'd probably still be here if it hadn't been for your mom finding out he was screwing you, too."

Terri turned to walk away, and April fairly launched herself from the ground. She did not advertise her attack; she just started swinging. Her first punch slammed into Terri's skull, almost breaking her best friend's head and her hand simultaneously. The pain didn't matter, she swung again anyway, catching Terri on the back of her neck and making her head slam forward.

And Terri laughed. She laughed even as she fell to her knees. April kept swinging her fists; through the tears that tried to blur her vision and the pain that ran up her hands every time she hit, she kept swinging, not ready to stop until Terri either took it all back or died. She would have said as much, too, if she'd been capable of speaking at all.

V

Terry Palance looked on as Jack Michaels opened his cell door. He didn't move, he didn't say a word, he just watched. Michaels looked at him with an expressionless face and shrugged. "Talked to Terri Halloway this morning. She says she wants to drop the charges against you."

"Excuse me?" He just knew his ears were deceiving him. He'd been in here too long now, and obviously his mind was starting to hear things like a man in the desert starts to see mirages.

"She doesn't want to press charges. Without her wanting you locked away, there isn't enough evidence that anything at all happened. So you're free to go." Michaels stepped back from the door of the cell and raised one eyebrow for half a second before he lowered both of them over his narrowed eyes. "But she might change her mind. If I were you, I wouldn't make any plans to go anywhere for a while. And I'd make good and damned sure to stay out of any other sort of trouble." Michaels threw down an envelope that had all of his possessions—wallet and car keys in this case—and walked back toward his office. He didn't respond when Terry said thanks.

It might be that there were a million forms to fill out in New York City or in Utica, but in Serenity it was as simple as walking out the door. That was exactly what Terry did. He walked out of the constables' offices and started for home. No muss, no fuss.

And he wished desperately that it was just that easy. As it stood right now, he was the next best thing to Jack the Ripper in the eyes of at least half of the people he knew. He was also screwed academically and at the very least had a mark on his record that would have people looking askance at him for years if he couldn't get it removed.

He should have been ecstatic, but instead he was racked. Everything that had been right in his life before he got locked away was now just off kilter. It wasn't a good feeling, and there wasn't a damned thing he could do about it. Every hour of every day in the lockup had been that much more time for him to think about how completely screwed he was by what Terri had done to him. There was a knot of heat in his stomach that kept growing hotter and tighter whenever he let himself think about the situation.

I'm not free, and I can't just wash all of this shit away. I'm screwed. No matter what I do, what I say, there's no one around here who'll ever believe I didn't rape Terri and leave her for dead. Thanks a whole fucking lot. There was a part of him, a small part, that wanted to just let it go, but there was a much larger part that wanted to know, by God, why she'd done it. A part that wanted answers and wanted an apology. Some people had accused Terry Palance of not being the brightest of men. They were not unduly harsh in their accusations.

The wind was picking up, and the air was cold enough to make him desperately wish he had a coat with him. He walked faster, aiming for home. Several colorful pieces of paper were skittering along in the wind, and one of them finally managed to catch his attention. He grabbed it as it pushed against the back of his leg and was ready to throw it away until he saw the words written on it. The illustration showed a smiling clown with red hair, a red nose, and a smile that was broad and friendly. The legend above the grinning visage was simple. It read: "Back by Popular Demand and for a Limited Time Only, the Alexander Halston Carnival of the Fantastic." Written in a dark red, bold print that ran over the clown's oversized belly was another message: "Free Admission! You don't want to miss this!" There was fine print at the bottom, too, but he didn't bother to look at it before looking away.

He frowned and stared at the picture. Who the hell would take a carnival to this shithole? The notion had a certain appeal, give or take the weather, and he thought maybe he'd give it a try later that night, if only to let him recover from the last few weeks. He sighed and folded the flyer, pushing it into his pocket without another thought.

He walked past the Donut Hut without giving it a second thought. His mom was probably busy, and he really didn't want to talk to her right then anyway. She'd left him in the cold when he needed her, and while he knew he was being unfair, that she really didn't have the money to post a bail for him, he felt like being selfish about the entire affair. It was juvenile, and it would cause more problems later, but he didn't care.

Somewhere along the way, as he walked and let his mind drift, he managed not to head toward home. His feet carried him down the road and off to the left, and before he knew it, he was in front of the school, looking at it with a weird blend of nostalgia and dread. Inside those halls, he was someone. Or he had been at least. Now? Who could say?

The sound of laughter drifted to him from the side of the building, over where the smokers gathered for their daily dose of nicotine. He shuffled in that direction, curiosity winning over his lethargy.

Terry rounded the corner and saw April Long pounding all hell out of Terri, who was laughing at her beating as if it meant nothing at all. Terri's clothes were disheveled, and she was bloodied in the face. Whatever had possessed April to start beating on her was apparently winding down a bit. Her fists still lifted and fell back down to hit Terri, but the blows were light and ineffectual.

Something finally clicked in his head, and Terry moved over, pulling April—who wanted to struggle but didn't really have the strength left—off of Terri. His ex-girlfriend laughed still, tears falling from her eyes, and sat up. Her

face was bruised and battered, her clothes torn and bloodied. Her body shook with the fading sound of her laughs,
and while it annoyed him, he couldn't help but notice how
nicely her breasts shook within the confines of her exposed bra.

April Long looked at him and sniffled miserably. "She
had it coming. She said nasty things to me." It was hardly a
convincing argument, but Terry just nodded and left it at that.

"Maybe you ought to go on home, April. Go and get
yourself cleaned up."

April nodded, too worn out to argue, and shuffled toward
her house, barely even taking the time to grab up her purse.
She might have been on the winning side of the fight, but she
moved like an old woman suffering the weight of her long,
miserable life.

Terry turned to Terri—Isn't that too cute? He could just
hear his mom saying it to one of the regulars at the diner.
She'd always been so tickled by the idea of him dating a
girl with the same name—and stared at her. He wanted to
offer her comfort and he wanted to slap her and he wanted
to scream in her face for the way she'd screwed his entire
life up.

Instead, he stood perfectly still and just looked at her.

And she looked back and smiled weakly. "Hi, Terry. I
see you got out."

"Yeah. Thanks for dropping the charges." What the hell
else could he say? She had him on the ropes, and anything
he did to make her unhappy, well it would be his ass on the
line, not hers.

"Seems only fair. You weren't the one that raped me.
But I was angry with you. You deserved to be punished. You
let me get taken away into the woods. You let him get me."

"Who was it, Terri? Who got you?"

"Constable Bill Karstens." Her pretty, bloodied face got
bitter right then, losing all of the happiness that had been

there an instant before. Why she'd been laughing he couldn't hope to guess, and he really wasn't too sure he wanted to know.

"Why didn't you report him? Why did you let him go?"

"Because I wanted you to hurt like I was hurt, you son of a bitch." She shook again, this time with anger instead of whatever twisted joy she'd gotten from April beating the crap out of her. "You left me there. You dumped me like a goddamned bag of trash, and he got me. You have no idea what he did to me, Terry! You can't begin to know what he did!" Her anger collapsed into bitter tears, and despite himself, he went to her. He wanted her to know how sorry he was. The anger didn't matter. The ruination of so much of his life was nothing next to the grief she was suffering, and despite everything she'd done to him, he still loved her.

He pulled her into his arms, and she melted against him, her tears hot and wet against his chest, her face pressed to him and her body shuddering with what had to be the worst sorts of memories.

"I'm sorry, Terri. I'm so sorry. I was so fucking stupid. I wish I could take it all back." He spoke softly, his words mumbled into her hair, which smelled as sweet and felt as soft as he remembered. He wanted to stay angry with her, wanted to hate her for what she'd done to him, but really, hadn't he been far, far worse to her? His eyes started stinging, the birth of tears that wanted to fall, tears shed for one stupid act and an even dumber bet that had led to him leaving her alone on a darkened road. Alone and vulnerable.

"I know you are, Terry." Her voice was so soft, filled with a deep loneliness that he felt he could understand. For just a second her hands wrapped against his, and her sweet face looked up, placing a kiss on the side of his mouth, while she looked deeply into his eyes. "But it's not enough."

Then she pushed back from him and screamed bloody

murder, her nails raking across the exposed skin of his forearms and down over his hands. Terry stepped back, shocked by the sudden outburst.

He was even more shocked by the sudden appearance of Principal Wortham. The man's normally friendly face looked as stunned as Terry himself felt. But the look changed quickly enough. Wortham's eyes scanned over the two of them, and then he looked straight at Terry, and his face grew angry and mean. Everything else aside, that was what shook Terry the most. He'd never seen Wortham look anything other than happy.

And he'd certainly never imagined that the man could hit that hard. He heard Wortham say, "You sick little bastard," and then he saw the man's fist blocking out everything else. Something white hot exploded across his face and knocked his whole world on its ass. The principal of the school might well have beaten him to death right then and there if it hadn't been for the screams coming from the classroom where Stan Long breathed out something that should have never been allowed to exist.

Terry felt himself lifted by his neck, and while he tried to remember how to think or really do anything at all, he was hauled down the small hill to the closest school entrance. He wasn't sure, he couldn't be over the sound of screams and the way his feet kept tangling over themselves as Wortham hauled him into the school, but he thought he heard Terri laughing softly behind him.

Maybe she was right. Maybe some sins couldn't be forgiven. Terry Palance cried like a child as he was dragged into the junior high school wing of the building and away from the girl he'd once dreamed of marrying when he wasn't just dreaming of being famous.

VI

The energies disappeared after they hit Barry LeMarrs. Or at least that was the way it looked to the students who witnessed their reemergence into this world. More accurately, they changed, dissipated to a certain extent, and continued on their way. Jonathan Crowley could have seen them, but he was still moving through the woods, outdistancing Joey Whitman and dodging past every potential obstacle with almost unnatural grace. He could have described the energies to a person who wanted to know what they looked like, and he could have told anyone who asked him what the energies were, too.

He could have explained what he thought he'd figured out about what was going on and what the man he'd been speaking to in the woods had done. He could have explained that the man—he wasn't really comfortable calling him MacGruder, for he was pretty certain it was just a cover name, a way to hide in plain sight, as it were—had decided to play hardball when it came to his curse. The energies he'd seen trapped before were all of those who'd been wronged by Serenity. Every person who'd been killed or maimed or violated by the people of the town over the years. How had he come to that conclusion? Well, for one thing, he'd already dealt with them once, and he had a certain *knack* for knowing these things. Sometimes he made mistakes in what he deduced, but he had a pretty damned good track record, all things considered. He knew they weren't the citizens of Serenity Falls, not even the ones who'd been murdered, because he'd guessed where they were, too, just as soon as he'd seen the wooden figures in Havenwood. One look at the tiny carving of Amy Blake had confirmed that for him, thanks very much.

Oh, to be sure, Crowley had a notion about most of what

was going on in the town, and he understood well enough now why he couldn't see the ghosts that should have been haunting the area. He couldn't see them because they hadn't been there. Something in the curse—or more accurately curses because he was almost certain one solitary curse couldn't manage everything that was going on in the town—had trapped them away and given them time to contemplate what had been done.

He could have explained—though he likely wouldn't have because he seldom did—that the dead were now freed and very set on only one thing. They wanted payback. But no one asked Jonathan Crowley, and he didn't really have the time to stop anyone and explain anyway, because he felt it when the energies came back, and he saw them as they soared above the town and streamed across the horizon heading to the east of the town proper toward where the farms nearby were situated.

But it should be known and he would be the first to admit it to anyone he felt he could trust, which was no one, thanks just the same, that Jonathan Crowley can make mistakes. He took one look at the great gathering of energies that illuminated the skies in a spectrum unseen by human eyes, and he decided to follow it. He needed, he felt, to stop it before it could become something more, something truly deadly as opposed to merely dangerous.

So he ran right past the school without a second's hesitation and left behind a few surprises that would come back to haunt him all too soon.

He left behind the fragments of the river of torn and bitter souls that stayed behind and found new homes. The dead had been busy for a long time, discussing what had to be done when the time came, and they were in no way ready to forgive and forget.

Throughout the high school several couples sat bolt upright at almost the exact same second. Aside from this small gesture, there were no visible signs that anything strange had happened to them. Eva Spinelli, Chris Parker, Meg Brown, and Glenn Harrigan, and the rest of the teens who'd been torn apart and remade by something in the woods, struggled within themselves, fighting against what had animated their bodies since they'd been killed. In many ways it was rather like fighting against themselves, and the fight was desperate. But to the other people in the classrooms with them, also engaged in taking their final exams, it looked like nothing more than several kids sitting up and getting more comfortable.

VII

It didn't take long for the call to go out from the school to the medical center and from there to the constables' offices. Once again understaffed, Jack Michaels himself was the one who answered the call along with Tom Norris. The morning had already been hectic and filled with strange news. Why should he hope it might actually get any easier? His first call this morning had been to let him know that something had happened to the bodies of the town's dead that had been held in Utica. He'd barely had time to hear that before the next call came in about the body of Penelope Grey being discovered inside her house. And there was no sign of Lawrence Grey anywhere. He'd already called in the rest of the constables because, frankly, he didn't know if just he and Norris could handle it. A very exhausted looking Victor Barnes was coming over from the medical center to handle calls.

"Will you tell me what the hell is going on with these damned flyers everywhere, Tom? Please?"

"I don't know. They're advertisements for a carnival that says it's going to set up at the Pageant farm."

"Yeah? Well, remind me to fine the morons when they show up. I am not going to have people littering in this town likes it's a goddamned dump."

The wind picked up and scattered what had to be several hundred of the flyers through the air in a veritable wave of colorful illustrations and grinning clown faces. Jack scowled and turned toward the school. Now and then he wished they hadn't decided to gate the cemetery. He could have just crossed right on through before the vandalism. He got to the school just in time to see the second ambulance pull up. The ambulance service might be located right next to his offices, but that didn't mean they usually got to places at the same time. One or the other was normally on the road, and this morning it had been both of them. He nodded to Walt Greene and Doug Laimo as they got out of the ambulance and headed toward where one of the teachers was waving frantically. It seemed like almost half of the student body was out on the lawn and sitting along the sides of the building, but he didn't really take the time to count them. Bill Wortham headed straight toward him, with Terry Palance in tow, looking like a caught rat in search of an escape route. Jack felt his stomach sink.

"I wish you'd told me you were letting this one out, Jack." His voice was low, but loud enough for Jack to tell he was truly shaken. "I caught him in the act of trying to rape Terri Halloway."

"What?" Michaels looked at the boy and felt himself start getting angrier. "Tell me he didn't succeed."

"I don't know, she was looking a little beat to hell and back, but I don't think she'd actually been . . . violated." Every word he said was penetrated by another shake of the beefy hand on Terry's collar. Terry looked scared, but he didn't actually try to run. That was just as well, because at the present moment Jack would likely have shot him dead where he stood.

Through clenched teeth and narrowed eyes he looked at Tom Norris. "Take this piece of shit back to the cell. Read him his rights, and don't touch him." He looked back at Terry, and the boy flinched as if he'd been slapped. "You take him right now, before I do something stupid." Then back to Bill Wortham. "Where is she now, Bill?"

"I've got her in the nurse's office." He must have seen what went through Jack's mind, because he hastily added, "Don't worry. She hasn't been touched or treated, just put someplace safe. I figured you might want to check her for evidence."

"What the hell else happened? Why do you need two ambulances?"

"I don't really know. Barry LeMarrs is dead, and so is Stan Long. I don't know what the hell happened, Jack. It looks like they got electrified and worse, but I don't really know."

"I'll deal with that later if I have to. Right now I need to check on Terri Halloway." Oh, he could barely believe this was happening. He could hardly imagine that he would have to deal with anything else happening to the poor girl and worse that Terry Palance might be responsible for it. He could scream for having let the boy go. But what else could he do? Both Gene and Terri had told him that charges wouldn't be pressed, and there just hadn't been enough else to go on.

He moved toward the nurse's station and balled and re-laxed his fists a dozen times as he walked. A few of the kids tried to say hello to him, and one teacher considered trying to ask him about what was happening, but they all changed their minds when they saw the look on his face.

VIII

Out beyond Havenwood, there was a small army of men working on restoring and testing all of the equipment that had to be serviceable for when the real work at the quarry started again. They were ahead of schedule, but they wanted it to stay that way. The powerful belt saws were working just fine, but the pumps for clearing away the waters had been sporadic at best. Even now they were fighting every attempt to get them flowing properly. It was frustrating and worse, because they needed those damned pumps if they ever wanted to actually get to the granite they were going to be cutting. The saws sure as hell wouldn't work under fifteen feet of water or more.

Amelia Dunlow and Mike Blake watched as the men pulled on this hose and twisted that bolt and finally, after almost four hours of failure, got the primary pump going. The industrial engine belched black smoke and then roared into nearly deafening activity. Still, they could hear the men cheer, and they got into it with them, excited that so much was finally going right. Marty Fulton walked over with a smile twice as broad as usual on his tobacco-stained teeth and slapped Mike on the shoulder in a way that was both companionable and rough. The man had arms like a gorilla's. The foreman of the site looked so exuberant that Mike feared briefly he would try to kiss him. Instead he looked over at Amelia and smiled. "I don't figure it'll take us much more than a few hours to get the worst of the water drained out, and then we can look into picking the best place to start cutting."

Amelia smiled warmly and placed her hand on his beefy shoulder. "You're a saint, Marty. I swear if I had a sister I'd have her marry you right now."

He chuckled and winked. "I think the old lady might

want to veto that one, boss." Marty's wife was a mystery to everyone. He never said what her name was, and he never showed her picture, but it was obvious that he loved her every time he spoke about her, even when he was teasing.

"How much does that pump handle, Marty?"

"In laymen's terms, I'm guessing about a swimming pool every two or three minutes." He smiled, strutting like a rooster he was so proud. "Gimme about five minutes, and I can show you what it looks like in action. We still have to get the main drainage hoses in place before we really get to work."

The falls were about to go into overtime. What had long since been a gentle stream of water falling from the side of the hill a quarter mile away was about to become something akin to the Mississippi River for the next week or so. The farmers down below where the water spilled out had already been alerted and were ready to report if any flooding took place. Some of them might not have been thrilled about the idea, but they were as prepared as they could be, and all of them understood the necessity.

Mike smiled and watched the activity. Amelia smiled beside him and broke her own rule, taking his hand in hers. It felt nice to hold her hand, so fine and delicate under the calluses. The weather was still preposterously cold, but even the chill over his skin didn't hamper his good mood.

It took Jonathan Crowley to do that. Crowley came up the side of the hill, where no one sane would consider walking because the ground was so damned treacherous, and looked right at them for half a second before looking toward the sky again. He stopped next to the two and stared down to where the waters from the pump would be falling soon enough.

"Hi, kiddies, I can't stay. I just wanted to warn you to watch yourselves. It's very possible that something bad is coming your way." He looked at Amelia, and for an instant his normally harsh expression softened a bit. It was gone too quickly for Mike to know for certain if it had been anything more than his imagination. "I found out what's wrong with this town, and I don't think it's very happy about me interfering."

"Why would that mean we have to be careful?" The question just sort of jumped out before Mike could stop it.

Crowley looked at him and grinned. "Because I only know a few people in town, Mikey, and I was told it might try to distract me by putting anyone I'm close to in danger." He stepped forward and pointed to Amelia. "That means I'm trusting you to watch out for our girl. Get me?"

Before Mike could respond, Crowley was in motion again, running past the work crew and down toward where the falls proper started.

Mike watched him for a second and then realized that Amelia was in hot pursuit. Cursing under his breath, he followed. Crowley moved like an animal with good reflexes, climbing over anything that got in his way and making it look easy. Amelia wasn't quite as graceful, but she did a far better job than Mike. By the time he'd caught up with the two of them, he was panting.

Crowley looked down into the valley and at the farms on his left and the town almost dead ahead, both well below their current height. Mike never really gave too much thought to the falls. They were pretty enough when the sun caught them the right way, but by and large he was like almost everyone else in the area, and only really saw them when he felt the need to. The town spread out nicely from here, affording a view that made the whole place look like a railroad train set model that had been carefully built. He could see the schools and the cemetery, the drive-in in the distance, and the spread of houses that ran off into the wooded areas. He could also see the farms down below, spread out and organized in a way that nature seldom managed on its own.

The wind was biting along the precipice of the falls, and the cold was even more sharp and obvious. He looked at Amelia, barely breathing hard, and Crowley, who had apparently been running for a while, and wished he had a tenth of their stamina. Crowley's face tracked over the land below and settled on one of the farms closest to the center of town.

"Damn. It's already happening."

"What is, Jonathan?" Amelia had that look on her face again, the one that said she felt something more than just intimidated when she was around the man. Mike pushed it out of his head and made himself remember that she was here with him, not with the man from her past.

Crowley pointed to where a black shape was growing in the field near the farmhouse. "I don't know, Amelia. But I know it can't be good. That thing is growing."

True enough. When Mike looked, he could actually see it shift and change in the distance. It looked almost like a line of three trees barren of all but a few branches when he'd first seen it. Now it was changing. The thin lines sprouting from the top of the thing were growing wider in a way that made him think of a bat spreading its wings slowly. Streamers of darkness moved from one line to the next, blossoming into something that made his skin crawl, though he was too far away to really see it clearly.

"Well, looks like it's time for me to go down there and see what's up." Crowley sounded weird, his voice not as overly cheerful as usual.

"Do you need a ride?" Amelia's hand almost touched Crowley but then pulled back at the last second, as if afraid she'd get burned.

"No. Whatever's down there might take advantage of me having someone I know nearby. I'll just walk."

"Walk? Christ, Crowley, it's almost two miles away." He didn't want to laugh at the man, but his voice cracked at the idea.

"It's almost two miles if I take the nice, long roads across town to get there. But if I go from here, it's not that far at all." Crowley looked at him, his normal smile back in place. "The ground's level, and I've run through a few fields in my time."

"If you go from here you've got a ninety-foot drop straight down to the base of the falls, and that will take time." Mike looked over the side of the cliff at the sheer granite that slid down to rocks he knew from his past were sharp and close together. Anyone falling from there would be dead, even if they managed to hit the water.

He looked back toward Crowley and Amelia, ready to say as much, and stopped himself. Crowley was gone. "Where the hell did he go?"

Amelia looked at him and shrugged, pointing with her finger over the side of the cliff.

Mike looked over again but saw nothing, no one. "You're kidding, right?"

"Jonathan isn't a patient man. He had somewhere to go."

Mike had no answer to that one. He looked over the side for another minute and then shook his head. Together, the two of them walked back toward the quarry proper. Up ahead of them the guys were celebrating. But between Crowley's words of warning and the sight of the black thing that seemed to grow out of the ground like a cancer, neither of them seemed much in the mood for joining in any longer.

IX

It was a short day at the school, which was just as well after the chaos of the early morning. Funny thing about your average institution: things tend to get chaotic in them when two people die under unusual circumstances. Throw in the new allegations of an attempted rape, and tense situations just get worse from there.

The school day ended amidst a great deal of disorganization and rumors. What walked inside of Rebecca Glass's body loved every minute of it. The body had actually come close to an orgasm when Stan Long started dying and had reached full-blown, body-shaking delight when that miserable bastard LeMarrs did his little detonation all over the wall. No one had noticed, of course, because everyone was screaming bloody murder when she came.

After that it was just a matter of waiting around and enjoying itself.

Funny thing about the separation of its spirit into different parts: each part had developed a new personality. That just wasn't at all what it had expected. But then, nothing that had been happening since its return to the world had been what it expected, so why should this be any different? All it had wanted was a return to what it had been. What it got instead was something that seemed more like a bonus than a punishment. It got a body that could feel, truly feel and experience real sensations beyond emotional gratification. In all of its existence it had never expected that. Just thinking about the body it inhabited and what that body could enjoy was enough to make it shiver with pleasure.

Becky walked out through the double doors in front of the school and spotted Lawrence across the parking lot, doing his best to look inconspicuous, which was pretty damned good, actually. Lawrence was naturally the sort of person most people seemed to look through rather than at, and the entity inside him had made this natural quirk into an actual ability. People walked around Lawrence, noticing him just enough to avoid collisions and unpleasant physical contact, but not enough to really pay him any attention. Becky only saw him because of their connection.

Being the same person made it easier to see what wasn't supposed to be seen. Not that she really wanted to see him anymore. She rather liked what she'd become, actually. Oh, she understood what he wanted, and to a certain extent even agreed with what he felt was necessary, but that didn't mean she liked the idea.

And she wasn't at all sure she wanted to reunite with her other parts, even if the two of them could manage to get the Joey-aspect away from the Hunter in one piece, which was rather doubtful.

Lawrence wouldn't want to hear that, and she didn't really much care what he wanted. What she wanted—and maybe what the Becky Glass persona wanted, too, if what she was feeling was right—was a chance to actually live for a change. No hiding, no fear, but actual life.

Lawrence started walking across the asphalt of the parking lot, his face pinched with an expression that looked like it was one part determination and three parts constipation. The longer Becky looked at him the less she liked what she saw.

"I've been trying to get in contact with you . . ." His voice was, if anything, even more annoying than his face. She tried not to think about the fact that she actually disliked a part of herself enough to really be annoyed by him.

"I've been busy, in school, trying to assess what's going on. I think it's finally begun."

"That's a little obvious, isn't it?" His eyes narrowed with contempt as he looked at her, and she wanted to swat him.

"Don't act superior to me. We're the same being."

"No, we're not. We've been . . . contaminated by these forms." He looked around, his thin arms gesturing wildly. "We might even be stuck this way, unless we can get back our other self."

"Just calm down, Lawrence. Nothing's written in stone here." She felt her lip pull back in a sneer and wanted to weep with the pure pleasure of it. Physical sensation was a miracle, and she intended to savor it for as long as it lasted. "And knock it off with the attitude problem. There are worse fates than being trapped in these bodies."

"You're enjoying this, aren't you?" He looked surprised, and she found that vastly amusing.

"Shouldn't I? Are you telling me you aren't reveling in the feelings?"

"No, as a matter of fact I'm not. This body is frail and pathetic. How could I possibly enjoy being stuck in it?"

"How can you not enjoy it? All of that time lost to ourself. All of that time before Crowley killed us, trapped in a body that couldn't feel anything at all. I love it!" Becky stepped up to him, looking down on his slightly shorter frame. "And I know what you did to that body's mother. I know you enjoyed that well enough, don't I?"

"You should talk. You can't even keep yourself from touching your body every chance you get."

"Why would I want to?"

"Because we have work to do. We have to pull ourself together and get on with this."

"Why? So we can get back that wretched thing we used to call a body?"

"YES, damn it, YES!" His voice was raised, and she was sure someone nearby would start paying them closer attention, but they just kept walking past. Lawrence apparently got the lion's share of the power that should have been evenly distributed. Joey had managed to control the dogs they'd reanimated—though she wasn't quite sure how they'd managed that feat as it was something they couldn't have done in the past—and Lawrence got almost everything else. Try as she might, she hadn't yet discovered what, if any, of the powers left had gone to her. "I don't want this! I want what we were before!"

"I don't. I like this new body, and I like being able to use it."

"It doesn't matter. We're going to be rejoined, and you can't stop it from happening."

"Oh, but I can. You can sense me, and I can sense you. That means I can avoid you."

"Not likely." He snorted, his face managing to look arrogant and constipated at the same time. She wouldn't have thought it possible if she hadn't seen it for herself.

"Don't cross me. I know what you're capable of, I know what you've done in the past, and I can make sure you suffer dearly for anything you attempt to do."

Lawrence looked ready to have an aneurysm. Becky turned away from him and started walking, finished with the argument at least for the time being.

He made no move to follow her or stop her but instead just watched her go.

If she thought it was over, she was very mistaken.

X

Dave and his family watched on as the police showed up and took to investigating the thing growing in the field. It hadn't been very impressive when it first started growing, it had just been weird. Now, on the other hand, it was a sight to see. It was getting bigger for one thing, and it was sort of radiating menace.

It was also starting to look like something, but he really couldn't quite decide what. It vaguely resembled a tent, but if that was the case, it was enormous and it wasn't complete. Yes, it looked like a circus tent, but one that had been brutally attacked by a madman with an eraser. There were gaps large enough to walk through all over the place, and he could see clear through from one end to the other if he walked to the proper angles. He'd even tried it a few times, just to prove it. But if it was a tent, it was an empty one. The only thing he saw inside was grass and air. Not, he was grateful to see, any sign of Marco or his pals.

There was a small part of him that still wanted to tell someone what had happened, but it wasn't the time. There was too much going on, and he was pretty sure his father would decide he was being a freak about the whole thing. Well, at first at least. His father knew him better than that, but he might forget he knew him better than that for a while. Parents tended to do that when there were other adults around. It was like magic; one second he was someone an adult could talk to, and the next he was reduced to a kid, merely because another person old enough to shave showed up. It was frustrating, but it was also a part of life, and he knew only time would change that particular fact.

He saw the freaky guy when he came toward the farm, eyeing the tent thing dubiously. The man had a few stray leaves and the like stuck to his clothes, and his skin was flushed like he'd been doing strenuous work. Or it might have just been the cold.

The man walked right past the constables and his parents and moved directly toward him.

"Shouldn't you be in school?"

"Shouldn't you be driving a car?"

"Can't trust cars. They blow up at the dumbest times."

"I'm gonna have to trust you on that."

"What's your name again?"

"Dave. And you're the parapsychologist guy."

"That's about it."

"Have a name?"

"Call me Jonathan."

"Why are you on my property, Jonathan?"

"Curious about that thing over there."

"The tent?"

"You figure that's what it is?"

"Looks kind of like one."

"You're probably right. Besides, it goes with the flyer."

"What flyer?"

Crowley pulled a folded piece of paper from his back pocket and showed it to Dave.

"Hmmph."

"Mmmmm?"

"Didn't have no one come by and ask if they could put up a Carnival of the Fantastic around here."

"Maybe your dad didn't tell you."

"Sure. Have a guy come up and ask to put a circus tent on the property and then not tell your kids about it. That's like having Santa Claus drop by and not mentioning it to the kids. That'll work."

"Maybe he was trying to surprise you."

"You don't know my dad. He's about as happy with surprises as you are with dirty clothes."

"What do you mean by that?"

"I mean if you was a cat you'd be licking your paws and having a cleanup party." He pointed to Crowley's pants. "Got a leaf stuck on your left hip." Crowley pulled the leaf away and let it drop. "See? Can't stand to be dirty, can you?"

"What makes you say that?"

"You just got that sort of face. Look like you'd sooner bite into a rotten apple than let any dirt get on you."

"You're still a strange kid."

"Yeah, and you're still a snot. But it happens."

The man looked at him for a long second before finally grinning. "Strange, but okay."

"Snotty, and I'll get back to you on the rest of it. But you helped Stan, so you can't be all bad." He looked over at the stranger and readjusted his Phillies cap. The sun was starting to creep through the clouds, and he hated getting too much glare. "What you figure's gonna come out of there when it's done?"

"Bad stuff."

"That helped."

"Well, I'm always trying to be helpful . . ." Jonathan sighed. "I think it's going to be a bad situation if it finishes whatever it's doing."

"Cops are here. They'll take care of it."

"You have a lot of faith in the local constables?"

"Well, we don't really get a lot of crime in Serenity Falls."

Jonathan laughed. "Read the papers much, do you?"

"No. I just watch the news."

"Read the paper, kid. You'll get more details."

"Stan said something about you saying we had a lot of murders per capita around here."

"Did he really say 'per capita'?" The man looked at him over the edge of his rimless glasses.

"No. I managed that one all by myself."

"Should have figured."

Constable Michaels walked over, looking at Jonathan and completely ignoring Dave. That was about what Dave had expected and merely confirmed his earlier suspicion about the ability of adults to relegate kids to second-class citizenry in an instant.

"What brings you out here, Mr. Crowley?"

"Dave's circus tent."

"Circus tent?"

Crowley showed the flyer to the man.

"Ah. I hadn't made the connection."

"Neither had I. That was all Dave."

Michaels looked at Crowley and smiled tightly. "What do you make of it?"

"It's bad news. Personally? I'd suggest burning it to the ground."

"Too much risk of starting an ugly fire. There really aren't any fire hydrants this far out."

"Then I'd think about knocking it down before it finishes becoming whatever its growing into." Crowley stood up and looked in the direction of the growing black mass. "I don't think letting it finish whatever it's doing would be the best idea for keeping the peace."

"You think it's trouble?"

"As a rule, when something black and smelling like that pops out of the ground, I can't help but think it doesn't have the best intentions."

"Good point."

"Oh, and I'd seriously suggest you get the people on this property somewhere else before that thing finishes whatever it's trying to do. I don't think this will be a safe place for anyone in a few hours."

"Dave's dad over there is already planning on everyone taking a few hours to eat in town."

"I'd also block off the road or at least the driveway to this place."

"Why?"

"The small print on the bottom of the picture says the carnival is here for one night only. I'm just guessing, but I suspect tonight might be the night."

Michaels looked at the man for a moment and then turned back to the big top sprouting from the ground. Dave looked, too, and saw that most of the holes he could have stepped through earlier were now much smaller or gone completely. As he looked on, one of the splits in the strange-looking fabric closed before his eyes. He thought he could see shapes in the material and moved closer.

Crowley sighed. "I wouldn't get too close, Dave."

Dave nodded and stopped a few feet away, squinting and looking as closely as he could. "There's bodies in this."

"Excuse me?"

"The tent. It looks like someone sewed it together out of bodies."

Crowley looked sharply at the growing tent and shook his head. Michaels came closer to the tent and all but pushed Dave away from it, as if it might suddenly leap forward and grab him. Dave might have been upset about that, but he'd already decided he didn't like the idea of being as close as he was to it.

Sure enough, the fabric of the tent seemed almost to writhe, to dance as the growing wind caught it and stretched it taut. Though it was faint, there seemed to be an impression of bodies—or at least the skins of bodies—sewn together crudely in an overlapping patchwork. It wasn't easy to see, but it was there just the same, and Michaels would have sworn that it hadn't been there just a few minutes ago.

"What the hell do you make of this?" Who exactly Michaels might have been talking to was anyone's guess, but Crowley answered him.

"I think you've got some seriously pissed-off dead people around these parts, Constable."

"Pissed off about what?"

"Being murdered." Crowley walked toward the tent and poked the thing. Dave would have sworn he heard the sound of voices whispering in the air at that exact same second. "I think the dead are about to have a payback party around here."

"There haven't been that many murders in Serenity Falls, Crowley."

"Are you sure about that, Constable?"

"Well, I've been in the police department here for fifteen years or so, and I think I've only dealt with around ten murders in that time."

"Ten that you know of."

"What do you mean?"

"I mean there are a lot of empty houses around here. I understand all about the quarry shutting down and all of that, but are you sure all of those houses were left by people who actually moved away?"

"Pretty sure."

"Mmm-hmm." Crowley looked at the constable and smiled. Dave watched Jack Michaels flinch as if he'd been slapped. "And how many of those people have ever come back to visit?"

"I have no idea."

"I'm pretty sure that at least a few of them are about to visit your fine town, Constable Michaels. I just don't think they're going to want to shoot the breeze while they're here."

"What do you know that you aren't telling me?"

"Not much. Nothing you'd likely believe, either."

"So. You think closing off the road would be a good idea and blocking off the farm?" Michaels still looked a little dubious.

Crowley grabbed the tent again and pulled hard this time. The air filled with a short burst of screams and wails and hisses of anger. "I think so, yes. I think that would be a fine idea. Don't you?"

Michaels nodded and reached for his radio. Dave's father called from near the house and told him to grab a few things. They were going on a trip.

Dave didn't argue. Leaving was sounding better all the time.

XI

Jessie and Charlee saw the flyers everywhere. They were almost impossible not to see, as there were dozens of them on the walls and on the telephone poles along their route home. School was mostly done, and both of them thought the carnival would be fun, but neither of them really had much desire to go. They were both in mourning.

Stan was dead. Stan, who normally managed to lighten almost any conversation with his little jokes—the quiet kind that seldom if ever had anything derisive about another person—and his easy good looks. Stan who always remembered to at least say hello to someone, even if he wasn't very fond of them.

Stan, who was the best friend of Dave, was dead.

And it just shouldn't have happened. Stan should have been a happy kid, and he should have been there for a long, long time, because, when you got right down to it, Charlee had sort of daydreamed that they'd date someday.

Neither of them really spoke, save for an occasional comment or sigh. They'd spoken earlier about what had happened, and Charlee had described the details in a monotone voice that gave the facts without dwelling on them. Then she'd started making little hiccuping sounds and broken into tears on Jessie's shoulder. That was all right. Jessie didn't mind. It gave her an excuse to do her own crying.

Dave hadn't been at school.

Dave probably didn't know that Stan was dead. One thing led to another, and now they were heading toward the Pageant farm. Well, Jessie was headed there to let her new boyfriend know what had happened. Charlee was just sort of along for the ride.

"Think he'll be okay?"

"I dunno. I hope so." Jessie shrugged her thin shoulders.

"I mean, I know he's strong and all, but this is Stan. You know? This was his best friend in the world."

"Yeah." Charlee looked away from the road and away from her feet and away from her friend. For some reason all three of the places she normally looked were making her very uncomfortable. She kept feeling the need to say something, just to hear a response, and it bothered her. It felt like a sign of weakness.

For a change of pace Jessie spoke first. "Joey wasn't at school today, either. Neither was Lawrence." Her eyebrows couldn't seem to decide if they should go together or lift up from the center, almost like she couldn't decide whether she should be thinking or worrying. "I hope they're all okay."

"I thought I saw Lawrence at school. Him and Becky were having a fight of some kind."

"Lawrence was fighting?"

"Yeah. Weird, hunh?"

"I didn't know Lawrence even knew Becky that well."

"No one knows Becky that well. I didn't think he knew how to have an argument."

Not far away, they could just make out the edge of Dave's place. Though the hill nearest them hid the farmhouse proper, it no longer hid the black thing growing near it. Several cars that would normally have passed by were parked on the side of the road, their drivers and passengers all watching the activity up ahead. There were flashing lights, red and blue and likely from police cars. The fire engines and ambulances in the area were exclusively red.

"What do you think's going on?" Jessie's voice sounded like it was on the verge of a full-scale panic.

"I dunno. Let's see what we can find out." They walked forward into the small gathering of pedestrians who desperately wanted to be drivers, and listened to the complaints. It only took a few seconds to learn that there was a roadblock up ahead. Well, roadblocks are all good and well, but they've never been very good at stopping people who got off the road. The two of them walked on, backtracking and then going over the side of the hill out of sight from where the constables stood.

Not too much later, other people started having the same idea and moved over the field, abandoning their cars and heading toward the Pageant farm. Many of them had already spoken to the local law, knew that they weren't allowed anywhere near the farm, but that has seldom stopped people in the past. Curiosity is a powerful thing. Just ask any cat.

CHAPTER 4

I

The sun started setting, hitting the edge of the foothills and fading away, leaving a cold night to grow and flourish. Those people who still commuted to jobs away from Serenity Falls repeated their daily routine and came back home, often cursing the traffic and sometimes just enjoying the ride. More than a few of them noticed the fact that the air was colder around Serenity, and a few even pondered why that might be, but life and the distractions it offers soon made all but the most painfully curious push the odd temperature shifts out of their mind. Besides, the weather wasn't as unseasonably cold as it had been at least. It was no longer necessary to wear a heavy coat, and that was a plus.

To the west of town there was a growing number of people who pulled off to the side of the road and grumbled about the situation. Access to Serenity was limited as far as car travel was concerned, and going around the Pageant farm meant backtracking by a few miles to get home. Most of them weren't pleased by the idea, and a few were pissed off that no one had bothered to call the radio stations in the area and give them advance notice.

Bob Steinman and Tom—no longer Tommy now that he had a real job, thanks just the same—Lassiter couldn't have cared less. They were tired, and they were bored. Bob handled most of the complaints, especially after Tom Two (Norris was the first Tom, and Lassiter had to deal with it) called one of the disgruntled motorists a few choice names and almost got into a fight. It's fair to say that neither of them was exactly in the running for any top cop awards, but eventually they both noticed that there were quite a few cars sitting empty on the side of the road.

Maybe there might have been a decision to do something about it, but neither of them really had the initiative to be bothered. That, and the Pageant girls were very distracting. Amber and Suzette were treating Tom like a real human being ever since he'd become a constable, and he was easily swayed away from paying much attention to the road. Both of the twins had gone to work and been informed by phone that the family was going to be staying in town until something was done about the thing in the yard. That didn't stop them from coming out to the farm to see what the hell was what. Nothing much could have done that. They were curious by nature. Still, as it became full night, they grew bored with Steinman and Lassiter and decided to head on their way.

What the good constables hadn't counted on was that the flyers everywhere around town would actually really attract any attention. There were people aplenty who headed toward the farm to see about the one-night-only affair. Most of them didn't bother with actually seeing what was causing the traffic jam, they just parked at the end of it and moved across the field. Surely the Pageants could have been better prepared if they were going to have a carnival, but really, there was only so much space in front of their farm, and having to walk wasn't exactly a challenge.

II

Amelia and Mike got back to Havenwood to find Crowley waiting for them. He had his pets from the pet store in his lap and looked almost guilty to be having fun with them. The rat was nibbling on a chew stick, and the kitten was batting at his fingers. Mike bit his tongue on a comment about how cute the scene was. He didn't feel that Crowley would take it well. He was, of course, absolutely right in his assessment of the situation.

Amelia walked over and smiled warmly. Crowley looked back and managed not to smile. "I can't stay. I wanted to leave you a few instructions."

Amelia nodded. "I'm guessing this has something to do with your little friends?"

Crowley looked daggers at her. "Good guess. I want you to let the rat go in back of your house in around an hour. I want you to keep the cat with you, right here. And if you feel you must go outside, take the cat with you."

"Rather cryptic, isn't it?"

"I'm a cryptic sort of guy, Mike." Crowley smiled for him, but it wasn't a nice smile. "I have reasons for everything I do."

"I'm sure you do."

Amelia made that little half-sad face she did whenever he and Crowley went at it, so he made himself behave. Everything about Crowley pissed him off, and there wasn't anything he could do about that, but he could at least fake it for Amelia's sake.

Crowley stood up, setting the rat back in the small carrying cage that had become its house in the last few days. "I have to go to the medical center. A little bird told me that the Parsons were having a few problems. Figured I'd stop by as a professional courtesy."

"Who?" Mike hadn't the vaguest notion about the Parsons. He knew most of the families in town to one extent or another, and to the best of his knowledge had never met anyone with the last name of Parsons.

"Some parapsychologists who came into town to help a local kid with a possession problem."

"Uh-hunh."

"No, really. I know it's not as reputable as, say, banking, but it's an honest field sometimes. They did their best, and they blew it, but they were smart enough to ask for my help." Crowley's smile was pure venom, and Mike returned it. Amelia sighed, but they both ignored her for the moment. "You should keep an open mind, Mike. It's good for the soul."

"Jonathan, please be careful." Amelia spoke as the man rose from his seat and headed toward the front door.

"I always am. Or at least mostly. The rat goes out, the cat stays in, understood?"

"Yes, Jonathan."

Crowley looked at her for a long second, his face carefully neutral. "Stay away from the little carnival at the Pageant farm. That's where I think this is all going down. Oh, and if it looks like you're going to have some sort of trouble out here, don't go into your bedroom. I've set up a few surprises in there that you don't want anything to do with."

Mike blinked in surprise and started to make a comment, then remembered he was supposed to behave himself for

Amelia's sake. It wasn't easy. Amelia simply nodded, her eyes downcast.

Crowley left a moment later, whistling to himself.

"What is it with him, Amelia?" The words just sort of crept out of his mouth, bypassing his common sense on the way. "What makes you so different around him?"

"He was someone special to my family once."

"See? That's exactly what I'm talking about. You're one of the most direct people I know, but whenever it comes to Crowley, you suddenly become vague. I have to tell you, I don't like it much."

"I know, Mike, but please . . . It's best if you don't know some things."

"Was he your lover?" There, it was out in the open now.

Amelia shook her head, playing with the kitten and deliberately not looking in his direction. "No. Nothing like that. More like an uncle."

"An uncle?" He shook his head and let out a half-laugh of contempt. "He isn't that much older than you. How could he be like an uncle?"

"He's much older than he looks."

"He'd have to be." Mike sighed and looked down at the rat in its cage, nibbling at the wooden stick. "He doesn't look any older than me."

"He was older than you before your father was born."

The words were stated very calmly, and Mike turned his attention to the back of Amelia's head, watched her graceful hand and the kitten that she kept engaged with play.

"What is he?"

"I can't discuss that, Mike."

"Is he human?"

"Sometimes . . . I think."

Mike might have asked another question, but there was a knock at the door, and Amelia went to answer it. Mike walked closer to see who was at the door. Despite the fact that he didn't like Crowley, the man had warned them to be careful, and Mike intended to do just that.

Amelia opened the door and looked down at Lawrence Grey. Lawrence smiled, looking up at her. "You have something of mine in this house, I'd like it back now."

III

There was silence at the Long house. In the emptiness of a house that was no longer a home, nothing stirred. Jason Long had seen the note his wife left for him shortly after he'd heard about the death of his son. He was spared the pain of seeing his son's body. There had been enough witnesses to eliminate the need for a positive identification from the family, and he was grateful for that.

Addy was gone.

April had come home and seen the note, too, and left a short time later without saying a word. Her hands were bruised. He'd noticed, but it really didn't register until after she'd vacated the premises.

Addy was gone.

Jason should have gone after April. Should have gone after Addy. He didn't have the strength. He sat down on his favorite recliner and stared at the wall blankly.

Addy was gone.

Three times he reached down with his hand, expecting to pet Beauregard's furry head. He touched nothing but air.

Addy was gone.

It was supposed to be a good day. He'd had enough shitty days of late, and when everything started going right, he'd allowed himself to dream that they would stay right. He'd landed a major break at work, had gotten word from Mike Blake that there was a lot of paperwork that had to be filed and that he was going to get to do the lion's share of it. It was what he did, the sort of thing he enjoyed as a lawyer. Simple, easy, and rewarding work that would keep a roof over the family's head for a while: filing for all the business licenses and permits that would have to be filed and making sure that everything was 100 percent kosher. A small victory for his little law firm. Hooray for the good guys.

Addy was gone.

He'd been on the way home from the Brick Oven, a little-too-expensive restaurant that happened to make the best damned food in three towns, when he got the call on his cell phone letting him know that Stan was dead. Oh, they hadn't actually just blurted out that his son had died; they'd just said it was urgent that he head over to the medical center immediately. He'd tried calling home but had no luck reaching anyone.

Addy was gone.

So he'd spoken to someone—a doctor he thought— who'd told him in soft tones that there had been some sort of freak accident and his one, his only son, was dead. And was there someone who could give him a lift home? Did he need to sit for a while? Would he like something to drink?

They were still asking questions when he left. He drove the rest of the way home remembering Stan's face and forcing tears back where they belonged, because real men don't cry. His father had taught him that at a very young age, and it was a lesson he'd taken to heart. Real men don't eat quiche, and they sure as hell don't cry.

Addy was gone.

He'd gone over in his mind how he was going to tell Adrienne about Stan something like a million times in the ten-minute drive home. The smell of the Brick Oven's French onion soup permeated the interior of the car, and he drove on autopilot, forgetting all about the special dinner for the family.

Addy was gone.

He opened the door to a quiet house and saw the note on the kitchen table, waiting for him.

The words took a while to focus. "I need some time. I'll call soon. I don't know if I'll be coming home. I love you April. I love you Stan." The note wasn't signed. It didn't need to be. The only person who came close to having writing as neat and precise as Adrienne's was April, and he'd just recently come to recognize the difference between the hand-writing of his wife and his daughter.

Addy was gone.

Jason Long killed himself just shortly after the sun went down. He ran a very sharp knife up from his wrist to his el-bow, severing veins and arteries in the process. He left no note. Real men didn't cry, and they didn't leave notes.

IV

April Long sat down in the waiting room of the medical center, waiting for someone to see her about her brother.

Jonathan Crowley walked past her and into the elevators without giving her a single thought. He moved up to the room where Jacob and Mary Parsons both rested and looked at them. Mary slept in an uncomfortable chair, her legs curled up under her body and her head resting on one hand. She was prettier when she was asleep. Her face lost its slightly harsh edge, and her features softened enough to make her look like a schoolgirl. Jacob lay in a deep sleep, the sort that some people never wake from.

He walked over to where the couple slept and stood over

Jacob. His hands never touched the man, but they ran above his prone form and felt the differences that were there, just under the surface. Then he nodded his satisfaction.

When he'd made his first visit to the farm earlier, he'd felt something was wrong with the head of the constables. Jack Michaels had been acting the way he always had, in Crowley's limited encounters with the man, but there was something decidedly off kilter about him. Crowley had felt it before, but that meant nothing. He'd run across a lot of that in Serenity, and part of the problem was that he could feel the curse that covered the town. The other problem, naturally, had been the big damned tent that was blossoming out of the ground. Things like that made it difficult to casually sense anything out of the ordinary. It was sort of like trying to feel a candle's heat from ten feet away when there was a bonfire only five feet off to the side. Still, he'd sensed something was wrong with the constable, and now he felt it again on the man in front of him.

Mary Parsons stirred in her sleep and shifted her body. He saw more of her leg than he was comfortable with as her gray flannel skirt rode higher, and he turned his back to avoid the temptation to enjoy the view. Professional courtesy and all that.

He felt the markings more than saw them, but he knew them for what they were. Jacob Parsons had become part of the problem. He and the constable both were touched by the curse and were now being used to feed it.

It wasn't all that unusual, really. Curses took energy, and that energy had to come from somewhere. The odds were good that every generation in Serenity had at least a few people marked with the sort of message written under Parsons's skin.

"Mr. Crowley?" Mary's voice was soft and slurred just a bit by sleep. He turned and looked at her as she adjusted her skirt and looked at him. "I didn't expect you to show up here."

"I heard about Jacob being attacked and figured I should at least show my respects."

"Thank you."

"Are you holding up well enough?"

"As well as can be expected, I guess."

"If you want to stretch your legs or answer nature's call, I can wait here."

She nodded and yawned and stretched herself with all the grace of a cat. He wondered why it was that she hid herself in baggy clothes and walked like she was holding a can between her knees. It was none of his business, he supposed, but it almost seemed a shame that a woman that attractive was determined to hide the fact. "I think I'll take you up on that. I really appreciate it. I just, I don't like the idea of him being by himself right now."

Crowley nodded a bit and managed a very quick smile. "I've been where you are. It's never easy."

Mary Parsons rose from her seat and moved to the doorway. "I'll be back in just a few minutes. Thanks again."

"No problem. Take your time." He waited until the door had closed and then pushed his hands against Jacob's round abdomen. "Jake and me needed to have a quick chat anyway."

Jacob Parsons's body heaved itself up in a spasm, and Crowley pushed him back down, his hands feeling like they would catch fire at any moment. Parsons's eyes flashed open, showing nothing but white, and his body twitched like a bird caught on a hot wire in an electrified fence.

Crowley had just finished when Mary came back into the room. She smiled prettily, and he smiled back. "I think you might want to call a doctor, Ms. Parsons. I think your husband is doing a little better."

She rushed over and saw that Jacob's countenance was changing a bit. In the last few days his hound dog face hadn't so much as twitched, and in comparison his features were practically doing gymnastics.

Crowley left a few minutes later, wishing a speedy recovery. He'd have stayed, but his hands still felt like they were about to combust, and he wasn't exactly feeling like being pleasant.

Besides, he had a circus to attend and a few other tasks to handle on the way.

V

Lawrence Grey walked into the house uninvited and moved toward the stairs. Mike started to protest, but Amelia shut him up with a glance. Crowley had said he had set things up in the bedroom. She wasn't willing to take any chances.

Lawrence moved past the two of them without bothering to give them the time of day. He knew what he wanted, and he intended to get it. Somewhere upstairs a portion of his essence was waiting to be rejoined with him.

The people in the room didn't bother him, and that was just as well. He felt tired and irritable enough without having to actually kill anything just at the moment. Lawrence went into the master bedroom of a house he hadn't dared even consider entering since his father had tried to kill him there, ready for any traps the Hunter might have set up. He knew who the people downstairs were, and he knew that at least one of them meant something to the Hunter. He could smell Crowley all over the place.

The bed was large enough to park a car on, but that wasn't important. The room was tastefully decorated in a fashion that screamed interior decorator, and he ignored it all, heading instead toward the door off to the side. Exactly in the center of the door was a piece of notebook paper placed with a single strip of clear tape. The paper was folded over on itself and had "To whom it may concern" written in neat, old-fashioned script.

Lawrence didn't hesitate to grab the folded message and read it almost as fast as he could unfold it.

> *Dear Rebecca and Lawrence,*
>   *Nice trick with the dogs. I liked it better than the nonsense in Camden and New York. What you want lies behind this door. Come and get it.*
>   *No worries about bombs or the like. You know I hate it when kids get hurt.*

Lawrence crumpled the paper and threw it aside, then pushed the door open. He could almost hear the Hunter laughing as he did it.

Inside the room was a large collection of wooden figurines, each nearly perfect. Each of the figures moved, hissing or screaming unintelligible noises from mouths too tiny to carry the sound far enough for him to clearly hear. It almost sounded like a crowd cheering for their favorite team, only from several blocks distant.

Lawrence moved into the room, pausing long enough to realize that these, too, were part of the curse that had been mucking up the gears for his plans since he came to Serenity. The figures moved away from him, surely terrified by the thought of anything as large and potentially clumsy as a child around them. He looked for the carving Crowley had made earlier and saw nothing. Lawrence stepped farther into the room and heard the door slam behind him with an almost thunderous finality.

The door hardly mattered. When he and his other part

were back together, they would be able to escape, even if the door was somehow ensorcelled. The Lawrence-thing frowned in concentration and tried to focus on where, exactly, the other part of his self was hidden. When exactly had he started thinking of himself in a masculine sense? He wasn't at all sure and didn't much care at that moment.

Instead of locating himself, he found another note. This one was taped to the shelf at roughly the same level as his eyes. He grabbed it, already tired of the Hunter's games and ready to get on with the work of destroying that most hated of creatures.

Dear Rebecca and Lawrence,

By now you've found the little darlings roaming throughout the room. I hope you like them. I finally deduced what they are only a little while ago, while I was contemplating what to do with that part of you that you are here to find. They are, I believe, the dead of Serenity Falls, or at least a portion of them. What better way to make sure your enemies don't know peace than to capture their souls as they die?

Each of them is an individual, and while there is a part of me that regrets what I've done, I felt it the best way to keep you out of my hair. It's not that I'm not enjoying your little guessing game (Well, okay, I'm not really having a great time with it, but I wasn't expecting to. Nothing personal.), but I really have much more important problems to deal with right now, and you have become something of a bore.

Are you looking for what I stole? It's right here, in front of you. All around you most likely. Those little buggers can't seem to stand still. All you have to do is capture each of the dollies around you and take back what's yours.

Good Hunting,

Crowley

Lawrence screamed, and the figures around the room scattered quickly, trying to find places to hide in the room. There weren't any, really, but they tried anyway. He reached forward and grabbed one that was a little too slow for its own good. The miniature man-shaped thing let out a tiny squeal of panic and beat ineffectually against his hand. He ignored it and concentrated on seeing whether or not Crowley told the truth.

"Damn you, Hunter!" He threw the figure down, taking some small satisfaction in the way it bounced and screamed as its legs snapped away and revealed their wooden interiors. It tried to crawl feebly away, and that part of Lawrence that was still purely Lawrence felt a rush of glee, like a kid playing Godzilla in a sandbox.

It was true. Lawrence looked around the room and knew it was true. Some small part of his essence was in each and every one of the wooden figures that was doing its best to get away from him.

He reached for the one he'd broken and called forth the part of him it held. The wooden figure crumbled in his hands, and he felt something leave the room even as his self was made stronger by being rejoined.

He grabbed for the next figure, and it dodged, crawling nimbly away from his groping hand. He had to admire the Hunter to a certain extent. This was likely to take a while. He grabbed again and felt satisfaction when the next one was in his hands.

As he squeezed his own essence from the tiny, struggling figure, he heard a low, light hiss ripple through the rest of them. Lawrence frowned, the sound not quite meshing with what he'd expected. The idea—in his mind at least—was that they might try to run, but they couldn't really hide. It was sort of like trying to get away from Godzilla in the middle of the Sahara desert. He would stomp down, and they would break, and if they were lucky they might dodge for a while, but basically, the little critters were screwed.

All around him the minuscule figures stopped running and looked at each other. Then they turned almost as one and looked at him. Lawrence dropped the one in his hand, barely feeling any satisfaction at all as the ruined husk bounced off the floor and broke into even smaller pieces.

He looked closely at the nearest of the figures, amused and a little surprised as it approached him. The speck of a face raised itself to study him in turn, and then the eyes flashed brilliantly for an instant. All around him the eyes of the wooden effigies flashed.

And then the wave of force slammed Lawrence against the wall hard enough to knock several shelves loose. He fell to the ground dazed for a moment but was quick to recover.

They were just as quick to attack. An army of tiny people might not intimidate Godzilla, but Lawrence Grey found them decidedly unsettling. He also found them painful. None of them could do much to him, their hands were too small to make more than a scratch, but hundreds of tiny scratches can add up quickly. Lawrence lashed out with wide sweeps of his hands, knocking the figures over with ease. Most of them got back up, and even those that didn't still struggled their best.

A few of them gathered together again, nowhere near as many as had done so for the first attack, and pushed at him with their power—*MY power! They're using my own power against me!*—managing to cause him more inconvenience than pain. They were delaying him, making this take longer than it should have, and again he found himself cursing the Hunter.

VI

Becky Glass walked the nighttime streets of Serenity without fear. Her mother was not home yet. She had gone into Utica and left a message that she would be late. There was something of a quandary about what she should do when it came to Becky's mother. The woman would surely get in the way, but not so much that she wanted to hurt her. The Becky part of her would not be happy if that happened. That was the least of her concerns.

Somewhere out there, Lawrence was trying to figure out how to make her become one with him again, and she had no desire to do so. She sighed, still enjoying the feeling that every single action she took brought to her. Oh, she knew it couldn't last, the endless fascination with sensory input, but she intended to enjoy it while she could.

The streets were mostly empty, which struck Becky as odd. Normally there were people moving around, shopping or eating or just wandering through the town. It was what they did, and that was one of the reasons she was here. She wanted to see them, wanted to experience their world. Being around them while they lived their lives was almost like getting an education. In her time the creature she'd been had feasted on flesh and reveled in the fear of the humans. It had never really given much thought to what made them what they were or why they should cling so desperately to life. They weren't really much of a concern beside the fact that they tasted good, and she liked to hear them scream.

She thought for a minute about her alternatives. They weren't really anything she wanted to use, but they were in place. Earlier in class, she'd sat next to Charlee Lyons. They'd talked for just a few minutes, but it was long enough. One little touch of her hand on the other girl's arm, and she'd set herself up with an escape route. Well, at least she'd set herself up with something. It took only a little effort. The thing inside of Becky Glass searched through her thoughts until it came up with the right phrase: contingency plan. She wanted this body, this habitat. She was comfortable with being a part of Becky. But she had Charlee now, if she needed her. That took a lot of the fear away, and it diffused some of the trepidation it felt about Lawrence and the Hunter.

A group of kids a few years older than her body walked toward the west side of town, talking excitedly about the carnival, and it finally dawned on her. They were off to enjoy the clowns and the elephants.

They were on their way to their deaths.

She had no doubt whatsoever about that. The carnival was a ruse, like the pretty scent of a Venus flytrap. It was a lure, and not even a very original one. Had she understood about what had happened in the past at the Pageant farm, she might have thought otherwise, but that little chapter of Serenity's history was well before her time and not something she had ever studied.

She was distantly aware that the Hunter was nearby and also understood that he had done something to Lawrence. Directly connected or not, she could feel that much about her other parts. Joey's aspect was gone, hidden away by the Hunter, but Lawrence she could feel, and if she wanted to, she could even know his thoughts.

She had no desire. His mind was a cesspool of vile notions, including what he wanted to do to this body. She'd never tried anything like what was going through his mind, but was fairly certain she wouldn't enjoy it.

Something else stirred at the edge of her mind, and she let herself drift to where it was. There, the hound. The one she'd called forth and delivered into a puppy when she first came to town. It was waking, at last, from the deep sleep it had gone into. Whatever it had done to the other dogs in the area had taken a great deal of effort, and it had needed to recover the strength it used. She didn't pretend to understand the nature of the beast; it was merely a convenient tool when she needed one and easily brought back from the death it had suffered long ago. It, too, had unfinished business in Serenity, which was the main reason she'd given it a body. It had been a good tool and might be again. She called out, and it responded, shaking itself free of the ground where it had gone to rest.

Becky moved through the streets, unbothered by notions of the Hunter or Lawrence. She moved toward the makeshift fairgrounds at the edge of town, knowing that the hound wanted to go there as well. The kids up ahead of her moved on, and now and then one of the boys would look back at her, his eyes lingering on her form. He wanted her. She understood that, but she didn't care. For now it was enough merely to walk.

VII

The Pageants had long since vacated the premises and taken everything they could with them. The animals were all pastured together in the farthest field, except for the chickens, who were locked away properly in the coop. Dave and his brethren were staying at the Serenity Inn, a small but comfortable bed-and-breakfast that was suddenly filled for the first time in weeks. There were only two rooms they didn't actually take over, and both of those were being used by other guests.

They were safe enough, as far as their patriarch was concerned. At least he hoped they were. Earl was not a young man anymore, and he had spent a great deal of time contemplating what he and the others had done on his farm so many years ago.

Andrew was understandably upset by the whole sordid business. It was ages ago in his mind, and he had done everything he could to suppress it. Earl thought that was a fine idea. He didn't want his son to think about his father as a murderer. They had never spoken of what happened the night Earl and the others went out and took care of business. They didn't need to. Andrew knew and understood why his father had helped with the killings, but it wasn't really the sort of thing that they could exactly chat about in polite society.

The thing was, all of that was supposed to be in the past. And now it was back. And it scared Earl to no end to think about it. Marie was long dead and in her grave, and though ten years after she'd gone he still missed her, he was grateful she wasn't here for this.

He looked to the west, saw the people on the road who drove or walked toward where his family farm was, and prayed everything would be okay. Earl turned away from the window and instead focused on the news on the television. Some fella with perfect hair was reporting on the latest news regarding the war on terrorism. Thinking about the World Trade Center was even worse than thinking about what was going on at his farm in some ways. He still couldn't really grasp the magnitude of the deaths that had happened in New York City. He didn't want to. Still, it was better than thinking about the blood on his own hands.

Earl Pageant settled down on the bed and watched the television, making himself think about what was going on in other parts of the world. The farm was too close to his heart, and so ghosts of the past were haunting him too much. In other rooms he could hear the sounds of his family moving around and making noise. The location was wrong, but the sounds were comfortable.

Outside of the room where Earl Pageant contemplated the past and the present and did his best to think of other things, his family moved and shuffled around him. Amber and Suzette were not there, but they were supposed to join the family later, and a room was waiting for them. Dave was no longer there, either. He'd crept out at the first chance after dinner. He wanted to see what was happening at the farm. He needed to know. He needed to understand.

Dave walked the road for quite a while, surprised by the number of cars and trucks parked along its side, more surprised by the number of people who had apparently decided to investigate the farm and the tent.

He started across the field that he'd walked more times than he cared to think about and saw, even in the darkness, that many of the young plants had been trampled by the feet of people who should have known better. His father would be pissed, but it looked like most of the damage wasn't the sort that would ruin the crops. Dave figured they had to be pretty damned durable anyway, especially since they had grown so well in the unusual cold weather they'd been having lately.

Which got him to thinking about the fact that the weather was finally warming up just a bit and about the fact that summer vacation was almost upon him and he was still forced to wear a coat to stop from freezing his balls off. As was often the case, he stopped moving while he thought. He simply stood where he was, looking toward the top of the hill, and contemplated the unusual weather. Just a few weeks ago it had been warm enough to go swimming at the quarry. He knew that, because Stan had almost drowned in the quarry and only managed not to because there had already been other kids swimming in the waters.

Now, looking back on the matter, he realized that the air

grew colder just after Stan's dip in the waters. Around the
same time as the vandalism at the cemetery and the visit he
and Stan paid to Havenwood. Even thinking about that still
gave him the creeps. The summer should have gotten pro-
gressively warmer, and while he could accept a few flukes
in the temperatures, he had to seriously wonder what the
hell had been going on.

He thought he knew the answer. He was almost certain
of it, but it wasn't something he really wanted to dwell on.
Still, it was there, and it didn't really seem to want to go
away. Dave started walking again, and soon he crested the
hill he'd been staring at.

He saw what had grown from the ground, now that it
had come to full bloom. He'd been right earlier, when he
decided it must surely be a circus tent. But now, in the
darkness, it had colors. Thick stripes of red and green and
white ran from the ground and joined together at the apex
of the tent that wasn't quite what it should have been.
There were no anchoring cables running outside of the
canvaslike skin, and there were no pegs holding down the
fabric. None were needed as it seemed to go well below
the level of the grass. Dave noticed all of this as he moved
down the hill and toward the thing. An even, pale light
spread throughout the entirety of the structure, glowing
enough to let him see that there were shapes moving inside. Human shapes.

That was disturbing. Dave had seen the flyers, seen the
message on them about the carnival, but he also knew the
constables were supposed to be stopping anything like this
from happening. Someone had screwed up, and he didn't
figure that would be a good thing for anyone in the tent.
He'd just wanted to see it, to see what it had become. He
never in a million years figured people would go in there.

Dave started backing up, not really wanting to leave—
that part of him that drank in knowledge wanted to see

what would happen—but feeling it might be best to actually call the constables and let them know that people had gotten through.

He stopped very abruptly when the body behind him pushed forward to end his retreat.

VIII

Serenity Falls Part Fourteen: Actions and Consequences

The time came in Serenity Falls that the curse laid out almost three centuries earlier came to pass. Or, rather, came to its final stages. The dead of Serenity Falls did not know the peace of the grave or whatever might lie beyond that final resting place. They knew instead an endless imprisonment and an awareness of what happened around them. They were locked in effigies of their own likenesses and forced to endure a world in which they were little more than children's playthings left abandoned in room without a child.

They were not amused.

Those murdered in Serenity knew a different fate and one far less kind. They knew that they were held against their wills in a place that was definitely not Earth and surely could not be Heaven, for there were no angels and there was no peace. And there they stayed, impotently raging against the unkind fate that had let them die.

Until now, when they were finally freed to seek answers to their questions and, far more importantly to most of them, retribution against the ones who killed them. But if there were answers to be had, they would have to wait. They were called now, drawn to the circus tent against their will in many cases and forced down into the great shell of misused charnel flesh.

First among them was a man who'd done all he could to make people smile in the worst of times, and he took his murder very poorly indeed. He'd died at the hands of cowards who used fire as their weapon, locked in his own simple trailer and roasted alive, screaming and begging for mercy that did not come. Cecil Phelps had been a nice man in life. He was less pleasant in death. As the people started gathering in the circus tent that was larger by far than any Cecil had ever known, he drifted lower and finally was drawn into the very ground to seek a new form, one that would allow him a chance for his final revenge.

In the ground beneath the big top, Cecil Phelps, better known as Rufo the Clown, found the perfect instrument for his needs. The boy was handsome and strong and a fitting receptacle for his rage. The boy was also desperately lonely and scared, trapped for most of a day under the ground wrapped in still more of the rotted flesh made dark miracle, sealed in a womb built for just this very purpose.

Marco DeMillio had fought hard to keep his life and his sanity. He'd managed to keep his life at least, until Rufo came for him. Had he violated Nancy Lyons? Yes, he certainly had. He'd used her and killed her, never questioning until that very moment if there would be a price to pay for the pleasures he took by force. He'd laughed as she cried and reveled in the sounds of her muffled screams, in the feel of her flesh struggling to be free from his abuses. He'd never once during that time considered the pain she was certainly experiencing as anything more than a source of enjoyment for himself and his friends, content in the knowledge that Bill Karstens would keep him safe from harm.

Payback, as has been said, is a vicious bitch. Had he violated Nancy Lyons? Yes indeed. And now the thing that came to him in his strange black shelter returned the favor, sharing with him the dubious pleasure of being on the receiving end of a violent rape, not only of the body but of the mind and soul. Oh, how he wanted to scream as the spirit forced itself into him, tearing his own soul into shreds in the process. Marco tried to scream but found that no sound could come past the forces driving themselves deeper and deeper into his flesh. His body twisted and warped under clothes that went through their own changes, practically boiling away as steam only to resolidify as a proper outfit for the master of ceremonies at a circus held over from Hell.

Not far away from him, other bodies—those who had for a brief moment been the proper terrors they had always wanted to be, both feared and admired for their brutality—twisted and screamed beneath the ground, fighting and losing in a struggle to keep themselves whole and unchanged. Karstens had lied to them, led them down a path where they could never hope to find their way to safety. To the very bitter end, they blamed the constable for the worst of their woes, never accepting that they had walked that trail willingly.

They could not know that Karstens had been taken by another entity himself, or that that very being, drawn back from its destruction and given new life again, was merely a pawn to the very curse that finally killed them in the end.

Albert Miles had vowed that every soul would scream before his work was done in Serenity Falls. The local bullies were among the first to keep his promise.

But there would be others. Miles had been thorough in his planning, you see, and while he knew a few would possibly escape from him, most of the people in Serenity would be made to pay for his suffering. The town's founder had taken the only woman he'd ever loved from him, and he was determined to make sure that the retribution was legendary. In order to make certain that he had his way, he used every possible means to an end.

The lead that had held his wife's screaming body had long been one of the most powerful tools of his revenge, for it held her pain and her tortured essence within its very molecules. The lead had done what it was meant to do when the people of Serenity had used it so long ago. It had bound her spirit and stopped her from ever having revenge. It had also worked in much the same way as the curse her husband later cast: it had prevented her ever knowing peace. In his effort to prevent an angry spirit from haunting him in his later years, Niles Wilcox had damned an innocent woman well beyond her death and had sealed the fate of his descendants for generations to come.

He had given all of that anger and hatred and impotent fury a way to be used by a person knowing the right methods to implement it. Albert Miles used the last of the lead from his wife's tortuous death as a fine powder, ground down and mixed with other ingredients best left uncontemplated, to lace the paper of every colorful flyer laid out for the Alexander Halston Carnival.

A simple spell, really. One that made the idea placed in a person's mind—by say a colorful flyer—stronger. *Going to the carnival could be fun* became *Going to the carnival WILL be fun and I WILL attend* in the minds of most who touched the paper. It wasn't a perfect plan, mind you, but it worked well enough in most cases. The exceptions were a few older people who remembered the carnival from before and had remembered what had happened when it was in town. They, and a few people who had a fear of clowns that became a full-blown phobia as a result of the enchantment.

Those people stayed away, as did the ones who had work to do and those who never actually touched the flyers. Damned near everyone else in Serenity found a reason to get there. They wanted to have a good time and maybe a few surprises.

IX

Jonathan Crowley was staying very, very busy. He had to run back to the quarry for one thing; there were some pumps he wanted to see in action, and it only took a few minutes of trial and error before he managed to get them up and running. The water might be able to disrupt a few of the dead on their way. There was some truth to the legends about ghosts not being able to cross running water. It didn't always work, but now and then it helped. Then there was the possibility of a fire to consider. That tent was big enough to be a problem if it caught ablaze.

He passed Havenwood on the way and was happy to sense that things were progressing the way he wanted in the doll room. Even from twenty feet away and through a wall, he could feel Lawrence's dissatisfaction with the method of regaining his power.

He still hadn't found Becky Glass, and that was annoying but survivable. He hoped.

He was there when Amelia let out the rat. He saw it run off into the woods, but he didn't stay long. He had to hope Amelia would be safe. He couldn't stay to find out for himself. She hadn't asked for his help, and he already had something else to do. Rules were rules, and he had to follow them or suffer the consequences.

Besides, there was a carnival he didn't really think he wanted to miss. Crowley ran, breathing easily as he covered the ground, and considered what would be waiting for him.

X

Terry Palance was making a lot of noise again, and he was seriously considering trying his hand at police brutality to shut the little bastard up. Ever since he'd been brought back in, the kid had alternated between crying fits and hysterical laughter, and both of them were wearing his nerves down to frayed, stretched wires.

Victor Barnes stood up, biting his lip against the scream that wanted to slide out of his mouth. His leg felt like it had been sawed half off where the freak had chewed on his calf the day before, and he really didn't want to stand on it, but there weren't a whole lot of options. He couldn't stay in the medical center when they were this understaffed, and he couldn't very well roll his little office chair all around the place and call it getting anywhere.

So he walked, and tried not to whimper, and moved across the office to where the holding cells were, and looked down at the kid inside who was doing his best to actually flood the cell with his tears. "Will you PLEASE shut up!"

Palance barely even acknowledged him.

"You had your chance to get the hell out of jail, and you blew it. Get over yourself and your poor, pitiful life, and deal with it."

"You go to hell." The kid's voice was muffled by the fact that he had his face buried in his hands, but the words were clear enough.

"Don't give me a reason, loser. I'm about up to my teeth with you."

The kid's only response was to start crying even louder, and Barnes moved away in disgust.

Victor Barnes gave up trying to get an answer on the radio a little after sunset. He'd hailed the morons at the Pageant place easily a dozen times and gotten no response.

Enough was enough. He limped out to his truck—once again dismayed by the amount of damage it had suffered in his short time with the police force—and started driving out that way. Jack Michaels could kiss his ass if he wasn't happy about it. There was something weird going on out there, and he was damned if he was going to let it just happen.

He'd had an uneasy feeling all day, and now it was worse. And besides, it didn't take a genius—thankfully— to figure out that people were heading in that direction, out to where the farms were to the west of town. Either they were all of them headed toward the quarry, which was unlikely, or they wanted to see the strange thing he'd heard about from Michaels and the others over the course of the day. He didn't figure the quarry could be all that exciting late at night, and he guessed the fucked-up train thing he'd seen bury itself in the ground might well be the cause of whatever was out there now.

Barnes drove like a madman. He hit the flashers and the sirens and tried to make contact with Michaels, Steinman, Norris, or even Lassiter. "This is Barnes. I'm leaving the office. I haven't gotten a response back from any of you in the last half hour, and I need to investigate what's going on. If you're looking for me, try the Pageant place."

There was no response to his call. He hadn't really expected one, but felt he had to try. Almost half a mile before he reached the area where the farm proper started, he saw the cars on the side of the road and saw the people walking down the side of the street or crossing into the fields leading toward what he was looking for.

Even from this distance he could see the lights out there, bright enough to light the way across the crops or the asphalt without too much worry about unexpected pitfalls. He was forced to pull his truck over a few hundred yards down the way. Apparently some of the locals had decided to make the entire road a parking lot, and the way was completely blocked.

He grunted and climbed out, moving between the parked vehicles and doing his best to get where he was going without actually bumping his calf against anything. He kept one hand on his nightstick and the other on the butt of his pistol, because he was sure as hell not trusting the people around him to be themselves. A few of them were still moving up across the field, and while they all seemed fully capable of thinking, the way they looked toward the light coming from beyond the top of the hill was too much like the same expression he'd seen on a few fundamentalist churchgoers for his comfort.

It took a while, but eventually he made it all the way to where the two cruisers were blocking the road, or had been once upon a time before the other cars around them took care of the problem. There was no sign of Steinman or Lassiter. "Well, isn't that just peachy." He looked inside the cars and saw no sign of trouble. Then he looked off toward the hill again and started walking. If they were there, he was going to knock a few heads together. He'd worry about the rest of it later.

Barnes turned around and called Mossiman's Garage. Every last one of these bastards had to get towed off to the side, and if Mossiman wanted to bill each and every owner, that was okay with him. Mossiman said he'd be there in a few minutes and that he'd bring out the reserves if he could get hold of his boys. That suited Barnes just fine.

He was panting and wincing by the time he reached the top of the hill. He almost forgot to breathe when he saw the big top tent and the droves of people lined up to get inside. Even from here he could smell cotton candy and popcorn and sawdust. He could hear the overly cheerful sound of circus music braying from the tent and into the surrounding farmlands.

He didn't like this one little bit. Not at all. It looked like most of the damned town was down there, and those who weren't were working on it. From the top of the hill he could see still more cars coming and observe their passengers climbing out and heading up toward where he stood, looking down on the carnival and the farm beside it.

He heard the sudden roar of applause from the circus tent below and looked that way, but there was nothing new to see. Then an amplified voice called out, welcoming the people of Serenity Falls to the show.

"Well, well, well. This should be a fun time for all of us, hunh, kiddies?" He knew the voice instantly, the sarcastic tone that made his skin want to crawl. Barnes turned around and looked at Jonathan Crowley, who stood right behind him and smiled brightly at the tent below, which reflected itself in his rimless glasses.

"Mr. Crowley."

"Constable Barnes . . ." Crowley put his hands on his narrow hips and rocked back and forth on the heels and balls of his feet. "Aren't you going to see the show? It looks like all the fun is about to begin."

"I don't think this is going to be fun, Mr. Crowley. I think there's going to be a whole lot of trouble down there."

Crowley's smile grew a little broader, and he shrugged his shoulders. "One man's fun is another's bad time. I tend to have trouble differentiating between the two myself."

"You aren't going down there, are you? Because I don't think I need another person to get to safety."

"Constable Barnes, you can barely walk. What on earth makes you think you could stop me if I wanted to go down there?"

"I outweigh you by a little over a hundred pounds, and I have a black belt in Tae Kwon Do."

"Lah-dee-dah."

Barnes looked at the man and sighed. "So you're going down there?"

"Of course I'm going down there. It's what I've been waiting for since I got here."

"You knew there was a circus coming here?"

"Not hardly. I just knew something interesting was going to happen." Crowley frowned for a second. "Say, where are the rest of your group?"

"I think they're already down there."

"Well, that could make this awkward."

"Why?"

"I'm not a hundred percent sure they'll be on our side."

"You think we're on the same side?"

"You want to protect and serve the people of Serenity Falls?"

"Yes."

"Then we're on the same side." With that, Crowley started walking down the hill. Barnes followed him a minute later.

XI

Tom Norris looked over at his boss and gnawed his lower lip in worry. Jack Michaels was never an open man, certainly not the sort to shout out his feelings to anyone who wanted to listen, but he was also not normally a brooder. And that was exactly what the man was doing: brooding. He wasn't being at all his normal self, and he hadn't been himself since the cemetery got all tore up that second time around. Tom had been bothered by it, but Jack seemed to have taken it to heart.

Or maybe it was that bug he was trying to get over. The

boss might be back at work, but he wasn't very energetic. Norris looked over at Michaels as his boss eased the cruiser around a corner and contemplated whether or not he should say anything. In the end he kept his mouth shut. If Jack wanted to talk, he would. Until such time, it was none of Norris's business.

Jack drove out of the town proper and down the quarry road, moving right past Havenwood and onto the old access road that used to actually go somewhere when the quarry was still fully active. Tom wondered if the road would be used again for hauling supplies when the business started in full operation, or if they'd go back to the railroad tracks that were rotting away in the woods nearby.

Tom watched the sides of the road, just as he always did when Michaels was driving. Jack didn't always go down this way, but now and then, just to make sure all was well, he took the long way around to wherever he was driving. Norris was expected to keep his eyes open to potential problems, and that was exactly what he intended to do. His lip felt tender where he'd been using it to ruminate, and he made himself stop nibbling. It wouldn't do to get chapped lips with the weather like it had been lately. He'd always been the sort to get split skin whenever the weather was cold, and all the ChapStick in the world didn't make a damned bit of difference if you never used it.

He was drifting into childhood thoughts when Jack finally spoke up. "How long have you been on the force here, Tom?"

"I dunno . . . maybe twelve years, give or take." He had to think about it. Yeah, a dozen or so was about right.

"So we've known each other over a dozen years, right?"

"Yeah . . ." He didn't really know where this was going, but wherever it was, he didn't like it. He kept having images of Jack leaning over to kiss him and confess his secret love. Not exactly an idea that was conducive to his relaxation. He couldn't help squirming a bit.

Jack smiled as he looked in his direction. It was a very small curl of the lip, but it *was* a smile. "I swear I can read you like a book sometimes. I ain't making a move on you, calm down."

Tom laughed it off, but even to his own ears his voice sounded relieved. "Shit, I never thought you were, Jack, it's just you don't normally ask questions like that." Jack didn't respond, just kept driving. After a few minutes he pulled the car to the side of the road.

"I was wondering about how long we've known each other, because I need to know how well I can trust you with a secret." Jack's voice was soft but carried through the cruiser with ease. The air was still, and the woods were almost preternaturally quiet. Tom could hear the sound of his own throat swallowing.

"Well, shit, Jack, I don't think I've ever given you reason to doubt me along those lines . . ."

"No, you haven't. But some things are harder to keep quiet about than others."

"Look, you know if you need an ear to bend, I'm here. No one will hear about anything that's said."

"I appreciate that." Jack looked at him and remained silent for a long minute. When he spoke again, his voice sounded strained. "Thing is, I've been contaminated."

"What? You mean you got the clap or something?"

"No. Not infected, contaminated. I—someone did something to me, and I can feel what they did working on my insides, like a worm crawling around under my skin. No, like around a million worms." Jack looked at him and shook his head. "I can't explain it better than that."

"Well, maybe we better get you to the clinic, Jack, see what's what."

"I don't know if it would do any good." He frowned

down at the meters on the dashboard and seemed to drift
for a moment. "I think I know how to fix the problem, but
I'm not really sure that the cure is any better than the disease in this case."

Norris looked at his boss and frowned. "Well, how bad
is the cure?"

Jack looked back at him, his brows lowered over his
blue eyes. He held one hand up, and Tom watched as shadowy discolorations shifted under the skin. "Jack, what's
wrong with your hand?"

"It's like I told you, it's under the skin, Tom. And it talks
to me." A few minutes earlier he'd been worried that maybe
Jack was making a pass at him, but now that seemed positively juvenile. Jack Michaels, one of the least imaginative
and most trustworthy men he had ever met, was looking a
little like Renfield in a Dracula movie. It was just possible
the man wasn't playing with a full deck. After everything
that had happened lately, including having to shoot Karstens
dead, it was just possible that the chief constable had taken
a swan dive into the deep end of the not-all-there pool.

Jack clenched his fist, and the odd little shadowy shapes
expanded and compressed with the flex of his muscles. Or
at least he desperately hoped it was the play of muscle and
bone, because if it wasn't, the darkness under Jack's skin
seemed determined to move on its own, and that was not a
pleasant notion.

"Um, what does the voice say, Jack?"

"Voices. There's more than one."

"Okay . . . What do the voices say?"

"They say I need help, Tom. They say I need someone
else to carry the burden."

"What burden, Jack?" Oh yes, there were definitely
a few bricks missing from Jack's load, and that wasn't
a comforting thought. Jack carried a gun, and he could easily
outmuscle Norris. His hand crept toward the pepper spray

on his belt. Blasting the damned concentrated pepper oil in
a confined area wasn't exactly the best idea in the world,
but if he had to do it, he figured the backlash from the stuff
was better than a full-on hit with it. It sure as hell beat the
idea of having to do something lethal to Jack, or having
Jack do it to him.

Jack looked at him with feverish eyes and blinked rapidly several times. "I've got to shoulder the responsibilities
of the town, Tom. But I don't think I can do it alone. I need
your help."

Tom looked at Jack and nodded his head. "Okay, well,
we have a town council for that sort of thing, Jack. You and
me, all we have to do is protect and serve, right?"

"God, I wish it was that easy."

"Well, what else is there?"

"Punishment. We have to be here to make sure that the
punishment is fair and just."

Tom nodded again, and his hand finally reached the canister on his hip. He'd just flipped off the locking strap and
the safety when Jack's hand changed. Small wounds, almost
like toothless mouths, blossomed across the skin, and from
them something dark writhed out like thin cobras. Tom forgot all about the canister of Mace as the lengthening black
strands—which, by God, matched up exactly with the shadows under Jack's skin—whipped through the air and struck
him.

Tom screamed and remembered the spray. His hand
pulled the Mace free from its holster and aimed at Jack's
face, pushing down the trigger as the shadows tore into his
skin. Jack had started to say something about being sorry
for what he had to do, but he cut himself off with a scream
of outrage. One hand reached for his eyes to wipe away the
burning pain. The other reached for Tom and caused him
the sort of suffering he'd never imagined possible.

Needle-fine cuts broke through Tom's skin and cut

deeply into his left eye, sending screaming waves of nausea through his entire body. He was right; the backlash from the pepper spray washed over his face around the same time he felt his left eye implode. Whatever he might have thought he knew about pain was nothing but a prelude, and from there, it only got worse.

XII

Dave looked over his shoulder and saw Becky Glass standing behind him. She touched his shoulder lightly and shook her head. "You shouldn't go down there, Dave."

"I wasn't gonna. I figured to call the constables. No one's supposed to be out here."

"Most of the constables are already here. I saw two of them go up the hill just a little while ago."

"Why are you here, Becky?" He looked at her, watched her face, and wondered what she was thinking.

"It's complicated. I just know that some of the people here are supposed to be here and some of them shouldn't be. You shouldn't be."

"Why not? Looks like everyone else is."

"It's a trap."

"Well, I didn't figure it was just a nice visit from the circus. Tent grew right out of the ground, and it smells like shit. That ain't the best way to get your customers to come see you."

"Dave, please, you were always nice to Becky. Leave here."

"I was always nice to you? Of course I was, you're a nice person." Why was she talking about herself like she wasn't really there? He hadn't the vaguest notion.

"There's bad things coming here, Dave. Really bad."

"Are they here yet?"

"No . . . I don't think so."

"Well, then if they are coming, and they aren't here, and they'll cause trouble, there are at least a few people down there that should be warned."

Becky looked down, her face giving nothing away. "If you're gonna do something, you better do it fast." From somewhere behind her, in the fields but too far away for him to see, he heard a deep, low growl. "I think he'll wait a little longer, but not much more than a few minutes."

"Think WHAT will wait a little longer?" He had felt his stomach clench at the sound of the growl. Whatever had made it sounded about the size of a truck, and he thought about poor Beau torn apart by that pack of dogs and wondered if maybe this was going to be a bit more than he would be able to run from.

"I'm not really sure, but he's big and has a lot of teeth, and he wants to go down there."

"Guess I better get down there."

"I don't know if that's smart, but I'll do what I can to slow him."

"Thanks, Becky."

She looked like she was going to say something else, but she stopped herself and backed away. Dave ran down the hill, moving around to the side of the tent without really giving thought to what he was going to do.

The line to get into the tent was long, but it seemed like everyone got in free of charge. At least they were moving quickly. The people around him—faces he'd known as long as he was alive—were all too happy. They were, to the last person, looking at the opening into the tent as if it might be their road to salvation. He didn't like that weird expression on their faces, but what could he do about it?

After only a few minutes he was inside the big tent and looking around at what had grown from the soil of his family home. The posts that held the tent up were as thick around as a tractor tire and looked like they were carved with hundreds of faces and bodies wrapped around each other in a way that was both arousing and obscene. The bodies wore no clothing, but most of their privates seemed to be covered by hands and feet from others around them in the carved wood. Wood? No, probably more of the same stuff that made the tent. He didn't like that notion and would likely have gone into one of his deep thought modes and stood perfectly still if he hadn't been nudged from behind by Mr. Waters from the bank. Off to the left he saw Jessie and Charlee, sitting on one of the lower bleachers that had also crept up from the ground during the hours since he'd had a chance to look at the tent.

He walked over fast, dodging around a few grown-ups who were milling around and trying to find good seats. Jessie lit up when she saw him and gave him a smile that just about made his whole day better. "Hi, Dave! I was wondering where you were."

Charlee looked at him with a puzzled expression. Like everyone else, they had that strange cast almost pressed into their features. He wondered if that was the same look that people got on their faces when they believed they'd made contact with the divine and suspected it was. The notion wasn't comforting.

"We have to leave, Jessie. Right now."

"What? The show hasn't started yet."

"There isn't gonna be a show; the police are coming to break it up. These people aren't supposed to be here. It's dangerous."

Charlee snorted laughter, looking at him, her face still wearing that odd blend of puzzled and rapturous. "The carnival is only here for one night, Dave. We haven't had

a carnival here, ever. It's practically a once-in-a-lifetime
chance." She spoke with the patient tones of a teacher with
a particularly dense student, and Dave realized that she almost always spoke that way. He didn't like her much just
then. She was cute as all get out, but maybe not the nicest
person. He could see why Jessie sometimes got angry
with her.

"Charlee, there isn't going to be a show. There's going
to be a mess. We have to go." He was trying to be calm, but
the looks on both the girls' faces was just annoying the hell
out of him. He grabbed Jessie's hand and pulled, and despite her protests, she rose up and came with him. "Are you
coming, Charlee?"

"No. I'm not going to miss this."

"Fine. See you next life."

Jessie struggled a little, but not much. Fighting wasn't
really her style, and that was one of the things he liked
about her. He got enough fighting around his family with
all of the small squabbles. And speaking of his family, he
saw Amber and Suzette sitting not far away, talking with a
small herd of guys, most of whom were doing a damned
fine job of staring at their tits. He called out to them, and
they ignored him for about a minute.

They listened when he dragged Jessie over and threatened to tell their grandfather they were here. The carnival
might be fun, but there wasn't a kid in the Pageant household who hadn't felt the sting of his leather belt across
their asses at least a few times. After that it took nothing at
all to get them to head for the exit of the tent.

Of course, actually getting out proved to be a little more
difficult.

Just as they reached the opening, the crowd started
cheering. Dave turned along with his sisters and his girlfriend just in time to see the spectacle at the center of the
three rings. A light that was nearly as bright as the sun cut

from the closest post and beamed down to the center ring. From that spot the ground itself was rising in a swollen bulge, and then it started peeling away like the rind of an orange.

A stage was growing from the ruptured turf. Almost ten feet wide and easily as deep, it rose smoothly through the rising applause of the people. One figure rose with it, a tall, almost gaunt man with dark, curling hair that fell to his shoulders in a thick cascade. He wore a top hat and tails, gaudily festooned with sequins and done completely in red. His back was to Dave and his gathering, as he lifted the hat from his head and swept the hat to his side in a graceful bow worthy of the royal court of England. He rose and turned ninety degrees, now facing to the right of where he had been, and bowed again. Then he turned again and faced the exit of the tent, his eyes burning brightly.

And Dave damn near fainted.

The skin on the face was drawn tight, stretched over bones to the point where he was surprised not to see the skull beneath as the flesh tore away. Thick greasepaint covered the flesh, painting the features titanium white except where other colors had gone over the first layer. Dark blue triangles replaced the clown's eyebrows and were mirrored below pale blue eyes. His aquiline nose was normal save for a single red dot the same color as his outfit, and his lips were painted into a crimson smile that was broken only by the perfect white teeth revealed when his real lips parted. Three earrings that looked very familiar twinkled in his left ear, and Dave got the sinking feeling that he knew what had happened to Marco and his pals.

"Ladies and gentlemen, boys and girls!" The voice seemed to come not only from the clown but from the tent itself. "Welcome to the Alexander Halston Carnival of the Fantastic!" He paused for the renewed applause, his eyes seeming to bore right into Dave's, cutting through his

glasses and sinking like teeth into the very soul of his being. "Mr. Halston regrets that he cannot be with us tonight.
He has a previous engagement in town, but he wanted me
to make sure you all have a wonderful time!"

Again the crowd went crazy, and Dave even heard Jessie
and his sisters cheering. He started to back away, started to
leave the tent again, as the clown started speaking.

"My name is Rufo, and I will be your host tonight. We
have quite a show planned, and one that simply wouldn't
be possible without the help of some old, dear friends."
He jabbed a white-gloved, long-boned index finger directly
at Dave, and his smile grew even wider as his voice practically purred. "Can we have a special round of applause
for our guests of honor, Dave Pageant, his lovely lady Jes-
sica Grant, and his stunning sisters, Amber and Suzette!"
The applause got even louder still, and several people
moved closer to them, crowding them with congratulatory
applause and pats on their backs. "If not for the kindness
and hospitality of the Pageants, we wouldn't even be here
right now. I'd say they deserve the royal treatment,
wouldn't you?"

Dave felt his stomach do a long, spiraling drop and
shook his head. Behind him, Amber and Suzette suddenly
let out little squeals of delight, and he turned to see two
more clowns handing them bouquets of black roses. An
enormously wide clown licked his lips and looked down at
Jessie before handing her a similar bouquet. All three girls
took them happily, not seeming to notice anything out of
place about their host or the twisted expressions the clowns
wore under their makeup.

"We have to go." Dave spoke and knew he couldn't be
heard over the sound of applause. He tried again, desperate
to make himself heard. "Jessie! We have to go, right now!"

It was Rufo who answered for her. "Nonsense, young
Master Pageant! This show is for your benefit, our way of

celebrating the history of Serenity Falls and the people
who made it all possible. We wouldn't dream of having
you leave now."

The sound of heavy rustling and snapping came to
Dave's ears, and he turned away from Rufo again, facing
back to where Jessie and his sisters were beaming happily
in the attention they received. The tent entrance was closing, sealing itself like an opening wound moving in reverse.

"Bring our special guests to the center ring, fellas! Let's
show them what a good time is all about!" Rufo's cheerful
words sounded like a death knell in his ears. Gloved hands
grabbed Dave roughly, and he was lifted off the ground and
carried through the crowd that parted for him. Jessie and
his sisters followed behind him, a clown escort walking
them through to where Rufo stood like an executioner in
red, smiling lovingly down. His eyes tracked their progress.

The stage on which he stood changed as they moved
forward. The edge seemed to cave in on itself and collapse
into a ramp that was perfectly smooth. Dave would have
been enjoying the show if he weren't so damned scared.

He was set down before Rufo with a flourish, and the
clown smiled even more brightly before leaning down until
they were eye to eye. This time when the clown spoke his
voice was not amplified. It was a hiss meant for his ears
alone. "Your grandfather should be here, boy, but you'll do
in a pinch." Long, bony fingers gripped his chin and forced
his mouth into a pucker. Rufo's voice was once again
booming from everywhere when he spoke. "Isn't he just a
doll, ladies and gentlemen? Couldn't you just eat him up?"
The crowd continued their applause, and Rufo's eyes narrowed in his smiling face. "I know I could."

CHAPTER 5

I

Amelia jumped a bit in her seat when they heard the sound of something heavy falling and breaking upstairs. Mike grimaced and forced himself to stay seated. Crowley told them not to investigate and to stay out of the bedroom, and he figured it might be best to listen to the man.

Amelia was nervous, and he couldn't really blame her. It was frustrating waiting for something to happen. He wanted to do something, almost anything, and he wanted a drink.

He always wanted a drink.

He wouldn't have one though. He knew better.

"What do you think he's doing up there, Mike?"

"I think he's pissing me off. I don't care how young he is, that little shit needs his ass kicked."

"Mike, I don't think the boy is responsible. I think he has something else inside him."

Mike sighed. "I know, I know . . . he's possessed or some

such nonsense." He was trying to be good about the weird-ness, he really was, but mostly Mike just wanted the world to make sense again.

"Mike, this is what Jonathan does. This is what he's al-most always done. He wouldn't have warned us without good reason."

There was a knock at the door, and Amelia rose from her place on the couch and walked that way.

"Listen, let me get the door. Crowley said there might be trouble for you." She nodded hesitantly and stepped back. Her face was worried, and he hated that look on her. She should have been happy and carefree. Or at least not worried about whether or not she was going to live through the night.

He opened the door to Jack Michaels, who nodded to him and then to Amelia. "Hi, Mike. This is going to sound like a weird question, but have you seen a kid around twelve or so?"

"This is gonna sound like a weird answer, but yes. He's upstairs."

Amelia came over to the door, almost allowing herself a smile. "Is he in some sort of trouble, Constable Michaels?"

"Well, if he's who I think he is, that's a possibility. Penelope Grey was found dead earlier today, and we haven't been able to find her son, Lawrence. A few people have seen him though, and they said he was acting as calm as could be. That might not be a problem, but his mother was killed sometime yesterday, as near as we can figure."

Michaels stepped into the house, moving past Mike and into the foyer, the cold of the night fairly radiating off his body. Still, the chill was less than it had been of late. Michaels looked around the room, his eyes barely blink-ing, and finally nodded his head. "Where would this boy be now, can you tell me?"

"He's upstairs in the master bedroom, I think. There's a small room off to the side, and I imagine he's in there."

Amelia stepped back from him and let him pass. Jack nodded his thanks and moved toward the stairway. A moment later he was gone from sight.

"Not exactly a visitor I was expected . . ." Mike frowned and looked outside. The sky was dark, and there were no streetlights this far from the center of town. He could barely make out the shape of the police cruiser in the driveway.

"He didn't seem that brusque the last time I saw him." Amelia's eyebrows knitted together in a V, and her bottom lip pouted out just enough to make him want to kiss her. She had a very sexy pout. Mike pulled her into a soft embrace and kissed her forehead. She nestled against him in the nicest way.

"Well, I know he's been a bit understaffed lately, and with all of the strange things going on around here, I'm not too surprised." Amelia's fingers stroked his chest affectionately, and he hugged a little tighter.

"Well, I don't know him very well. It just seems like he's not having a very good day."

The sound of a car door slamming from outside caught Mike's attention, and he looked outside through the open door to see Tom Norris heading their way. He wasn't walking very well. He had a limp that was very pronounced. "I think that's Tom Norris. He looks hurt."

Amelia turned her head away from his chest and looked in the same direction. "It is, and you're right, he does look hurt." She moved to the door and through the threshold, with Mike a few paces behind her. "Constable? Do you need help?"

The man looked feverish, like he'd been put through the wash and left to dry in a pile. Mike could see that his clothes were badly wrinkled, even in the darkness. His voice was faint and strained when he spoke. "Not . . . That wasn't him . . . You've got to run."

Mike frowned. "I can't hear you, Tom. What's wrong?" They walked closer and could finally see some of the damage that had been done to him. Tom's face was battered and swollen, his left eye forced shut by the swelling. His mouth was split and covered with dried blood. The limp was caused by the fact that his left foot was dragging, practically flopping at the end of his ankle, but still he was moving toward them, half hopping whenever his left leg settled on the ground.

"That's not Jack Michaels . . . he isn't himself. He's doing things, and you have to leave before he gets to you." The words were still strained and slurred a bit. "Get away, take the cruiser if you have to."

The voice from behind them shouldn't have been very surprising. Mike knew Jack was in the house, but for some reason it still caught him off guard. "Damn it, Tom, didn't I tell you to stay in the car?"

Mike turned just in time to see the pistol come out of Jack's holster.

"Jack, what the fuck?" Mike slid himself back, moving to shield Amelia at the same time.

Norris reached for his own revolver, but it had disappeared somewhere along the way. Jack Michaels pulled the trigger, and Mike watched as Amelia's chest blossomed in a spray of bone and blood. Three more explosions came from the muzzle of the .38 in the constable's hand. Each and every one of the bullets fired tore into Amelia as she fell.

Mike didn't even have time to scream before she hit the ground. Michaels looked at him and shook his head. "I'm sorry about this, Mike. I really am. But some things are beyond my control." He aimed again and fired. The bullet hit Mike Blake across his brow and sent him into the darkness.

II

Terry was still in his cell and still feeling miserable about the way his world had crumbled. She'd screwed him again and laughed about it. And there was no one on the planet who would ever believe he was innocent, not now.

He was pacing again. He'd gone through anger, hysteria, and depression about a hundred times by his reckoning, and he felt the anger coming back again. That bitch had ruined him, there was no other way around it. He was as good as convicted, and if there had ever been a chance of him getting off with doing only a few years, it was gone now. Because now they'd pulled his skin from under her fingertips and now there was a witness to the crime. Now he would be considered not only as a rapist but as a stalker.

There was nothing he could do about it and no way a jury would consider him as anything but the worst kind of scum. He couldn't get past that single thought. It had become the focus of his world, and not all the begging and pleading in the world was going to get him off the hook this time around.

Eugene Halloway walked into the office and moved across to the cells, never saying a word.

Terry looked at him and returned the silence. There was nothing he could say that would make the man believe him.

After a few moments of the silence, Gene Halloway spoke up. "She's at home, if you're wondering. Damned near everyone in this town is at some sort of carnival, but my little girl is lying in bed and barely speaking."

"I didn't do it."

"You shut your mouth, you little pig. Don't you dare speak to me." Mr. Halloway was as mild-mannered as anyone he'd ever met, but not anymore. The man standing in front of him was the Mr. Hyde to the Dr. Jekyll he was used to seeing whenever he went around to pick up Terri. "She had to convince me to let her drop the charges. She started saying she wasn't really sure it was you, and that there wasn't enough evidence, and that she never wanted to think about it again. And so I agreed. I let you off the hook, you little shit, and you did it again." His voice shook with anger. His entire body seemed on the edge of collapse he was trembling so much, but his voice stayed soft and low, and that scared Terry more than anything else.

"Look, I know you don't believe me, Mr. Halloway, I wouldn't even believe me, but I swear to you, I never hurt Terri." He was trying, at least. He had to try. He wanted to make it clear to the man that he was innocent, even though he knew there wasn't a chance of ever convincing him.

"You don't listen very well. I thought your mother raised you better than that." Halloway scowled at him and clenched his hands into fists. "Then again, if she'd done her job properly, you wouldn't be behind bars, would you?"

"My mother isn't the one causing the problems here. Your daughter is. Terri played me. She set me up and made sure it would stick, and you won't ever believe me, but I never hurt her."

"You got caught red-handed this time. I might have believed you before, hell, Terri had me convinced that I should give you the benefit of the doubt, but you went ahead and tried to rape her again. You should have bought yourself a whore. I'm sure your mother could have set you up."

And there it was again, using his mother against him. There were many, many things in the world that Terry could ignore, but messing with his mother wasn't one of them. "You go fuck yourself. You leave my mother out of this, you prick."

"You should have left my daughter out of it. That's what you should have done, mister."

"I didn't touch the bitch!"

"You did. You did, too, you sorry little fuck. And I'm gonna make sure you never touch her again."

"Did you find the key for the bars? 'Cause I'm not walking any closer to give you a free shot." Terry scowled and crossed his arms. He'd always liked Mr. Halloway, but there were limits to his patience, and they had been exceeded.

"I don't need the key, you bastard." Halloway reached into his coat and pulled out the strangest looking gun Terry had ever seen. It had a huge barrel and that was enough to make Terry worry. That was all that mattered. "Try raping another girl, you sick little shit."

Halloway aimed directly at his head, and Terry froze, unable to think of a damned thing he could do to get away. He stood with his hands in front of his face and prayed his hands would deflect the bullet.

Then Halloway lowered his aim and fired the missile from his flare gun directly at Terry's crotch. At first it felt like he'd been kicked in the groin, and Terry let out a grunt and dropped his hands, reaching to protect his masculinity. He yanked his fingers back when the heat from the flare burned them, and then he let loose with a scream loud enough to make his throat raw as the burning pain erupted in his crotch. The heat seemed to claw its way deeper and deeper into his body, and there was nothing at all he could do to stop it. Terry slapped and danced and screamed and finally fell backwards against the commode, his ass falling completely into the bowl of the toilet.

He felt himself start fading, felt numbness start swallowing him whole. Through slitted eyes he saw Mr. Halloway walking away from the cell. He didn't see the man place a call to the medical center. He wasn't conscious when the paramedics came in or when they finally managed to find a spare key for the cells in Jack Michaels's desk. He wasn't aware of the short ride to the medical center or anything else for the rest of the night.

III

Crowley and Barnes reached the tent just in time to watch the only entrance seal itself from within. They stopped short and looked carefully, Crowley even going so far as to run his hands over the entire area in an effort to find the spot where the opening had been.

"It sealed itself shut. I could get the impression we weren't welcome." Victor Barnes looked at the shorter man and saw a smile spreading across his face that made the sarcasm in the words even more evident.

"You might think this is funny, Crowley, but I don't."

"Am I laughing? No? Then I don't think this is funny. Not really." He shrugged and glanced back at Barnes, his plain brown eyes unreadable. "I just don't believe in getting all worked up over something until I know the score."

Barnes looked at the tent and touched the material, repulsed by the feel of it. The stuff was warmer than the air and felt slightly wet. "How do we get in?"

"Got a knife?"

"No. But I have a big gun."

"And I'm sure that will protect the people inside without any trouble at all, big guy, but it might not be any good for cutting a hole in this thing."

"Point taken. Do you have a knife?"

Crowley pulled his whittling blade from the back pocket of his jeans. "I never leave home without it." He flipped the blade open and reached for the canvas but stopped when he heard the new voice behind him.

"I don't think he wants you to do that." They both turned and looked at Rebecca Glass, who was standing only a few feet away with her arms crossed over her chest.

"Well, well, well, look what finally showed up."

"Crowley, what the hell are you talking about?"

The man ignored him. "Becky Glass, am I right?"

She nodded. "I wouldn't try to open the tent if I were you."

"Why not?" The man's voice was positively patronizing as he looked down at the girl. She looked up with anger in her eyes, apparently not liking to be treated like a kid, which, of course, she was. Though the way she carried herself and the look on her face said otherwise.

"Because my very big friend over there," she pointed over her shoulder with her thumb, "doesn't want you to."

"Isn't that a pity? Well, let's you and me have a talk about what you've done to the girl you're hiding inside, and then I'll talk with your buddy."

"We've come to an understanding, Becky and I have. You leave us alone, and we'll let bygones be bygones."

Crowley snorted laughter, pushing his glasses up to the bridge of his nose. "Yeah, that could happen."

"You don't believe me?"

"Not in this lifetime, cupcake."

The girl sighed and shook her head. "I tried to let you off the hook, but since you won't let it be, I guess we'll just have to do this the hard way."

"I already took out one part of you. What makes you think I can't handle you without breaking a sweat?"

"I never said anything about *me* handling it, did I?" Becky Glass smiled and then let out a loud whistle, which was muted only by the sound of applause from inside the tent. She stepped off to the side and promptly dropped to the ground on her hands and knees.

And then it came charging from the darkness like a speeding truck. The beast she'd helped bring back into existence without really knowing exactly how or why came to Becky's aid. Victor Barnes let out a yelp and stepped backwards, reaching for his pistol as the hellhound charged. Its eyes blazed with green fire, and thick gouts of steam bellowed from between lips peeled back from teeth as long as his middle finger.

Crowley hopped back just in time to avoid having the jaws of the thing snap shut on his head. No dog Victor had ever seen prepared him for the sheer mass of the beast in front of him. If the hounds he'd dealt with before were big enough to dent the side of his truck, he wasn't thrilled with the idea of what this thing could do. As if to prove him right about its strength, the beast swatted him with a paw and sent him sailing through the air, the pistol he'd been holding lost along the way. He tried to twist around and land on his back but didn't quite make it. Instead he landed on his ass and his legs and felt the injury in his calf ignite with new pain. The pistol landed a few feet to his right, just out of reach.

The four of them—girl, stranger, big damned dog-thing, and Barnes—all waited for the next move. Crowley was grinning, the girl was still crouched on the ground, her eyes trying to watch everything at the same time, and Victor climbed back to his feet as fresh warmth ran down his leg from where he'd landed and torn stitches. The demonic Cujo was eyeing Crowley and panting heavily. Barnes tried to understand how something that big could get around in the woods—let alone in the fields around the farm—without being seen. He also took the liberty of reaching for his pistol as he tried to figure it out.

Fido took the gesture poorly and turned toward him with a roar that lifted his hair and half deafened him. The muzzle on the beast moved toward him and opened wide, giving him a much better view of the inside of the animal than he'd ever wanted. Vic's leg decided it was a good time to not work, and he fell backwards. He saw the mouth lunging for him and closed his eyes. Staring death in the face wasn't on his agenda, and he was damned if the last thing he wanted to think about was the thing in front of him.

Something grabbed the back of his belt and pants and hauled him out of the way before the teeth could slice his face off. Constable Victor Barnes, who had done time as both a military policeman and as a biker in his wilder days, let out a shriek worthy of an adolescent male who'd zipped himself and went sailing backwards.

When he could look again, he saw Crowley facing off against the monster. Both of the opponents had their teeth bared in feral grimaces. The hound roared again, and Crowley backed away a few steps. His smile was still firmly in place, but he looked a little nervous. Barnes couldn't blame him.

"You have interesting friends, Rebecca. Why don't you call Fifi here off, before this gets ugly? I have things to do." Afraid or not, he sounded remarkably calm.

"I have no control over the thing, Hunter. The best I could do was keep it calm until you disappointed me." The voice coming out of the little girl was completely wrong, gravelly and almost sibilant. "Now it is free from me, and you'll have to deal with it alone."

Crowley jumped backwards, covering almost seven feet from a standstill, and the place where he had been was filled with gnashing teeth and steam. Vic tried to stand again, but his leg told him to go to hell. Failing that, he started crawling. The pistol was only a few feet away. He figured he could reach it if he tried.

The little girl had other ideas.

She reached down for him as he moved and, fool that he was, he thought she was trying to help him. Instead, her hand clawed into his hair and she pushed his face toward the ground. He was caught off guard but quick to respond for all the good it did him. He pushed back with his full body strength, but may as well have pushed against a stone wall. The thin arm of his assailant didn't budge, and all he got for his trouble was a bruise on the back of his head.

"Jesus Christ, kid! Knock it off!" He pushed again, trying to force her away from him, but instead found his head pushed even lower. She made a sound like a ruptured steam pipe, which broke apart into laughter. He didn't know anymore if he should be terrified, angry, or just humiliated. Finally he reached out with his hand, letting her push him farther down as a result of giving up the leverage, and grabbed her ankle. His hand was big enough to cover half of her calf as well, and he yanked hard, pulling her from the ground and dropping her next to him.

She had no choice but to let him go as she fell, and he rolled away, shaking his head and trying to get the feeling back in his neck. He looked toward the girl again, unsettled by the cold look on her face. "I'm sorry about this, but you have to die now."

"Not really what I had in mind . . ."

He never had a chance to finish the comment. She hauled her leg around and kicked him in the side of the face. Vic's head snapped around, and he rolled, his face feeling half numb and his leg burning in protest as he moved it the wrong way again. He grunted and got to his knees, looking at her. She rose from the ground and stood up, brushing off her jeans. "It's nothing personal. I just can't have any witnesses . . ."

"Kid, if you don't knock it off, I'll have to put you in cuffs." Somewhere behind him, he heard Crowley cursing and remembered that there were worse threats than a little girl on speed. He had to fight the temptation to look behind him, but he managed it. "You need to calm down right now."

"Oh, please . . ." He barely saw her move. But one second she was shaking her head and looking at him petulantly, and the next she was on top of him again, pushing his face with her little hand and knocking him on his back. "Let's just make this quick. I have things to do." He wanted to laugh at the absurdity of the situation but knew the feeling was brought on by panic.

What the hell am I supposed to do, hit a little girl? Cut me a damned break here! He pushed back, using his body and mass to shove her off balance. It was a nice theory, at any rate. She didn't budge. "Will you fucking fall down?!"

Her voice sounded a little strained, but not enough for his satisfaction. She pushed harder and sent him sprawling. "No. YOU fall down!" Little Becky Glass stomped down with her foot, planting it firmly on his calf and tearing all hell out of the remaining stitches. Her heel twisted and ground down harder as he screamed.

Well, that was about as far as he could take the kid stuff. Screw the fact that she was barely touching puberty. He backhanded her across the face. Becky lifted off the ground, her body spinning a little over halfway around, with a stream of blood running from her mouth and nose. He would have felt a lot guiltier about it if he hadn't been damned close to passing out from shock. The first nauseating wave went through his body, running up from his leg to his crotch and then through the rest of him. Barnes fell forward onto all fours again, retching and trying not to let the world go gray.

From the corner of his eye, he saw Crowley backpedaling. He might have thought the man was retreating willingly from his enemy, but his feet were off the ground, he was moaning, and the front of his shirt was gone, replaced by patches of bloody cloth.

Crowley slapped against the side of the tent not ten feet from Victor and then shook his head, grinning like an angry baboon and standing back up as quickly as he slid to the ground. "You little shit . . ." The man danced to the side with footwork that would have made Muhammad Ali in his prime envious, and then started back into the fray. Barnes saw the big black thing snarling, shaking its massive head and crouching low. It charged like a bull, head down and teeth bared, ready, no doubt, to lift that mouth and take half of the man in a single chomp. Crowley spun off to the side, dodging as the muzzle lifted and opened. His hand shot forward and reached, coming dangerously close to that bear trap full of teeth, and his fingers clawed into the animal's green, burning eye.

The hound roared in a high-pitched fit of agony, rearing back and knocking Crowley through the air again. He rolled and came up on his feet, jumping back again as the animal slammed down to the ground, both massive forepaws pounding the earth hard enough to leave dents. Green filth spilled from the beast's ruined eye socket and from Crowley's hand. There was no pause to appreciate pain or the minor victory; the two of them charged each other again.

And while Victor Barnes let himself get distracted, Becky Glass recovered from the brutal backhand and moved in closer. The old Becky might have just laid back and given serious thought to how much her face was hurting—the taste of blood was thick in her mouth, and it felt like a few teeth were loose—but the Becky that had formed from the unusual union with the supernatural wasn't quite as quick to call the fight done.

Barnes let out a loud yelp as she grabbed his wounded leg and hauled him off the ground with ludicrous ease. Her thin fingers felt like barbed hooks as they dug into the open wound on his calf. In the occasional cartoon he'd seen growing up, there were characters that would grab another animated figure and swing it overhead like a baseball bat, only to slam it into the ground. He was the only person he knew who got to understand how those cartoon characters felt when they met the turf. It was a lot funnier in the cartoons. He hit hard and felt several ribs break under the impact. Everything went out of focus except for the pain.

"Uhhh" was about all he could manage, but it was supposed to be a warning for her to stay back. In addition to feeling like he'd just been hit by a wrecking ball, he was finally getting over his problem with hitting a preteen. Guilt be damned when the girl in question could pack that sort of wallop. He blinked several times, trying to remember where he was and why he was on his back. All he really knew was that he had to get up and take care of matters right damned now, thanks very much. Moving hurt, and he made a few loud noises as he rolled onto his stomach and started pushing up. His leg refused to move, and that was inconvenient, but he saw her when she braced her own legs to try another round of hit-the-planet-with-the-cop. He grabbed his nightstick from its loop on his belt and brought it down across her knee.

Rebecca Glass dropped like a sack of potatoes, and as she hit the ground he used the stick again, this time across her flat stomach. She gasped and made fish faces while she tried to catch her breath. He hit her twice more, careful not to strike bone, because, despite his anger, there was a little girl in there somewhere, and he didn't need the extra guilt. She curled up on herself and stopped moving. He crawled over and pinned her in place, reaching for his handcuffs. *Not that they'll do much good, but every little bit helps.* He looked up and saw Crowley and the beast were still going at it. Crowley's shirt was bloodier than before, but now it was speckled with that same green crap he had on his hand. *I want to wake up now . . . this shit is getting too weird.*

Crowley's arm got swallowed by the dog-thing. He could actually hear the sound of bones breaking through the howl of pain that exploded past Crowley's lips. He jumped and thrashed like a man with his arm in a meat grinder, which was, basically, what he was at that moment. The dog shook its head, throwing Crowley around like a chew toy.

Barnes crawled across the ground and looked for his pistol, cursing his game leg. While his head was turned away, Crowley did something that made the monster scream. He looked back to see Crowley doubled over in pain, clutching the ruin of his arm, and the hound vomiting up a thick stream of greenish black bile.

Crowley stumbled his way and fell to his knees. The man was pale except where he was bloodied. His glasses were nowhere to be seen, though Barnes wasn't too surprised by that. Crowley grinned at him and slapped him on the shoulder with his good arm. "Tag team time, Vickster. You get to shoot the big pooch, and I get to play with the girl."

"I can't do shit, man. I can't even find my gun."

"It's two feet to your right. Now move and do it fast. Hit that fucker before he decides to stop coughing up blood."

. Barnes knew, absolutely knew, that the gun hadn't been there a few seconds ago, but when he looked, it was exactly where Crowley said it would be. He grabbed the .38 and pointed it at the black dog just as it shook all over and lifted its face again, looking for the man who'd put a serious hurt on it. The one eye seemed almost as bright as a sun and looked at him with a glare of pure hatred.

Crowley completely ignored the thing, putting his faith in Vic's abilities. The strange man reached out and clutched his unchewed hand over Becky's mouth, leaning in close and whispering to her. Whatever he said had an instantaneous effect. She went into convulsions, her arms trying to pull away from each other, the cuffs at her wrists cutting deeply into her flesh.

The black furry mountain charged, teeth bared and spilling flecks of green-tinged foam, billowing out that glowing steam from its maw as its clawed feet cut into the ground and took out chunks of turf. For one perfect moment, the world was in absolute focus. He heard Crowley whispering words that sounded beyond merely obscene, heard the gasping breaths of Becky Glass and the sound of his own heartbeat, the deep thumps of the monster's paws as they hit the ground. He saw the wide-eyed fear in the girl's bloodied face, saw the loss that spilled from her eyes in the shape of tears. There was a part of him that wanted to make the pain go away, but he pushed it aside. He saw the wounds on Crowley's arm—and were they smaller than before? Possibly, just possibly—saw the blood that spilled from tears and holes and gashes across the man's chest and neck. He saw the pure, sadistic glee that lit the man's eyes as Becky Glass bucked and tried to escape his touch. Saw the animal looming larger and larger as it stormed his way, that one burning eye focused on him to the exclusion of everything else in the universe. He saw his finger flex against the trigger of his weapon, felt the kick of the pistol in his hand and, by God, could almost make out the bullet as it cut through the air and left a vacuum in its wake. It was an instant only, but in some ways it was longer than his entire life. Four times since he'd been born he felt that nearly omniscient clarity. Each time it happened, he knew his life was an instant from ending. Each time he had no regrets when he looked back.

The bullet hit its mark. The green orb of the hellhound's remaining eye exploded from its socket, and the back of its thick skull bulged outward before blossoming into a dark wound. It took several more steps, but he could see they were only reflex, and it tilted hard to the left, falling on its side before it hit him.

And then he was back in the real world, and all the pain was back and the monster was still dead, but he didn't have the strength to celebrate, he was too busy trying to keep his grip on the pistol, which suddenly weighed about as much as a limousine.

Victor Barnes hit the ground and stayed there, his eyes

shifting to Crowley and the girl. The world was sideways from this perspective and half hidden by thick grass, but he didn't mind. He could see enough. Jonathan Crowley held something in his hand that glowed a sickly orange and writhed as it tried to get away. Becky Glass lay on the ground before him, no longer struggling but seemingly sleeping peacefully.

Crowley's skin was still covered with wet streaks of blood in two different colors, but there were no wounds on his body. They were all gone. The man looked at him and winked. "Figure maybe you want to sleep this one off?"

"Mmmmn."

"That's okay, Vicky. I'll take care of the rest."

Barnes closed his eyes. He wanted to make a snide comment but figured it could wait until he wasn't unconscious. He drifted away with the sound of calliope music cheerfully blending with the screams that were coming from the tent.

IV

Jonathan Crowley winced as he walked toward the tent. There were parts of him aching that hadn't been touched, but muscle strain and exhaustion were doing their part to kick the bejeezus out of him. It didn't help that he hadn't really wanted to fight the hellhound. It was justifiably angry over having been murdered, and it told him as much even as it attacked. Oh, no one else would have heard or understood, but it made itself very clear to him.

He reached into his pocket and pulled out his whittling knife again. The thing in his hand was determined to get free, but he didn't really want that happening. If that meant he had to endure a few more minutes of stinging pain as it tried to burrow though his hand, well, he was capable of holding on long enough to bind it. He folded the entity around the blade and closed the knife back up before pocketing it again. It was a temporary solution at best, but would give him a little time to figure out what to do with it.

The music from inside the tent was boisterous and loud and just exactly annoying enough to make him want it gone. He couldn't use his knife just then, so he grabbed the material in his hands and tore a new entrance into the big top. The leathery fabric screamed as it opened, and he caught a whiff of putrescence under the carnival smells.

Crowley stepped through the opening and smiled tightly.

He had no idea in hell what he was going to do about the situation, but it definitely needed rectifying, immediately if not sooner.

The kid with the glasses—Dave, that was the name— was up onstage with the two girls who looked to be twins and another girl, maybe the age of the one outside. Dave was being held by a corpse in clown makeup while the females around him were escorted by a menagerie of unusual figures. Five clowns in all, each with a different style of makeup and each looking a little on the mummified side. All around the stage there were people in bleachers looking at the show with big smiles on their faces. Oh, to be sure there were a few who looked like maybe they could sense that something was wrong, but most of them were having a grand old time.

Nice of the ghosts to give them a few good memories before sending them to their deaths.

"Hi, there." He called out loudly and made sure he was heard over the noise of the crowd and the music. The people in their seats didn't notice him, but the clown posse did. Most of them just frowned, one of them actually growled in his general direction, and the one in the fancy tuxedo smiled warmly.

"Well, howdy, stranger! Looks like we have a new friend, folks. A man who just couldn't resist joining us for the show!" The lanky figure strutted away from Dave Pageant and moved in his direction, his arms gesturing to the audience. "Let's give him a big hand, ladies and gentlemen! You have to admire that sort of enthusiasm!"

The air fairly vibrated with applause, and Crowley saw the happy faces looking his way at last, acknowledging him. He smiled and walked toward the center ring, shaking his head slightly. Sometimes the things he dealt with had egos, and this one was reaching new heights. "Well, howdy right back, cupcake. Would you like to discuss the agenda for your show, or should we just get to the part where I kick your ass?"

The gaudy ringmaster laughed out loud, and the crowd ate it up. He was pretty sure the clown could have started cutting parts off of the kids on the stage, and the audience would have cheered just as strongly. *The lights are on in Serenity Falls, kiddies, but there's nobody home.*

"You must be Jonathan Crowley, am I right?"

Crowley smiled and took a small bow. When in Rome and all that rubbish.

"I had a long talk with our benefactor. I know about you." The broad smile grew wider, and sky-blue eyes fairly sparkled with pleasure. "We really don't have anything against you, Hunter. Why don't you go ahead on your way and leave everything alone?"

"Well now, I can't really do that. I have this problem with dead things that want to get up and play when everyone around here just knows they're supposed to stay dead." He shrugged and smiled back at the thing in the top hat. "I just can't seem to let it go. Call it a character flaw."

"Oh, it's definitely a character flaw, my good man. And

one that could get you in a lot of trouble." It waved one
white-gloved finger in his direction, shaking its head and
making tsking noises. "It's the sort of thing that can bring
nice little kids into the hands of big, bad torturers, too."

"Oh please. You want me to believe you were going to
let them go?"

"Well, it would be nice if you did, but I can see your
point." It shrugged and walked around the stage, arms
thrown behind the back and practically strutting like a sequined rooster. "Still, you can't say we didn't give you a
chance to leave. I mean, I've heard a few stories about how
tough you are, but do you really think you can take on all
of us?"

"What? Five clowns? I've taken on six or seven clowns
a few times, including once at a Ronald McDonald look-
alike contest. Man, those guys get pissy when they lose out
on a free Big Mac."

The clown looked at him, puzzled by the reference, and
then shrugged it off. "I don't just mean a few clowns, you
know. I mean the rest of the circus, too, and a few hundred
others besides."

Crowley looked around, shrugging. "I only see five
dorks dressed up in bad makeup and cheap clothes. The
rest I can worry about when they show up, if they show up."

"They're already here." Rufo the Clown touched his
nose with one fingertip and winked. "They're already
here."

"How very special for them. At least let the kids go. I
can't imagine a one of them caused any deaths around
here."

"Here's a BIG surprise for you . . . WE DON'T CARE!"
The smile faded away from his face as he spoke, and
the scowl that replaced it was enough to even draw
down the corners of the red lips painted across his skin.
"They might not have pulled the trigger on the smoking

gun, but there isn't an innocent among them!" He jumped, clearing the stage and landing only a few feet from Crowley. The people in the tent made appreciative noises as Rufo moved forward until his face was just out of easy striking distance. "We're getting biblical today in sunny Serenity Falls. Sins of the father revisited on the son, as it were."

"Why?"

"Because we can." The clown smiled broadly, his voice a grating purr. "And because there are a lot of really angry people around here who were just minding their business when the fine, fine citizens of this little hamlet decided to make a meal out of their lives." He was sounding downright angry now, and that made Crowley feel good.

"That sounds just swell, Mr. Clown. Heck, I guess since it happened to you, it's all right to do it to someone else who never did anything wrong."

"You don't know anything, Mr. Crowley. You don't know, and you don't understand."

"Oh, I get it. Boo hoo hoo, my life got taken away, and now I want revenge. Only, sigh, my murderer is dead, so I guess I'll just take it out on someone else."

Rufo's eyes narrowed down to angry slits, but his smile came back. "You can think whatever you want, Mr. Crowley. But I learned the rules. You need someone to ask for your help, and no one in this little gathering will do that."

"I was already asked to help."

"Yes, you were, with other things. No one asked you to help against us. You were asked to help a little boy who is no longer among the living, and that means you weren't invited to this particular party."

That took him off guard. Stan Long was dead, and he hadn't expected anything along those lines. Still, he shook his head. "I'm willing to take that risk if you are."

"Well we've always been willing, Mr. Crowley, we were

just trying to be nice about the whole thing." He walked
back toward the stage, dismissing Crowley as if he no
longer mattered. "We only want revenge. It's not like we're
actually evil or anything. You need to get some perspective."

"I need to get some perspective?" Crowley chuckled.
"Little man, if you had any less perspective you'd be a
proper fanatic."

"You aren't even interesting anymore. Go away."

Before Crowley could respond, he felt hands grabbing
him, pulling him toward the ground. He looked behind him
and saw, sure enough, that the rest of the carnival and what
looked like a few hundred other dead people were there.
He felt a thick sheet of ice grow over his stomach lining
and made himself swallow the fear. It wouldn't do him any
good to panic. They weren't solid, not made of flesh like
the clowns, but they were there, and they were not at all
happy to see him. None of them were distinct, they were
little more than wisps of mist in the air around him, but
they had enough physical mass to pull him down and keep
him there. If he tried, he could probably have deciphered
individual faces. He didn't try. He didn't care. They
weren't people; they were the enemy.

Rufo strode back up to the stage and moved over to
where Dave Pageant sat with his arms held back by one of
the other clowns. Crowley pulled hard against the spectral
hands clutching him, but there were too many of them. He
might as well have been superglued to the ground for all
the success he had at getting up.

All around him the people of Serenity cheered and
stomped their feet, ecstatic at the turn of events. He knew
they were under the influence of the dead brought back by
the curse, but he also sensed there was something more to
it than that. He just didn't know what it was.

"Well, folks, that about covers the preshow entertainment. Let's get on with the part you've all been waiting for,

shall we?" Crowley looked at the clown again and listened
to what it had to say as the barely visible bodies pressed
him down to the ground. "It's time to pay back you fine
people for each and every murder ever committed in this
town. And we're going to start with one of my personal fa-
vorites, the grandson of the man who orchestrated the murder of me and my whole gang of merry men."

The clown pulled the hat from his own head and set it
on Dave's tousled hair. "Dave Pageant, this is YOUR
death!" The crowd was nearly orgasmic in their reaction,
screaming and stomping and cutting lose with shrill whistles as Rufo reached into his coat and pulled out a knife as
easily as a magician did a rabbit from a hat.

Dave screamed the first time the blade cut into his face.

And Crowley watched, unable to help despite his best
struggles.

V

Lawrence Grey grabbed the last of the wooden figurines
that was still mobile and pulled it close to him. He wanted
to scream in triumph, but he was feeling just a little too
harried and hurting a little too much. His body was covered in blood, all his own, thanks very much, and he could
not escape the stinging pains that ran in waves like a feverish shiver from cut to cut. Finally, after what seemed like
hours, he was going to have the final part of himself that
the Hunter had stolen. It was a wonderful feeling. Still, he
knew he'd have to be cautious. He could already feel his
energies scorching the very body of the boy he possessed.
He? When did I become a he? He shook the thought away,
casting it aside like a used rag. No matter that he called

himself a he, or that the last part of him that was still missing called itself a she. It was time to become fully united
again. Time to have his revenge on the Hunter for killing
him in the time before his death and resurrection. *Besides,
I almost always take a male body. Why shouldn't I think of
myself as a he?*

He looked down on the broken wooden toys, trinkets
carved decades ago, which had grown in number with
every death in Serenity. Every native of The Falls who was
murdered wound up here, and quite a few who had died of
natural causes as well. Not all of them, there were a few
missing, but not many. How many there had been when the
original creator of them had died he had no way of knowing, but he suspected it was substantially less than he'd just
had to destroy.

He looked to the delicately carved wooden woman in
his hands, dressed in wedding finery, with dark hair and
tiny dark eyes, and smiled. That part of him that truly was
Lawrence noted that the doll looked a lot like the woman
he'd seen when he entered the house and wondered if she
were dead and if this last figure came after Crowley had
pulled his latest stunt.

It didn't really matter. He would pull the trapped essences
from the effigy, and if they belonged to him or could be absorbed, he would take them. Either way, this demented little
prison was now emptied of captives, and the one who'd cast
the curse over Serenity Falls in the first place could suffer an
eternity or two of hellish pain for all he cared.

He could sense it, the malevolent presence that was
watching over the town even now, reveling in whatever was
happening where the black tent had formed. He'd be heading there himself in just a moment, because the time for
games was over now, and he knew that Crowley was down
there somewhere. Crowley had to die, and he had to be the
one that killed him. He owed the bastard.

As he left the ruined collection of carvings and passed through the master bedroom in the house, he let his mind drift back to the night when he and the Hunter had met.

The details were still hazy, but he knew he'd been summoned from somewhere and called to do the bidding of some mortal or other. He never really cared who summoned him, so long as there was blood involved. Blood and death and the sweet, carnal stench of fear were all that he'd ever lived for. It was what he was created to cause and what he used to feed himself and stay strong.

Where had he been? London, perhaps. Or maybe in Düsseldorf. He'd taken the simple route on this case, stealing the body of a human and using it as both his tool and his camouflage. It had been centuries at that point since he'd been allowed from his personal darkness and into the realm of flesh and light. He'd fairly screamed with enthusiasm, and his host's handsome face smiled almost constantly as he walked the streets of the city and found new victims. The summons had been not to kill an individual or to destroy a family or even a neighborhood, but to destroy the verminous poor who littered the streets and choked the life from the city with their mutual misery. In some ways his killings were almost a mercy to the victims. He was quick with the kill and creative enough with the mutilations to leave even the strongest humans petrified. Hardly really worthy of being called work when he was enjoying it so much and feeding so well on the terror he inspired.

And then Crowley showed up and ruined it. One of the women he'd torn through actually had someone to care for her in her miserable life, and that someone—he never knew who, or he'd surely have found and devoured that wretch by now—had called upon the Hunter and asked for help.

He'd heard of the Hunter, of course. There weren't really that many creatures out there who hunted down his kind, but most of them were known and avoided whenever

possible. But he'd never imagined that he'd meet the Hunter
or that even half of the rumors could be true.

Jonathan Crowley came out of the shadows, stalking
him as if he were the prey and not the one that everyone in
the city feared. It had been enough to enrage him, and the
smiling taunts from the Hunter only made him angrier.

Still, anger was not always enough to eliminate caution.
He'd learned long before his latest spree that rash actions
lead to death or worse. His nature was to be creative, not to
be impetuous. He would have left well enough alone and
merely taken his leave of the entire situation if the Hunter
had allowed him that luxury. Instead, he was confronted,
assaulted, and soundly beaten down.

And when the Hunter was done with the beating, when
he'd begged Crowley for mercy, the Hunter had done to
him what he had done to so many victims over the centuries and torn him to shreds, pulling him from the body of
his host and shattering his existence. There was no sleep,
no sweet merciful darkness when the Hunter was done
with him. There had been only endless pain and constant
burning light, until something had pulled him from that ra-
zorfield of suffering and dragged him back into this world
in Silver Springs, Arizona, and bade him to bring the town-
ship death and suffering.

In exchange for this small trifle, which he'd have gladly
granted for free, he was given the name the Hunter used
and told where he would be and how best to strike at him.
How could he possibly have refused?

He had a second chance, and this time he had an ally of
sorts, even if that ally thought to use him as a pawn.

It should have been simple. He should have spread his
chaos and fear to all who inhabited Serenity Falls and
drawn the Hunter into his web, but nothing had worked
the way it was supposed to, and in time he came to understand why.

It was the curse. The curse stopped him from having his way with Serenity Falls. The curse was hungry and wanted all of the fun for itself. He'd been foolish to think that the breath he gave to the small dog was his doing. That, too, had been the curse, working to build a defense against him committing too many acts of fear and violence. He'd summoned a powerful beast with his breath, given it new life and power, but it had never served him, never let him take complete control of what it did or the minions it created from the flames that burned within it did.

Oh, but it had fooled him. That damned thing had tricked him and let him believe he had governance when in fact he merely had a casual alliance. Why? Because the true master of the beast had been the curse, and every single act it did was done to serve the creator of the curse.

Lawrence Grey left the house he'd come to, where, once upon a time, his father had tried to cut his heart out. He looked at the two still forms on the lawn and in the driveway, saw the two policemen, one badly hurt and one looking down at his victims, and smiled.

He could feel the fear and agony on the bound constable, could taste the flavor of his dread, and it was sweet.

But the other one was free of him, protected by the powerful words written under his flesh and kept safe as a living battery for the very curse that had thwarted him. The injured one was written upon as well, but the words were not finished, and they had no power until they were complete. He was a replacement for another, and without him the curse was not as powerful as it should have been, as it had been ever since long before its creator had summoned him to this place.

Lawrence walked past Jack Michaels, who stood trembling, his eyes on his service pistol, wide and filled with a dread that Lawrence could not enjoy. The man had not meant to do anything to either of the prone figures now behind Lawrence; he could sense that. But he had done it anyway, and now he was becoming finally fully aware of the fact that he was merely a pawn.

Lawrence let him live, because he understood that sort of confusion and knew the man wasn't really a danger anymore. The nature of humans was simple to understand. The man wasn't a danger because he was too lost in the act that he had just done. There was blood on his hands now, and he couldn't grasp how it had come to be there. Some humans might have lashed out under the same circumstances, but this one was too busy feeling guilty.

Lawrence, though he could sympathize with the confusion, felt no semblance of guilt. He could understand Jack Michaels's dilemma, but empathy was beyond his personal scope of experience.

He was not as kind with Tom Norris. The man looked at him and for all the world seemed to want to warn him of the danger that Michaels presented. Lawrence, still a little giddy from the power he'd retaken from the dolls, reached out with adolescent hands and touched them to the man's swollen face. He smiled up at Norris's worried face and whispered softly to him, "Die, Constable Norris. Rot away for me."

Where his hands had touched a moment before, dark black patches grew on the man's skin. Norris sucked in a harsh breath and tried to remember how to scream as the flesh necrotized, decaying away from his cheeks and jaw in mere seconds, and finally managed a weak scream as the rot grew like a hyperactive fungus, spreading over his face and down to his neck. Lawrence looked lovingly into his eyes as the skin ruptured and began spilling pus and blood like tears. He devoured the pain and panic that spilled from the constable in nearly palpable waves. He drank in the agony and breathed in the smell of the grave as Thomas J. Norris puddled into ruin before his very eyes.

The curse and its maker had been foolish to think he wouldn't take being misused and discarded personally. Neither Lawrence Grey nor the thing that possessed him had ever been very forgiving.

"The Hunter is mine. You won't get a second chance to fool with me." He spoke to Jack Michaels, but the man made no response. The constable was still trying to understand what had made him draw his gun and fire on two innocent people.

Lawrence moved toward the quarry, his short legs covering preposterous distances with each stride. He never noticed the cat watching everything he did. He never saw the rats moving in the same direction as him. Even if he had, he'd have thought them beneath his concern.

We all make mistakes.

VI

Dave Pageant screamed as the knife cut into his flesh, drawing blood, slicing muscles, and scraping bone. Rufo pulled the blade back and smiled. "There. That wasn't so bad, was it?"

Dave made a mewling sound and blinked. Beyond that there was no response from him.

Crowley, pinned in the audience, was not as quiet about the entire affair. "Oh, you're quite the terror. Listen, I'm trying to be reasonable about this, but if you don't lay off the kid, I'll make it my personal goal to kill you slowly."

The ringleader smiled and tilted his head a bit as he looked toward the man. "I told you, this is none of your concern. I know the rules, and I know you can't do a damned thing to stop us. You haven't been asked."

"Look, why don't you just give the kid a cell phone and have him call his grandfather if that's really who you want so badly? Why should you want to take it out on a little boy when you can take it out on the guy who did you in?"

"What's a cell phone?"

Crowley arched an eyebrow, and Dave looked his way, finally beginning to calm down enough to breathe again. Their eyes met for only a second, but Dave nodded his head a bit.

"A cell phone, you moron. A portable phone. You can make calls from almost anywhere. All you have to do is tell the old man his grandkids are here, and I'll bet he'll get his wrinkled old ass over here in a jiffy."

"They make portable phones?" The clown seemed genuinely shocked.

"Yeah. Half of your audience probably has one." Crowley rolled his eyes. His face said it was like talking to a slow and very annoying toddler.

Rufo looked at the man for a second and then looked back to Dave. "Is he serious?"

"Yeah . . . He's for real."

"Isn't science wonderful?" Rufo called out to the audience, asking to borrow a cell phone. While roughly a dozen people all held theirs up, Dave looked directly at Jonathan Crowley, who was staring in his direction with an expectant look on his face.

"Help?"

Rufo turned his head fast, glaring at him with venom in his blue eyes, and Crowley grinned. "I thought you'd never ask."

The clown whipped his whole body in Crowley's direction, his face almost comically shocked. Dave turned, too, just in time to see the man stand up, brushing off the spectral hands that held him in place. There was a loud roar of defiance from the amassed gathering of—What? Ghosts?

Maybe. They always looked like white splotchy things in photographs, and those things were white and splotchy—and they surged forward, a tidal wave of ectoplasm seeking to drown him.

Rufo practically danced around on the stage, watching, as the man was overwhelmed. Through the thick, white whirlpool of the ghostly images, Dave could see the solitary figure of Jonathan Crowley lifted from the ground and spun around again and again by the fluid energies writhing around him. He was tossed as easily as a handkerchief in an industrial dryer.

They were pretty in a weird way, the figures that moved around him, half-formed shapes that seemed to swim across and through each other like crosscurrents in a turbulent tide pool. But he could feel the cold coming off of them and knew that what he'd suspected before was true. They were the reason for the weather. Ghosts were supposed to draw energy from the world to manifest, and he guessed it took a lot of energy to let that many ghosts become even partially substantial. But if they drew in energy, did that mean life force, too? And if it did, what were they doing to Crowley caught inside their prison?

Whatever it was, he wasn't enjoying it. His face looked distorted by the forms surrounding him, but Dave could still see the anger there. The hatred growing. Dave could see enough through the thick, misty air to know he never wanted the man mad at him.

Rufo put a hand on his shoulder, the bony fingers digging into his flesh. "See what he's going through, boy? What he's enduring is nothing. We had a lot of time to discuss things, and all of us agreed. We don't just want revenge, we want our lives back."

"What do you mean?"

"I mean we're just going to kill him, but we're taking what was taken from us." He leaned in closer still, his eyes

like marbles, and Dave would have sworn he saw things
writhing under that skin, long and narrow, like worms bur-
rowing just beneath the surface of the clown's paint. "I'm
not going to kill you, Dave, I'm going to be you." He
looked over at Jessie and Dave's sisters and winked. "And
then I can have some *real* fun."

"You sick motherfucker!" Dave didn't even think about
it, he just hammered his forehead into the clown's nose.
Rufo let out a bark of pain and clutched at his face. Dark
red ran down from behind his clutching hand and ran over
his lips, leaving darker trails of scarlet over the crimson
paint. The clown holding on to Dave's hands let out a grunt
of surprise, and Dave took advantage of the momentary
shock, yanking his arms free. There were only a few things
that could honestly make Dave Pageant lose his temper,
and Rufo'd found one of them. Dave stood up, and Rufo
started pulling back. Dave helped him along with a knee
to the chin that damn near dislocated his kneecap in the
process.

The crowd went crazy, whistling and cheering, and even
though Dave knew it wasn't really applause for him, he
liked the way it sounded. He took a swing at the ringmaster's head with his left hand and realized almost instantly
that it had been a bad mistake. The clown caught his wrist
in his free hand and let the bloodstained glove covering his
face drop away. Instead of seeing a broken nose or a fat lip,
he saw the same twisted face with a nosebleed and a smile
that made his testicles want to pull up and hide away.

"I didn't know you had it in you, boy. You've got spirit."
Rufo yanked on Dave's wrist, and as he was pulled toward
the clown, the bloody hand became a fist that slammed into
his face like a brick. The punch would have been painful
anyway, but one knuckle caught the fold of skin where
Rufo had cut him before and peeled back the exposed lip

of flesh. His eyes started watering, and it felt like he'd just had every nerve in his cheek electrocuted. Dave shrieked at the pain, and any delusion he had of hoping to fight the man was lost.

He was, after all, only a twelve-year-old boy. He never really had a chance, but it was a nice dream while it lasted. The painted man hit him again and then a third time, and Dave went down. He wasn't unconscious; he just couldn't get his damned body to move.

Rufo helped him along, grabbing his arm and rolling him over onto his stomach so he could see the show. Just to make sure he didn't go anywhere, he planted one well-polished shoe in the small of Dave's back and pressed down hard.

So Dave got to watch as Crowley decided to fight back at last. The man just stopped doing his imitation of a load of laundry on the spin cycle and suddenly righted himself in the thick bubble of ectoplasm that surrounded him.

The clowns on the stage made varying noises of disbelief, the most eloquent of which came from Rufo himself, who said in a subdued voice, "He can't do that. That's impossible."

Dave smiled through the pain. "Yeah? So's coming back from the dead, asshole."

Rufo, apparently too distracted to really take offense, merely thumped him on the back of the head and warned him about using dirty language.

Jonathan Crowley looked toward the stage and smiled, an expression that was easily as sadistically gleeful as Rufo's had been a moment before. Then he said something. The distortion around the man made it impossible for Dave to figure out what it was, but the result was impressive.

For one second, everything that surrounded him was highlighted in a corona of red. Each individual shape within the pool glistened with its own Kirlian aura. And then every one of those shapes flew away from him in a comet trail of energies, screaming in what Dave guessed was pain. They sounded a lot like he did when Rufo punched him in the open wound.

Crowley hit the ground and landed like a gymnast pulling off a perfect dismount. He looked at Dave and winked and then looked toward the painted ringmaster standing above him and nodded. "Thanks. I figured it was something like that. I mean, why not just kill them all at once unless you wanted to have the bodies for yourselves?"

"We'll have the bodies, Hunter. There's nothing you can do to stop that."

Crowley crossed his arms and shrugged. "Well, you'll have bodies at any rate." There was a deep rustling sound from where Dave was, and he looked past Crowley at the disembodied things that still moved like they were in pain, the weird red glow around them flickering and sputtering now. Beyond the ghost-things, there was the audience of people Dave knew very well, all of them still applauding and laughing as if they were watching the best damned circus ever; the greatest show on earth as opposed to a few freaky clowns and a handful of their friends. Beyond the townies, there was the tent, which now writhed and rippled as if hit by hundreds of softballs that were trying their best to get into the place.

"What do you mean?"

"Oh, I mean I figure the bodies are a part of the curse. There isn't a one of you I can see or half see that looks like you could pull that sort of thing off without help. You get bodies, sort of like payment for services rendered is my guess."

Rufo stood with one eyebrow raised, his real lips smirking underneath the greasepainted smile. "You don't think there are enough people on the bleachers?"

"On no, there are plenty. You just won't be able to do anything with them."

"Well, we certainly can't all fit in Dave here." He pushed with his foot again, and Dave let out a whine as the air in his stomach was forcibly removed. "And we sure can't fit in you. We tried that at the hospital, remember?"

Crowley's smile grew wider. Dave couldn't help but wonder if his mouth was hinged like a snake's. He figured if the man smiled any harder, he'd almost certainly split his own lips. "Oh you'll have bodies. You'll have plenty of bodies . . . If you can get past what's waiting outside."

The tear Crowley'd made earlier suddenly grew wider, and though he saw nothing, Dave could feel the rush of something spilling into the big top. Voices drowned out the applause, which started fading almost as soon as the hole opened. The voices sounded angry and then some. They sounded a lot like the voices of the things that had surrounded Crowley.

Dave felt the clown take a step back, finally freeing his back from the weight and letting him get a deep breath of air.

"What the hell have you done, Crowley?"

Dave turned and saw Rufo looking all around the tent, his eyes wide with surprise.

"Where did they come from? How did you do that?"

Crowley smiled and wiggled his fingers. "Hocus-pocus, sunshine. Say hello to the rest of the local residents." He leaned just a little more toward the ringmaster and whispered conspiratorially, "They don't much like it when people pick on their families."

VII

Lawrence stopped well before he reached the tent and the
land where it sat like a bloated pustule. He still intended
to get there, but there was something going on at the
Serenity Inn that caught his attention, and he crept closer,
his curiosity winning in a brief struggle with his common
sense.

The house-cum-bed-and-breakfast stood three stories
tall, with a widow's walk and enough shingles to look positively scaly. It was beautiful but looked like it belonged to
another time. Lawrence Grey had seen the place only a few
times in his sheltered life, and it had always appealed to
him. The part of him that was new to his mortal shell
couldn't have cared less, but a certain amount of placation
was necessary, even now. The boy was incredibly strong-
willed, and he wanted to see what was inside the building.

And so he did.

Lawrence walked in through the front door, his pallid
face set with a look of almost childlike wonder. Inside the
place, the Pageants had just about taken over. There were a
few of them in the lobby, moving around and trying to get
comfortable in the unfamiliar and almost claustrophobic
confines. They were used to the farm and the three houses
there. This was different. This was rather like sitting in a
bus. Oh, they might know everyone along for the ride, but
there was none of the elbow room they were used to, and
it just didn't sit very well. So they made do, spreading out
from the bedrooms and practically commandeering any
and all available spaces.

A few members of the family actually took the time to
look over at Lawrence, but seeing only the boy and what he
wanted them to see—which in this case meant a boy who
was not partially shredded and smeared with blood—and

not what resided inside him, they went back to whatever it was each of them was doing.

Lawrence looked at them just as casually, and after scanning the room with his eyes, he focused on Earl Pageant. It wasn't that Earl himself was all that interesting, but the ghostly figure behind him was enough to catch almost anyone's attention, provided they could see it. The spectral man looked enough like Snidely Whiplash—archenemy of that cartoon do-gooder Dudley Do-Right—that Lawrence almost snickered. From his long, hawkish nose to the muttonchops, from his fancy clothes to his top hat, the figure beckoned from another time. The humorous aspects faded quickly if one could see the sheer insanity that fairly burned across the features of the handsome face.

Lawrence looked at the translucent figure and pondered why it was there. The part of him that was newly back from the place beyond the mortal realms reached out with its mind and asked. The figure snapped around, looking away from Earl Pageant and staring harshly at the young interloper.

Who are you? The eyes seemed almost to bore into Lawrence, demanding an answer. Lawrence shrugged and gave his name.

What do you want here? Why are you interfering?

Lawrence raised one eyebrow and smiled softly. *What makes you think I'm here to interfere?*

You can see me when no one else can. Are you the Hunter?

Not likely. I'm here to see that he dies. I'm just passing through.

Him you may take. But Earl Pageant belongs to me. I will have him.

Why?

He let us die. All of us. He murdered my whole family and buried us where we burned. They weren't exactly words so much as flashes of memory that were shared.

Lawrence understood immediately what was said and knew that the ghost of Alexander Halston sought retribution for what was done to him and his carnies. *I will make him suffer, and he will know why he suffers before I take back what was mine.*

He's of no concern to me. I only want Crowley. I have no argument with you.

He meant every word of it, too, but sometimes actions speak louder than words. Before Halston had a chance to make a reply, the dead freed by Lawrence roared past the bed-and-breakfast on a gust of wind that led them toward the black tent and the Pageant farm. Halston turned his attention away from Lawrence and watched, his face growing angrier by the second. The dead of Serenity Falls—those who had been born to the cursed place and endured the imprisonment of their spirits, their souls—were moving in a very deliberate course, and Halston could tell where they were headed. They were going to where he had come from, where the rest of his carnival performers and the others murdered in the town had set up their site for retribution.

He saw them, and he recognized a few as the very people who had burned his traveling world to the ground and taken him with it. He spun back around and stared at Lawrence. Perhaps some part of the spirits he'd released in taking back his stolen self had been absorbed when he took back what Crowley had stolen. He honestly couldn't say. If that were the case, he had no way of knowing it. But something, some taint from the dead of Serenity's natives apparently connected him to the seething energies moving past him.

And Alexander Halston was not amused. *LIAR!* The call was so loud, so filled with hatred, that even the Pageants, who could neither see nor sense Halston, looked up and stared for a moment at the spot where the ghost stood.

The owner of the dead carnival got a running start and charged Lawrence, intent on punishing him for the events that were beyond his control. His hands reached into Lawrence, sliding through soft human flesh and leaving no marks. And those very same hands grabbed the entity within Lawrence's body and started clawing, trying to rip him from his safety within the boy.

And the thing that Jonathan Crowley had killed, the very thing that had come to Serenity Falls for the sole purpose of destroying Crowley, decided that being attacked by someone—anyone who could so easily start pulling him from his chosen host—was not to be considered a minor threat.

To the Pageant family, it looked as if the boy who'd come into the Serenity Inn was having a fit. They did not see the razored claws that moved from within him, gripping the arms of the equally unseen Halston. They did not see the form that was half torn from Lawrence's body as it fought back against the ghost of a carnival owner. What they saw was Lawrence Grey twitching spastically, his face going deathly white. What they heard was his strained cries of pain. The Pageants were good people by most standards. They moved almost as one to help the boy who'd come in out of the dark. Earl was the first to touch the boy. He dropped to his knees next to the fallen youth and reached out to calm him down. And that simple act was enough to get him into a great deal of trouble.

It was enough to let Alexander Halston into his body and into his mind. That would have been the end of him, too, if it hadn't been for Lawrence. There was no charity in the act, there was no kindness toward the stranger who'd come to his aid. There was only the need for retribution. That which possessed Lawrence reached out, spectral hands cleaving through flesh, reaching for the ghostly enemy that dared violate the sanctity of his host. Alexander

Halston was once a man, brought back to a semblance of life by an ancient curse. The thing in Lawrence was never a man but had been brought back by the same means. It tore Halston's spirit out of his hiding place and roared, then devoured the spirit of a man wrongly murdered.

And if the spirit of the head of the Pageant clan was torn and sliced in the process, that was just an added bonus. New power swelled within Lawrence's body, and he felt the strain on his human form increase, but knew he had no time to stop. The dead moving toward the Pageant farm could not be a good sign as far as he was concerned. It seemed almost certain that where they went, Crowley was sure to be. And if the dead moved with such purpose, there had to be a cause.

Whatever the purpose, whatever the agenda of the dead, he was also certain that it would work against his own goals.

Crowley was his to kill. End of discussion.

Lawrence stood up and walked away from the confused family. They paid him no heed. They were far more worried about Earl, who fell unconscious, a line of drool spilling from his mouth.

Lawrence walked at first and then began to run. He would not lose this time. He could feel it. The Hunter would be his to kill and maybe even to feed on. Not far off he heard the sound of calliope music. The skin of his host was stretching, heated almost to the point where it would burn. He could feel the changes starting to take place within him and hoped that the body would last long enough. He wasn't really sure if he could take on another host if he wasn't complete. He'd only managed the three children because they had opened themselves to him, had invited a miracle of sorts and gotten him instead. Finally, he was ready.

Finally, Jonathan Crowley would pay for his sins.

VIII

The five clowns on the stage looked around, and four of them grew fearful. Rufo merely grew angrier. This was not what was supposed to happen. They had all been promised new life, new bodies, in addition to their chance for revenge. He intended to make sure it worked that way.

For early fifty years he'd been held, locked into a place that made no sense and forced to endure the last moments of his life again and again. He'd almost gone insane in there—well, okay, maybe more than almost, but he was feeling better—and he would surely have lost his mind completely if he hadn't been the one to speak with their benefactor and plead their case.

Rufo was the only one of them who remained truly conscious throughout the long ordeal. He'd even been given a certain amount of freedom, been allowed to leave for short times and visit the living world of flesh, the better to prepare the others when the time came. It was both a sacrifice and a reward. For a time there had been some among them who would have been content to merely accept death, but Rufo worked on them, convinced them that a second chance was what they needed, just as their benefactor had convinced him.

He was their leader, and even Halston had accepted him as the general of their army. And he was damned if he'd let them down now because of the actions of one smarmy freak with a mean grin and a modicum of power.

He'd had Crowley where he wanted him, safely out of the way to allow the whole group their chance, but somehow that damned whelp from the Pageant family had ruined everything. When he'd asked for help, the whole game changed. One moment the Hunter had almost been theirs, and the next he was knocking them aside like they

were nothing more than guppies in a pond where he'd been
dropped in like a freshwater shark.

Rufo called out silently, rallying the troops—or the
troupe, depending on how one looked at the carnies—and
they responded, rising from their agony and moving toward the crowd of living, breathing killers in the stands. So
the Hunter interfered and spoiled some of the fun, so
what? They could still have their new bodies. They could
still get their revenge and cast the people of Serenity Falls
into the hell where they'd been stuck. The souls of the murderous town would be forfeit, and they would live again, albeit in new bodies and with new names.

Rufo allowed himself a smile as the victims of Serenity's sins charged, touching their new forms and pushing
forward, ready to cast down the very wretches who had
taken their lives. The cheering crowd continued laughing,
seeing what he wanted them to see and reveling in the
pleasure of a good carnival. Wouldn't they feel differently
in a few minutes, when the dead took hold of their
wretched lives and fed on their souls? His grin was so
broad that he thought he might actually tear a muscle or
two, but that was okay.

His smile died quickly when he saw the spirits he'd led
to this time and this place pushed back before they could
even gain a foothold on the bodies they sought as their
own. His dead grin became a scowl and then a roar of outrage as his brethren discovered along with him that the
Hunter had done something more than cause a little pain.
He had barred them from what they were promised.

There were limitations. Even the most powerful curses
have drawbacks. Once freed, once they managed the impossible and rose from death, the victims of the town had
only until midnight to gain new flesh or forfeit all they
had worked toward. There was still time, true, but not much

and certainly not enough to find new hosts for their spirits.
Rufo was fine, the four who were with him were fine, but
the rest would be screwed, and hard, if they couldn't find
new bodies.

And to complicate the entire damned situation, the dead
of Serenity, the people who'd brought them to this predica-
ment in the first place, joined them in the big top. They
were not here for new bodies. They were here to stop Rufo
from finishing his duty to the others.

They attacked, generations and generations of lost or
captured souls poured into the tent and attacked the troupe,
ready, it seemed, to do whatever it took to stop their descendants' possession and demise.

Spirit versus spirit, in a battle for the very life of
the town. And below him standing in the midst of it all,
untouched and smiling like a jackal, was Jonathan Crowley, the Hunter. The man spoke softly, but his voice carried
through the din. "I promised you'd have bodies. Here they
come."

Rufo looked around and saw nothing save the battle between the warring dead and the cheering crowds of people
who should have already been taken. Then, at last, he spotted them, the hosts that Crowley offered.

Rats. A seething mass of vermin vomited into the big
top, crawling over each other and the people who stood on
the ground nearest the entrance. The people kept laughing
and applauding, gasping with delight at the imagined show
Rufo granted them, unaware of the hundreds and hundreds
of rats that swarmed into the tent, chewing their way
through the leathery material and scurrying across the saw-
dusted ground, their faces glazed and their bodies moving
almost mechanically as they came.

Crowley turned away from him and walked toward the
opening in the tent, a tear made larger by the rodents still

swarming into the place. The man was laughing out loud now, his voice filled with good cheer. "Get 'em while they're hot, old son! They're the only ones your friends are going to get!"

Rufo screamed, infuriated, and came close to simply attacking the man, but he knew that was what the Hunter wanted. Instead he chose discretion and beckoned the rest of the clowns to do it for him. As always, they listened.

It took effort, more energy than Rufo should have spent, but he felt the time had come to end this before everything they'd worked so hard for fell apart irreparably. He called to their benefactor and felt the distant response. A moment later the four clowns began to change, becoming something more than merely possessed humans.

Crowley walked away, unaware of what was heading his way.

It was Rufo's turn to smile again.

IX

Lawrence stopped, the nerve endings in his body stretching taut and sending waves of pain through him. The entity within him felt a brief surge of panic, but it didn't last for more than a moment. His kind was never meant to possess a mere human for long. The energies that made up his essence were simply too powerful for most bodies to accept, and even those that could take them never lasted for more than a few hours under most circumstances. Being divided had weakened the force of his being enough to allow the mortals inhabited by him to retain their shape without fear of simply burning away. But now that he was partially complete again, the strain was proving too much for

Lawrence. That was a pity, really; he'd grown rather fond of the boy's form. Much as the part of him in Rebecca Glass had said before, he'd become rather attached to feeling human sensations. They were interesting and pleasantly distracting.

He looked around and saw that he'd almost reached his goal. The tent where Crowley and the rest of his essence were was just ahead of him. Between his goal and his body, he saw three items of moderate interest. The first was Becky Glass, now devoid of the energies that he'd granted her. She was battered and unconscious, her arms bound behind her back. The Lawrence part of him thought decidedly perverse things about the potential for fun with her in that condition. The part of him that held sway over the body saw instead a more sensible use for her. The second thing of interest was the unconscious form of Victor Barnes. The man was huge and could potentially make an ideal body for use in fighting Crowley.

And then he spotted the other body, the ruined creature that had been reborn from his breath. Lawrence smiled. There was enough here to take care of his problems. He just had to use it the right way.

Lawrence sat down on the ground, nearly oblivious to the sea of rodents that washed across the farm and battered at the tent. They came from every part of the area, drawn to the circus as surely as if the Pied Piper had called them. They were inconsequential.

He spoke softly, the lips of the host body splitting with each word as his power manifested more completely. The host didn't really matter anymore. He had a new idea. The rats started avoiding contact with him when his clothes began to smolder.

X

The four clowns moved toward Crowley with violence in their eyes and a promise of death in their every stride. "Hey, rube!" The words matched up with the actions of the first clown. The flabby but muscular man who first got to meet the Hunter on the field of combat grabbed his shoulder, spinning him around and swinging a meaty hand at his face. Crowley dropped backwards under the swing, his leg moving up in counterpoint and kicking the clown in the stomach. It was rather like kicking a stone wall. Whatever else could be said for Rufo and his friends, they definitely weren't pushovers.

Crowley liked that. He hated when there wasn't a challenge involved in the job. He pushed with his foot against the gaudy abdomen, having to satisfy himself with the body staggering backwards. The clown, red hair flying and bright smile converted into a snarl, landed hard on top of one of his cohorts. Crowley took the opportunity presented to get back to his feet properly.

He got into a proper stance just in time for a short, bald clown with a painted-on five o' clock shadow and a battered old derby to take a jab at his face. Crowley's head snapped back, and he felt a wash of blood flowing from his nose. The clown grinned and jumped toward him with a whooping battle cry. He was dead a few seconds later, his neck and arm broken.

Crowley didn't wait for the others to think about it. He attacked with a ferocity that was nearly impossible to believe. Bert Calhoun—Dexie the Dunce while in his makeup—a large, angular man with more bone than meat under his baggy pantsuit, tried to take a bite out of Crowley's hand. He got a mouthful of his own teeth instead when Crowley drove his fist forward hard enough to slice the skin on his own knuckles. Dexie stepped back with both hands over his mouth, mumbling obscenities past what remained of his split lips, and dropped like a stone when the blade of the Hunter's hand cut across his esophagus. Crowley enjoyed devastating him; his grin was almost glowing when the man fell, his back broken and his face bloodied and pulped. Rufo shook his head, unbelieving. This was all going wrong, horribly wrong, and their benefactor was nowhere to be found.

As Crowley broke the third of his friends, Rufo began to feel the first real inklings of fear. The man was both efficient and sadistic, his smile eager and pleased with each sound of things breaking that he heard coming from the clowns he grabbed. Mikey let out a shriek of agony when the Hunter drove stiffened fingers into his brown eyes, and only stopped screaming when Crowley forced his head back until his neck broke under the merciless pressure. Rufo wasn't liking this one little bit. "Damn you! Why can't you leave us alone!"

Crowley landed on Punch's chest with both knees, knocking him into the ground and rolling off the stunned clown with the grace normally only granted to cats. "Because Dave asked me nicely."

Rufo started off of the stage himself and then stopped when he saw Crowley drive the heel of his foot into Punch's sternum hard enough to let his shoe sink in by several inches. There had to be a better way. That thing wasn't human, no matter how it looked. He wasn't ready to die again, not after so short a time back in the world.

And then, as Crowley kicked into his latest target, a voice called out, loud, almost booming, and Rufo grinned. The voice came from outside of the tent proper and was high enough in the air that it couldn't possibly come from a man.

XI

Do the dead dream? Possibly. The hound had been dreaming just moments before, a lovely mental movie of chasing
down the bad man who had killed those children in this
very location so long ago. It was a dream he'd had a thousand times or more over the years since he'd been pushed
from his body.

His dreams were the only thing he'd had for a long time,
until the strange thing had come and drawn him into its
body and then breathed him on the pup. After that his
dreams had faded for a while, replaced by the joy of actually being alive, actually doing something again for the
first time in decades.

He was not without direction. He'd been summoned by
the strange thing to do the bidding of the voice that even
now echoed in the back of his head like a distant buzzing
noise that wouldn't leave him alone. He'd been hesitant to
do what the voice told him at first: despite what most people believed of him, he was not normally a killer. But in
the end he'd had no choice. The voice got louder and
louder if he disobeyed, became a thunderous roar that
deafened him to everything but the command it uttered,
until he did as he was told. It wasn't merely inconvenient;
it was excruciating.

The voice was still there even as he woke from his
dreams and was drawn to the strange thing again, commanded by the otherworldly voice inside the human pup
and forced to touch the strange thing that hid within the human pup's skin. He did not like the strange thing. It was not
a pleasant creature, though he found it oddly appealing
when it was in the girl-pup's skin.

He was summoned, and the siren call of the voice min-
gled with the summons from the strange thing, becoming

one demand. He was drawn to the man-pup and did as he was commanded; his essence moved into the body occupied by more than it should ever be able to hold and grabbed the strange thing in his jaws and pulled it to him. There was a strange feeling of tearing, a wrenching away from the anchors of the flesh to the spirit, and then he was free, his prize held in his jaws, to go back to the ruin of his own body. And as he settled once more into his own flesh, the strange thing swallowed him and was in turn swallowed by him.

There was heat and there was pain and there was the sudden twisting pull of being reborn a second time, given another chance to live and breathe and finally see his friends again, the ones who had traveled with him and fed him and kept him safe.

The strange thing's voice was gone, replaced by thoughts that were both his and not his. But then, even his body was different now, stronger and structured in ways that made little or no sense. He could never have walked if the strange thing had not had practice with this new form, so different from what had always been in the past.

The hound rose on two legs, flexing arms instead of forepaws. It sniffed the air and looked toward the gaudy tent that grew from the ground. Its muzzle shifted into what could best be called a grin and then, because it felt good to be alive again, it howled, the sound almost loud enough to drown out the voice.

Legs that were wrong and awkward moved forward, hands that should never have been flexed reached for the dead-smelling canvas, tearing it aside with ease. The hound reveled in the feeling and at the same time realized that it had no say as to what exactly the body did. That was all right. That was just fine. For now it would be satisfied to see old friends and to seek out the one who had killed it last.

The hound had never taken well to being hurt, and being killed just plain pissed it off.

XII

The behemoth that came through the tent's fabric roared its challenge, and the hair on Dave's head vibrated from the sheer volume. Dave Pageant looked at the thing that tore through the tent's side and blanched. He recognized nothing at all about the creature that snarled and gnashed at Jonathan Crowley. The thing stood almost nine feet in height, and if he had to make a guess, it weighed in at roughly the same weight as his father's tractor. The body wasn't human, but there were similarities. It had two arms, two legs, and a torso; beyond that . . . not really all that much. The arms were massive, thick with muscles that corded beneath a layer of fur. The legs were all wrong, looking more like they belonged on an animal than on anything remotely akin to Homo sapiens. The feet were little more than paws that stretched up into powerful calves that bent backwards and grew up to knees shaped in ways that made little sense. The thighs were easily as thick as Dave's waist, and led up to a furry abdomen that looked more like a barrel than a stomach and hips. The chest was heavily furred and led up to a head that belonged on the meanest dog Dave had ever seen in his nightmares. But there was something wrong—aside from the fact that the damned thing shouldn't have existed at all— with the hide on the thing. It was flaking and splitting in places where the joints moved too much, almost like a snake's skin that had dried and was ready to fall away.

Crowley turned his whole body, breaking the last of Rufo's reserves in the process. The last clown fell, dead again, as the Hunter turned to face the thing in front of him. All around them, the rats swarmed.

"Enough! I have had enough of you and your damned games, Hunter!" The voice was one part growl and two parts hiss past lips that belonged on a canine. It spoke with Lawrence's voice. Dave watched the thing moving toward Jonathan Crowley and heard the tones and inflections of Lawrence—albeit a large and rabid Lawrence—and wondered what exactly was going on.

Whatever Crowley was—and Dave had already decided the man wasn't quite as human as he looked—the thing he was up against was apparently willing to turn him into confetti. It hit him hard, the flesh on the thing's body splitting away to reveal something dark and covered in viscera with claws like knives. The claws scraped down Crowley's chest, leaving bleeding trenches in their wake. The thing hit him four more times before he could react, hissing like a boiler ready to blow the entire time.

Crowley went down, and Rufo started grinning. He shifted around so that his face was close to Dave, and Dave could see that disturbing smile go wider and wider. "Maybe this won't be so bad after all, young Master Pageant." He placed his foot on Dave's back again, just as he was trying to stand, and pinned him in place.

Dave watched as Jonathan Crowley went down and lost what little hope he'd had going. This was going to be bad. The monster's hide sloughed off in heavy flakes of skin and fur even as it made a wet, steamy noise and slammed into Crowley's prone form, practically climbing on top of the fallen man like a lover. "I'm going to feast on your heart, Hunter. I'm going to shit on your body, and then I'm going to burn what's left of you."

Dave tried to stand up, but there were things in him that were hurting more than he would have ever thought possible. He made a few noises of his own, sounds that were too much like when his father had killed Porky, his almost pet pig, a few years ago for a family get-together. It was embarrassing, and he hated it.

Rufo moved around a bit and promptly sat on his back, his legs sprawled out to either side. "Where do you think YOU're going?"

"Guh-get offa me . . ." His voice was a squeak. The thing was skinny, but it was heavy! He pushed with his arms but couldn't get any leverage. "Damn it, Amber! A little help here, please!"

He heard Amber gasp, a sound he was familiar with. She made that exact noise every time she woke up. Sometimes he wondered if it was something that was unhealthy, like a breathing problem. Right then, he was just glad to hear it. "What? Hey! Get offa him!" He'd never been so glad to hear his sister's voice.

Amber Pageant was slim and pretty and just about the right build for a model. There was a reason that so many of the local boys tried to get into her pants, and it wasn't just because of her reputation. What more than a few men had learned over the years was that she was also much stronger than she looked. Amber grew up on a farm, and she had done her share of chores since she was knee high to a grape. She was also raised in a large family that was known for settling arguments with their fists when necessary.

Loosely translated: when she tackled Rufo, he noticed. He and she both rolled off Dave and hit the hard stage floor, rolling once before she wound up on top of him. She cocked back her fist and hit the clown in the face, but as with her brother before, it seemed to have little effect. Rufo reached up and grabbed her around her neck, lifting her just enough to make her choke and gag against his bloodied glove. Amber's face turned almost as red as her hair, and she started struggling, shaking and bucking her body as her hands clawed at the sequined sleeve of his jacket.

That was enough for Dave. He got up, his eyes tearing and his vision getting all wonky as he charged the clown.

Rather than trying to hit him again, he got up behind his sister, pressing his weight down on her shoulders to help with his balance, and cocked back his leg.

The punt he landed on Rufo's testicles would have done any kicker in the NFL proud. Amber kicked away, choking and gagging, her lungs taking in great gasps of breath. Rufo was making similar sounds, but they didn't sound quite as healthy. Dave kicked him again and again, his blurred vision shifting toward red.

Then he jumped back, fully expecting the clown to attack again. Fortunately, Rufo looked a little occupied.

The air all around them moved; the cloudy figures that had once surrounded Crowley looked almost like they were dancing in zero gravity. But if so, they danced without partners. Or at least without partners he could see.

Dave grabbed Amber's arm and pulled, but stopped that nonsense just as soon as his ribs started trying to break out of his chest. Something had to be broken. He couldn't figure how anything could hurt that much and not be broken. "Uhh . . . Owwwie . . ." He blinked back tears and looked to Amber, where she was starting to rise. She grimaced at him and grabbed his hand, pulling him faster than he really felt good with.

Dave looked over his shoulder and saw Rufo still on the ground, holding himself and rocking slowly. It was nice to know the bastard could feel real pain. He looked over farther and saw what had been the dog-thing holding Crowley to the ground, his fingers driving hard into the soft flesh of the man's shoulders. Only a few shreds of the previous skin remained, but what was underneath was sleek and gray and seemed to have a skin that was scaly in the same way as a lizard. Even the face had changed, becoming less canine and more reptilian. The rats were everywhere, crawling over each other, a writhing carpet of living things that left half of Crowley buried under them. And still the crowds in the stands cheered on, oblivious to what was happening. He wondered what they were seeing and hearing, but it really didn't matter too much. He had to get to Jessie and Suzette. Amber pulled him on, and he lost sight of the thing that was still changing, becoming a different nightmare even as it continued its onslaught on the man pinned under it.

But he still heard Lawrence's voice in the monster as it screamed at Jonathan Crowley, "Give me back! Do you hear me? Give me back!"

Crowley was lost from sight, but he heard the man laughing in response.

Dave reached Jessie at the same time that Amber let go of his hand and started shaking her twin. Both of the girls seemed to come out of the sleeping state they'd been in with ease. Both of them looked around and almost immediately started to panic. Dave glanced around and decided he couldn't really blame them.

There were four dead bodies on the ground, but unless you knew it, you wouldn't be able to tell. Between the misty figures moving around in the air and the sea of rodents, it was almost impossible to see much of anything.

Then he saw the lizard thing rise from the sea of chaos, screaming, his hands clutched to his face, the wicked talons on his fingers completely ignored as he tried to stanch the flow of blood from his eyes. The sound he made was something between nails scraping roughly down a chalkboard and an eagle's screech. Crowley came up after him, and even through the murk, he could see the gaping wounds all over the man's body.

Crowley was just attacking again, planting a savage kick into the monster's scaly face, when the ocean of rats suddenly froze. The air stopped its turbulent activity, growing still, and the figures that had been fighting moved

slowly, their vague heads looking down and seeking something, though Dave couldn't have said what.

The only sound that came to him was the scream of the
thing over Jonathan Crowley, and Dave felt for him in that
instant but forced the thought away. It had the voice of
Lawrence—not so much in pitch but in speech patterns—
and if it was the kid he saw at school all the time, then it
was fair to say that Lawrence wasn't Lawrence anymore.
He was something different, and Dave didn't figure much
of Lawrence was left beyond what stood there with blood
vomiting from its eyes, if his ears weren't deceiving him.
He grabbed Jessie's arm, and they ran, with him leading
Jessie and Amber leading Suzette. There wasn't any way
around it, so he made his way to the stage stairs, climbing
down into the frozen rodents and forcing a path through
them with hard kicks of his legs that swept the animals into
the air and away from them all. The path didn't last for
very long. More vermin fell into the vacant space, filling
the void as quickly as Dave made it. The feel of the hot
furry bodies against his legs and feet was enough to make
him want to curl up and die.

He pushed on anyway, oblivious to the tears in his eyes
and the fact that he was screaming himself hoarse. He
pushed past Crowley and the Lawrence-voiced thing, trying not to see the almost tarlike skin under the few places
where it still had remnants of the previous flesh. Whatever
the Hunter was doing was taking time, but it was also apparently working. The nightmare seemed to have shrunk in
size again.

Jessie was screaming, and he lost his grip on her when
she fell and landed on still more rats. The animals didn't
even flinch, they just lay flattened by her weight as she
fell, breaking the bones of over a dozen of the animals.
He thought it would never end, but eventually they got to the
opening where the vermin had forced their way in, and

he pulled Jessie through after him as he climbed outside of
the great tent.

Dave made it another four feet before he fell to the
ground, not overly far from where Becky Glass and Victor Barnes both lay unconscious. He joined them in the
darkness.

XIII

Rufo rose just in time to see his hopes and dreams for retribution shattered.

As he managed to stand himself back up—a feat that required more than he would have imagined when it came to
concentration—he surveyed what was left of his forces.
The dead of Serenity Falls were paying a visit to the dead
murdered by Serenity, and it didn't look like either side
was exactly winning. Familiar faces—those he loved and
those he hated—struggled against each other, but there was
really no way to decide if one group or the other was going
to win the struggle.

And then everything changed. One second he was watching the strange dance of the dead, a war between those who
had lived in town and those who merely came to visit. The
next second the tides of battle shifted in a way that he'd
never have expected. He felt his very essence pulled at,
clawed at roughly, and he held onto his new body only
through desperate strength and a will to continue living
again. The others did not manage to stand so well. His ears
nearly felt ready to shatter from the sounds of their
screams, a cacophony that none of the living could hear,
save perhaps for the Hunter. And did Jonathan Crowley's

smile grow wider in that moment, even as the demon beating on him ripped into his side with barbed talons? Yes, Rufo was almost certain it did.

The spirits of his friends and fellow escapees from death were drawn down, pulled roughly, their forms tearing apart and their very beings ripped into jagged fragments. Each spectral ally was granted what had been promised but not in the way expected. The ghosts of Serenity Falls' victims were drawn into the rats that survived. No exact number was needed to let Rufo know that there were far more rodents than there were wraiths. A fraction of a spirit went into each of the vermin.

The battle was over, and the verdict was a draw. The dead of Serenity Falls, the only ones left, fled the tent, almost as if they were drawn away from it by something too strong to resist.

Rufo stood in the center of the ring and stared, his face impassive but his eyes showing his hatred.

All around him the crowds of living natives to Serenity continued their celebration of the carnival that only they could see. Slowly Rufo smiled.

All was not lost. At least there could still be revenge.

Rufo didn't need to fight his way through the rodent army. They were scattering on their own. He noticed the bodies of his friends among the casualties. The rats had apparently been hungry. They seemed to have liked the flavor of the other clowns in the big top.

Rufo didn't need a door, either. He merely touched the surface of the tent, and it opened for him like an eager lover ready to obey.

XIV

Crowley finally lost his patience. He'd hoped that he could save all three of the children that had been taken by the thing in his pocket. The creature in front of him was looking a lot more familiar, though he couldn't quite place all of its parts just yet. He knew the hellhound was in there, and he was pretty sure Lawrence Grey was in there, but he was still trying to puzzle out the last part. The part that mattered most to him was the boy, though that was going to change and soon if the thing didn't stop tearing into him. He was trying to defend himself and not hurt it, but there were limits. He felt what had been Lawrence Grey sink teeth into his neck and gave up any hope of bowling a perfect game. The fact that he still couldn't figure out what it was or how it knew him was no longer important. It was frustrating but not a priority. The only thing that mattered was the pain.

Crowley brought both of his hands up and shoved his thumbs into the canine ears on the monster's head, pushing hard and hooking his nails into the tender insides. It let go of his throat with a bark of pain, and he struck it on the snout with a blow from his forehead. As it tried to recover from the double assault, Crowley bucked his body hard, unsettling it from its perch on his stomach.

He wrote himself a mental note about the kid and promised himself he'd see to a proper burial if he had to. Then he went on the offensive.

Crowley swayed on his feet and still managed to grin. The wounds he'd suffered earlier in the evening were now gone. And his more recent ones were closing, though the warmth running down from his throat was a little worrisome. It lashed out, slamming its meaty hands into his shoulders, trying to push him back down to the ground. He reached out and started playing dirty again. His hands hooked into the eyes of the thing, and it reared back, taking a few inches of his hide with it when it let go of his shoulders. Still more monster crap covered his hands, and he was too tired to properly enjoy it, but he took some small satisfaction.

He moved quickly, dodging the thing's wild swings. It blinked bloody eyelids and shook its long head, trying to clear its vision. Crowley looked for an opening and then closed in fast.

"You know what you did wrong, sweet pea?" Crowley grabbed the head of the thing and held it tightly in his hands, forcing the damned thing to face him. "You never told me your name."

He whispered the words right into the creature's ear and felt the power of the words assault it. His hands bucked, knocked away from the thing that had been Lawrence Grey, and saw as well as felt the presence that had given him chase since New York City forced from the boy's ravaged body.

The monster's—*Lawrence Grey's?*—corpse hit the ground and stayed there. The entity that had been giving him so much trouble looked for another form to possess and, finding none, tried to flee. He couldn't afford to let it go free, so he snatched the pulsing thing from the air and gripped it in his hands again, feeling it writhe and sting and fight back against his grip.

Crowley turned away, no longer smiling. He was disgusted and bitter. He'd failed again. True, he seldom let himself dwell on the failures, but this one was fresh, and it annoyed him. The crowd was still cheering for a few moments, but even as he noticed them, their almost frantic applause and laughter started to fade. The audience slowed until finally the sounds of excitement were abruptly replaced with confusion and murmured questions. The people of Serenity and the few visitors who found themselves in their midst started looking around as if they'd suddenly found themselves in a foreign place. Several of them stood up and moved toward the hole in the side of the tent. They stumbled as they walked and muttered dazedly to themselves. Others started to follow, almost instantly creating a bottleneck, but changed their minds when the leathery wall sealed itself.

Crowley looked around, his eyes scanning over the crowd and looking in all the places he could think of to check and saw that the circus clown with the top hat was gone. He frowned, trying to figure out what else was wrong. The people inside were starting to panic, and that distracted the hell out of him. "Do you mind? I'm trying to work here." The words were mumbled and muted. Surely no one around him even noticed, especially not with all of them looking so panicky.

They were doing their best to find the exit based solely on where it had been. Their best wasn't very good. Crowley pushed past a few of them and finally made his way to the flexing leathery wall. It actually smelled worse than it had before, and he had to fight off the urge to retch.

He grabbed the stuff between his hands and pulled, but this time nothing happened. He tried again, his hands tugging and his arms straining, feeling a little satisfaction when it started to tear at last.

The satisfaction was short lived. Half a second after the wall was torn apart like a tissue paper wall, he saw Rufo outside smiling broadly. "You had your choices, Hunter. I'd expected better from you."

Jonathan Crowley felt the gasoline hit him, splashing across his face and spraying out over the ground around him. He turned his face quickly, his eyes closing against the pain he knew was coming his way. His eyes only caught the smallest amount, but still they watered and felt like they were on fire. All around him the people who'd been doing

their best to get through to the outside were now beating a
hasty retreat, and he just couldn't blame them. The very
thought of burning again made him want to run, to scream.
He could still feel the memory of fire ripping across nerve
endings and boiling over his eyes. Crowley whimpered, his
hands moving fast to protect him from any flame that might
come his way. Oh God, he never wanted to feel that again,
not in a million years. He backed away even farther, and
then made himself stop. How long had it been since his
knees actually shook? He couldn't say, but they were doing
it now. Still, there were responsibilities to take care of, much
as he might loathe them. There was more to consider than
his own comfort.

His mind made up, he headed for the newly torn entrance
again, just as Rufo smiled warmly and produced a Zippo
lighter. Jonathan Crowley had just enough time for his eyes
to go wide before the grinning clown dropped the lighter
and danced away from the spillage near his own feet.

He heard the *fwoomph!* of the gasoline catching ablaze
at the same time that the heat ran across the ground and
reached his own body. Once the danger was there, his mind
cleared of panic. He'd have understood everything about
those four moments in Victor Barnes's life, the ones where
everything around him became so very crystal clear. For
Crowley, it had happened many more times, but the experience never lost its intensity.

The flames ran across his body, burning only the gasoline for the moment, but he knew that wouldn't last. The
people around him caught fire as well, most of them frozen
with panic and understandable fear. The blaze ran greedy
fingers over the tent, and the wall near him, so determined
not to give way to him a moment before, apparently didn't
have the same durability when it came to fire. Crowley
threw himself over the floor and rolled again and again,
trying to extinguish the flames that were covering him. He

held his breath, knowing better than to even think of inhaling. His heartbeat pounded in his skull like a bass drum, and the world kept tilting over and over as he rolled. The gasoline was both a curse and a blessing. On the one hand, it burned too damned well for his comfort. On the other hand, the oily fuel actually gave him a small amount of protection: the flames burned the fuel first, and then aimed for the flesh. He managed to get himself extinguished before he got more than minor injuries. He looked around with wide eyes, panting harshly and stepping back from the pool of fire that was turning the grass near him black.

The good folks of Serenity Falls were starting to burn and starting to scream. Pain broke paralysis with ease, and pure unadulterated terror was quick to take the place of shock. Several people were rapidly becoming full-scale conflagrations, beating at their own bodies with hands that only helped spread the fires. Others were trying to escape; beating at the parts of the tent that weren't already on fire. A woman he'd last seen going into church on his first Sunday in Serenity charged toward the growing wall of burning tent and tried to push through it, her eyes closed and her voice calling to the Lord for protection. It's just possible He was listening; she tore through and stumbled out into the cool evening air without actually setting herself ablaze.

Crowley took a deep breath and followed her, darting through the opening and again slapping at the parts of his clothing that reignited. There was nothing he could do for any of them from inside the tent, and very likely little he could do for them from outside it, but he would at least try. He saw Barnes standing next to the tent, almost roasting alive from the heat, and was amazed. The man was a walking list of injuries, but he kept coming back for more. He figured he could like a guy like the constable, if he were to allow himself the luxury of friends.

Crowley managed to barely miss tripping over Dave Pageant, who was flat on his back and breathing heavily. He saw several people on the ground, more than he'd expected. In addition to the girl he and Barnes had been forced to knock senseless, he saw the Pageant boy, his twin sisters, and his girlfriend. Dave had been in a fight and had been wounded, so he might be excused, but the twins and the little girl with him had barely seen anything remotely like combat. There was something more than injuries or exhaustion at work and, frankly, he was getting a little tired of the whole mess.

He promised himself he'd do something about it and soon. First, however, there was the fire to consider. He could hear the sound of the runoff from the quarry and the falls splashing heavily and was glad he'd decided to start the pumps earlier. Ghosts and fire were both present, and running water had its advantages. He grabbed the woman who'd dodged through the fire and screamed at her to get the people to the river. Dazed as she was, she nodded her round face and started pointing at them and yelling. The water was half an acre away, but it would have to do and at least the way to it was mostly level. He looked down at Dave Pageant and then crouched over him. His hand slapped hard enough to rock the boy's face. Dave let out a yelp as Crowley's fingers touched the cut on his cheek, and his eyes fluttered open. "Your farm, boy! Get the sprinklers or whatever the hell you have going, and do it now!" To his credit, the kid got up and ran for the farmhouse.

That was all he could do, really. He couldn't go back into the massive burning tent. His skin was still coated in gasoline, and he wouldn't do anyone any good dead, least of all himself. Besides, somewhere out there a clown was cackling at having caught him ablaze, and he didn't like that one little bit.

The tent screamed as he started running back toward

Serenity proper. He shivered at the idea that it had felt everything from the beginning, and shivered again at the thought that it was feeling the flames that were burning it apart. Crowley ran faster, his legs cutting across the distance at high speed, telling himself it was just the need to get other things done that made him run so hard.

XV

Victor Barnes woke up to the sounds of panicked screams. His reflexes took over, and he awoke quickly, alert and ready to act. At least mentally. His body still hurt like hell. He looked to his left and saw the girl he'd been fighting, lying unconscious on the ground. To his right, the tent was burning, rapidly being swallowed by flames that didn't just burn but consumed everything around them. There were more people outside than there were before, but not as many as he would have liked. He rushed toward the burning big top and tried to pull the doors open, his leg dragging behind him and barely supporting his weight. The blood was still flowing freely, and he felt lightheaded as he moved. He got to the entrance of the tent—which apparently was not as close as he remembered, since he had to move much farther than he'd expected—and pulled it open, his fingers singeing almost instantly.

Barnes pulled hard, feeling the fabric tear as he threw his weight into the task of opening the damned tent completely. As soon as the hide was pulled back, the insides of the thing began spilling out. Smoke and flames and heat assaulted him, and so did the sight of people burning. Jonathan Crowley was the second one out, after a woman who screamed out to Jesus as she ran. Crowley's hair was singed and his face blistered. What little clothing he had left on caught ablaze as he dove through to the outside. He rolled across the ground, slapping at the licking fires that moved over him.

The heat was worse than Barnes could have imagined; his fingers felt like they were bubbling from the intensity, and he had to let go of the tent. He watched Crowley grab a middle-aged woman with a face as round as the full moon and bark orders at her, and for a moment he felt the world go gray again. When he could see clearly once more, Crowley was running away from the tent and the farm, and Dave Pageant was moving into the main house, his blood-ied face determined.

Vic shook himself and bit down on his own bottom lip, taking the sharp pain like a slap on the face and letting it direct his mind back to the present. He yanked at the tent's opening again. The fabric he held in his hands seemed to fight against him, determined to slip from his scalding fin-gers. He watched people pouring through the wound in the material, some actually burning as they ran, and saw the moon-faced woman Crowley had spoken to pushing them down the hill, away from the farm and toward the distant stream. Some of them moved quickly, others fell and had to force themselves back to their feet or get help from still others. The tent writhed against his hands, the fabric pushed by the people spilling out into the cool, fresh air. With a mind of its own the peeled-back material bucked and writhed, finally pulling free from his hand where it flapped back against the rest of the tent, leaving a trail of smoke to mark its passage. As it landed close to the rest, the damned thing sealed itself. He grunted and reached for it, making himself focus on the people inside and not the pain he was about to endure. Just the same, he heard himself whimpering.

But as if it were reading his mind, the flames from the

tent grew brighter and hotter, spilling outward amid the screams from the people still trapped inside the leathery, reeking tent. The colorful big top blackened, the color and illusion of mere fabric falling away as it caught fire.

Victor Barnes was forced back, the blazing tent becoming too hot to even stand near. From within its depths he heard wailing screams of pain, tortured sounds that were loud enough to almost deafen him. Lord, how he wished they would rupture his eardrums to get away from the cacophony. The hair on his head smoldered, and he backed away again as the tent started splitting, great gaping holes appearing in the sides and billowing out sheets of fire that roared at the heavens. Whatever truly held the massive structure together collapsed, sending flaming streaks of matter into the air and fire belching from every rent in the material. From inside the screams continued, and Vic hopped backward, slipping and falling to the ground, helpless to stop it. In a matter of moments, it was too late for anything that might still be alive inside the ruin. The tent fell in on itself in an explosion of flaming debris, cinders rising toward the heavens and spiraling away from the heat on massive gusts of escaping air. Less than three minutes after it started, the fire claimed the lives of most of Serenity's population.

A minute after that, the sprinkler system for the farm kicked in, spraying jets of cold water through the air in arcs that carried for twenty feet or more. Dave Pageant had finally managed to get the waterworks started, just exactly soon enough to be of no use. Victor Barnes stared at the blazing mass not fifteen feet away from him, blinking back the cool drops of water that splashed over him.

CHAPTER 6

I

Mike Blake awoke to a pounding headache that centered itself just above his left eye and insisted on doing what it could to drill through the center of his skull. His eyes felt glued shut, and he soon realized they were. His own blood had started to dry over his face, and the resulting mess was decidedly sticky. He tried to sit up and knew half a second later that he'd made a hideous mistake. Whatever else was wrong with him, his stomach was feeling particularly treacherous.

He stayed exactly where he was, barely breathing, until his insides decided they were calm enough to let him move again. Then he used his hands to pry his eyelids apart and took a look around him.

And remembered where he was and what had happened to the woman he loved. He crawled over to Amelia, barely aware of the whimpering sounds he was making. He looked down at her slender body and the blooms of drying blood across her stomach and chest and felt the tears threatening to spill. In his mind he saw Amy's body skinned and tormented, superimposed over the form of his lover. Mike's mouth opened and closed, trying, he supposed, to make prayers to a God he'd long since given up on. The words wouldn't come, and that seemed appropriate somehow.

His hands tore at her blouse, ripping the delicate material away in an effort to assess the damage. His eyes looked at the flesh he'd caressed, kissed, and adored, looked at the dried gore that covered it, and he tentatively reached out a hand to see if he could find a pulse. He found no heartbeat, but he also found no wounds.

"A-Amelia? Honey?" His voice shook, but there were words again. His mind was slowly sliding back onto the tracks and moving forward, though cautiously. *I saw the bullets hit . . . I saw her shot . . . Where are the wounds?* Mike's breaths came faster and faster, his mind starting to really make connections. *'S not possible, but they're gone . . . her skin is perfect.*

Mike settled his head down between her breasts, trying to hear anything at all, a weak breath, a single heartbeat, any sound that might say there was still life in Amelia's body.

Amelia moaned softly, her eyes opening and closing a few times before recognition came to her. She smiled, and Mike pulled her close, holding her tightly, his entire body trembling. "Oh, God, I thought you were dead, uh . . . I I thought you were dead . . ." He broke apart then, letting himself cry. And she sighed softly, her thin arms going around his neck, hugging him closer still and rocking him. From somewhere off in the distance he heard the sounds of people screaming faintly, a noise he'd normally have gone off to investigate, but that at the moment meant nothing at all to him.

A short while later, Amelia broke the hug and pushed

him gently away, looking around at their surroundings. If her torn clothing bothered her, she showed no sign of it.

"Where's Jonathan?"

Mike looked at her and shook his head. "I dunno. Maybe he's still at the hospital."

"Where's the constable, either of them?"

Mike frowned, letting himself remember what all had happened, letting himself remember being shot, Amelia's getting shot right in front of him by Jack Michaels of all people. "I don't know . . . Why the hell did he shoot at us?" He shook his head, puzzled, and was aware of the painful throb of the wound he'd received in his scalp. He let his fingers slide past the drying tears on his face and felt the bloody mess and the growing knot under his skin. "Maybe we should go to the hospital ourselves, Amelia . . ."

"Oh, Mike, honey . . ." She was there in an instant, her delicate fingers touching the edges of his wound, her face frowning. "Yes, I think the hospital is exactly where we need to be."

They started toward Mike's old car, his hand fishing into his jeans. "Maybe I better let you drive." He staggered a bit, feeling a wave of dizziness crawl through his skull.

Amelia got behind the wheel, and they were off a few moments later. She drove with care, and Mike admired her ability to be calm. At least when he wasn't considering the fact that he'd seen her die. He made himself ignore the latter part, not really sure if he could trust any of his memories after taking a bullet across his head.

"There's a fire at the edge of town . . . down where we saw that thing growing."

Mike looked through the trees and saw that, sure enough, Amelia was right. A blaze from down where the farms were was burning furiously. But even as he watched the blaze from between the trees, he could see the fire getting smaller. He also saw something else; a thick column that looked almost like smoke breaking away from the trail of sparks carried by the wind. It was fully dark out now; the sun had set and the moon was barely risen, but he could see the smoke clearly, almost as if it glowed. The breeze moved a column of sparks and black smoke away from the town, but that serpentine second trail moved toward Serenity proper. *Bullet hit me harder than I thought. First I'm imagining my girlfriend is dead, and now I'm seeing glow-in-the-dark smoke trails. Good thing we're on our way to see someone about it.* His stomach did a few backflips deep inside of him, and he grunted.

But even as he thought the words, he knew they were wrong. Something was moving against the wind, and it looked like it was on a collision course with where he was going. The car turned hard to the right as they left Blackwell Road, and Mike felt his brain turn in the opposite direction.

He drifted into unconsciousness while wondering if the cloud heading toward Serenity Falls was dangerous. It was.

II

Joey Whitman was lost. There was just no way around it. He should have been able to find his way through the woods with the greatest of ease—he'd traveled through them for years, after all—but it wasn't working out that way. Jonathan Crowley had left him on his own, and he'd been fine with that at first, certain that he would get back to his house long before dark. But now it was well past sunset, and he was stuck in the woods, and there was no way in hell he was ever going to get home unless he stumbled across a path.

The problem seemed to be that all of the paths were gone. Even the ones he knew should be off to his right and just ahead of him. If he were walking through a pencil sketch, the trails couldn't have been better erased.

He was okay with that. Not really thrilled, but it was survivable despite the bitter cold weather. He was just fine with the whole thing, except now he was hearing other sounds in the woods. Sounds like heavy footsteps and the occasional deep laugh that seemed to echo from damned near everywhere.

Fair to say that Joey was a decent kid and certainly not a coward, but there were limits to how much he really wanted to deal with at this point. He'd been trapped with something else in his body, and he'd been stuck with one of the scariest men he'd ever met for half the day.

He was scared, and the longer he kept hearing the sounds, the worse it got. But he was also tired of what was going on and slowly getting angrier and angrier. *The good thing about the woods,* he mused, *is that there's always something around you can use as a weapon. Sticks, rocks, the occasional thorn bush.*

Joey found a nice, heavy stick that looked like it could cause a little damage and kept walking. He figured if the footsteps got too close, he'd just swing first and apologize to anyone he shouldn't have hit later.

He had to stop himself from taking wild swipes at every noise he heard, wanting to make good and damned sure that when he did attack, it would count. It was easy to be deceived by the almost perfect silence. Mostly he heard the wind sighing through the trees or the sound of his own footsteps crunching through the grass. He didn't want to turn around, didn't want to risk letting whoever or whatever was following him know that he was on to that little fact. And while it was easy to think strategically, it was much, much harder to follow through on his own plan. Almost as hard as it was not to just run screaming or break into tears.

But he managed to be calm enough to execute his plan properly. He listened, and made himself take small breaths, and when he heard the sound of someone moving behind him shuffling through the mulch and small plants, he made himself be patient to the point where he thought he would surely scream or have a heart attack while waiting.

And when that someone was close enough that he could hear their breathing, he swung his makeshift bat as hard as he could. The sound of the stick cutting air was almost as loud as the scream that came from the person following him.

Either his aim was off or she was faster than he'd ever thought possible. The thick branch slammed into Charlene Lyons's crossed forearms with enough impact to make him drop the stick. Her loud shriek didn't help him steady his nerves.

Under most circumstances, Charlee Lyons would probably have kicked his ass roughly two seconds after he'd pulled a stunt like that. She wasn't known for being mild mannered, and he'd seen her take down a guy or two in her day and for far smaller offenses.

But then, she wasn't normally already hurt. His eyes had long since adjusted to the darkness, and he could see her well enough to know that something was very, very wrong. Her hair was too short, less than half the length he was used to seeing, and her skin looked mottled. Joey moved in closer as she fell to the ground in tears, trying to hold both of her arms in her hands and sobbing openly.

He lowered himself down next to her and saw that the strange discolorations were blisters. Her clothes were scorched, and her flesh had taken a beating, too. He stood up and lifted her as gently as he could, helping her to her feet. There was no way in hell he could carry her anywhere; she was as tall as him and at least as muscular. But he could help her. He knew he could.

He looked around in the near-perfect darkness and saw the paths that had eluded him before. It was only around a mile or so to the medical center from where they were. He was pretty sure he could find his way.

Despite her burns, or maybe because of them, she was shivering. He took off his shirt and wrapped it softly over her shoulders as she slowly wound down from her crying jag. He didn't speak, and neither did she. They just walked.

III

There were sounds out there, in the distance, leading toward the farm. The Pageant family heard them and despite the urge to go out and investigate, they listened to the patriarch of the family when he said they had to stay inside. Earl Pageant was not a man to be ignored when he said the way things were going to be.

They gathered in the lobby, one and all, a large family, to be sure. And while it became clear that the twins and little Dave were missing, still no one left to find them. Earl had spoken, and they obeyed. Besides, the air had a feel to it that seemed to sap courage right out of the whole lot of them.

Dan Barrister, the proprietor of the inn, had left for the night. He knew the Pageants and knew them to be good people. He took advantage of the few hours off to go home to the small house behind the Serenity Inn and relax with his family.

So he wasn't there when the front doors of the inn opened wide, and Cecil Phelps stepped past the threshold. He was dressed in jeans and a dress shirt, and he was all smiles. He walked casually over to the small reception desk, slid the register book around, and signed his name in big block letters—Mr. Cecil Phelps—and tinged the bell sitting there three times. Earl Pageant was the man who answered him, and Mr. Phelps smiled broadly at that. He looked at Earl with bright blue eyes and nodded amiably.

Earl shook his head sadly. "Sorry, mister. There aren't any rooms left here."

"Are you sure? It looks like a jungle out there with all the cars along the road, but they all looked like they were parked for the circus just down the road."

"Well, that circus is over at my place, and it isn't really something we expected. Might be able to find something a little closer to town though." Earl studied the young man in front of him, a sense of déjà vu whispering at the edge of his mind. There was something about the man that was decidedly familiar.

"Well. I suppose I can walk a little farther. It can't be that far, right? But maybe I'll check out the big top first. I do love a good show . . ." Those blue eyes looked over the room and slowly toward the doors Cecil Phelps had entered. "I think I might just have to do that, yessiree bob."

"Oh, I wouldn't go there, mister. I don't think it's the best place to be." The man looked at him straight on, and there it was again, the feeling that they'd certainly met somewhere before.

"Not much on the circus?"

"Not this one. I hear the police think it's crooked."

"Really? Well, maybe I should stay away from there. I've seen what cops can do when they decide they don't like a carnival." He winked at Earl, his fingers tapping a rapid tattoo on the wooden reception desk. "I've heard stories, too."

"Yeah?"

"Yeah. Did you ever hear the one about the clowns who were burned to death in their trailer? Seems there was a carnival in this small town, and a few kids went and got themselves killed, you see, by snooping where they shouldn't have. So the people in the town, well, they got a trifle upset you might say, and they went and barricaded one of the trailers. Oh, I don't suppose it mattered which trailer, so much. Just any of them might have done the job. They snuck up close—three of the townies I think it was, yeah, three rubes—and they spilled a little petroleum and paint thinner all over the whole trailer. And then, just for grins, they lit that bad boy up."

Earl blinked but did nothing else. His heart was feeling a little funny in his chest, and his knees were sort of watery. He looked at Mr. Cecil Phelps and felt the strange familiarity again, a profoundly disturbing experience. The man reminded him of the stranger he'd seen his grandson speaking to; he smiled too much, and it wasn't really a very pleasant affair, that smile of his. It was all teeth and blood-red gums, and was that a little cotton candy stuck at the corner of his mouth? Where would he have gotten cotton candy around these parts? And he remembered the carnival at his farm, and his eyes grew a little wider. He studied the man again. He was a thin man, rather tall, with skin that was a little pasty looking, really, and long, dark curls of hair that would have made most women jealous. His hair was so black it was almost blue.

The rest of the Pageants were doing their own things, but now and again they looked over at their patriarch and the stranger.

Mr. Phelps spoke again. "You'd think someone at the farm where that little carnival was set up would have heard the screams, wouldn't you? Five men dying in a burning trailer can't be too quiet. Can you imagine what they must have felt? The panic when they realized the doors were blocked and the flames were starting to get through? Can you even guess what that was like?"

Earl Pageant shook his head mutely in denial, his eyes

going a bit wider as he started to realize what or who he was speaking with. Mr. Phelps wiped at his own brow and took away a layer of flesh-colored makeup, or maybe it was skin, and revealed a dead white color underneath. He let out an exaggerated gust of breath and smiled. "Is it hot in here? Or is it just me?" He wiped his face again and pulled away still more flesh, exposed more of the titanium white under it, and the odd blue triangular markings that seemed a part of that very same newly exposed skin.

Mr. Phelps pulled the rest of his face away, and Earl was too busy watching to even notice that the rest of his family was turning his way to see what was happening. He wasn't even really aware when he started backing away, shaking his head and moaning low in his chest. Like a magician with a few tricks up his sleeve, Mr. Phelps pulled the register book from the reception desk and tore a page from it. The single sheet of paper seemed impossibly large, big enough to cover the man's entire body. Only his face showed as he rattled the sheet of paper, making a riffling noise in the air in front of him.

"I used to be a clown for a while when I was younger. Did you know that? I was pretty good, too." The man looked at him with a knowing smile and held up both hands for Earl to see. For just a moment the paper sheet in front of him started to collapse, but then it righted itself. And how had a piece of paper just big enough for signatures grown as big as a dressing room screen? Well, that was a new one on old Earl. "Wanna see a neat trick?"

Mr. Phelps winked and ducked low behind the paper. The only part of him that showed was his hand holding the top edge of the paper again, which was as white as his face had become—or was that a glove? No, it couldn't have been a glove; Earl had seen the fine, dark hairs on that hand only a moment before.

Cecil Phelps let the paper fall, and as it drifted to the

ground he stood up to his full height, the jeans and shirt gone, replaced by a glistening crimson tuxedo. His face was all wrong, and Earl let out an honest-to-God scream when he saw the stage makeup fully revealed.

"It's been a lo-ong time, Earl Pageant. Did I ever have a chance to thank you for the hospitality you showed me and mine?" Rufo's hands moved quickly, folding the immense paper with a dexterity that would have shamed most prestidigitators. He folded and tucked and folded again as he walked slowly toward Earl.

"You—you can't be here. I saw you die!"

"That you did, my good man, but here you are, and here I am."

"Pa? What the hell is going on?" Andrew Pageant was not a man who believed in violence, but he understood it. He knew that sometimes it was necessary. He had taught his children to understand that as well. He got to his feet and moved toward his father's side, determined to make sure that nothing happened that shouldn't.

Rufo looked at him and grinned madly, his teeth fairly gleaming in their field of crimson paint. "Andy! How nice it is to see you again!" He nodded his head amiably, and his hands kept moving and folding and tucking and dancing around the paper he held. "Me and your pa are just going over a little unfinished business. Why don't you scuttle your butt right back over to that couch and watch the boob tube, okay?" If his tone was patronizing, he hid it behind the menace that showed in his eyes.

The clown looked back at Earl and whispered quickly, "Is this between the two of us, Earl? Or does it involve the whole family?" He stepped closer, and Earl tried to step back but was having a little trouble convincing his legs to move.

"Just between us, I think." The voice was so faint it took him a moment to realize he'd spoken at all.

"As long as your son agrees, I think we can play it that way. But if he moves another step toward me, I'll pay my respects to everyone. Do you understand me?"

"Andrew, you go sit down. I can handle this matter." His voice was stronger now, because it had to be.

Andrew didn't seem to want to agree. He started forward again, and Rufo grinned broadly. "Well, Earl, old son, I gave you a chance. Pity your children can't mind you." He winked lewdly. "Of course if they could, none of this ever would have happened."

Rufo opened his hands, and the thing he'd been folding opened with them. It wasn't paper anymore. It wasn't paper, and it certainly wasn't small. The folded thing fairly jumped through the air and wrapped around Earl Pageant like a wave of canvas. In less time than it took for Earl to let out a gasp of surprise, he was wrapped neatly into a straitjacket that was festooned with ribbons of every color and decorated merrily.

Andrew didn't wait to see what was going on; he merely moved toward his father where he was now trapped. "I have to admit, Earl, that I'm better with balloons, but this isn't half bad." Andrew closed in at a full charge, and Rufo stepped to the side, easily avoiding the first rush.

"Please, mister. Please, just let them go!" Earl's voice was desperate, and even he had trouble recognizing it.

"Two men were guilty of hurting your kin, Earl Pageant!" The voice that came from the clown was deep and powerful, charged with hatred that had simmered for a long, long time. "Two men killed five, and you and yours killed fifty!" The clown sneered, his scarlet-stained lips peeling back from teeth that belonged in a shark's mouth. "And you dare ask me for lenience?"

"They didn't do anything!"

"Neither did I!"

Andrew tried charging again, and this time Rufo's

white-gloved hand reached out, grabbing Earl's son by the face and stopping his forward momentum. Andrew let out a cry of protest that quickly became a scream of pain. The man tried to pull back from the clown's hand without any luck at all. "Neither did I, Earl! I was just a kid out to have a little fun and keep everyone happy! I didn't deserve to die for that, and neither did the rest of them! But I was watching you, Earl Pageant! I was already dead, but I was *watching* you! I saw what you did to my family, my friends! Now I guess it's time to let you know how that really feels!"

Andrew bucked as hard as he could, his feet sinking into the rug and kicking back for all they were worth. It didn't make a bit of difference. He was stuck like a fly to a spider's web. "All my hopes, all my dreams," the clown shouted now, spittle flying from his lips as he leaned closer to where Earl was held. "Ruined by you and your good neighbors!" His gloved hand squeezed, and Earl heard the sound of his son's face breaking and imploding under the pressure the clown applied. Even over the sound of his own screams and those of his family, he heard his son's last rattling breath. "Everything I had, crushed and burned!"

Rufo let go of Andrew's face at last, and the ruined pulp that had been the skull and flesh of his oldest son fell before Earl like so much meat in a slaughterhouse. The clown shook his hand and sent bits of Andrew's crushed head sluicing across the faded antique rug and Earl's straitjacketed chest. "So, guess what, Earl?"

Earl was screaming, his heart broken as his son fell dead. He looked at the clown and felt the tears start falling even as he lowered his head to take the demonic visitor back to Hell himself if he had to. Rufo slapped him backwards, and he staggered until he hit the couch to the left of the reception desk.

"Can you guess, Earl? I'm going to return the favor.

This time you get to watch!" Ricky Pageant fell to his knees next to his dead father and screamed hoarsely. Ricky was not exactly normal, true enough, but he was not feeble enough to miss what had just occurred. Rufo made his death quick, simply twisting his head until the vertebrae ruptured in a series of pops. There was just a brief flash of regret on the clown's face, but it was there, and then it was gone, erased as if it had never existed. Tina let loose a scream that was shrill and filled with more pain than any nine-year-old should ever know. She tried to crawl through her mother as she backed away from the horror of watching not one, but two of her family members murdered. Earl moaned and cried and did all he could to pull his arms free from the canvas bindings.

Lisa Marie Pageant, who had married into the family, screamed and ran for the front doors, but they would not open. She pounded with her fists and clawed with her nails and kicked and even body-slammed the doors, but to no avail. Her husband Brian, cousin to Andrew, was torn between going to her aid and killing the clown. He tried the latter, but it didn't work. Rufo ripped his arms off with all the casual skill of a child pulling wings off a fly. The red paint around his mouth was soon joined by a different shade of red that ran like tears across his face.

Earl Pageant watched while each member of his extended family was killed. The clown didn't seem to much care how he killed them, just as long as they died. And in the end, the clown came for him as well.

And in the end what he did to Earl Pageant seemed like a mercy.

And maybe it was.

IV

Jonathan Crowley ran for all he was worth, his eyes narrowed against the cut of the wind in his face and his legs pumping hard as he headed toward Serenity Falls. Somewhere up ahead of him a freak with a greasepaint smile was moving this way as well, and Jonathan Crowley wanted to kill him. He wanted to kill him slowly and listen to the bastard's screams. The remaining gasoline on his skin and on the few shreds of his clothes was evaporating, but it still hurt. His eyes were puffy, and his skin felt like someone had shrunk it by a few sizes and then forced it back over the rest of his body. His mouth tasted like the interior of someone's broken-down garage, and his muscles seemed to be under the impression that they were being drawn through a taffy puller.

He'd felt better.

Then again, he'd felt worse more than once.

The stinging pain in his palm told him he still had a grip on whatever had been grieving him since he'd arrived in Serenity and before, but for the time being he didn't have the time to deal with it properly. It was doing its best to escape him, but he wasn't about to let it go. For the present he willed the agonizing sensation to stay just under the surface of his palm's flesh, and while it wanted to get away, he was winning the battle.

Overhead he could see a cloud of energies that he knew couldn't possibly be a good thing. He had a suspicion as to what the source was but no idea whatsoever where it was headed or what it was meant to do. He'd handled the dead from out of town, but the locals were a different story entirely. They were still around and moving, and they were very likely a lot stronger in numbers.

How long had they been trapped in that house, locked

away in the small dolls that served as their prisons? Were they even coherent anymore? He didn't know; he only knew they had to be eliminated one way or another. As a general rule ghosts weren't more than a nuisance. Most of the ones he'd encountered—and he'd run across hundreds over the years—were little more than animated memories. They were stuck in certain locales and forced to repeat some act that had been significant in their lives or their deaths. The exceptions could be nasty, but not very often. But this was new to him. This wasn't one spirit, this was hundreds of them, hundreds that had been tortured for who knew how long, and hundreds that would want some sort of payback.

Considering the murder rate in Serenity Falls, he had doubts that any of them would be in the mood to have a pleasant chat. Indefinite incarceration with optional torture seldom left one in a good mood. He knew that from experience.

One nightmare at a time, old boy. He ran harder, seeking any sign of where Rufo might have gone. The clown was not right in the head, and worse still, he was in the mood to cause a lot of damage. He'd taken being beaten very poorly, and Crowley doubted that burning one tent was going to be enough for him.

From behind him a good ways, he could hear the echoes from a few sirens. Someone had managed to make a call to the emergency services. That was good. It helped with the whole leaving everyone behind to live or die on their own thing. Priorities. He had to stop what was causing the damage, not just work on what had already happened.

He reached the edge of the cemetery and stopped running, looking around the oddly centered graveyard, his body almost perfectly still. There was something going on in there, but he couldn't see anything. It was just a feeling. Jonathan Crowley had learned a long, long time ago to trust his feelings.

He grimaced, waiting as patiently as he could for the sound of his own pulse pounding in his ears to calm down. Frankly, running a couple of miles after a long fight tended to make his heart go a wee bit faster than he liked, but there it was. He took slow, deep breaths and waited. There was the sound of the sirens, growing more distant; there was the sound of a car coming down the road and his own diminishing heartbeat. Nothing else. Not a bird, not a cricket, nothing, though with the recent weather in Serenity, he wasn't too surprised.

Still, with all of the activity outside of the town proper, there should have been something going on in the center of the damned place. He was having the same problem as before when it came to his abilities to sense the unnatural. There was too damned much of it around to really be able to distinguish one mess from another. It was hard to see a candle's flame when the sun was out.

So he had to trust the rest of his senses to make up the difference. So far that hadn't been working too well, but it was possible he'd manage it anyway. Maybe.

The car he'd heard coming his way finally showed up. He turned and saw the occupants as the gray Mercedes-Benz pulled to a stop. Amelia stepped out almost instantly, heading his way with a frown of concern.

"Jonathan? Are you all right?" As soon as she got close enough, he felt the itching start deep inside of his body, felt the healing begin.

"I will be in a minute." His eyes ran over the length of her body, unconsciously admiring her form as he noted the drying blood on her torn blouse and pants. "How about you?"

She nodded, her loose hair moving in the growing

breeze that, like most breezes in the town, was far too cold
for the season. "I'm fine. But Mike isn't doing well. I think
he has a concussion."

"So get him to the medical center. I'll be along in a few
minutes if I can."

"Will you be all right?"

He shot her a look that reminded her of exactly who he
was, along with a smile that stated very clearly for her that
he had plans to stay that way. "Of course I will."

That was, naturally enough, when something decided to
prove him wrong. Amelia was just starting to climb back
into the car when the pain lanced deep into the soft meat of
his shoulder, and something scraped across the bone of the
joint. Crowley hissed, his smile turning into an entirely different sort of expression as he fell forward. "Ahhh! Shit!"

"Jonathan!"

Crowley fell hard, grunting as he slammed into the
concrete edge of the sidewalk. He felt the hot flow of
blood spilling across his shoulder and down onto the
ground below him. His eyes damn near bulged from their
sockets at the pain. There was no healing itch, just the
pain deep inside him that seemed to be growing bigger
and bigger.

Amelia started moving toward him, and he tried to warn
her back. Whatever had hit him felt like it was trying to
carve through his entire torso, and he didn't want her getting a dose of the same treatment. But his voice just didn't
want to listen to any nonsense about working.

Amelia moved closer and then stopped, her eyes going wide.

The voice of Jack Michaels came to Crowley from the
same direction as the pain that was overwhelming him.
"You need to step back, ma'am. I don't want to hurt you,
but this is something that has to be done."

Crowley tried to push himself back up into at least a

kneeling position. His arm gave out, and he landed on the ground a second time. He heard the sound of the pistol in the man's hands being cocked. "These are hollow points, if that helps, Mr. Crowley. I'll make it quick."

V

The room was quiet, and try though she might, Mary Parsons couldn't quite make herself relax enough to sleep. Jake was unconscious, his breathing regular and steady, not sounding at all troubled any longer. She was grateful for that. Grateful to Jonathan Crowley, though she couldn't really be sure that he'd done anything. It was just a feeling, really, that he'd done more than watch over her husband when he relieved her for a few minutes.

With a soft sigh she rose from her seat near the hospital bed and walked over to look out the window. It was dark outside, and the air was clear and dry. She guessed she could probably spend hours just counting the stars she could see from this one opening alone.

Mary shook her head lightly and breathed in deep. She was tired and wanted to sleep, but her mind wasn't quite going along with the program. If she let herself think about it, it would surely annoy the hell out of her. So instead she let her mind drift to what had happened since she'd come to Serenity Falls with her husband. She couldn't think of much that had gone right, save for meeting Jonathan Crowley, who she knew only by reputation as one of the finest parapsychologists ever.

Even if he did scare the hell out of her. Not so much for what he said or how he acted, but just because he seemed to almost breathe out menace wherever he went. She wondered

idly if he were even truly sane or just capable of faking it
better than most.

She was still lost in her thoughts when the door to the
room opened. She only became aware of the change because
of the light from the opened door reflecting on the window
she faced. It was a hospital. You came to expect a few inter-
ruptions. She didn't bother to turn away from the view.

Jake snored softly behind her, and she sighed, almost
envying him.

When the voice came from behind Mary Parsons, she
almost screamed. Despite knowing that someone was in
the room, she was still caught off guard. She turned around,
her eyes wide, her heart beating faster than she liked to
think about, and faced the source of the words she hadn't
even heard clearly.

He was an older man, in his late forties if she had to
take a guess, with steel gray hair and kind eyes the same
color. He wore a lab coat over his suit and had a stethoscope around his neck, but she'd never seen him before. He
smiled, looking just a little apologetic for the interruption.
"I'm sorry, I didn't mean to startle you."

"Oh, that's all right. You just caught me daydreaming."
The man moved over to her husband's sleeping form and
placed the stethoscope against his chest, his face going almost blank as he concentrated.

"I was glad to hear Jacob was doing better. Comas are a
nasty business."

"Thank you. Yes, they are."

"Still, he had something I needed, and I'm going to
need it again."

"I'm sorry?" She blinked, his words worming past the
slight daze she was in.

"I'd marked him, you see. He was supposed to be making sure everything went the right way against the Hunter."

"Against who?"

"Crowley. That fellow Jonathan Crowley." His voice was still pleasantly conversational, but the words rang to a different tune. "He's really become something of a nuisance."

"What are you talking about?" She heard the edge going into her voice, and that suited her just fine. This man, whoever he was, couldn't possibly belong in the same room as her husband. He was going on about taking something of Jake's, and that wouldn't happen while she was alive to stop it.

"It's really very simple, Mary. I need your husband's soul. I'm not nearly done yet, and the Hunter has made it almost impossible to get anything finished without enough energy to properly handle the matter. There's still a great deal I have to accomplish before I'm content."

Mary contemplated his words for all of three seconds, and then grabbed the closest available weapon. Her hands gripped the IV stand that had been attached to her husband until a few hours ago, and she put her whole body into a swing that would have made most major league batters proud.

The heavy wheeled base came across the man's scalp with a loud smack. He staggered backwards, his eyes wide and his mouth hanging open, as if the last thing in the world he expected was that she might take offense to what he was saying. Some people, perhaps even most people, would have left it at that and reached for the call button to get a nurse.

Mary Parsons was not to be numbered among them. She hit him again. This time the wheels spun across his upper back and shoulder, and he grunted loudly as he fell back, trying to block the blows with his thick hands. Mary wasn't having anything to do with it. Adrenaline was kicking into her system like a flash flood, and she intended to take full advantage of it while she could. Her anger bloomed into life and burned brightly when she thought of what poor Jake had already been through. She slammed the long pole over the man's back as he fell to his hands and knees, bending the metal into a new shape with the blow. He fell flat on the ground, his hands twitching and his legs kicking faintly.

She hit him twice more for safety's sake, the IV frame in her hands bending with each blow. She hated to think about the cost of replacing it, but next to Jake's life, it wouldn't be very much. Mary Parsons set down her weapon and hit the button for summoning a nurse. When the man at her feet twitched, she picked back up her trusty IV stand-cum-club and stood guard, waiting for help to arrive.

There are people in this world it doesn't pay to mess with. The stranger with the kind eyes learned that lesson the hard way.

VI

Serenity Falls Part Fifteen: Absent Friends

There was a storm gathering over Serenity Falls, and it had been building for years. John Blackwell had spent the last few years of his life carefully carving figurines that would have shamed many of the artists in the world who had been formally trained. He'd strained his eyes almost daily, and he'd used the self-control of a surgeon to honor the people of Serenity with likenesses that most of them never saw until their own deaths.

And after that they saw them all too well. Looking at the wooden figures every day, locked into their own likenesses but unable to feel the touch of others or to speak coherently amongst themselves. They'd spent time as prisoners of their own lives, forced to reflect on what had happened to them and forced to endure the endless span of time in a room where they had no power, no control over anything at all, save their own limbs when they concentrated hard enough.

And then one day they were freed. A giant of a boy came into the room and shattered their wooden prisons.

They'd escaped and been drawn to the black tent— a tent created by their captor for the sole purpose of destroying their families—in order to stop what Albert Miles wanted to see happen. A good number of them didn't actually have family members at the place where they were drawn, but that was all right. They went along just the same in an effort to help the others who'd been imprisoned with them. They went along because, really, there was nothing else for them to do. They'd been alone for far too long, locked away close enough to touch their friends and families but forever refused that privilege.

Mostly though, they went along for revenge. There were old disputes held in by the dead that had to be taken care of, and many of the very people they had arguments with were in that black tent. They knew it, could feel it, and sought to ease the anger that burned within them.

Only to have their vengeance taken from them before they could satisfy themselves.

The very beings they sought to confront were destroyed before their eyes, shredded and seeded in a small army of rodents. And they knew who did it. They could see him below on the ground with a bullet in his shoulder and another soon to go into his skull.

Some of them considered lingering, waiting for his death and then tormenting whatever came out of him. Others, wiser ones, remembered what he'd done to the ones who'd sought to possess their kin and went about their remaining business.

The storm that had been building for almost as long as Serenity had existed finally broke. The dead went their own ways, and in many cases they sought the reasons for their deaths.

Stephen Wilkins sought the woman who'd murdered him. Most of the people in town were under the impression that he'd moved away—and in truth he *had* moved away, but he had come back to see her one last time at her request—some believed he'd committed suicide. He had not. He had been murdered and very craftily by the one of the women he loved. Oh, he knew he'd been wrong. He knew that he was playing with the hearts of different women who deserved not to be used so shallowly, but the sad fact for him was that he'd loved them both. Sadder still that they had been related.

He thought of her, and then he felt himself drawn to where she lay sleeping. Adrienne Long had spent most of her early evening consuming more alcoholic beverages than she did in a month. She wasn't just unconscious, she was blitzed.

The Scotch she'd consumed wasn't the only spirit to enter her that night.

In her booze-induced dreams she relived the last minutes of the time she spent with her lover, the man she'd found out a few days before had been successfully seducing her daughter. The difference in this case was that he lived in her dreams.

Instead of carefully arranging his body for the local police to find, he got back up after she'd finished with him. Instead of the razor cuts she'd drawn down his arms helping him bleed to death in the bathtub they'd shared for one last tryst, the wounds had sealed themselves, and he'd forced her under the bloody waters until she bucked and gasped in water instead of air. In her dreams he held her down beneath the surface of the waters until she was dead.

And in Serenity Falls, they found her body two days later, where she'd choked to death on her own vomit. No one noticed the fingerprints around her neck. The outer surface of the skin was fine. It was only deep inside where the trauma took place.

Stephen Wilkins left Serenity for the last time a few moments later. He only stopped once more, to look at April where she lay asleep in the hospital waiting room. Her dreams were far more sedate than her mother's. At least that night.

Throughout Serenity the dead paid visits to old friends and family members. It was a night few would ever forget. Dana Glass, the mother of Rebecca Glass, was visited by the spirit of her husband, Marty, who told her that she had to stop moping around and get on with her life. He was dressed just like he had been on the night of their first date, as handsome as ever, with a smile that could melt her heart. There was another man in the dream who agreed completely with her husband and swore that he would take care of Becky over the next few hours. In her dreams, Dana and Marty danced and reminisced before he had to leave. They parted with a kiss and the promise that he would be with her again someday.

Earline Waters dreamed she was with her Alden as she slept. He came to her with that little boy look on his face that said he'd done something wrong and asked for her forgiveness. She was so happy to see him that she forgave him in an instant, not really knowing why he felt the need to apologize. She held him closely, and they stayed together through the heart attack that took her in her sleep.

Bill Karstens came home, too. Back to his wife and children whom he'd loved so well in life. Bill was not really the bravest man in the world, nor the kindest, but he had always loved his family dearly, and the idea of being without them caused him more fear than ever should have been possible. While they slept in their beds he concentrated with all of his might and managed to blow out the pilot light on the gas stove. It took effort to turn the valves to open the gas lines, but he managed. He was there for each and every one of his family members as they died in their sleep. He took them with him when he left.

Gene and Bethany Halloway were asleep in their bed. Bethany made small noises and dreamt of running away with her first love. But it was only a dream. She would never leave Gene. She loved him, despite his faults. He'd been there for her when every part of her life wanted to crumble and had given her the strength to see through every crisis that came her way.

Gene moaned in his sleep, thinking about what he'd done to that sick bastard that hurt his little Terri. She meant the world to him. She was his legacy, and she was his pride. She loved him despite the fact that he'd failed her in every possible way. In his dreams she accused him of letting her die, letting her go to her death screaming and begging for some kind of mercy that she was never shown. In his dreams she accused him of ruining poor Terry. And when he thought the worst of it was over, she let him see exactly what had been done to her in the darkened woods by Bill Karstens. She let him feel every second of her torment and let him know that what lay in the next room was nothing more than her body, captured and used by a force that wanted all of Serenity Falls to suffer and die.

She let him see the truth, in other words.

In the end he begged her for forgiveness. In the end she forgave him.

He woke up quite a long while before his wife did. And Gene sat in his bed for almost an hour before he left the room and went to see what had happened to his daughter.

Terri Halloway lay in her bed, her body covered in sweat and her bedclothes glued to her lean form by the strain of being used as a living battery. He looked down on his daughter and wept silently. In the darkness of the room he could see the strange writing that lay under her skin, glowing through her flesh like a nightlight through a paper bag. The markings made no sense to him, but he knew they were vile things, evil in every sense of the word.

Gene leaned down and kissed her sweating lips, felt her hot breaths gust against his face as he looked at her. And though it shattered his heart to do it, he put his little angel out of her misery. With hands that normally did little more work than tapping the keys on a calculator or looking through the volumes of law books on his shelves, he reached down and pulled the pillow from beneath her writhing body. He planted a knee on either side of her hips and leaned forward, holding the pillow over her face. She struggled, thrashing about on the bed until he was certain the noise would wake Bethany, but still he held her down, pinned in place by his weight on top of her and by the pillow he used to stop her breathing. The sound of her last breath leaving her body was nothing in comparison to the sound of his heart shattering inside his chest.

The strange light that spilled from under her skin faded as quickly as her life did. Gene walked slowly from her room after covering her remains with the sheet she'd kicked to the floor in her sleep.

Gene looked in on his wife for a moment, studying her face. Was it possible to love someone so much that it hurt? Of course it was. If ever he needed proof, all he had to do was ask Jack Michaels about how it felt.

He left the house dressed only in a pair of dirty jeans he took from the laundry room and his jogging shoes. He had unfinished business to take care of, and now was as good a time as any to handle it.

Terri had told him other things while he slept, you see. She had told him what she had done to Jack Michaels

while he suffered through his delirium. She told him that
Jack was marked, too, and that he would do things just as
she had if he wasn't stopped in time.

It could be said that Gene Halloway left his home that
night looking for many things. Forgiveness, perhaps, for all
that he had done wrong in his life. Maybe just a chance
to make one thing go right after all the bad things he'd
done. Or maybe he went out there because of what Terri
confessed to him. How she'd gone about leaving the marks
on Jack's body. She was his daughter, after all, and the
thought that any man had touched her was enough to make
him angry.

In the end it is hard to say exactly what drove him into
the darkness. He never left a note and never said a word to
anyone about what made him seek out the man he'd once
called his best friend.

Some questions just can't be answered.

VII

Jack Michaels looked down at Jonathan Crowley and shuddered. The man was down and should have been out, but he
was still moving, despite the hole in his chest. He wasn't
just moving, he was actually trying to stand up.

Deep in the recesses of his brain, the constable was
screaming. He couldn't believe what he'd just done, couldn't
imagine what would make him load his service weapon
with the sort of bullets that could drop a bull elephant and
shoot a man who'd been trying to help him keep order in the
town.

But that panic and that absolute disbelief never reached
the surface of his mind. It was buried along with the rest of

his morals. He had a job to do, and he knew that he would finish it one way or another.

He aimed the pistol at Crowley's head, tracking the man's jerky movements. Not twenty feet away, the woman who'd come to town to make everything all right was looking on, her long-fingered hands covering her mouth, and her dark eyes wide with disbelief. In the car she was driving, Mike Blake looked his way and grimaced, his eyes narrowed.

Even as he kept pace with Crowley's motions, it registered with him that the woman should be dead. He'd killed her not an hour ago. That place in the back of his mind, buried deep below his consciousness, went a little crazy right then. Like a pressure cooker left unattended and unvented for too long, things started rumbling deep inside of his brain, in the parts untouched by the sorcery used on him. *I killed her? Why in the name of God would I do a thing like that?* The constable's hands trembled slightly. Not much, but enough that he had to focus hard to take proper aim at Crowley again. Damned if the man wasn't looking at him, his brown eyes almost burning with intensity.

The man was saying something under his breath, each word a strain and most of them enough to make him cough blood. Despite the fascination he felt for the effort involved, his eyes were drawn back to Amelia Dunlow, a woman whose clothes showed the signs of what he'd done to her, and whose body was as perfect and flawless as he'd imagined. Her hands covered the lower half of her face, but the motion left most of her chest exposed. In the worst possible situation, his libido insisted on looking. He forced himself to find another object to study, anything that wasn't so damned distracting.

He found Crowley. The man was still looking at him, but the pained expression on his face had faded a bit, and he could almost swear he saw a hint of a grin past the blood that trickled from the stranger's mouth.

"Why is it . . ." Crowley panted hard as he spoke, each word now loud enough to hear and each one of them spilling bloody froth from his mouth. "Why is it that every time I meet a lawman I could maybe get to like, he ends up being a weak-willed little prick?"

"I didn't want to do this to you . . ."

"Then why did you?" Michaels blinked hard, not believing his eyes. The man was actually trying to stand up. He felt a brief flash of panic, that lower voice screaming about impossibilities again. But then Crowley slid back down hard, hitting the sidewalk and the road again.

"I don't have a choice . . . she made me do this."

Crowley laughed; it was an unpleasant, bubbling sound in his chest. "That's just perfect. Your type always finds a woman to blame it on."

Michaels practically flinched at that comment, the feelings of guilt over what had been done to him—and he knew full well that he'd had no control over the situation, but he also knew that he'd enjoyed it—blossoming in his chest. "You need to not talk about what you don't understand."

"Michaels . . . I have a present for you." Crowley sat up again, wincing in pain. Jack couldn't quite see through the man's chest, but he almost felt like he could. The blood flow was still heavy, and he didn't figure the stranger for being alive in another few minutes. *Just like the Dunlow woman is dead! That worked pretty fucking well, didn't it? Yes sir! He'll be at least that deceased, won't he, Jack? And aren't you glad you keep listening to that goddamned voice? The one that keeps making you do things you know are wrong? The one that keeps saying it's just best if you go ahead and shoot Crowley again? Maybe you better listen, Jack. Maybe you better listen good, because I don't think you can trust this freak as far as you can throw him!* He shook his head to shut the voice off. It wanted him to kill an innocent man, and he didn't want to listen to it. He didn't know how Amelia Dunlow had lived through the shots, and he didn't really care. He was just grateful. The idea that he'd become a murderer had been haunting him since he left Havenwood, and that was one ghost, at least, that he no longer had to worry about.

Jack Michaels leaned closer in on Jonathan Crowley, fully prepared to receive whatever present the man had to offer, even if it wasn't the sort he'd really enjoy getting.

The only thing that stopped him was the sound of Gene Halloway calling out to him. "Jack, please. Stop this. I know what happened between you and Terri. I know what she did to you. She told me all about it. Now please, stop, before someone else gets hurt."

He looked at his long-ago friend and looked hard. Gene was the last person he expected to see on the street in the latter part of the night, dressed in wrinkled pants and nothing else. Good old Mike—who was still trying to understand everything going on around him if the expression on his face was any indication—was a far more likely candidate for acting stupid in the middle of the night. Hell, Mike had a track record for it. But Gene? Hell, at his worst in high school, Gene was still about a straitlaced as they came and never one to be seen in anything less than perfect clothes. It was almost as unsettling—though nowhere near as blatant—as the idea of Crowley standing back up or Amelia Dunlow being alive.

He turned away from Crowley and walked toward Gene. "Gene? What are you doing out here? Go home to Bethany before she starts worrying."

"Don't worry about that, Jack! Jesus, listen to me. You have to stop this! You're not acting like yourself!"

Jack frowned. He knew what Gene was saying was absolutely true, but he also knew there wasn't a damned thing he could do about it. He'd tried fighting the voice, tried hard, but he couldn't. It was stronger than he was. Even now he could feel the pull of the voice calling to him, telling him to turn back to Crowley and finish what had to be done.

His ears were practically burning. He could hear Crowley whispering again, that soft chanting sound, partially distorted by the blood that was in the man's lungs. He turned to look, his gaze going from Gene to Jonathan Crowley. The man was still sitting up, but his face looked paler than before. He held his hand tightly closed, a fist that trembled as he winced. There was a pocketknife in his other hand, but the blade wasn't really a threat on the worst day, and right now the hand holding the blade was limp.

But Crowley was staring right at him again, his feverish eyes glinting like brown marble. Gene was still talking to him, but he couldn't hear the words. There was something glowing in the hand Crowley clenched tightly shut. Jack had no idea what it was, but it worried him a bit.

"What's in your hand, Crowley?"

"Something special . . ." He wheezed, his voice barely above a whisper. "Just for you, Constable Michaels."

He aimed the gun at Crowley's head. "Drop it."

"Certainly . . ."

Gene's hand touched Jack's shoulder from behind and he turned his head, surprised by the contact. At the same time, from the corner of his eye, he saw Crowley's hand opening.

Gene was speaking again, his words urgent, the look on his face one that Jack had never expected to see again. It was the look of a friend who was worried about another friend. It left him feeling strangely empty and at the same time, angry.

Something shimmered in the air just above Crowley's hand. It glowed like a firefly, blinking and flashing at a hyperactive pace. It was even the same pale green color.

Jack looked at Gene, watching the green thing from the

corner of his eye. Gene's mouth moved, but the words didn't seem to ring out very clearly. He couldn't make sense of them. Maybe it was the flashing light that streaked his way, moving in a jagged line that cut through the night's darkness like strobing lightning and arced directly toward his head.

When it hit him he screamed, his body spasming and the pistol in his hand firing a bullet into the air. Through the pain he saw the bullet rip away from him, missing Crowley's head by a few inches.

Jack Michaels screamed louder still as his skin began to smoke. There were patterns of heat on his body that seemed to start on the inside and work their way to the surface of his flesh. He noticed that his right hand, which was plainly in his view, was smoking, wisps of pale white rising from the odd symbols that started blackening on his epidermis.

He fell to his knees, wanting to slap at the burning spots but having no idea where to start, even if he could manage to make his arms move. Through the pain he heard Gene's voice calling out with concern, felt the man's hand gripping his shoulder again, saw him leaning closer to see if he could help.

And nearby, he heard Crowley call out, "Oh, I wouldn't do that, mister. That might not be wise." And why was it, he wondered, that the man sounded amused?

"You're not me, and he's hurt."

"He'll get better, but if you don't let go of him, you might not."

"What would you know about it?"

"Ever heard the term 'he's got a monkey on his back'?" Jack turned his face, looking at Crowley, trying to make some sense of what the man was saying. It wasn't exactly easy going. The pain was starting to calm down to a level slightly lower than agony, but it was still damned hard to concentrate. "The good constable doesn't have a monkey. He's got a curse."

"He's got a what?"

"A curse." Crowley stood up in one easy motion, the blood flowing from his chest increasing in volume as he did it. Gene backed away quickly. Apparently he hadn't noticed that the man talking to him was burned, blistered, battered, shot, and mostly naked until just then. Either that, or it was the expression on Jonathan Crowley's face that made him suddenly skittish.

Crowley's hands snapped out and grabbed Jack's shoulders. Where he touched, the pain flared up until Jack prayed for unconsciousness. No such luck. He felt everything and heard everything.

"What the hell are you talking about?" Gene's voice managed to sound scared and angry at the same time. His face was doing a good job of keeping up with his tone.

"Watch and learn, sweet pea."

Crowley looked into Jack's eyes—which were practically bulging out of their sockets by that point; the pain was getting worse, and he thought for sure he would actually catch fire—and he leaned in close enough for Jack to see the white of his teeth beneath the thin crimson stain that still poured out when he spoke.

"Do you hurt, Constable Michaels?"

"Uhhh . . . yah . . . hurts bad . . ."

"Good. That means you're still alive." The hands on his shoulders patted down placatingly. "Now, this is going to hurt an awful lot. But that's okay, too. We'll call it payback for the hole in my lung." His smile grew broader, and he whispered a word in Jack's ear. It was a word that he'd never heard before, and the sound of it was like a thunderclap across Jack's brain. The sound seemed to grow louder and louder, and the world around the constable turned so bright white that he couldn't see anymore. Not that he would have been paying attention anyway. Something inside him started twisting and clawing, and he felt certain his heart was going to explode.

The markings in his skin flared up, and he bucked hard, trying to get away from the hands that held him in place. Was it possible to die and keep feeling? He didn't know, but he was afraid he was about to find out.

VIII

Mike Blake watched Crowley get shot in the back and saw everything else going on around him with a drugged sort of detachment. He wanted to focus. He wanted desperately to pay attention, but nothing seemed to make much sense. The only solid truth left to him was that his head hurt, and his heart seemed to be trying to crawl out of his rib cage. Every time he tried to move his eyes he got dizzy, and every time he actually moved his neck or anything above it, he felt like he was getting a bad case of the bed spins. Which would have maybe been acceptable if he'd been drinking, but he'd behaved himself admirably, thanks just the same. Everyone around him was looking at Crowley and Michaels. Amelia was looking at the two men like a spectator at a tennis match. Her head practically followed the words that each spoke like a ball in play.

"Do you love her?" The voice was in his head, he knew that, knew it because he could hear it so clearly, despite the noise all around him. It was a cultured voice, smooth and used to speaking to people. It was pleasantly masculine, almost amiable.

"Amelia? Yes. Of course I do." He couldn't be sure if he was actually speaking or just trying to talk. Whichever the

case, the voice seemed to hear him without any trouble at
all. And whichever the case, he knew he was speaking the
truth. He loved her.

"Good. Love is important. Here's a question for you.
Does she love Jonathan Crowley?"

"I—I don't know."

"Maybe not as a lover, but maybe like family?"

"I think so. I think he's very important to her."

"Is she important to him?"

"I think she's the closest thing he has to a friend." He
wasn't sure if he liked the way this conversation was going.
He didn't know who the voice belonged to, and he was almost sure that if the person behind that voice wanted to
know something about Crowley, it couldn't be a good thing.
Hell, nothing about Crowley was a good thing as far as Mike
was concerned. He meant to lie when he answered, but instead he uttered the truth.

"How about you? Are you important to him?"

"No. I don't think he cares if I live or die." And that,
too, was the truth. He didn't like Amelia's friend Jonathan,
and he knew the feeling was mutual.

"Good for you." He hadn't realized there were hands on
his shoulders. He'd heard the voice clearly all that time and
never noticed that someone was touching him. That couldn't
possibly be a good sign. He only noticed them now, because they were massaging his skin. Long, bony fingers that
pressed down with enough pressure to hurt even through
everything else. Painful enough to make him start coming
around from his daze.

"What are you doing?" The hands left his shoulders at
the same time that the question left his mouth. This time he
actually heard himself speak.

"Doing? Why, I'm going to kill your girlfriend . . ."

"What?" The word this time came out loud and clear,
and the fuzzing around his skull seemed to burn away. He

turned his head, fighting through the dizziness that accompanied the move. He saw a flash of dead white skin and a smear of red and bright blue eyes that moved from his view as the interior of the car tumbled a few times inside his skull. He heard the car door slam and reached for his own door, desperate to get to Amelia, to warn her before it was too late.

Mike pushed and finally managed to open the passenger's side door of the Mercedes. Actually getting out of the vehicle was a bit more challenging; the wound on his head was throbbing and everything around him insisted on tilting to the left harder than he could compensate for. Was it a concussion? How the hell would he know? He was having trouble remembering his name right at the moment. He got to his feet and kept them, and looked around to see what, if anything had changed around him. Crowley was holding on to Jack Michaels, and the constable was thrashing around like someone had decided to electrocute him. He twitched, and his mouth was opened wide in a shocked expression, but he was mostly just lying there with smoke coming off his skin. There was a man with them now, one he thought he should recognize, but he looked wrong, and it was hard to focus with everything around him moving like a Tilt-A-Whirl on overdrive.

He finally spotted Amelia—she hadn't moved much, but damned if it wasn't a challenge anyway—and though he looked, he saw no one near her. Crowley and the rest were easily fifteen or more feet away, and the only firearm he saw was lying on the ground, forgotten. It lay between where Amelia stood—her face still almost stuck in that worried expression—and where Crowley was holding Jack down.

"Amelia? You have to run." His voice was sounding as faded as he felt. That wasn't good. Amelia didn't even hear him. He moved toward her, his heart thudding heavily and his stomach threatening to expel everything he'd eaten in

the last year. *God, please let me reach her . . . Please let me
get Amy safe . . . NO! Not Amy, Amelia! I can't think . . . I
can't even fucking see. Help me, Lord . . .*

He moved toward her, his legs shifting his stride to
compensate for a tilt that wasn't there. He wound up running in a half circle instead of a straight line. When he
stopped and managed to reorient himself, he was standing
a few feet to Amelia's left.

At least she'd finally turned to notice him. That was an
improvement.

"Mike? Mike, you have to get back into the car. You
look like you're ready to pass out." Her brows drew together over her eyes, and she moved toward him. He
opened his mouth to speak and got out a wavering sort of
sigh instead of words. *Just how badly was I hit? This is getting stupid, and I don't have time for it.* He was exasperated
and then some.

"Amelia . . . You have to run. There's someone out to
get you." Finally! Actual words coming out of him, and
they were coherent.

"Mike, I can't leave right now. We'll get you to the medical center in a few minutes, I promise, but I can't leave just
at this moment." Her eyes darted out to where Crowley was
finally taking his hands from Jack's shoulders. Jack had
looked better. He was out flat, and his body was convuls-
ing. He still had streamers of smoke coming from his skin,
but they were weaker than before at least. "Jonathan? Is
everything all right?"

Crowley looked at her and lowered his head. He was
breathing hard, and there was a wound that should have
killed him that was still bleeding freely. His what-the-hell-
kind-of-question-is-THAT expression spoke for him as
eloquently as words would have managed.

She shook her head, looking slightly embarrassed. Mike
managed not to start giggling hysterically only because he

was worried about her. "Do you need to go to the hospital with us?"

Crowley frowned. "Are you hurt?"

Before she could answer, a clown popped up behind her like a demented jack-in-the-box. Long, spidery fingers snatched a handful of her dark, curly hair and yanked her head back savagely. Mike stepped back, the appearance of the red-tuxedoed clown throwing him even more completely than Crowley talking with a hole in his chest. "She's just fine, Mr. Crowley." The voice was smooth and silky, a purr of pure pleasure. The clown smiled broadly, his eyes almost burning behind the pancake makeup over his skull-like face. "She's just dandy tasty, thanks for asking."

Amelia started struggling instantly, and the gloved hand in her hair pulled roughly, twisting her head and neck to the side, exposing her throat to the grinning face above her. She let out a startled scream that was at least half pain.

Mike heard himself growl and took a step forward. Crowley was moving at the same time, reaching down for the pistol on the ground.

The clown's free hand moved in a graceful arc, his fingers gesturing with all the skill of a master prestidigitator. Mike watched those fingers fairly blur in the air and for the life of him had no idea where the knife that bloomed into their grasp could have come from. But he saw the cold, shiny blade rest against Amelia's throat and froze where he was.

Crowley hadn't been motionless. He held the pistol in one hand, the barrel aimed directly at the clown's head. Gene Halloway looked on, his face almost unreadable and his skin goosefleshed from the lingering chill in the night-time air.

"How long the little lady stays alive and well is entirely up to you, however. Which will it be, Mr. Crowley? My life and hers? Or do you let me walk away from all of this?"

Mike looked at Jonathan Crowley. The man was staring a hole through the clown, the firearm unwavering. For once Crowley wasn't smiling at all. He looked all too willing to kill someone.

IX

Gene Halloway was doing his best to understand what had just happened. He was so addled he'd even left his car running, which just wasn't at all like him. One minute he's walking toward Jack Michaels—and don't ask how he knew where to find the man, because he had no fucking clue—and the next Jack is shooting a man in the back. Now, it's fair to say that he never expected that sort of action from his high school chum. Hell, if Jack had ever had a reason to shoot a man, well, Gene knew better than most. And shooting someone from behind, someone who wasn't even armed? Nope. Not a real possibility. It couldn't have just happened, but it had. And now he had to deal with that.

But to make matters worse, or at least more surreal, the man then got up and had a conversation with Jack and then took him down. Managed to throw some sort of glowing spitball, for all Gene knew, and then pinned Jack to the ground and sent him into seizures. Not just seizures, oh, no, the sort of spasms that apparently caused perfectly normal skin to blister and smoke.

Gene was doing his best, he really was, but after a busy day of blowing the balls off an innocent teenager and murdering whatever possessed his only daughter's body, he just wasn't really in the right frame of mind for any more *Outer Limits* special effects and convoluted stories.

He looked at the naked, scary, wounded man and then at

the unpleasantly mean-looking, smiling clown holding the
justifiably nervous woman in front of him like a shield.
He looked at Mike Blake—and could that really be Mike
Blake, for God's sake? He was sober. That hadn't happened in years!—who was staring daggers at the clown.
Then he looked down at Jack, who was doing a damned
fine impression of roadkill at the moment.

"Excuse me?" No one bothered looking at him. They
were all too busy doing Mexican standoff routines. "Excuse me? Would one of you PLEASE tell me what the hell
is going on here?" He waited for an answer, and none came
his way. If he hadn't actually known better, he'd have
thought the people in front of him were figures in a wax
museum. "I'm serious here. I need to know when everything around this town went completely bat shit, or I might
have to do something irrational."

Jack Michaels let out a very small moan, and that was
good. It was nice to know that Jack was alive. He'd been
meaning to talk to Jack about something, but at the moment he couldn't for the life of him remember what it was.

No one else seemed to care much. Gene reached down
and touched Jack's face. His skin was almost burning
hot—not exactly a shocker, as he'd been frying a few seconds ago—and the eyes that looked at him showed more
confusion than anything else. "Jack? What should I do?
Who's the bad guy here?"

Michaels looked at him for a second and blinked slowly,
the confusion going away. He sat up, bracing himself with
arms that looked about strong enough to pick up a golf ball
without too much effort. Damnedest thing Gene had ever
seen—well, weirdest thing within the realm of possibility
at least—Jack's face went stone cold and hard right before
his eyes. The hazel eyes that had been clouded over became as sharp as a hawk's, and he assessed the situation in
an instant.

The clown coming out of nowhere had been a shocker. Jack Michaels moving from prone to standing was almost as much of a surprise, but that was nothing next to the constable pulling a second pistol from the back of his belt. It wasn't just that he had a second gun—that happened all the time in the movies—it was how damned fast he was. Jack had always been agile, certainly he'd always been faster than Gene, but the draw and aim was almost too quick for Gene to actually see, and he was standing right there with the man when he did it.

Everything happened all at once.

The woman reached her arm behind her back and grabbed the front of the clown's sequined pants, her fingers sinking into the fabric and clawing hard at his crotch.

The clown gasped, trying to pull back from the sudden pressure and drew the blade in his hand across her throat. A fountain of blood practically exploded from her neck and spilled down over her exposed breasts.

Crowley pulled the trigger on the gun in his hands.

Jack Michaels pulled the trigger on the gun in his hands.

Mike Blake let loose a scream and ran madly at the clown.

The clown didn't back up, he flew backwards, a hole appearing in the arm that held the knife and half of his face just vanishing even as he spun and stumbled and fell flat on the ground. The knife he'd held in his gloved hand seemed to hang in the air, spinning on an unseen axis and catching every iota of light in the area, casting it back as a hundred tiny flashes before it finally fell into the brown grass at the edge of the sidewalk.

Mike Blake never made it to where the clown lay face-down on the turf. He stopped at the woman who lay on the grass nearby, her body trembling as her lifeblood spilled out. He pulled her close to him, her blood staining his clothing, the thinning stream spilling over his rugged face and blinding him as he tried to look at her.

The man the clown called Mr. Crowley was there half a second later, pushing Mike out of his way and grabbing the bleeding woman in his arms. Lifting her, and running. He'd made it across the street and halfway up the lawn to the medical center before Gene was fully conscious of what was happening. Mike and Jack took off after him, running hard. Poor Mike slipped and fell on his face in the lawn before he managed to get any real footing.

Gene watched them go, having absolutely no idea what had just happened around him but suspecting it was more important than words could express. He watched until all four figures entered the building, and then he walked over to what was left of the clown in the grass.

The back of his head was blown out. It looked like someone had gone at a ripe tomato with a melon baller and been a little too enthusiastic. He could see the bloody grass through the hole in that head, and that thought fascinated him. He bent closer, the giggles he'd felt earlier starting to spill from his mouth in soft chuffing noises.

He'd gone into a full-scale attack of hysterical laughter by the time the clown turned around and looked at him with his one remaining eye. And oh, that was just too much. Still laughing, he tried to back up and slipped in the gore from where the woman had bled out all over the grass. He landed hard on his ass, and even that seemed outrageously funny.

He was still laughing when Rufo's hand wrapped around his throat.

And then the clown was laughing, too.

My, the night had certainly been full of surprises.

X

Crowley hit the emergency room doors with his back, shielding Amelia's body with his own. He didn't bother with administrations; he just grabbed the first white coat he saw.

The man looked at him with wide, terrified eyes, but listened when Crowley told him Amelia needed help. One look at her ruined throat was enough to make that clear.

He backed away when the crowd of medical personnel got too heavy. By then Mike Blake was there with him, and so was Jack Michaels. Both of them looked worried, but Mike's pain was obvious on his face.

Crowley scratched at the insane itching going on in his chest. He couldn't get to it, not anymore, not since the outer skin had started growing back, but he wanted to.

Amelia Dunlow was dying. No way around that, but he could say he'd tried. So far that was pretty much all he could say about anything that had happened in Serenity Falls. He'd tried.

And he'd failed.

He had that damned handicap the bad guys almost never seemed to be saddled with. He had to play by the rules. They could cheat as much as they wanted to, and the man behind everything that had happened in the town was very good at cheating.

Mike Blake was a gibbering wreck behind him. He was crying his eyes out and fighting against the doctors and nurses who were trying to work on his skull. Crowley didn't know how bad the injuries to the man's head were, but they were bad enough that he was fighting back even through his grief. At least he hadn't actually started posturing. Not yet. Maybe not at all.

If he'd had to hazard a guess, he'd say Mike might have

a chance if there wasn't too much bleeding going on under his skull. But the way he was acting, the way he was moving, led him to think there was something wrong that went beyond just a concussion.

He should have kept the cat with him. He should have listened to me.

Crowley forced the thoughts away. Like as not Mike Blake thought the cat was for Amelia. He didn't know about her. Jonathan Crowley wasn't going to be the one to enlighten him, either. That wasn't his job, wasn't his place in the world. He was just a Hunter. He did damage control.

Jack Michaels had a haunted look on his face. He figured the man would look that way for the rest of his life. However long that might be.

Jack had been through a few things, not the least of which was getting a demon shoved down his throat. But in Crowley's mind, that had been a better idea than the alternative. If he hadn't let that damned thing loose on the man, he'd have had to kill him.

He still didn't know what the demon was. He knew it had a grudge against him, but that was all. Had a grudge. Now it didn't have anything at all. You don't always have to know a name to destroy something. It helps, but it doesn't have to be there. In this case, he'd forced it into Jack Michaels's body and then let it do what it wanted to do in the first place. He'd let it destroy.

The curse on Serenity had called for sacrifices. If he'd been inclined and had the time, he could have calculated exactly how many through the years, but it wasn't worth the effort. All he needed to know was that it took four people at any given time to be the focuses of the curse. Jack Michaels had been one of them. The demon had taken care of that when it tried to possess him. Crowley had taken care of the spell that bound Jacob Parsons. The poor slob had been trying to do good in the town, and one of the other people locked into the curse had spread it to him like a virus. Jack Michaels was the likely candidate. He couldn't be sure it was the constable who infected him, but he was the likeliest choice.

That was two conduits down. He felt the third one nearby, and the fourth was gone. Just gone. He had no idea where. He closed his eyes and breathed in deeply, letting his mind and body relax, even as he shut out the sounds of the trauma team working on Amelia and the blubbering, fighting screams of Mike Blake.

The third one was coming closer, coming to him for a change of pace, instead of him having to hunt it down. When the doors to the already overburdened emergency room opened up, Crowley saw the person who was being used to hold what was left of the curse together and smiled.

XI

Joey urged Charlee on for the last few steps. She was ready to collapse, and he wasn't far behind her, but he wouldn't stop until she was safe.

He pushed the doors to the emergency room open and stopped. The sight before him almost overwhelmed him. There was a group of medical folks holding a screaming man down, strapping him to a gurney as he fought and cursed and howled angrily. It took him a minute to recognize Mike Blake as the one doing all the fighting. In the next alcove over, all he could see was the backs and sides of a group leaning over another examination table. They were crowded together so tightly he couldn't hope to actually see the patient. But it had to be bad, if the heavy stream of blood leading to that small room was any indication.

Constable Michaels was pacing like an expectant father waiting to hear his child had been born. And the man he'd led into the woods earlier was sitting in one of the cheap plastic chairs of the waiting room off to the right, smiling in his direction. The man was naked and bloody. He looked completely insane.

When he stood up and came at Joey, that was all she wrote. Joey grabbed Charlee by the shoulders and turned around, ready to take his chances with getting her an ice pack. She'd made it this far without dying; he was pretty sure she could make it the rest of the night.

He didn't even clear the threshold of the entrance into the emergency room before Crowley was all over him.

The man's bloodied hands clenched his shoulders and pulled, almost knocking him off his feet. Joey screamed as loud as he could, his eyes searching for a way to get pretty much anywhere where the stranger wasn't.

He almost broke into tears when the man pushed him aside, despite the fact that he hit the wall and slid down bonelessly. What stopped his joy was that he was now reaching for Charlee, and she was in no shape to defend herself.

Joey didn't let himself think about the fact that a bloody, naked man was the one attacking. He didn't let himself think about the smile that he'd seen enough times to give him nightmares. He just lunged, grabbing the back of the man's head in both of his hands and doing his best to pull him away from Charlee, who was looking back at Jonathan Crowley with a shocky, pale face and eyes as wide as a scared rabbit's.

"Getoffa her! Getoffa her, you faggot!"

Crowley ignored him, pushing Charlee to the ground, her face and chest crushed under his weight, pressed into the bloody linoleum. She was screaming like a pig led off to the slaughterhouse, and he couldn't blame her in the least.

Joey reached down and sank his teeth into Crowley's ear.
The man was too damned big for him to really hurt with his
hands, and desperate times called for desperate measures.
He felt skin and cartilage break under his bite. Warm blood
spilled into his mouth, and he thought for sure he would gag
right then and there. This was a hypochondriac's nightmare.
God alone knew where this man had been and whether or
not he had AIDS or something even worse. The taste was
raw and wet, and Joey bit even harder as the man suddenly
jerked back.

"You little shit!" Crowley hit him. Joey had been in exactly five fights in his twelve years. He'd won three of
them, and in every one of those cases they'd been more
like pushing matches than actual fights. He'd lost two of
his brawls over the years. The first had been to Charlene
Lyons after he'd called her a slut three summers back. She'd
been an important lesson in the fact that some girls know
how to hit. She'd pushed him, he'd pushed her, and she'd
promptly gut punched him and followed through with a
roundhouse across his chin. That had hurt, but it had been
more surprising than anything else. The second fight he'd
lost had been to Perry Hamilton, who was two years older
and had punched him in the balls as soon as the fight
started. That one had been bad. He'd been waiting to piss
blood for about a week after that little incident.

He'd never in his life been hit by an adult before. First it
was a mild head butt that sent him back just a little and
made him let go of the man's ear. Then Crowley's fist
slammed squarely into his nose and sent him staggering
back. He couldn't see anything except the bright lights going off in his head. He couldn't taste anything but Crowley's blood in his mouth. He couldn't smell anything at all,
and the only thing he heard was a solid, loud ringing in his
ears. But he felt the wall he bounced off of, and he felt the

floor when he hit it. And he felt his muscles telling him to fuck off and die when he tried to stand up.

A few seconds later he heard Charlee screaming, and then he felt strong hands grabbing him under his armpits and lifting him off the tiled floor. "Easy there, easy does it." He recognized the voice as the constable's. "Let's get you to a chair, son."

Charlee screamed again. He forced his eyes back open and saw her feet kicking up and down, the toes of her shoes slapping against the bloodied tiles and Crowley's butt pinning her thighs in place. For half a second he thought the man was raping her. He fought hard to get up, but the constable held him down and warned him to sit still.

And then it was over. The naked man stood up and backed away from Charlee, who was looking at him with the strangest expression, like she'd just seen a ghost and the idea was pleasing to her.

It took him a second to realize she didn't have any more swelling or bruises on her body. All the spots where Joey himself had beaten on her were gone, and so were the burn marks that had covered her.

He looked at Crowley coming his way and tried to understand what was going on. The man was frowning, not even looking at him. Joey opened his mouth to speak, and just like that Crowley had a finger pointed at his face. "You say a single word, and I swear I'll beat you to death. You're already on my shit list for the dogs. Biting me isn't making it any better."

He had the good sense to keep his mouth clamped firmly shut until Crowley left the emergency room, still naked and bloody and not looking at all pleased.

CHAPTER 7

I

Serenity Falls Part Sixteen: When the Dust Finally Cleared

It's hard to think good thoughts about anyone after a massacre. The day broke feeling like a summer day should feel for the first time in weeks. The air was warm and working toward hot at a frightening pace. After an extended stay in winterlike conditions, most people had no idea how to handle that.

But it was a minor concern at best.

The death toll was what was on everyone's mind that morning. No one really knew where to even begin counting. The massive tent was gone, and it had taken several hundred people with it. The eyewitnesses, including Victor Barnes, Jessie Grant, Dave Pageant, and his twin sisters Amber and Suzette, knew that there were a lot of people trapped inside when the structure collapsed, but like everyone else, they would find themselves hard-pressed to tell anyone exactly who had been caught by the flaming debris.

Certainly the coroners would try to figure it out, but the fire had been so intense that there was little left but cooling puddles of body fat and an occasional bone to work with.

It would take time; that was all there was to it. People had already been reported missing, and the long list of cars that had been abandoned along the road would help narrow everything down a bit with any luck, but that didn't mean much to the families involved.

It was bad for Dave and his sisters. They had lost every member of their family who stayed away from the farm. The only family left to them was each other, and only because all of them had chosen—or been drafted as it were—to avoid following the rules. Of the survivors, Dave was the one in the worst shape, and it only took a few stitches to set him to right. Physically at least. Survivor's guilt knows no age boundaries, and the fact that he had done all he could to help put the fire out didn't take any of the sting away.

Becky Glass was one of the few people there who didn't really have a lot of trouble with being a survivor. She'd been unconscious for a lot of it and had had the strangest dreams while in her slumber. Her father came to her and told her he loved her, and then another man came to her. He was almost familiar, though she couldn't for the life of her figure out why until much later. In her dreams he explained that she was a good person and that her family had been kind to him when he needed the help. He'd been a visitor to Serenity back before it was called Serenity Falls. He knew her great-grandparents and thought the world of them. He never said his name but told her that he would be nearby if she needed him, and he would know when the time came. He claimed he had a debt to pay and that watching out for her was part of it. Three years later she ran across his picture in an old family album. His name was Darryl McWhirter, and he had been dead for a long while.

Somehow that knowledge didn't bother her as much as she'd expected it would.

There was a part of Becky that missed what had been inside of her. That spirit had given her something she never really knew she lacked until she had it and then lost it. It had given her confidence. She hid the loss well. Though she wasn't drawing the eyes of men like she had when that thing had been in her—for which her mother Dana was grateful once she had a chance to look back at how oddly her daughter had acted for a few days after her father had died—she squared her shoulders and made a point of looking people in the eye. After a while it stopped being a con-job and became a part of who she was, but it took time.

Joey Whitman and Charlee Lyons stayed the night at the hospital. They learned later that they were orphans. Their parents had all gone to the circus the night before. None of them got away from the fire that broke out under the big top. Nancy Lyons's body was found a few days later. Charlee lost everyone in her family in one brutal stroke.

Joey stayed with his Uncle Bob and Aunt Lisa. They were good people, and in time he recovered well enough. To many of the people in town it seemed the biggest change for him was that he no longer worried quite so much about whether or not he was getting sick. He just started rolling with the punches. Charlee didn't recover as quickly. She drew in on herself a lot. She had nightmares, and she had screaming fits for quite a while. She had no family in town, but it worked out eventually. She wound up staying with the Grants. Jessie was her best friend, after all, and both of Jessie's parents were calm and patient and loving with her. It took time, but eventually she was back to her old self.

April Long packed her bags and left Serenity Falls. She was too young to be on her own, but she walked away just the same. She took her father's car and cleaned out the bank accounts for the family. No one in Serenity ever heard from her again.

Victor Barnes was the only constable who managed to survive the fire. He wasn't much help to Jack Michaels for a while though. He had been beaten, bitten, and burned too badly to do anything but go to the medical center and stay there for a few weeks.

Barnes had a roomie at the center: Mike Blake, who wound up with a hole in his skull to ease the pressure from internal hemorrhaging. Mike didn't recover well at first. Before he became Barnes's roomie, he spent a week in the intensive care unit in a coma. His time in a deep sleep was filled with strange dreams and stranger thoughts. In the most surreal of the dreams he saw Amelia and Amy walking together, looking for all the world like twin sisters, though when he saw them together he could tell the difference between them with ease. He was not surprised to learn that Amelia Dunlow died on the operating table. She never came back to consciousness.

He was not surprised, no, not a bit. When the situation was explained by Jack Michaels, Mike simply nodded and stared at the wall. He may have been out of his coma, but he was hardly livelier.

Three weeks after he entered the clinic he was released. He stopped on his way back to Havenwood—as he had no place else to go save an apartment that meant nothing to him—and picked up a large bottle of vodka. He didn't drink it on the way to his home, but as soon as he got there he twisted off the top and poured himself an eight-ounce shot, hold the rocks.

He'd just put the bottle down and reached for the glass when Jonathan Crowley's voice reached his ears. "Oh, that'll do the job, Mikey, but maybe you should try something a little faster instead." Crowley dropped a knife on the coffee table, directly next to the water glass. "If you

run it from the wrist to the elbow, no one will have a
chance to save you."

"Fuck yourself."

Crowley sat down on a chair across from the sofa where
Mike squatted and smiled. "Not really my style, but I appreciate the suggestion."

"What are you doing here?"

"Just wanted to make sure you weren't being a complete
asshole about everything and to let you know I'm leaving
town." Crowley snorted a half laugh out of his nose and
shook his head. "What's left of it anyway."

"Did you find out who killed Amy?"

"Yep."

"What is his name?"

"Albert Miles. He used her, along with a lot of other
people over the years, to keep his curse going strong until
he could get everything set up the way he wanted it."

"And is he still alive?"

Crowley tilted his head to one side and looked out the
front bay window, his eyes moving over the asphalt. "I
think so." He shrugged. "If not, he's good at faking it."

"Have an address for him?"

"No. And if I did, I wouldn't give it to you anyway."

"That's what I like about you, Crowley, your compas-
sion."

"I'm being very compassionate. I'm stopping you from
falling off the wagon. Trust me; for me, that's compassionate."

"Yeah? So why would you care in the first place?"

"Frankly, I don't. But Amelia does."

"Amelia's dead, right? I don't think she'll be too worried one way or the other."

"Well, that just proves that you don't know shit."

"What do you mean?"

"I mean Amelia's not as dead as you think she is. That's

the other reason I'm here. She wanted me to give you a message."

"You're not funny."

"Of course I am. When I'm joking. Which, just to make sure you're getting this, I'm not."

"I saw her die."

Crowley got that get-a-clue look on his face again. "And you saw me get munched by dogs and shot in the chest."

"You didn't die."

"Neither did she. Not really. But there are rules she has to follow, and one of those rules is that she can't ever come back to Serenity Falls."

Mike closed his eyes, almost refusing to believe what he was hearing. "So, if this is true, I can go to see her?"

"Yes, Mikey, you can. But I can pretty much guarantee she won't have a thing to do with you if you're pickled."

Leaps of faith are always deadly things. Mike had learned that a long time ago. Still, it was that or drink the booze that he was close to salivating over. Given a choice, he thought he'd prefer to risk it and see if Crowley was just a sadistic bastard. "So, saying I believe you. Where would I meet her?"

"Connecticut, where her family home is."

"And would you have an address?"

"Yes. And I even have a copy for you." He put a folded slip of paper into Mike's shirt pocket. "Use it in good health."

"Where are you going now?"

"Not Connecticut, if that's what you're worried about."

Mike shrugged. "Can't say it breaks my heart." Both men were silent for a moment, and Crowley rose from his seat. He looked ready to speak again, but Mike beat him to it. "What happened here, Jonathan?"

"Bad mojo. But don't worry. The worst of it's gone." He shrugged. "There was a curse, and it required certain things that I took away from it. Now it isn't here anymore."

"Why did you do it?"

"Why did I do what?"

"Take away the curse?"

"It's what I do. Besides, there's a kid out on a farm who asked for my help. I have a soft spot for kids."

"Any other reasons?"

"Why did you quit drinking, Mike?"

It took him by surprise. Not the question, but the fact that Crowley called him *Mike* instead of *Mikey*.

"I got angry instead of just depressed."

"Welcome to my world." Crowley slapped him on the shoulder and headed for the door. "She said to take your time. There's no hurry to get to her unless you want to hurry."

"Why would she think I wouldn't hurry?"

"Because some people have trouble dealing with the fact that she's not human."

"What is she then? What is she if she isn't human?"

"Not for me to say. That's between the two of you. Make up your mind and handle it. Oh, and Mike?"

"Yeah?"

"Do I have to mention how badly I'll hurt you if you fuck with her?"

"No. No, you don't."

"Good. Then we can leave on pleasant terms. Have a nice life, Mike."

"You, too, Crowley."

The man laughed softly as he left Havenwood.

Mike left town the following day. He didn't return. There was nothing in Serenity Falls for him.

Jack Michaels did not leave town. He stayed there. It was home, no matter how screwed up it was. He was there for Gene's funeral. They found him on the grounds of the emergency center with his neck brutalized and a substantial chunk of his skull missing. There was no sign of the clown that had been shot the night before. He didn't dwell on that too much. Except when the lights were off and the night came creeping in. It was one of the many things that gave him nightmares.

Bethany and the constable got together for a while. They dated, and they made love that was as near to perfect as he'd ever hoped for, but the past was too far gone, and there were still a few places in their lives that haunted both of them. Eventually they went their separate ways. But they became friends, and they stayed friends, and that was more than he'd ever really expected.

And he found a certain closure in that friendship. He even got a surrogate daughter out of the deal. Terri Halloway was a sweet kid, and if she was quiet a lot of the time, that was all right. She'd been through all kinds of hell, and it would be a long time before she could really trust a man in any serious way if he was right in his guesses. Near as he could figure, he was right more often than not.

As for Terry Palance, he lived through the devastating injuries he received at the hands of Gene Halloway. He was prosecuted for his crimes against Terri, and he was found guilty and sentenced to twenty-five years in a maximum security penitentiary. He served four years of his sentence before getting himself stabbed to death. He'd tried to fight off the affections of a few of the men who thought he was just a little closer to being a real woman than the rest of them were. They took him and then they killed him when he took the rape personally. His mother didn't attend the funeral, but several others did, including Terri Halloway, who was escorted by Jack Michaels. She cried a lot of tears when he was lowered into the ground. If a few of the sounds she made sounded almost like laughter to Jack's ears, he didn't let it show.

Life went on in Serenity Falls, but it was never quite the same for most of the people in the town. There were holes in their lives, wounds carved by a man who could not forgive the sins committed against him even after three centuries had passed.

His actions left them as scarred as the actions thrown against him. Albert Miles wasn't even a memory to most of the people in town. Mary Parsons saw him, or at least the body he'd chosen to occupy while he paid his respects to his first wife's memory. The only name she heard for the man was Arnold Holiday. No one knew what the meter reader was doing in the medical center that night, but there were no charges pressed against Mary for braining him. His body had apparently been dead for over a week. It was just one more surprise that had no solid answer. The town had endured a lot of surprises. Mary and Jacob left town as soon as he was released from the medical center. They've written a lot of notes about the case but haven't figured out quite how to piece it together well enough to make a proper book. They've tried getting in contact with Jonathan Crowley on numerous occasions, but to date they've had no luck.

II

They'd stayed away from the carnival, just like they were told to. They waited patiently at home, watching as their parents moved to their deaths at the big top. The voice had told them to avoid it, and they had listened. They were almost human still, but the changes that had been made within them were necessary for the tasks that lay ahead. The voice spoke, and they listened. Aside from that, they were as they had always been. Eva Spinelli and Chris

Parker were still crazy about each other and still fighting like mad every other day. Both were fully convinced that they were in love with the other, and both were constantly worried that the other would leave them. To that end they were constantly setting little tests to see if their significant other would pass or fail. That there were no rules for the tests was hardly surprising. Most teenagers fall victim to that unusual form of emotional torture at least a few times. What made it special was that the two of them were so damned good at it.

Meg Brown and Glenn Harrigan were still holding hands all the time. The difference was that they were now going a lot farther in their relationship than they had before the voice came along and told them it was okay to break the rules. Like when Glenn slit his father's throat. His mom was ready to go to the carnival and, by God, go she did. His father was feeling a bit under the weather and decided to stay home. That wasn't in the voice's plans, so Glenn fixed it. One kitchen knife and one sleeping parent met briefly. The end result was one dead parent whose body now lay in the basement, shoved into the crawl space next to the water heater.

They went on, doing much as they had done before the voice came along, before even the hounds controlled by the voice had torn them apart. The biggest difference was that they didn't go on in Serenity. While families suffered and died in the conflagration at the Pageant farm, they slipped past the massive parking lot that the road near the place had become, and they found the bus the voice had sent for them, exactly where the voice had said it would be. Each of them took two changes of clothing and nothing else.

The bus left town before the carnival went up in smoke. The teens went along for the ride.

Their new master had plans that had nothing whatsoever to do with Serenity Falls, and they were a part of those plans. They were looking forward to what the future held,

and they were looking forward to meeting their master. He
promised them great things in the future and freedom from
the rules they'd been forced to live by. Few teens have ever
been able to resist the promise of a brighter tomorrow, and
they were no exceptions.

Eva and Chris sat together at the front of the bus, directly behind the driver, who never even bothered to look
at them. They were holding hands, as at the moment they
weren't fighting. The bus left New York by nine in the
morning, and except for the driver, every person on the bus
was asleep when they left the state.

None of them ever came back to Serenity Falls. None of
them ever missed the place, either.

Their future was set for a different course, and Albert
Miles made sure he kept them busy.

III

Jonathan Crowley left Serenity Falls, too. He walked most
of the way to the town's limits before he realized he was
being followed. When he turned, the car that pursued him
continued on, matching his pace almost perfectly.

He ignored it for roughly ten minutes and then decided
his feet were too tired to continue walking when he didn't
have to.

"Nice of you to finally decide to join me."

The car gave no response, save to sit there and idle. Having no mouth, speech really wasn't much of an option for it.
Crowley opened the driver's side door and threw his suitcase
into the backseat. For the moment the car had chosen to be a
Mazda Miata. That was good enough. It was sporty and
would get him where he was going.

Crowley fastened his seat belt and searched the radio waves until he found a station that played big band tunes. Jimmy Dorsey's oddly cheerful and mellow sounds were soothing as he drove away, heading west again.

He liked heading west. It felt like heading home, and he could use the break.